Readers lo

'Ideal for fans of Richard Osman's books … this murder mystery will keep you guessing as the bodies stack up! Full of **red herrings, twists and turns, wonderful characters** and fabulous houses.'

'Set in the historic town of Stamford, this murder set in the antiques trade is a **brilliantly plotted mystery**.'

'**Mystery and intrigue** … written by a talented and gifted author.'

'**Absorbing** murder mystery … interesting information about Antique auctions was a added bonus.'

'A **thoroughly enjoyable** cosy murder mystery … I'm looking forward to the next book already!'

E. C. Bateman studied History of Art at university before starting her career in the strange, wonderful world of antiques. Having made the questionable decision to marry an auctioneer, she moved to Stamford and dreamt up the idea for this series whilst living in a converted Georgian flat overlooking St. Mary's Church in the heart of town. They've since decamped to the surrounding countryside with their two children, but can still be spotted around the cobbled streets on a regular basis, usually being dragged along by their effervescent cocker spaniel, Audrey.

instagram.com/ecbatemanbooks

Also by E. C. Bateman

The Stamford Mysteries

Death at the Auction

Murder Most Antique

BIDDING FOR MURDER

The Stamford Mysteries

E. C. BATEMAN

One More Chapter
a division of HarperCollins*Publishers* Ltd
1 London Bridge Street
London SE1 9GF
www.harpercollins.co.uk
HarperCollins*Publishers*
Macken House, 39/40 Mayor Street Upper,
Dublin 1, D01 C9W8, Ireland

This paperback edition 2025
1
First published in Great Britain in ebook format
by HarperCollins*Publishers* 2025

A catalogue record of this book is available from the British Library

ISBN: 978-0-00-877098-3

This novel is entirely a work of fiction. The names, characters and incidents
portrayed in it are the work of the author's imagination. Any resemblance to
actual persons, living or dead, events or localities is entirely coincidental.

Printed and bound in the UK using 100% Renewable Electricity
by CPI Group (UK) Ltd

Prologue

It was All Hallows' Eve, and Stamford couldn't have dressed more befittingly for the occasion. The English weather, usually so unreliable whenever clement conditions were desired, was in its element tonight. A dense violet fog enveloped the town's Georgian skyline, making it impossible to see more than three steps ahead along the twisting, cobbled streets. The handsome stone houses loomed out of the mist, transformed from their usual honey-coloured hue to a frosted silver. The wrought-iron lampposts were mere smudges of apricot, the spires of the four churches that dominated the centre utterly vanished. The River Welland, normally so bucolic and placid, was tonight a whorling, purpling mass of current, thrashing its way beneath the numerous bridges that marked its path through the heart of town.

Tonight, Stamford was another world, far removed from its usual role as a smart yet also down-to-earth country town. Tonight, it was ethereal and mysterious. Some might even say it had an air of magic about it.

That person, however, would certainly *not* be Margaret Creaton.

She huffed as yet another gaggle of excitable children barrelled past her stocking-clad legs, clutching their baskets of sweets, chattering and squealing in such a way as to make her ears ring painfully.

Halloween was a thoroughly nasty festival, in her opinion. Celebrating evil spirits and the undead and such like. If she had *her* way, Stamford wouldn't partake in it at all. It just wasn't *fitting* for a respectable town like theirs. She'd raise the issue at her next Pillars of the Community meeting with the mayor. The woman might be an asinine scatterbrain, in Margaret's estimation, but she did, by all accounts, possess a brood of children. Surely, as a mother, she could be persuaded that the festival just wasn't wholesome for young minds.

"Do come *along*, Colin," she snapped over her shoulder at the stooped figure of her husband, who was staggering along behind her. They were passing The George now, perhaps Stamford's most famous landmark. The ancient coaching inn was a beacon in the fog, a warm lemony glow emanating from the many windows staggered randomly across the building's facade. From behind the mottled diamond panes, Margaret could make out the flicker of firelight on the oak-panelled walls of the dining room, the flash of silver cutlery and crystal-cut glass as toasts were raised.

"Sorry, Margaret." She could hear Colin puffing along behind her, his slip-on shoes shuffling against the pavement. "It's just…" He hesitated, audibly gulping as he shifted the enormous hessian sack in his arms. "Are you *sure* they said they wouldn't deliver? It seems strange for a coal merchant not to."

Margaret declined to answer. As a matter of fact, the coal merchant *had* offered to deliver, but they'd asked five pounds to do so. Five pounds! The *cheek* of it. She'd been so incensed that she'd almost told them to cancel the order entirely, but a coal fire was one of her *very* few indulgences, and with the clocks having just gone back…

Colin didn't press her. Instead, he just staggered along dutifully, emitting the occasional death rattle-type wheeze. She didn't ask him if he was all right, and he didn't complain. Colin never complained, no matter what demands she made of him. It was a trait that ought to have endeared him to her, but, paradoxically, it only made her despise him all the more. He was so loyal, so puppyish, so utterly blameless. The lack of anything to legitimately hate only made her resent being stuck with him all the more.

They carried onwards in silence through the mist-bound streets. People passed them in clusters, laughing and jostling, many of them in costume. On their way to the pub, no doubt, or out to some god-awful Halloween party. Gradually, however, they began to thin out, their chatter receding into the distance as Margaret and Colin cut down a small lane. It was barely wider than an alley. There were no pubs down this way, nothing to draw anyone who might linger. It was flanked with elegant townhouses, but they were mostly shuttered, only the faintest glow visible around the joins, hinting at the cosy evenings happening within. Margaret felt herself breathe a sigh of relief. This was more like it; quiet, restrained, behind closed doors. The way life used to be in Stamford.

This town had always been such a tranquil place, a backwater, really; conveniently situated for stopping off on the route North to South for a spot of lunch or a cup of tea, but little more than that. But in recent years, that had begun to change. People had begun to discover it. Now, it was a – Margaret shuddered at the word – *destination*, a sort of living museum where one could marvel at the perfectly preserved Old English past while still enjoying the decidedly modern metropolitan comforts of artisanal roasted coffee beans and chi-chi boutiques. And it was only getting worse year on year. What with the Georgian Fair in the summer, and the horse trials in the autumn, and the papers forever harping on about what an idyllic place to live this was…

And come to live they did. Not just the classic wealthy retirees, either, whom the town had always attracted. But a whole host of other people. The wrong sort of people, as Margaret's grandmother would have put it, in ominous tones. Londoners. Young couples. Families. All changing the face of the town, upending the status quo. And now, to top it off, they were having murders here. They'd never had murders *before*, Margaret thought reprovingly. If you asked her, there was only one place to point the finger, and that was squarely at all of these incomers. Not that they were necessarily doing the murders *themselves*, she conceded, reluctantly. But still, it didn't stop them from being responsible.

Actually, maybe that was something else she could bring up with the mayor, come to think of it. A sort of tax, maybe, or extra restrictions…

Margaret's phone buzzed from the depths of her tweed pocket. The sound made her jump, falter in a way that would have seemed totally out of proportion to anyone who didn't know the strain she'd been living under for the past six months.

"Are you … all right, dear?" Colin's reedy voice asked

hesitantly, filled with a concern that made bile rise in her throat.

"I'm fine," she said shortly. "Just out of breath. You go on ahead."

She pulled out the phone, sick with dread as she clicked the button to bring the screen to life. It was the epitome of a basic model, capable of calls and texts – and that blasted snake game, which she couldn't work out how to get rid of – but little else. And that was more than enough, as far as Margaret was concerned. None of that smart nonsense that rotted folks' brains and turned them into posing idiots. She'd purchased it as one of a pair for herself and Colin, thinking it would be nothing more than a useful device for sending him commands while she was out of the house.

She'd never imagined it could turn into an instrument of utter terror.

It was a voicemail. She didn't want to imagine what message might be awaiting her this time. They seemed to be getting nastier and more threatening as time went by, her blackmailer wanting to remind her who was in charge. As if they needed to. As if she could possibly forget.

Margaret stared down at the phone in her whitened grip, resisting the urge to fling the thing onto the cobbles and stamp on it, over and over again, until it was smashed beyond recognition. But that wouldn't do any good. In fact, it would probably only make things worse. With the mobile as a means of communication, she was effectively keeping her tormentor contained. Without that, they might resort to calling the house phone, or worse, turning up on the doorstep...

With a shaking hand, she put the phone to her ear, forcing herself to listen. After a second or two, a jaunty tone came on the line, and she felt every muscle in her body sag with relief. It was just the plumber, telling her he'd got the part for the kitchen tap. Normally, she loathed the man's chirpiness, his insistent good cheer. He'd driven her half mad around the house last week, chattering away, oblivious to her curt replies. At the time, she'd thought that she'd be quite happy to never hear his voice again.

Now, though … it sounded like a heavenly choir to her ears. She sent a prayer of thanks to the oblivious man, reflecting that she might even pay his bill at the end without quibbling, as she usually did.

She composed herself, putting the phone away with hands that were still trembling, despite the danger having passed. She wasn't sure how much longer she could live like this. Her nerves were stretched to the limits, starting to fray.

"Colin," she barked, whirling around. "Let's…"

But the street all around her was empty.

Her husband of forty-two years had vanished.

Margaret's head whipped back and forth in confusion, eyes squinting, straining to see through the mist. She could already feel her fear fading, replaced with a familiar irritation. Where was the old fool? Couldn't she take her gaze off him for one minute without him bumbling off?

She stormed down the lane, muttering a string of unflattering curses that were decidedly in contrast to her wedding vows. And then something shifted to her left; a flickering of the light streaming from one of the windows. She looked across…

And what she saw there made her turn to stone.

Margaret Creaton wasn't a woman easily frightened. But the face that stared out at her was like something from the mouth of hell itself. A terrible, grotesque mask, crowned with two gnarled, curving horns. She gasped, stumbling backwards, the lamppost behind her the only thing preventing her from falling. Her back clunked into the cold metal, knocking the wind out of her, eyes squeezing shut in pain.

"Margaret?"

The thin, quavering voice floated through the darkness. Margaret forced her eyes open, just in time to see Colin peering at her, concern etched into his benign, bovine face.

"Are you all right, Margaret? Have you had a turn? Do you need to sit down?"

"No!" The word was harsh, ragged. She shoved him away roughly. "No, I—"

Suddenly, she remembered, her eyes flying back to the window. But it was empty. Just a blank rectangle of light. No demon. No nothing. She could feel her head starting to swim. For a moment, she genuinely wondered if she was going mad, if the strain had finally cracked her sanity.

"Let's just get home," she said shortly, not meeting Colin's eye. She couldn't bear it when he was all attentive like that; it made her skin crawl. "You know how I hate this time of year."

Really, she told herself shakily, as they continued through the shrouded streets. These Halloween costumes were getting more and more outlandish. There really ought to be some system, some way to make sure they weren't too inappropriate, too frightening. There were still a lot of elderly people around here; people ought to have some respect for that. Perhaps she could draw up some sort of rule…

Already rallying at the thought, she mentally added another item to her list of things to take to the mayor.

Chapter One

Twenty-four hours earlier

"A little higher, I think." Felicia stood back, tilting her head to one side as she surveyed the scene before her. "Can you get it into that niche there? Or maybe onto that shelf?"

Algernon, who was teetering precariously on a Victorian wheelback dining chair, waited patiently, pumpkin clutched in his outstretched hands, while his mother deliberated. He already knew exactly which spot she was going to pick, but in his twelve and a half years on earth he'd learned that it was better to let her get there on her own. Besides, it wasn't as if he had anywhere else to be. School finished at the end of this week, and autumn half term stretched before him in a glorious, russet-coloured blank. Most of his new schoolmates would be heading out of town. A good number of them were boarders, and home was in another part of the country; but even those who were local like him seemed to have somewhere else to be, their families making the most of the fortnight's break by jetting off to the Greek islands or the Canaries for some October sun.

Not that he minded in the slightest, Algernon thought happily, stretching out just a little bit further as the maternal gaze finally settled on the inevitable niche. He gripped the back of the chair as it wobbled, inching up onto his tiptoes. Because *he* would be here. His favourite place in the whole world. And more importantly, so would his family. All together, all in one place. Just six months ago, that would have seemed impossible.

"We need your father for this." Felicia decided suddenly, as she watched her son almost topple off the chair. She leaned back and called, "Dexter!"

A geranium-coloured leg appeared through the doorway, followed by a lemon-shirted torso. Not many men could dress like an ice cream parlour and manage to make it look dashing. But then, Felicia's ex-husband wasn't many men.

Thank goodness, she thought darkly. She wasn't sure the world could take more than one Dexter Grant.

"Fear not, I'm here." He bounded to a stop in front of her, sweeping into a mock bow. "How can I be of assistance, dear lady?"

Algernon giggled, and Felicia fought the urge to roll her eyes … even as she studiously avoided looking into Dexter's own, cobalt-blue pair. She knew exactly what they were like when he was in this mood, alight with mischief, the laughter lines that had appeared in the past decade only enhancing their rakish appeal.

Because her ex-husband was appealing. It was an uncomfortable fact, one she tried very hard to ignore these days. She'd been there, done that … and then she'd asked for a divorce. It was a decision she'd never questioned. After all, admiring Dexter from a safe distance was vastly different to actually being married to the man. And the former, she could testify, was the preferable of the two.

She tried not to look at Algernon, who was watching them, unable to keep the joy off his face. She knew how much it meant to him, having his father around. But Dexter was never one hundred per cent predictable, and if the bright lights of his television career came calling again … well, they'd been there before, and it hadn't ended well. His transformation from lowly – if dashing – art-history professor to the swashbuckling, fedora-sporting *Treasure Seeker* had taken off in ways none of them could have foreseen, much less kept up with. Looking back, it had all just seemed to happen so *fast*; suddenly, he was gone, chasing artefacts around the globe while she was left behind, picking up the pieces…

She pulled herself up sharply. No, she told herself, she was more than happy to leave him to his legions of fans. They could have him, as far as she was concerned.

"You can be tall." She helped Algernon down off the chair, handing Dexter the pumpkin, then pointed upwards. "It needs to go there."

He climbed onto the chair, then hesitated, pumpkin hovering in mid-air.

"Are you sure?"

She folded her arms, glowering up at him. Of course, she ought to have known he'd have an opinion. He'd never been one to simply take instruction.

"Yes, I'm *sure*. That's the biggest pumpkin. It needs to go front and centre."

"Ah, but bigger isn't necessarily better." He leaned across, scooping another pumpkin off the reception desk and balancing it on his fingers. "This, now … is clearly the superior gourd. It's quite resplendently warty."

"And blue," Algernon agreed, nodding his head in earnest agreement.

"Quite. Anyone can have an orange pumpkin. We don't want to follow the herd, do we?" And without waiting for an answer, Dexter positioned the interloper in pride of place. "There." He stepped down, sweeping an arm out grandly to indicate his handiwork. Any onlooker would have been forgiven for thinking that he'd slavishly decorated the entire thing, not simply placed a single pumpkin. "A masterpiece. Cup of tea, anyone?"

Felicia drew in a breath as she let her gaze rove around the vast marble foyer of the historic mansion that her auction house called home. Dexter might have his fans, she told herself, but she … she had this. And right now, it looked magnificent. Garlands of autumn leaves wound around the stately columns, splashes of vibrant scarlet and orange providing a dazzling contrast against the cool white stone. Lanterns were perched on the steps of the sweeping central staircase, each containing the flickering glow of a candle. And then there were the pumpkins. They were crammed across every available surface, all manner of colours, shapes and sizes. Spilling across the reception desk, stacked in artful piles in corners … it was like an explosion of autumn.

Betsy would have thoroughly approved.

The thought made Felicia blink, sudden tears catching her off-guard. This sort of thing had always been Betsy's job before. Her old saleroom manager – and friend – had been so creative; she'd made everything look so perfect, and so effortlessly, too. And she'd loved this time of year so much.

Felicia hastily gathered up some errant leaves that had fallen to the floor, hoping the action would prove distracting before emotion overwhelmed her completely. These moments still came upon her from time to time; the fresh realisation that Betsy was gone for good. That she would never walk back into the saleroom in a cloud of lavender perfume and lilac mohair, round face alight with beneficence. They were fewer and further between now, at six months after her friend's death, but the intensity of them didn't seem to fade. It was like waking from a bad dream, over and over again.

She could still vividly recall the last time it had happened. It had been three weeks ago, when she'd passed the chocolate-box cottage that had once belonged to her friend. Its front garden was bare at this time of year, devoid of the winter pansies Betsy would always pack into pots along the path, a splash of luminous colour against the weakening sunlight. But the house had no longer been empty. There'd been a wreath on the lilac-painted front door, Wellington boots by the mat, mud slowly cracking as it dried upon their glossy coating. Then the door had opened, and Felicia had found herself frozen, momentarily unable to move. Of course, she'd known the house would be occupied again one day; Betsy had only the one son, so probate wouldn't have been complicated. And he lived in Australia, so he wouldn't have a use for the house. But still, it was a shock.

He must have rented it out, she realised. No wonder it hadn't needed an estate agent's sign; it was in a beautiful location, situated as it was at the quiet end of Bath Row, its frontage gazing out over the green swathe of the Town Meadows. It would have been snapped up in an instant.

A woman had emerged from the interior, dark hair falling across her face as she turned back to speak to whomever was within. Felicia found she was holding her breath.

And then two children had tumbled out, laughing and squealing. The woman had turned, seen Felicia and smiled hesitantly. The spell was broken. Felicia found she could move again, and she'd nodded, moving on her way. Betsy would have liked to know there was a family living there, she'd told herself. Her friend had missed her grandchildren so much. Missed them with an intensity Felicia hadn't realised until it was too late.

She'd kept her head resolutely down as she'd passed the house two doors down. Grander in style, it nonetheless had a forlornness about it that only came from long-standing emptiness. Its future was set to be far more complex. After all, Evelina was still alive. And the house still belonged to her, even if she could never hope to live in it again.

"Are you all right, Mum?" Algernon, ever perceptive, was watching her carefully.

"Of course, darling." She crunched the leaves between her hands, pushing them into the bin as she pasted a smile on her face, straightening to place an arm around his slight shoulders. He took after her in build, finely boned and graceful, although, as of yet, he didn't have either of his parents' height. Just another mystery to add to the growing list that was her oblique, sensitive child. "It looks lovely. And soon, I'm about to get two whole weeks with you. What don't I have to be happy about?"

As though in response to her question, a crash came from

upstairs, followed by a litany of choice expletives. Felicia tried not to wince. Dexter smirked.

"Bloody hell!" Her father's not-so-dulcet tones bellowed from the office above. "Who put these paintings here? Are you trying to break my *other* leg?"

Felicia rolled her eyes to the ceiling and began to count slowly. It was a trick she'd had to employ a lot since her father had returned to the auction house following his six-month, doctor-ordered hiatus. She'd known the transition would be difficult; after all, the last time they'd tried running the place together, it had been such a disaster that she'd quit both her auctioneering career and the town she'd grown up in altogether, only returning the previous spring when Peter's accident had forced her back onto the rostrum, gavel in hand.

She'd never dreamed that it would become a permanent arrangement. Staying couldn't have been further from the plan, and yet suddenly, it had seemed like the only thing that could possibly happen next. She'd told herself she'd only done it because Algernon had asked, but the truth was that a part of her had always mourned the life she'd left behind, and the chance to have another go at it had been tricky to resist.

And she hadn't regretted it. Although it certainly hadn't all been plain sailing – starting with a murder here at the auction house on her first day back – she'd nonetheless found a foothold that had been missing in her existence for a long time. Finally, things had felt like they were falling into place. She was home. She was doing a job she loved. Algernon was happy. Even her strained relationship with her father had begun to fuse, slowly but surely.

Until he'd come back to work, that was.

Peter Grant appeared at the top of the sweeping staircase,

glowering. He was a striking man, broad and rugged, with sweeping white hair and piercing blue eyes set into a burnished face. A farmer by birth, he'd never lost the weathered appearance, nor the earthy bluntness, which came with the profession.

"I did warn you someone might trip over them when you moved them there last week," Felicia managed, with admirable mildness considering her teeth were gritted.

Peter's scowl deepened.

"Don't be soft, lass. Why would I do a daft thing like that?"

Why, indeed? Felicia wondered. When this had first started, it had genuinely worried her. Was her indomitable father beginning to lose his marbles? The enforced convalescence had been hard on him, she knew; Peter Grant was a man who liked to be up and doing, who was used to being in command of all that he surveyed. He wasn't one for being idle or out of things. His idea of a holiday was half an hour with a palate-rakingly stewed cup of tea and a bacon butty while he whisked through the Sunday morning papers. That was about as long a stretch of sitting down she'd ever known from him before his injury. He was a man who thrived on action and, as he put it – often rather pointedly in Dexter's direction – 'good honest hard work.' And yet, for months, he'd been forced to sit on the sidelines, with little else to do but twiddle his thumbs. It couldn't have been good for his brain, she knew. But could it really have changed him *so* much?

As it was, she hadn't had to worry for long. She'd soon been disabused of that particular notion. No, he was still as sharp as ever; he could recount every score from his weekly pub darts night upon coming home, and his business acumen was as quick and ruthless as it had ever been. He'd razed through the accounts for the period he'd been gone, complaining about everything she'd done – and a few things she hadn't – before storming around the auction complaining about everything else that was left. By the time he'd been back in the office an hour, there wasn't a figurative stone that hadn't been unturned, tutted over, and denounced 'bloody stupid' or 'bloody inefficient' or, in one particularly memorable case, 'bloody un-English.' She thought that might have been in reference to the new mug tree she'd bought to save them cluttering up the sideboard around the kettle, but her head had been whirling so much by that point it was hard to say.

Peter's verdict had been brisk, brutal, and unequivocally damning: everything she'd done was wrong. Even the things she'd kept exactly the same as before he'd left were wrong – and there were quite a few of those, because what with her living situation, and being short-staffed, and the two murder cases she'd been embroiled in since she'd arrived, she hadn't exactly had a lot of time for innovation. She'd just been plodding along, trying to keep everything running and above water. But somehow, apparently, she hadn't even got *that* right.

It was, of course, no less than she'd anticipated. But it hurt all the same, in a small, quiet way she felt too ashamed to voice. How naïve and foolish to entertain even the faintest of hopes that he might have reacted differently, like wishing for a white Christmas each year that never came. Whatever tentative rapprochement they might have made in their relationship over the past few months, her father was always going to be her father. He never changed, never deviated from course. She had to accept that.

"Come and see the decorations, Grandad," Algernon

called, his upturned face a perfect pale heart. "We've just finished."

Felicia watched in wonderment as her father's expression metamorphosised before her eyes, softening like melting butter as his attention focused on his grandson. At least Algernon never had to feel the rough raze of her father's sandpaper-like personality. She had to admit, there had been a small part of her that had worried, when Algie was small, and his delicate, otherworldly personality had become apparent, that Peter would struggle to engage with his grandson. After all, her father was a salt-of-the-earth sort, and he generally only had time for others who were the same.

Luckily, her son seemed to be the exception. Algernon was the only person who could bring out Peter's gentler side. She had to admit to being immensely relieved about that, although it did bring his treatment of *her* into starker relief. Why he could never seem to extend the same understanding to his own daughter was anyone's guess. But it was true what they said about motherhood; overnight, your priorities completely changed. You no longer came first. So long as Algernon was benefitting from it, she was willing to bite her tongue and bury her own grievances on the matter.

"Smashing, boy." Peter had descended the stairs and was ruffling Algernon's blazing bronze head with a proud smile. "Best we've ever had, I say. I'll bet nowhere else in town has as many pumpkins as this."

"I put that big warty one up there," Dexter ventured, obviously feeling the need to take some of the credit.

Peter stared at him stonily. Dexter visibly tried not to quail. The two men's relationship, never exactly chummy even at the best of times, hadn't been improved by Dexter's sanctioning the discharge of fourteen guinea pigs into Peter's sitting room in the summer. Knowing first-hand how long one of her father's grudges could last, Felicia sensed that any attempt at rapprochement on Dexter's part was going to be in vain for quite some time yet. But thus far, she'd neglected to tell him as much. It was *so* much more fun watching him try.

Without warning, the huge double doors flew open, accompanied by a blast of frigid October air.

The leaves on the columns shivered. Papers on the front desk rippled. From somewhere just outside, a dog started barking hysterically, and a car alarm began to wail. Anyone looking on would be forgiven for thinking that a minor earthquake was taking place. But the occupants of the auction house knew otherwise.

"I think," Algernon said, somewhat unnecessarily, "that Aunt Cass is here."

Chapter Two

"Christ!" Curls tumbling, scarf wrapping itself around the door handle – why Cassie still endeavoured to wear scarves was anyone's guess, as they were clearly her worst enemy – Felicia's oldest friend staggered into the foyer. "It's grim out there today. The high street's like a ghost town – no pun intended," she added wryly, casting a glance around the decorated hall.

Cassie had a flair for the dramatic, and Felicia suspected her friend's description wasn't entirely accurate. After all, Stamford's centre was never empty. Not these days. However, she couldn't deny that the auction had been quiet as a millpond all afternoon. It was, indeed, the kind of moody autumn day that positively invited staying in with the fire lit and a hot drink in hand. Preferably one laced with something warming.

"I wasn't expecting to see you this afternoon." Felicia put down a spice-scented pillar candle and advanced towards her friend. "Is everything okay? I thought you had parents' evening."

"Oh, I do. But it doesn't start for an hour or so. *Don't* ask me which one's it is," she added, as an aside to the assembled company at large. "I've already been to two this year." Cassie had three boys under the age of eight, which, combined with her teenage daughter Robyn, a husband and an uncommonly shaggy and badly behaved dog, on top of her duties as Stamford's mayor, made her a very busy – and very distracted – woman. "Honestly, they all start to blur together, unless something particularly memorable happens."

"There was a brawl at one of yours once," Dexter told Algernon wistfully. "Over the last chocolate biscuit, I believe. Jolly entertaining it was."

Algernon, who didn't entirely share his father's irreverent streak, looked faintly disapproving.

"Cup of tea, then, duck?" Peter suggested, already halfway to the stairs. It was a rhetorical question, really; Cassie had never been known to turn down a caffeinated beverage. "Kettle's just been on."

"Absolutely," Cassie agreed fervently, peeling off her coat. "I'll take a herbal. Nettle if you've got it."

There was a silence. Peter faltered, his foot on the bottom step. His face convulsed in painful confusion.

Felicia, who was well aware that her father was only cognisant of two types of hot beverage, neither of them bearing the slightest relation to a roadside weed, hastily stepped in before his brain exploded.

"It's okay, Dad, I'll do it." She took Cassie's coat and draped it over her arm. "Come on. We'll go up to the office."

She hustled Cassie up the staircase. Only when they were safely in the office, tucked away amongst the ancient eaves, did she turn to her friend with a half-smile.

"I think nettle tea might be a stretch for this place," she explained. "We are *literally* stuck in the past, remember?"

She was well aware that the space that surrounded them perfectly illustrated her point. The auction-house office was a long, crooked room, once the servants' quarters of a house much older than its Georgian façade would suggest – and therefore spared the renovations and updates various owners would lavish upon their own quarters downstairs. Here, you could see the bones of the original building; the gnarled beams holding up the sloping ceiling, the uneven walls, the deep-set mullioned windows, which once would have looked out upon the Stamford of half a millennia ago. Felicia loved this room. It was like a secret compartment, a hidden treasure no-one would ever guess at from its outer wrapping.

"I'll bring some next time I visit," Cassie said earnestly, appearing to completely miss the flippancy of Felicia's remark. "It's very cleansing, you know. Alain tells me it flushes all the toxins out." Cassie paused, then added, "You know, you should get your dad drinking it. His temper … he's probably *full* of toxins. It would do him a world of good."

Felicia looked at her friend, trying vainly to find any hint of irony in her tone, or mischief in her eyes. But there was nothing. She sighed internally, reminding herself that she was supposed to be being supportive of Cassie's newfound 'awakening.' But it was getting more and more difficult with each passing day.

After the tragic events of midsummer, Cassie had been referred to a therapist by the hospital. It had been less of a gentle suggestion than a firm requirement.

"You were almost killed," said a particularly brisk nurse. "And by your own employee, none the less. Someone you knew and trusted. You are *not* fine."

At the time, Felicia had agreed wholeheartedly. After all, what had happened was enough to shake even the most robust of constitutions – even that of her irrepressible, ever-buoyant friend. It was important to make sure she was processing it properly, not just bottling it all up.

Perhaps predictably, Cassie hadn't been of the same mind. Therapy, she'd insisted, was for moony, navel-gazing types, people with fragile minds. Not her. *She* was a practical optimist. She didn't need to *talk*; she needed to get on. She'd got through everything else life threw at her that way, and this would be no different. She'd dug her heels in with impressive, donkey-like stubbornness. But eventually, after a lot of pressure – and some hefty bribery from Robyn in the form of a family-sized chocolate bar – Cassie had agreed to go, although under voluble duress she made sure everyone was well aware of.

"One session," she'd vowed darkly, as she'd glared up at the smartly fronted practice on Star Lane. "I'll do *one* session. But that's it."

Felicia, who'd accompanied her – for the simple purpose of ensuring that she actually went inside and didn't bunk off altogether – had simply nodded indulgently and prodded her towards the door.

"Take your time. I'll be in the waiting room when you're finished."

The session had, to her surprise, overrun, and she'd just been getting engrossed in an article about Narcissistic Personality Disorder – which was ringing Dexter-shaped bells all over the place – when Cassie had finally reappeared.

"Well?" Felicia had probed, as they'd stepped out onto the

street. "How was it?"

"It was … not what I expected," Cassie admitted, cagily. "I suppose … I mean, I know I said… But I might go back for one more session after all. Just one, mind. Alain says there's more to unpack."

There'd been a strange look on her face as she'd said it, Felicia reflected now. She'd noticed it then: a sort of guilty, flushed expression. Slightly dazed. But she'd just been so relieved that Cassie hadn't stormed out of the session halfway through … she hadn't really stopped to analyse it. To realise what it might mean.

What it had meant, it soon transpired, was that her friend was now officially *in* therapy. One more session had quickly turned into two, then suddenly, it was once a week. From having to force her friend to go, Felicia was now struggling to keep the infernal *Alain* – whose name she was pretty sure was actually Alan – out of every conversation. It was like he had a hold on Cassie's brain.

She wouldn't have minded so much, Felicia thought, if it had actually appeared to be making her friend happy. She would have sat patiently through the unintelligible therapy speak, helped out with the cleansing rituals, bought every box of herbal tea in the supermarket. She would have done it all, and gladly, for her oldest and most beloved confidante, the woman who was more like a sister to her than her actual sister. But Cassie, for all of her insistence that she was a glowing new person, didn't actually seem all that radiant on the inside. Alain might have given her enlightenment, Felicia reflected, but he'd taken something else in exchange: her sense of humour. And without that, Cassie was … well, just *not* Cassie.

But of course, she didn't say any of this out loud. Instead, she replied airily, "Oh, I think it's already too late for Dad toxin-wise. I suspect he's pretty much made of pork pie by this point."

"Hmm." Cassie pursed her lips, an action which, four months ago, Felicia would have comfortably predicted she'd never see her friend do. "Well, if you haven't got nettle, peppermint will do, I suppose. Although it's rather a *mainstream* herb."

"I thought you always said it was like drinking a mug of toothpaste," Felicia couldn't resist pointing out, with a raised eyebrow.

"Did I?" Cassie feigned a sort of pious, wide-eyed innocence, of the sort that was designed to make her accuser feel very small and petty. "Perhaps I did. It sounds like something the old me would have said."

She uttered the phrase 'old me' as though it were a particularly virulent, buboes-sprouting disease.

"I'll see what we've got," Felicia said diplomatically, rummaging around in the kitchen cabinet with more hope than expectation. In this auction house, it was a choice of either builder's tea or instant coffee. And not even the slightly more luxurious Gold Blend at that. More the kind that looked concerningly like soil and left an acrid, burnt taste on the tongue for hours afterwards. Anything else, as just established, would probably give her father an apoplexy.

To be fair, it wasn't just hot beverages. Peter Grant's parameters for what constituted acceptable were tremendously narrow. Many things in modern life were decried under the damning banner of 'outrageous nonsense': colourful trousers, sourdough bread, topiary, digital kitchen-timers (a bit of a mystery, that one, but she knew better than to ask), bottled beer, dogs in coats, absolutely everything about Dexter…

"I'll even settle for camomile," Cassie was saying, with a magnanimous air. "Lemon verbena…"

Felicia found a desiccated bag of indeterminate breed lurking at the back and dusted it off surreptitiously before plonking it into a cup, where it immediately proceeded to turn the water an unappealing shade of khaki.

Cassie took a sip, letting out a satisfied sigh.

"Perfect."

Felicia eyed her disbelievingly.

"Really? I mean … wonderful. Glad you like it."

"Listen." Cassie put her mug down, looking suddenly hesitant. "I should mention … this isn't just a social call. There's something I need to ask you."

Felicia felt her heart sink. The last time Cassie had said that, Felicia had been dragged into the town's midsummer Georgian Fair. And, in quick succession, a string of four brutal murders. So she felt justified in the wariness she heard in her own voice as she replied.

"What *kind* of something, Cass?"

Cassie fidgeted with the papers on Felicia's desk.

"Do you remember a girl called Lucia Mills? She was in our house at school. Had those *really* dark eyelashes that the teachers used to think were mascara, so they'd make her scrub her face, but actually they were just naturally like that."

"Oh, yes." It was hard to forget a girl like Lucia. She'd been the ultimate queen bee, always surrounded by a gaggle of cronies – or admirers, as she'd probably preferred to think of them. She'd always had the latest, swishest version of everything, too. Felicia had a particularly vivid memory of a pencil case of Lucia's she'd fervently coveted as a twelve-year-old. She could still bring up an image of it in her mind's eye: bright pink and furry, with a clasp that looked like a lollipop. Meanwhile, Peter had made *her* use Juliette's old hand-me-down case; her elder sister having as little flair then as she did now, it had been a dreary grey thing, serviceable and depressing. The only thing going in its favour was that it had made rather a good pillow during the duller lessons. "Her father was some sort of hedge fund manager, wasn't he?"

"*Everyone's* father was some sort of hedge fund manager." Cassie smiled wryly. "Except yours and mine."

Peter Grant had certainly stood out amongst the other parents at their prestigious school, Felicia acknowledged, with his calloused hands and thick North Lincolnshire accent. She also knew that it must have seemed an odd choice to some, that a self-made man, so proud and outspoken about his working-class roots, would sacrifice nearly all of the hard-earned profits of his then fledging business in order to send his children to such an elitist institution. To someone who knew more about him, though, it wasn't difficult to understand. After all, no matter how proudly he might talk now about his days on the farm, about having to make his own way in the world, Felicia knew it hadn't been easy, and he would have done anything to avoid his daughters having to repeat that kind of hardship. In her fonder moments, she liked to think of him sending them to that school as his own, rather idiosyncratic way of showing love.

Cassie had always been one of the few people she'd never had to explain any of this to. After all, her friend had been in a similar boat. She'd been there on a maths scholarship; her parents would never have been able to afford the fees otherwise. The two of them had both been fish out of water, in their second-hand uniforms, their too-big shoes bought to last for as long as possible. And girls like Lucia Grant had made sure they'd been reminded of that, often. Which is why Cassie's next words surprised her.

"Well, anyway, she and I have stayed in contact over the years…"

"Really?" It was on the tip of Felicia's tongue to ask *why*. When Lucia had left at sixteen – to go to finishing school, of all places – Felicia had breathed a sigh of relief. She seemed to recall Cassie doing the same.

"Just Christmas cards, you know the sort of thing." Was it her imagination, or did Cassie seem faintly defensive? "The point is, now she's asked me to put the two of you in touch."

Felicia's surprise ramped up to astonishment. What could Lucia Mills possibly want with *her*? She was just a lowly auctioneer, very much small fry compared with the glitzy world her old schoolmate now inhabited. She thought she might have married some politician; a diplomat, maybe? "I don't see how I…"

"It's a bit … sensitive, I believe." Cassie dropped her voice, even though there was no-one around to overhear. "Basically, she wants some things valued. Quietly. By someone she can trust."

And suddenly, Felicia understood. Even without knowing the particulars. No-one knew better than an antiques valuer how easily loyalties could go out of the window when money and possessions were involved. Lucia certainly wouldn't be the first to resort to paranoid levels of secrecy.

"She's staying at The Aquitaine," Cassie continued, still slurping appreciatively at the murky sludge in her cup.

That diverted Felicia's attention. She felt her eyebrows raise.

"Wow. I thought you had to wait for someone to shuffle off the mortal coil to get into that place."

The Aquitaine Member's Club was simultaneously the town's least known and most legendary hostelry. Tucked away in a quiet back lane scarcely wider than a medium-sized car. From the outside, it didn't look like much, well, not by Stamford's standards, at any rate. Anywhere else, it would have been a standout building, with its huge sash windows, ionic-columned portico and elaborately carved friezes. Here, however, it was just another Georgian townhouse in a square mile jam packed full of them. But beyond those wide stone steps, through those glossy duck egg blue painted doors…

Well, the truth was, Felicia had no idea. Very few people did.

Generally, you didn't get to set foot in the place without being explicitly invited by a member. She'd heard things, of course. Fragmented descriptions of glittering chandeliers and plush club rooms where cocktails were served on silver trays in front of dazzling gilt and marble fireplaces. Needless to say, it was eye-wateringly expensive, although that was really neither here nor there. Lots of places in Stamford were expensive, and lots of things, too; it was that sort of town. The sort that drew money like a magnet. Old money in particular.

No, it was the secrecy, the inaccessibility, which made it so alluring, so fascinating. In a world where everything was on display, where nothing was private, The Aquitaine kept its doors firmly closed, its confidences close. Its online presence was minimal, and it never advertised. But then, it hardly needed to. Felicia had only been half-joking with the line about waiting for someone to die; rumour had it that the club operated a lengthy waiting list.

"Or be married to an ambassador, apparently," Cassie offered lightly.

An ambassador. *That* was it. So she hadn't been too far off the mark.

"Well, she always had her sights set high," Felicia remarked. "It sounds like she got what she wanted."

"Or did she?" Cassie drummed her fingers on the tabletop, looking like she was itching to say more. Her resolve didn't last long. She leaned in, saying breathlessly, "I get the feeling all isn't exactly *rosy* in the marital garden, if you know what I mean. She didn't say much, but…" She blinked then, as though emerging from a trance. The conspiratorial light dimmed in her eyes, and her face sobered. "But no, I *mustn't* gossip. Alain says that when we judge others, we only judge ourselves."

Felicia, who wasn't even entirely sure what that meant, took a long draught from the glass of water on her desk to save herself from having to answer.

"Anyway, she's staying in town for a few days," Cassie continued obliviously. She rummaged in her copious bag, producing a half-eaten packet of Monster Munch, an odd sock, and a screwdriver before finally handing Felicia an embossed business card. "Here are her details. She says drop in anytime. The club know to expect you."

Felicia looked down at the card. It was a pointless thing, really, in this day and age; a caprice, a status symbol. It was gilt-pressed, in swirling letters, and had clearly been expensive to produce. Now, it was creased across one corner, and emitting a faint aroma of pickled onion. Felicia felt her heart twang. Cassie's utterly chaotic lack of organisation was one thing that had thus remained impervious to Alain's efforts, and she fervently hoped it stayed that way. Once the ultimate test of her fond indulgence, it had now become, bizarrely, something to cherish, a last vestige of the old Cassie.

"Okay, I'll do my best," Felicia promised, trying not to wince as she sifted through her mental calendar. With only two weeks till the next auction, a catalogue still to complete, plus her usual round of home visits and valuations, *and* with her senior valuer Hugo still away on compassionate leave … to say she was run ragged was an understatement. "But I'm really not sure when I'll be able to…"

"*Felicia!*" A sonic boom – one with a distinctly Lincolnshire accent – shook the foundations of the building. Both women flinched.

"On second thoughts," Felicia stood hastily, already reaching for her coat. "Maybe I *could* find a gap in my schedule."

"Felicia!" The voice bellowed again. "Where are you? Come here and explain to me what the *bloody* hell has happened to my lotting system!"

"Right now, perhaps?" Cassie said, with a knowing smile.

Felicia flung her scarf around her neck with a nod, suddenly feeling a lot more enthusiastic about the whole endeavour.

"Absolutely. No time like the present."

Chapter Three

Felicia wrapped her pale pink coat more tightly around herself, her gaze moving upwards to Stamford's spire-studded skyline. The sun was already dipping low, despite it being barely five o'clock. It was always disconcerting how quickly the nights drew in at this time of year. That sense of winter hurtling towards one, almost without warning … the sudden prospect of unrelenting cold and dark stretching ahead… It was easy to see why humans had always felt there was something ominous and unsettling about this time of year.

Golden light shone on the cobbles as her footsteps paced across town. Down the high street, with its gaudy shopfronts decked out in full Halloween finery. Around the curve of St. Mary's Place, tucked away beneath the shadow of the Medieval church. Across the Town Bridge, with its sweeping views of The Meadows – a vibrant ribbon of croquet lawn, green in the daytime, now more of a chartreuse – and the river, which wrapped around either side of it like an embrace. She passed beneath The George's famous gallows sign, which spanned the roadway above. Dating from the eighteenth century, it had once served as a prominent warning to the numerous highwaymen who'd lurked along one of the busiest travelling routes in the country. These days, whilst less sinister in meaning to modern travellers, it was still an unmissable sight, and a unique welcome to a town famous for its idiosyncrasies.

The crowds thinned out noticeably on this side of the river, and as she walked up the steep thoroughfare of St. Martin's, she saw fewer and fewer people. By the time she turned off into the narrow side street where she knew The Aquitaine was situated, she found herself in an unusual situation for a town as bustling as Stamford.

She was completely alone.

She stopped abruptly in the middle of the street, relishing the novelty. Breathing in the solitude. Everything was silent, even the hum of traffic hushed by the dense stone of the buildings that huddled in around her.

Then she heard it: the crackling sound of a footstep meeting a leaf-covered pavement.

She sighed wearily, closing her eyes briefly against the glorious, burnished sunlight slanting against her face.

"I know you're there, Dexter."

A pause. She turned just in time to see him melt sheepishly out of the shadows.

"*Ah*. So you noticed me, then."

"I noticed you from the moment I left the auction house." Spy material he certainly wasn't, she added silently, even if he *did* always insist that he'd been approached during his last year at Oxford. MI5 had certainly dodged a bullet there, so to speak. She folded her arms, fixed him with a glare. "Why are you following me?"

"Just making sure you got here safely." He recovered quickly, as he always did, his reply glib as he fell into step with her, moderating his long strides to match her own. "It'll be night soon, after all. Don't fancy the idea of you wandering around in the dark alone."

"It's five o'clock," she replied stonily. "And it's Stamford. The only thing in danger of being viciously attacked around here is a cream tea."

"Perhaps once, dear heart," he wagged a finger – a gesture she was *convinced* was designed to annoy her – "but times have changed. Or have you conveniently forgotten all the grisly murders that have beset our fair town of late?" He shook his head sorrowfully. "No, these are mean streets these days. You really can't be too careful."

"I didn't realise you were so concerned for my welfare," she said slowly, eyeing him suspiciously out of the corner of her eye. His face was perfectly, sculpturally earnest, but then, that didn't mean a thing. Dexter might have made a terrible spy, but he would have excelled as an actor. Plus, she reflected, he would have much preferred the wardrobe of the latter. Blending in in a nondescript black coat would have been his worst nightmare.

"Anyway," she continued tartly, pointing her gaze determinedly ahead and picking up her pace. For all the good it did; she was tall for a woman, but he was taller. There was no way she was going to lose him. "It appears I've made it here in one piece. So you can be on your way now."

Her gaze moved up the handsome, slightly forbidding frontage before her. The club was in darkness, shuttered against the night. No sounds spilled out from within. If it weren't for the discreet gold sign next to the front door, glinting in the low lamplight, Felicia would start to wonder if she'd got the wrong building. It looked for all the world like an empty house, its owners away for the holidays.

"Not quite." Taking advantage of her distraction, Dexter linked an arm through hers, steering them gently but rather speedily towards the immaculate white marble steps before she had a chance to realise what he was doing. "After all, what sort of gentleman would I be if I didn't escort you to the door?"

"A very sensible one," she said darkly. "One who values his shins."

He pretended not to hear her, instead raising his hand to knock on the glossily painted pale blue door. Felicia's eyes widened in indignation.

"Wait, what are you doing? You are *not* coming in!"

He gave her a wounded look.

"Oh, come on, Fliss. Don't be such a spoilsport. I only want a *little* peek. You can't deny me the chance to get a look inside this place, surely? From what I've heard it's an historian's dream. Some of the stuff they're rumoured to have in there…"

"Yes, I can," she hissed, trying to wrench her arm from his. But he held fast. "And I will. Besides, you need an invitation to get in."

He gave her his lazy grin. The kind that made the gullible swoon and her want to slap him.

"Never posed a problem for me before."

It hadn't, either, she thought bitterly. Dexter always could sweet-talk his way into anywhere.

Except, she reminded herself, her heart. Not these days.

She pulled herself upright, steeling her gaze. His smile faltered. Just a little.

Before either of them could say anything else, however, the door in front of them swung open, apparently of its own accord. Dexter and Felicia looked at one another, then back at the glowing entranceway.

"How…" Dexter was scanning the portico around them, his dark brow furrowed. He was clearly looking for a security camera, but Felicia could already tell him there weren't any. The door was entirely free of any of the modern security features one would expect to find on an establishment such as this: no intercom, or keycard slot. Not even a doorbell. Just a heavy brass knocker in the shape of a fleur-de-lis.

Belatedly, a white-gloved hand appeared, followed by an arm. It was clad in the most exquisite livery: duck-egg blue with gold piping.

"Good evening, Ms. Grant. We've been expecting you."

Felicia felt her mouth drop open, the question of how he knew her identity already forming on her lips. But the footman's eyes were already flickering to Dexter. "And Mr. Grant, too, I see. What a … *surprise.*" Felicia thought she detected the suggestion that it wasn't an entirely pleasant one, but it was too subtle, too smoothly covered for her to say for sure. His blue eyes glittered as he stood aside, gloved palm gesturing them within. "Welcome to The Aquitaine."

Felicia and Dexter shared one more glance. Then, in tandem, they stepped into the inner sanctum.

Chapter Four

Annabel Drayford, manager of The Aquitaine, glided between the sumptuously laden tables, her critical eye taking in every minute detail. She inspected each snowy tablecloth, each mirror-bright silver candlestick. She tweaked an errant fork back into line here, an asymmetrical cruet set there. She primped the sprays of greenery and berries that adorned the centre of each table. Eventually, she stood back, allowing herself just the smallest nod of approval.

As underwhelming a reaction as that might appear, it was in fact the highest accolade. Annabel had once heard her standards described as celestial; an epithet that still made her glow with satisfaction every time she recalled it. But even she had to admit that there was very little to find fault with here tonight.

Of course, the Great Hall was a sight to behold at any time, but there was no denying that it really came into its own on a cold Autumn night, when the darkness pressed in outside, deep and thick. The room was one of the few surviving features of the small medieval monastery that had originally occupied this site, before the Reformation had seen it consigned to a near ruin. As with most things in Stamford, it had been given a neo-classical facelift by the Georgians, who'd turned it into the kind of blandly handsome, symmetrical townhouse they so adored. Luckily, though, the new owners had obviously had some sentiment for history, as they'd kept the Great Hall intact. They'd even managed to restrain themselves from painting the panelling, as so many of their contemporaries had, and the dark wood that lined the walls still bore its original rich, radiant lustre.

Overhead, the ceiling soared, vaulted and braced with a lattice of beams, each as thick as a tree trunk and blackened with 500-year-old woodsmoke – a seldom-noticed remnant of the open fire that would once have blazed in the centre of the room. Suspended from those beams were two enormous candelabras, each hanging from a hefty rope, the other end of which stretched down to a bracket secured at elbow height on the wall. This allowed for the chandeliers to be lowered every evening as night fell, so that their hundreds of candles could be lit.

Annabel watched now as the second chandelier was heaved back into place, inching higher and higher as one of the porters strained at the ropes. It was a job no-one relished doing, she knew, but it was well worth it for the effect. The Great Hall had never been wired for electricity, and was always lit solely by candlelight, suffusing the room with an intense, deep radiance that electric light could never hope to emulate; it danced around, turning the silver tableware molten, scintillating off the crystal glasses. It was heady, intimate … and so, *so* expensive it almost hurt to look at it. Especially for a woman like Annabel, whose own cut-glass accent had come out of a book, who saw jewellery on display here every night that cost more than the house she'd grown up in. Early on in her career, it had bothered her, made her feel uncomfortable. Now, she didn't even blink at it. This was her normality now. This strange, rarefied bubble, where the world was another place entirely. Where perfection was guaranteed at all times.

No, Annabel reconsidered, wrinkling up her nose at the word. It was trite, meaningless. Utterly insufficient. Anywhere could be perfect; The Aquitaine had to be more than that.

It had to be *sublime*. Every moment of every day. The woodwork had to glow with a lustrous layer of beeswax polish. The logs in the ever-blazing fireplaces had to be kiln-dried especially for the club, to exact specifications that would produce the requisite level of crackle and snap. Whims had to be catered to before the members had even thought of them themselves.

There was nowhere like The Aquitaine; that was so often uttered it had become fact. But what made The Aquitaine what it was … that didn't just happen. In reality, it was the proverbial swan, paddling furiously beneath a seamless, regal surface.

And it was Annabel's job to do the paddling.

She caught sight of her reflection in the foxed glass of the overmantel mirror and took a moment to survey herself. The crisp white shirt, the upright posture, the discreet pearl studs shimmering from each earlobe. Polished but unshowy. Annabel took a certain satisfaction in the knowledge that her own mother wouldn't recognise her on sight these days.

She tucked a strand of walnut-coloured hair behind her ear, turning her face this way and that to inspect her minimal make-up. Or at least, what was the illusion of minimal make-up. In reality, her face was no more natural than her hair – a genuine blonde, she'd discovered early on that she was taken much more seriously as a brunette. Plus, it made her look older – again, not something many women aimed for, but Annabel was more invested in her career than her vanity, and people liked the same qualities in their club managers as they did in their newsreaders: experience and gravitas.

With a last glance around the dining room, Annabel crossed the flagstones, automatically pasting a smile onto her face as she crossed the threshold into the library, or snug area, as it was affectionately known. The space was the heart centre of the club, the least formal and, perhaps as a direct result, the most consistently frequented. At almost five o'clock, the room was packed, as she'd known it would be. It was teatime, after all. That most English of traditions, and at this most English of establishments, still a major event in the day's schedule. In a few minutes, the brass gong in the foyer would be struck, and instantly, swathes of blue-clad waiters and waitresses would glide in, pulling trolleys piled high with cakes and scones. Others would carry teapots, piping hot and perfectly brewed with each guest's favourite blend. The whole thing was a decadent whirl, choreographed as carefully as a ballet.

Annabel strode through the snug, trying to set a pace that was businesslike but not harried. She nodded at several members, shared a warm greeting here and there, but didn't linger. She crossed the empty foyer, her footsteps becoming soundless as flagstones gave way to deep-pile carpet. Soon enough, she stood before an unobtrusive door tucked beneath the staircase. Its brass plaque bore a single word – *Manager*.

She reached into her blazer pocket for the heavy brass key

and fitted it into the lock, feeling the same frisson she always did at the sight of her own personal sanctuary. It was only a small room – barely bigger than a cupboard, really – but to Annabel, it might as well have been a palace for what it represented. It was a symbol of everything she'd achieved, what she was part of now. Her name was engraved on the wall, beneath all the others who'd held this position. Her chair, slotted neatly beneath the vast bureau plat, was the same chair that had been sat in by dozens of managers before her. For the first time all day, Annabel felt a genuine smile rise to her lips.

Then her gaze fell on the set of pigeonholes that lined the wall behind the desk, and the smile vanished, along with the warm glow of satisfaction, replaced with a faint feeling of nausea as she reached over and plucked the blank envelope out, holding it gingerly between two fingers as though it might be radioactive. She already knew there was no point in checking the window; it would still be locked, as it had been when she'd left the room. Just like the door. However they were getting in, they were careful to leave no traces.

She'd always known that The Aquitaine was a secretive place – it was basically its hallmark, after all – although until she'd taken charge of it, she'd had little concept of just what that meant. She slid a fingernail beneath the envelope seal, holding her breath.

A deep boom reverberated through the walls of the office. The gong. Annabel stuffed the unopened envelope into her desk drawer with an exhale of relief. She straightened her collar, smoothed her chignon, squared her shoulders. Prepared herself for her next mission.

Everything else would have to wait. For now, it was teatime.

Chapter Five

The foyer was like the inside of a diamond; a shimmering hall of mirrors, gilt and marble, reflecting back on itself endlessly.

Dexter let out a low whistle, and Felicia elbowed him in the ribs. The porter turned enquiringly, and Felicia smiled innocently back at him until he looked away again.

"Behave yourself," she hissed, between teeth still clamped in a faux smile. "Remember I'm here for a meeting. This isn't a jolly."

As usual, Dexter completely ignored her warning tone, head swivelling this way and that as he gaped shamelessly at their surroundings.

"It's even more astonishing than I'd imagined. I say, is that a Holman Hunt?"

"No idea," lied Felicia, who'd clocked it the minute they'd arrived, pinning his arm closer to her side before he could clamber up the bannisters to get a closer look at it. "Will you *stop* it? You're drawing attention to us. And not for the right reasons."

Dexter, who was firmly of the opinion that there was no such thing as the wrong sort of attention, rolled his eyes, but obediently allowed himself to be led in the wake of their guide.

"The snug," the porter announced grandly, leading them into a room with more chairs in it than Felicia had ever seen in a single space. They were everywhere: in front of the fire, by each window, arranged in clusters and pairs, some on their own, some by low tables set up with games of chess and draughts, and some by reading lamps, leatherbound volumes stacked in their sphere of light. Almost every seat was occupied. The room was an intimate one, low-ceilinged and small-windowed, with a gigantic inglenook fireplace that suffused the atmosphere with glowing light and faintly smoky heat. If she could overlook the hodge-podge of different furniture styles and ages, she could almost let herself be seduced into believing she was standing in a medieval tavern.

They were efficiently funnelled to a pair of brocaded banquettes tucked away in the corner.

"Mrs. DuFontaine has requested the booth for you this afternoon." Their guide whisked their coats from them with magician-like efficiency. "She'll be down presently; in the meantime, please make yourselves comfortable."

Felicia began to slide onto the plush bench, only belatedly realising that she was on her own. Dexter had vanished; something he was infuriatingly adept at. With a vague harrumph that reminded her alarmingly of her father – dear God, she had to watch out for *that* – she settled into the seat, tapping her fingers impatiently on the tabletop. The table, which, she realised suddenly, looked tantalisingly like it might be late Jacobean, although it was too hard to tell in this low light. Atmospheric it might be, but it was an antique expert's nightmare.

"*Felicia*?" A voice hailed her. "Felicia *Grant*? Is that you?"

Felicia, who'd had her head half under the table looking at the underside, bolted upright guiltily.

"Of *course* it's you." The voice was familiar; rich, with a slight gravelly smoke underscoring each word. As a woman materialised in the seat opposite, Felicia saw a face that she hadn't set eyes on in decades. "You look *just* the same."

Felicia suspected a heavy dose of flattery in that statement, but as she looked back at Lucia Mills – as she still couldn't help but think of her – she couldn't deny that in her old schoolmate's case, it really was the truth. There was the same handsome square jaw, the straight nose, the wide, generous mouth. The shining dark hair was still a raven's black, falling in a perfect liquid curtain to her shoulders, and she held herself in the regal manner she always had. In many ways, she looked exactly as Felicia would have expected: a grown-up, more polished version of the lanky teenage girl with ideas of grandeur. The make-up was flawless, the clothes clearly designer. Diamonds dazzled at her ears, throat and fingers.

"How long has it been?" Felicia said now, with a wry smile.

"Too long to think about deeply. Let's not do the maths." Lucia rearranged the layers of cashmere around her shoulders. She was dressed entirely in what, to the uninitiated, might be termed 'beige', but was in fact a complex and beautifully toned medley of shades, from butterscotch to toffee to clotted cream. The kind of shades only money could buy. "I hear you're back here for good these days?"

"Yes, life's circled around a bit," Felicia agreed lightly, leaning back in her seat as a waiter appeared seamlessly at their side, holding aloft a tray of tea things. He began to place them methodically – but no, Felicia decided immediately, that wasn't quite the right word. *Reverently*, that was more like it. The items were set down one by one: the Georgian silver teapot in its stand, the gilt-edged plates with hand-painted flowers drifting blowsily across their surface, the lidded sugar bowl with its delicate, seashell-shaped tongs … all part of a ritual that dated back hundreds of years. It was simultaneously soothing and fascinating, even to one who was reasonably used to it.

It was a truly pervasive myth that the English sat down to a full afternoon tea every day without fail, irrespective of flood, pestilence, war, alien invasion … or anything else, for that matter. The disappointing truth was that this wasn't so widely the case anymore, although admittedly in Stamford, haven to the past that it was, the decline was much slower. Felicia, certainly, had been raised to associate the five o'clock chime with putting the kettle on and searching for something sweet to go with it. Although most days, that was often something unglamorous like a biscuit or a slightly stale piece of fruit loaf. It was scarcely comparable to the performance that was going on in front of her now.

A lull had fallen between them at the waiter's appearance; as he departed, though, it remained, with a certain encroaching awkwardness. The conversation had been superficial, brittly bright, each of them feeling their way. Now the flow had been broken, it seemed that neither of them quite knew how to pick it up again. It wasn't perhaps to be wondered at, Felicia reasoned; after all, they'd been mere acquaintances at school, sharing a house and Set One French, but little else.

Besides, Felicia couldn't help but feel that this was all

merely a politesse, that they were acting out the pleasantries as one must. She could sense that beneath the poised exterior, her companion was in fact seething with impatience, dialling down the clock until she could decently get to the matter at hand.

"I've missed Stamford," Lucia sighed at last, gazing fondly at the spread in front of them. "Everything's done so very *properly* here. Nothing ever changes."

Felicia wasn't sure how to reply. In her experience, that could be both the town's greatest blessing and damnedest curse. But as it turned out, she didn't need to; Lucia was already carrying on, her eyes misty as she gazed out into the night.

"It's always been my own perfect little slice of England, this place. The one I dreamed about whenever I missed home. The thought of it was so comforting, when I was thousands of miles away, in a strange country."

"Being an ambassador's wife must be lonely at times," Felicia said softly.

Lucia opened her mouth, then shut it again. But before she could reply, an irate voice rasped between them.

"You shouldn't be here."

Surprised, the two women looked around. There, standing over the table, was a decidedly unfriendly-looking man. He was holding a volume – Felicia couldn't quite read the gold lettering on its leather spine from here, although it didn't look to be a light read – under his arm, and was glowering openly at them both.

"I beg your pardon?" Lucia said politely. Felicia had a flash of her as an ambassador's wife; beautiful, gracious, endlessly patient. Lucia had always been able to mould herself to a role. "Is there some sort of issue?"

"Yes, as a matter of fact, there is *some sort of issue*," he parroted the last four words in a sardonic way that immediately caused Felicia a shiver of dislike. "This is my seat. You're in it."

"There must be a misunderstanding," Lucia said smoothly, with a winning smile. If she'd noticed his mimicry of her, she didn't show it. "You see, I booked this seat for my friend and I."

He shook his head. He had, Felicia couldn't help but notice, the most magnificent head. Aristocratically shaped, with calcium-white hair that crested in great sweeping wings towards his temples. His features, too, were refined, the hand that held the book finely boned. His natural build, Felicia estimated, should have been slim, compact. Almost neat. But the signs of too much good living were apparent in the way his salmon-pink shirt strained over his middle, the swollen flesh of his fingers, the florid, slightly puffy face.

"My seat is not *bookable* by all and sundry. You can't possibly have done."

"Well, I did." Lucia's response was light, although there was a definite edge creeping in. "You're welcome to check with the club. Now, if you'll excuse us…" She began to turn back to Felicia.

"I don't think I will, no." He leaned on the edge of the pew, his shadow blocking out the light from the fire. "Not until you've vacated my seat."

"There are plenty of other places to sit," Felicia felt she ought to interject. Lucia was looking at him warily, and not without reason. Felicia herself was beginning to wonder if he was quite sane. And he was making her feel uneasy, the way he was looming over them like that. Although, she had a nasty suspicion that was the intention. "Equally comfortable-looking ones," she added, pointedly.

He looked at her properly for the first time. His gaze swept down her body, then back up again. He took his time, not making the slightest effort to pretend he wasn't looking. His eyes when they met hers were assessing.

"This isn't about comfort. It's about principles."

"*Principles* would dictate that you cede your seat to a lady," she informed him sweetly.

Surprise shimmered across his face, followed immediately by rancour. His lip curled in a sneer.

"Oh, my *sincerest* apologies. How *unchivalrous* of me." He swept into an exaggerated, mocking bow. "You'll have to move, *ladies*." The word positively dripped with sarcasm. He straightened, his face hardening. His next words were spat out like stones. "Now shove off. Before I have you kicked out."

Lucia gasped, her fingers flying reflexively to her glittering throat.

"*Dr. Rauceby!*" Their waiter was back with a tray of finger sandwiches, appal written all over his face. "This isn't … you can't just…"

"I can do what I like around here," was the snapped response. "And frankly, you should be asking yourself how this happened. It never would have in the old days." He looked disgusted. "This place used to be the best. Now it's going down the pan. I warned them what would happen; you let in the dross and standards are bound to slip." He gave the two women a meaningful look. "It seems I was right, as usual."

He stalked away, several gazes following him as he went. Although the altercation had taken place in an undertone, it had clearly been picked up on by the rest of the room. No doubt it would form the whispered talk of the club for the rest of the evening.

Lucia looked scandalised, as though her very honour had been besmirched.

"He called me *dross*!" Her voice was breathy with indignation. Her bosom trembled. "I am most certainly not… I've never *been* so insulted. How *dare* he?"

Felicia, who acknowledged that by the standards of this place she probably *was* dross, decided not to comment.

"I really can't apologise enough." The waiter's professional veneer was slipping, his freckled face ashen. The tray trembled in his hands, clinking against the buckle of the watch on his wrist. On the dial, a familiar symbol flashed under the lights: a small arrow, almost like a crow's foot. Felicia noted it with interest, then sternly reminded herself that she wasn't working right now. Well, not technically, anyway. "He should never have got near you. I turned my back for *one* minute…"

"Who is he?" Felicia couldn't resist asking.

"Does it matter?" Lucia sniffed, arranging her napkin on her lap. She'd regained some of her haughty composure, although there was a telltale tremor to her voice. Felicia got the impression that the incident had rather shaken her. Evidently, life as a diplomat's wife had accustomed her to being handled with kid gloves. She should try an afternoon working at the auction, Felicia thought with amusement. Grizzled old antiques dealers didn't go in much for courtly manners, and being a woman counted for little in their book. "A thoroughly nasty man; that much is apparent. I can't *bear* snideness. I hope

49

he's not here for the rest of the week. It will quite ruin my stay. I've a good mind to complain, actually."

The waiter gave her an agonised look. If possible, his face whitened even further.

"No, *please*…" he stammered, the last of his professionalism crumbling. His eyes were desperate, beseeching. "I'll make sure he doesn't come near you again, I *promise*. Just … my manager *can't* find out about this. She'll kill me."

Lucia looked unmoved by his pleas, so Felicia stepped in.

"I'm sure there's no need for that to happen," she said quickly. "After all, it wasn't really your fault. And we're not so hardhearted that we can't overlook a small mishap. *Are* we, Lucia?"

She stared at her companion pointedly until the other woman gave a pouty sigh.

"Oh, all *right*, I suppose…"

"Ladies." A slightly breathless voice rounded the side of the booth. The woman who followed it, however, didn't look breathless in the slightest. In fact, she looked as sleek and unruffled as a prima ballerina. Her brown hair, hovering somewhere between light and medium, was pulled back in a neat chignon that looked too old for her face. "Annabel Drayford; I'm the manager here. I'm so sorry for that unfortunate misunderstanding. Doctor Rauceby is one of our most long-standing guests. I'm afraid he's rather used to having things a certain way."

"That doesn't give him the right to be so objectionable," Lucia bristled, clearly having already forgotten her agreement not to complain. "Honestly, I've never *been* so insulted. It's not at all what I expected from this place. To be … *attacked* … in a public setting…"

She looked as though she might raise a hand to her forehead and swoon. Immediately, Felicia thought of her mother, who had the singular honour of being one of the most dramatic people on the planet. The faux swoon was her specialist move, used as a manipulative weapon whenever anyone had displeased her.

She wondered where her mother was right now. Not in Stamford, certainly. Not in what she called 'rainy old England' at all. She'd shed herself of her home country, together with all the other things that she'd so long resented – her husband, his auction house, the cramped cottage by the river – when she'd sailed away with the owner of a line of luxury cruise ships some years earlier. Felicia rarely saw her these days, although she did receive the odd, borderline inappropriate photograph of her mother and Juan posing in swimwear against the backdrop of some sun-splashed destination. Usually holding a mint julep.

"No, of course not. Please, allow me to apologise profusely on his behalf." Annabel Drayford spoke soothingly, understandingly, but Felicia thought she detected a faint flintiness creeping into her tone. "And your tea this afternoon is courtesy of the club, naturally."

Lucia still looked rather sulky, so it was left to Felicia to answer.

"Thank you. That's very kind."

The manager seemed to look at her for the first time. Then her eyes widened, the bland mask of her face finally registering an emotion.

Surprise, Felicia thought. But not necessarily the good kind.

"Excuse me, Ms. Grant." There had been a slight pause before she'd spoken; just a beat. She visibly recouped herself, twitching her lips into a smile that didn't reach her eyes. "I'm ashamed not to have recognised you immediately. But the lighting in here…"

Felicia waved away her halting apology.

"Not at all, really. I wouldn't expect you to."

"Oh, don't be *coy*, Felicia," Lucia piped up now, her humour quite rapidly restored as she poured a fragrant stream of amber liquid into her china teacup. "I hear you're quite the celebrity around here these days. Let me think, what do they call you? Lincolnshire's Lovejoy, isn't it? The crime-busting auctioneer?"

Felicia slid an appraising glance at her. The tone had been all sweetness … but did she detect a sour note in there? A sly, mocking tartness, disguised as gentle teasing. It reminded her, uncomfortably, why they'd never really gelled at school. Lucia Mills had been one of *those* girls. Nice enough to everyone's face, but behind their back…

"Not by choice, I assure you," Felicia replied now, with a glibness she didn't entirely feel. It was the *Stamford Bugle*, the town's most infamous – and borderline libellous – gossip rag, which she had to thank for those unwelcome sobriquets. "I'm quite content to be a dull, anonymous auctioneer, thank you very much."

Annabel Drayford didn't look convinced, but she gave a small inclination of the head.

"At The Aquitaine, one can be whatever one wishes." She stepped aside as the cake trolley wheeled into view. "Well, enjoy your tea, ladies."

"Isn't she a little young to be in charge of a place like this?" Lucia asked peevishly, as they were left to peruse the dreamlike confection that was a proper, old-fashioned display of sweets. Jewel-studded fruitcake crowned in shimmering gold dust. A sticky slab of gingerbread, diced into thick, treacly cubes. Lemon drizzle, a cut-out wedge revealing its pillowy centre, the top decorated with slivers of candied fruit… Felicia's head was spinning just looking at it all. Feeling rather overwhelmed, she selected a slice of marble cake and a brandy snap, balancing them on her plate.

"Perhaps she's older than she looks," she suggested, pouring milk into her tea, watching it bloom like pale, frozen mist.

"Well, she doesn't seem to have a very good grip on things here," Lucia said crisply, adding a dark chocolate Florentine to her plate. "I'd heard so much about this place, too. Perhaps that odious man is right, and things aren't what they were. Perhaps I ought to have stayed at The George after all, like I usually do. I came here for discretion, but that's gone out of the window, hasn't it?" Her lips flattened. "Half the club probably knows you're here by now."

Felicia put down her teacup. Finally, it seemed, they'd come to the all-important point.

"Why *am* I here, Lucia?" she asked gently. "Perhaps it's time you told me."

Chapter Six

Her companion looked at her for a long moment, then sighed.

"Yes, I suppose we ought to get to the point, unpleasant though it may be. There's no sense tiptoeing around it." She took a breath, as though to steady herself, then said, "I'm thinking of leaving my husband."

"I see." As bombshells went, Felicia had heard much worse, but then, she accepted that divorce for her had been a very different experience than it was for most people. It had been so indistinct, the breakdown of her marriage, so lacking in acrimony … and it wasn't as if the man was out of her life. She hadn't even managed to make it across town from the auction house to here without finding him at her side. Sometimes, she wondered if she really counted as properly divorced at all.

For Lucia, however, it would be another matter entirely. World-changing. She had gone from school to university to being a diplomat's wife. All her life, she had been protected, cossetted, safe in the knowledge that she knew exactly what her role was, where she fitted.

"Things between us have been … distant … for a while," Lucia said, haltingly, her voice dropping lower and lower as though afraid someone might overhear. "But recently, I've seen a side of his character…" She trailed off, her eyes far away for a moment, until she gathered herself again. "Let's just say that I want to have all of the facts at my disposal. Know where I stand, as it were. You see, he's a very powerful man—"

"I understand," Felicia interjected quickly. "You don't have to tell me any more if you don't want to." And honestly, it was better that she didn't. Divorces were complicated, chaotic things, and it was easier for Felicia to do her job if she wasn't plunged into the middle of them. To an extent, the less she knew, the better. "You'd like something valuing, I take it?"

Lucia nodded.

"My jewellery." She reached into her handbag and pulled out a midnight-blue pouch. For a moment, she looked as though she were about to set it down, then hesitated, holding it in her palm, looking at it with a rueful expression in her eyes. "The only real, tangible asset I own. I came to the marriage with nothing, you see." At Felicia's surprised look, she explained, "My father was an old-fashioned man. I was marrying a rich husband; as far as he was concerned, I was provided for." Her lips twisted. "But that's not how the world works now, is it?" She put the pouch down on the table between them. It gave a tantalisingly metallic clink as she did so. "I'd appreciate your opinion."

Feeling the by-now familiar flicker of anticipation she got in these moments, Felicia untied the pouch, letting it fall open. A moment later, she took a sharp breath.

A glittering mound of jewels scintillated at her. Felicia's eyes could barely take it all in; she just stared.

"Impressive, isn't it?" Lucia said, in a bored voice. She was inspecting her French manicure, apparently immune to the splendour before her. "Whatever my husband's faults, he has excellent taste. It's all the best of the best, you'll find."

Felicia ran her fingers across a pavé necklace, watching the fire flash within. She didn't need her loupe to tell her that these were top-tier diamonds; they were as clear and colourless as mountain spring water.

"Lucia," she leaned forward, instinctively putting a hand across the jewels protectively. "Do you think we should do this somewhere else?"

Lucia blinked at her, not seeming to understand. Felicia bit back a sigh, wondering just how sheltered her friend's life must have been to date.

"Somewhere more private?" Felicia persisted, pointedly, indicating the busy room that surrounded them.

"*Oh.*" Lucia's face cleared as she finally caught on. She gave a tinkling laugh. "I see. You think … dear Felicia! It costs an absolute *fortune* to be here. I'm sure no-one would … the very *idea.*" She crossed one leg over the other with a demure smile. "Besides, why do you think I requested this booth? We're quite sequestered in here."

Felicia briefly wondered whether to disabuse her friend of the notion that people who seemed to be dripping with wealth were always to be taken at face value. She'd lost count of the number of clients who lived in castles and manor houses yet dropped in to the auction regularly to sell off their prized possessions. All so that they could keep up the appearances they held so dear. The Wimbledon debenture, the luxury cars … or their membership to a club like this one. To drop it, after all, would be tantamount to admitting that there might be a 'problem' – and that would be unthinkable. No, Felicia was willing to bet that a good number of these people couldn't really afford to be here.

"I'm more worried about people spotting *me*," Lucia was saying. "You see, I told my husband I was staying at our chalet in Switzerland. I'm not supposed to be in Stamford at all."

"So that's why you didn't stay at The George."

It made sense now, Felicia thought. The town's famous landmark was like a highway. It was bustling, social, a place to see and be seen. You could even cut through the centre of it to get from one part of town to another. It was the definition of public. It certainly wasn't the place to go if you wanted to avoid seeing anyone you knew.

Lucia nodded.

"I confided in an old friend, who offered that I stay here under her account. She's a member, you see. She told me it wouldn't be an issue, that they're used to discretion, but…" She looked unsure of whether to say more. "Well, to be honest, since I arrived, I've been getting the impression that the club might not be as content with the whole arrangement as she suggested. Oh, they've been perfectly *cordial*, nothing too much trouble, but…" Suddenly, she drew back, with a shake of the head that sent her dark hair rippling. "Anyway, listen to me, distracting you from your work. I'll be quiet as a mouse from now on."

Felicia scarcely heard any of this. Her attention had been caught by something hidden within the pile in front of her. A dull, honeyed gleam, peeking out from amongst the scorching brilliance of the gemstones all around it. She pushed aside a sapphire tennis bracelet, fishing out the object. Compared to everything else, it was an unprepossessing sight: a ring, battered and dented, the thick gold band warped out of shape.

"Oh, *that*." Lucia looked faintly embarrassed, as though Felicia had found an old bra of hers accidentally lurking amongst the spoils. "Sorry, I don't know how it got in there." She held out her hand.

But Felicia held on, looking at her schoolmate with renewed interest.

"Your husband didn't buy you this?"

"*God*, no." Lucia looked scandalised. "He'd never get me anything so tatty. It's an old heirloom of my grandmother's; junk, of course, but one gets sentimental about these things. I've never been able to bring myself to throw it away."

Felicia held it under the light from the table sconce, turning it this way and that. It was of heavy, florid design, with a large oval cabochon to the centre.

"Ghastly, isn't it?" Lucia was spreading clotted cream thickly onto a scone. "I don't know how anyone could bring themselves to wear— What on *earth* are you doing?"

Felicia was probing the sides of the ring, pressing experimentally around the stone's setting. She really hoped she wasn't wrong about this, or she was going to look like a prize idiot.

Mercifully, just as she was beginning to worry, something shifted beneath her finger pad, and the face of the ring popped open.

Chapter Seven

The two women stared at it, momentarily stunned into silence. Lucia lowered her forgotten scone to her plate, eyes round.

"I had no *idea* it did that! What…"

"It's a poison ring," Felicia explained, carefully levering the hinged compartment further open with her nail.

"You mean … like the Borgias used?" Lucia looked horrified.

"It was rumoured to be a favourite method of theirs, yes," Felicia said. The idea was as fiendishly simple as it was terrifying; the unfortunate victim would be offered a drink, and while their host was pouring, they would surreptitiously flick the secret catch on their ring, releasing the deadly poison into the goblet below. It would have been the work of a moment, almost invisible to the naked eye. She peered gingerly inside, then let out a sigh of relief. "Empty, thank heavens."

Lucia went pale.

"You didn't *really* think there might still be…"

Felicia shrugged.

"Honestly? You never know."

Only the person who'd commissioned the ring would have definitely known that this was no ordinary piece of jewellery. The compartment was expertly disguised; there was a fair chance that she was the first person to have opened it in hundreds of years. And to think that the last time might have been over someone's drink… The thought sent a chill down her spine.

Lucia's gaze had turned sceptical.

"Now you're just scaring me." Her voice held a note of reproval. She shook her head decisively. "I mean, it must be some sort of fake, or copy. That's far more likely, isn't it? It can't actually be *real*."

"It's the most logical explanation, yes," Felicia admitted slowly. "The Victorians were rather taken with the idea and they appropriated it as a sort of whimsy. It's true that almost all of the examples you see are from then. Some people have even gone so far as to suggest that Renaissance poison rings were just a Victorian myth, that they never really existed."

"Well, there you go, then…" Satisfied, Lucia took the ring as Felicia held it out to her.

"But…" Felicia started, then stopped herself, wondering whether she really ought to say more. Whether she should just leave it at that. But the antiques valuer in her was too strong, and it was too late; she was already blurting it out. "Even so, I'm not convinced that *is* a copy." Before Lucia could interject, she hurried on, pointing out the details on the ring as she spoke. "Look at how the stone's been set, for one thing. And the way the band's formed. Even the colour of the gold; it's all spot on."

More than that, it just didn't *feel* Victorian, Felicia added, albeit silently. There was nothing in the working of the ring that hinted at romanticism, mysticism, wistful nostalgia … it wasn't easy to explain, or quantifiable; simply a combination of instinct, expertise, and good old-fashioned experience. Once you'd held enough objects, you started to get a sense for things. Of where they'd come from, the spirit of the age from which they'd emerged.

Sometimes, you held an object, and you just *knew*.

Obviously, something she'd said had struck a chord with Lucia, because her companion didn't simply dismiss her as she'd expected.

"Well, if you think … I suppose you *are* the expert." Lucia was eyeing the ring warily now, doubt written over her face. "But please, don't tell me that means…" She lowered her voice, "that people were actually *murdered* with this thing? That would simply be too horrid." She shuddered, dropping the ring onto the table as though it was radioactive. "I'm not sure I can bear to have it near me. I shall have to sell it now." Then, after what Felicia felt was a calculated pause, she added, casually, "I don't … I mean, it wouldn't be *worth* anything, I suppose? I mean, if it really *is* rare…"

Felicia opened her mouth to reply, but before she could, they were interrupted by a bright young voice hailing them.

"Hello. You two are new, aren't you?"

A girl's face popped around the side of the booth, surrounded by a sheen of pale blonde hair. She regarded them with open interest.

At the first sign of interruption, Lucia had pounced into

action, scrunching up the jewellery pouch and whisking it back into her bag with one fluid movement. Clearly, she wasn't *that* blasé about who might see it, Felicia thought.

"Usually, it's the same stuffy old people around here," the girl was saying, as though feeling more explanation were needed. "That's why I noticed you."

Felicia looked at her, immediately finding herself returning the interest. It wasn't difficult; the girl had a captivating face; almost pretty, yet too unusual to really be described as such. There was something alien-like in the exaggeration of the features: the chin a touch too pointed, the eyes a shade too wide set. The eyebrows were so pale as to be almost non-existent in this light. Felicia found herself trying to work out how old she was; her cheeks still had the plump youthfulness of childhood, but her face was just beginning to lean out, to take on a shape. Fifteen, perhaps?

"You're making the assumption that we're not stuffy," Felicia said, with a smile. "We might be the stuffiest people in here, for all you know."

"You're not." The reply was confident. "Not in *those* shoes."

Felicia glanced down at her pink suede ankle boots and couldn't resist a laugh. They were the kind of footwear her father would disgustedly decry as 'townie,' and indeed they had come with her from the capital, so she couldn't argue with him on that point. They were shamelessly un-countrified, but she wasn't ready to surrender to a life of stolid soles and serviceable browns just yet. Even if she *did* have to clean mud off the things almost daily at the moment.

"I'm just a visitor," she explained. "Hence the footwear transgression."

"Oh." The young face fell in disappointment. "That's a

shame. I'd hoped you were staying. It would have been nice to have someone interesting to talk to for once." She sighed the sort of put-upon sigh only someone under twenty-five could muster up. "It gets so *dull* here. It never changes."

Felicia knew better than to remind her that that was, for most people here, the main draw. Keeping things exactly the same was an almost impossible task; that's why people were prepared to pay for a place like this, where they managed it so seamlessly. But that was something you didn't appreciate until you were older. Constancy and nostalgia were an anathema to the young.

"Although, it's already a lot more exciting with you here," the girl was saying now, clearly trying not to look unashamedly thrilled about it. "I saw you having a run-in with Doctor Rauceby. He's a real pill, isn't he?"

"So we found," Lucia said tautly. Her tone wasn't impolite, exactly, but it wasn't encouraging either. Clearly, she wanted the conversation finished. But the girl seemed impervious, rattling on.

"I wouldn't take it personally; he's like that with everyone. Always spoiling for a fight." She cocked her head thoughtfully, the strands of blonde hair that had escaped from her French plait dancing around her face. "I once heard him call someone a canker on the face of humanity just because they liked blackcurrant jam on their scones rather than strawberry."

Well, at least he was loquacious, Felicia thought weakly.

"I wish I could say he was the worst here, but…" The girl trailed off, then let the pause sit, looking at them hopefully out of the corner of her eye.

Felicia could feel Lucia's impatience radiating across the table. She knew she shouldn't take the bait. But at the same time, how could she not? The girl was clearly bored, but more than that, she seemed a little lonely, too. Felicia's heart went out to her. Presumably, she'd been dragged here by her parents against her will, and there couldn't be much to entertain her in a place like this. She didn't see the harm in giving her what she wanted. So she leaned forward – deliberately avoiding Lucia's disbelieving gaze – and, dropping her voice to a conspiratorial tone, said, "Listen, we could use your help. My friend is going to be staying here for the next few days. Perhaps you could give her some tips. You know, who's who, what they're like. She'd find it really useful."

Their companion's eyes lit up enthusiastically, even as Lucia began to protest.

"Really, Felicia, I don't think that'll be necessary—"

But Felicia cut her off breezily.

"You don't want any more run-ins like the one we just had, do you?"

"I can tell you anything you want to know," the girl said eagerly. Now she was officially invited into the conversation, she moved closer to the table, rounding the side of the pew. It was only then that Felicia noticed she used a walker, leaning on it heavily as she manoeuvred it into position. She shifted her weight as she reached across for a slice of marmalade Swiss roll, biting into it whilst still talking, in that way teenagers have. "No-one notices me. I'm practically part of the furniture. I know everything that goes on around here." She was already reaching for another piece of cake – the first one having disappeared in a blur – and using it to point towards the fireplace.

"You see those two?"

Felicia and Lucia both shifted onto the edges of their seats, craning to get a glimpse of the two wingback chairs closest to the fire.

"Those two ladies?" Lucia said. "They look like nice, respectable sorts."

"Is it respectable to treat your sister like a slave?" The girl said flatly.

As if on cue, a querulous voice cut through the hubbub.

"I said a splash of milk, Sybil. A *splash*! That's more like a tidal wave. How can you still get it wrong after so many years?"

"I'm really *very* sorry Lavinia," another voice replied, sounding flustered. "My hand caught in this big loop of wool; I can't think what it's doing there. I'm *sure* it wasn't in the pattern. Oh dear, I must have got muddled up somewhere. Of course, you can't drink that; I'll ask them for a fresh pot of tea at once."

"Poor Sybil," their young informer told them now, in an undertone. "She's had a lot of bad luck. Her husband left her with nothing; she didn't find out until he'd died that he'd basically gambled away all their savings. She's so innocent; I don't think it ever occurred to her to think about money. Lavinia, now ... *she's* as rich as anything. But she's also mean as anything. When she offered to take Sybil in, there was nothing charitable about it. She just saw the chance for an unpaid worker *and* a whipping boy to take her temper out on all in one fell swoop." A shadow crossed her sweet face. "No-one should be pushed around like that, should they? Forced to live their life for someone else." She shook her head with a sheepish grin. "But listen to me! I'm making this place sound dire. Really, not *everyone's* as bad as that! Look ... those old gents at the chess set. That's a really sweet story; they're brothers who live on opposite sides of the country, but they were evacuated here during the war, so this is where they meet. They don't mix much; I think they just want to spend time together. But they're very nice if you get talking to them."

"And him?" Lucia pointed, and this time Felicia *did* have a decent view. It was a young man, still scribbling away, his black hair dishevelled and sticking up in tufts as though he'd been running his hands repeatedly through it. "He looks about your age."

Was it her imagination, Felicia wondered, or did their companion's young face flush slightly?

"Oh, that's … that's just Florian. He stays here with his mother."

And that, apparently, was all she had to say about Florian, because she moved on quickly to, "And then there are my parents. I should mention them, I suppose."

"Well, of course *they* shan't be on my avoid list," Lucia said, belatedly rediscovering her graciousness.

"Oh, no, they definitely should be." The reply was deadpan, utterly earnest. "Don't get into a conversation with Daddy unless you only want to talk about racehorses and how everyone in the world thinks they're superior to him. He's got an enormous chip on his shoulder, I'm afraid, and this place only brings out the worst in him." She raised a ghostly eyebrow. "We're new money, you see, and most people here made their family fortunes around the Norman Conquest. He's paranoid that all the other members here think he's common. Which of course they do," she concluded simply. "And Mummy…" She sighed. "*Where* to begin with Mummy?"

"Aurelia?" A fluttery, faintly panicked voice drifted across the room. "Aurelia, darling, are you in here? Where *are* you?"

Aurelia – a lovely name, Felicia thought, and one that suited her – pulled a face.

"As if I could get lost in this place," she said bitterly. "Where am I going to go?" Then she immediately looked guilty, explaining, "I have to keep reminding myself that it's not her fault. She can't *help* being a bag of nerves. Ever since…"

"*Aurelia!*" The voice was openly frantic now.

"I'd better go," Aurelia said, with visible reluctance. "She'll only get herself into a terrible state if I don't, and I'll have to spend all evening calming her down." She began to turn, the wheels of her walker gliding effortlessly across the carpet. Even so, Felicia saw her wince; clearly, she was in more pain than she let show.

"I hope you come and visit again," she said, looking Felicia straight in the eye. And then she was gone.

For a moment, neither of the women spoke.

"What a curious child," Lucia ventured at last, pouring herself another restorative cup of tea. "Really quite … odd."

"She's a teenager," Felicia replied. "They're *meant* to be odd. I have one of my own at home," she added, by way of explanation as Lucia looked askance at her.

"*Oh.*" Her friend's gaze dropped away, the curve of her eyelashes creating deep shadows on her cheeks in the candlelight. "I … I didn't realise you had children."

"Just the one. A son."

"How wonderful." Lucia's voice had flattened; a muscle quivered in her throat before the spoke again. "We never … I mean, with my husband's career, and the travel, there was just never quite the…" She met Felicia's eye with an over-bright smile, scrunching the napkin on the lap into a ball and placing it on the table. "You know, I might just powder my nose quickly, if you'll excuse me." She indicated towards the inglenook. "The fire…"

"It *is* rather warm," Felicia agreed tactfully, making a point of reaching for another scone. "Take your time. I'll be quite content here. Plenty to keep me going."

The minutes ticked by. Felicia toyed with her scone – which she hadn't really wanted – and wondered if she hadn't unwittingly put her foot in it. When Lucia had been gone a good fifteen minutes, Felicia reluctantly conceded that maybe she ought to go and check everything was all right.

The Powder Room, as it turned out, more than lived up to its rather overblown name. A row of pink marble sinks, crowned with gold taps, marched along the far wall. Behind them, clustered in baskets, complementary toiletries for every possible beauty-related emergency could be found. There was even a hairdryer station in the corner, although Felicia was struggling to imagine what would have to befall someone for them to do a full blow-dry whilst they were halfway through dinner. Then again, she reflected wryly, perhaps that was the point. Everything about The Aquitaine was pure excess; it wasn't about what was necessary.

One thing the opulent bathroom didn't possess, however, was any sign of her old schoolmate. Puzzled, Felicia left, intending to head back to the snug. But as her hand rested on the carved newel post at the head of the staircase, something caught her attention. A glint of light on dark shining hair. *Lucia*.

Felicia went to move towards her, then stopped as she realised her friend wasn't alone.

She was with Annabel Drayford, tucked into an alcove further down the hall. They were deep in conversation, their heads bent towards one another. Felicia couldn't hear what they were saying from here, nor could she see Lucia's face. But she could see Annabel's, and the expression on it wasn't a happy one. The manager was nodding, but her eyes were hard, her mouth set in a sombre line.

Suddenly, Lucia seemed to have had enough of the conversation, and she turned to walk away. With a bolt of horror, Felicia realised she would be right in her eyeline. She ducked behind a marble nymph, sucking in her breath.

And then a low voice spoke in her ear.

Chapter Eight

"What are we looking at, then?"

It was barely a murmur, but Felicia started so violently that she jostled into the nymph, which rocked precariously on its plinth. On the landing, Annabel Drayford paused, looking around her curiously. Her eyes raked her surroundings as though scanning them for any anomaly. Then, slowly, she began to walk straight towards the statue, her brow creased in a frown.

Felicia felt her heart drop into her suede boots.

But the manager stopped just short, scrutinising a fern on a polished occasional table. She reached into its foliage and with a single, brutal yank, plucked a browning leaf from amongst the green fronds. Her face smoothed in satisfaction at the restoration of order, and she turned, sweeping away abruptly towards the stairs.

Felicia sighed, allowing her shoulders to drop slightly in a moment of relief before she turned accusingly to the man next to her.

"Did no-one ever teach you that it's bad form to sneak up on a person, Jack?"

"I'm not sure you're in any position to be sanctimonious, given your current position." His lips quirked in a half smile, the closest his expression ever got to the real thing. "You know, the best thing about us is I never know where we're going to meet next. But I think behind the buttocks of a semi-pornographic statue has got to our best yet."

His hazel eyes were almost golden today, and alight with amusement; she was trying very hard to look anywhere but directly at them. That gaze had a tendency to suck her in, keep her where her logical brain knew she shouldn't be.

Because Jack Riding was trouble. And not just in the way the town had labelled him: the black sheep, the teenage tearaway, the boy who would never come good… No, to *her*, the danger he held was much closer and more personal. She steeled herself, running through the list of all the reasons why she'd promised they would never get this close to one another again. Not that she needed to; her pattering heart, traitorous thing that it was, was enough of a warning all on its own.

"I was avoiding someone," she said, sounding, even to her own ears, insufferably prim.

"That's just a grown-up way of saying that you were hiding from them. Or should I say, her." Jack riposted, indicating Annabel Drayford's retreating form. "What did you do? Break some of their priceless crockery? Accidentally call someone 'My lord' instead of 'sir'?" When she glared at him, he held up his hands. "Hey, look, I'm not judging. I spend a decent amount of time hiding from her myself. The woman's a termagant."

"You know her?" She looked at him properly, then, taking

in the camera around his neck. She'd been so surprised to see him – then so *distracted*, loathe as she was to admit it – that it only now occurred to her to wonder what he was doing here. "Wait, are you ... *working*?"

His mouth quirked up in wry acknowledgement.

"Ouch. Don't bother to hide your astonishment."

She flushed.

"I didn't mean..."

"Of course you did. But I can't take it personally; we both know that I'm *exactly* the sort of riffraff a place like this usually wants to keep well away from their polished floors and pocketable silver."

He said it breezily, but as ever, when they got onto this topic, there was an undercurrent of bitterness there.

"I just wouldn't have thought this would be your sort of commission, that's all," she said neutrally, keen to move the subject away from such tricky waters.

For a moment, she thought he was going to call her out on it, but then he shrugged, leaning against a marble thigh.

"You're right, it's not. But it'll pay my rent for a year. Even I'm not *that* unmaterialistic." He gave a hard smile. "Besides, it's still hardwired in me to take whatever work I can get. If you recall, it wasn't that long ago I could barely get hired to photograph a public toilet in this town ... apart from by your dad, of course," he amended, his face softening slightly.

"Yes, well, we know how he likes to be contrary," she quipped, although they both knew that wasn't really the reason. Not in this case. Oh, certainly, her father did have that streak in him; still a Lincolnshire farm boy at heart, he had no time for the stuffiness or pretension that could prevail in a town like this, and he took a certain mischievous satisfaction in creating awkwardness for those who did. Probably plenty of people at the time had thought that hiring the local scapegrace – as many still stubbornly insisted on seeing Jack, despite the many intervening years suggesting otherwise – was just another example of Peter Grant's slightly provocative sense of humour.

But her father, for all of his outward boom and bluster, was surprisingly astute when it came to judging the heart of a person. Since the day he'd started the auction house, Felicia didn't think he'd ever even glanced at a CV or reference when deciding whether to hire anyone. He would have employed Jack not just in acknowledgement of his merits as photographer, but of his character, too. A vote of confidence at a time when no-one else had any in the young man they'd all long since written off as irredeemable.

Felicia, she was thoroughly ashamed to admit, would probably have been of the same opinion, had she been in town at the time. After all, she'd been all too ready to take the rumours at face value earlier in the year, when her path had first crossed with that of the man standing in front of her now. She knew very differently these days. In fact, she was one of the only people who knew the full truth. That Jack's last, and most serious crime hadn't in fact been his at all; he'd been set up, and although he'd escaped prosecution, he'd been tried and found guilty in the court of public opinion, nonetheless. His punishment had been longer-lasting than anything the law could mete out, and the injustice of it had left its mark on him.

"It seems that since the Georgian Fair, my stock has risen considerably." Jack raised his fair eyebrows. "I still don't know what Cassie had to do to force the council to hire me for that, by the way. I'm figuring it's probably better I don't probe too deeply."

Felicia was inclined to agree there.

"Well, would you look at you." She smiled softly. She was aware of herself stepping closer, unable not to be drawn in. He was unrelentingly beautiful; she'd almost forgotten how closely his eyes matched his golden skin. Warning bells were beginning to sound in her head, reminding her of what had almost happened the last time they were this near to one another, but she barely heard them. "First an endorsement from the mayor, now an exclusive member's club. What next? The women's institute?"

"I'm currently dodging calls from several vicars," he admitted, deadpan.

"I'd say you're skimming dangerously close to becoming the bourgeois choice around here. You'll have to hang up your rebel's hat for good."

"I think I'm still safe for a while yet. I had to borrow a jacket and tie just to get into this place." He smiled, properly, for the first time, and her stomach flipped in response. She bit her lip, suddenly all too aware of just how small the alcove they were occupying was. And her hand… With a bolt of horror, she realised it was resting on his chest. How the hell had it got *there*? She could feel the warmth of his skin through his shirt, the steady thud of his heartbeat. It sounded remarkably relaxed compared to her own. She snatched her hand away like it had been burned.

"I'd better go," she mumbled. She could feel her face flaming, and she looked away. "I have a friend waiting downstairs."

And she all but fled; or at least, she would have done, if she hadn't been hindered by the ungainly necessity of having to squeeze past him to get out of the niche.

For a moment, she thought he was going to let her go, just like that. But then, suddenly, his hand closed gently around her wrist.

"You're definitely just here on a social visit?" His voice was low, no longer teasing. "It isn't … anything more?"

Lucia's commission jumped into her mind. But that was a private matter; she'd promised she'd keep it quiet. Besides, it was no business of Jack's.

"Why would you say that?" she asked lightly.

"Because I know you." His lips twisted. "And because I saw that *he's* here." Felicia didn't need a name to know he meant Dexter. "You two … you're not on the trail of something, are you? One of your mysteries?"

"No, we're not." This time, she didn't have to lie. She pulled her wrist away with a frown. "Why are you *asking* me all this? What's this about?"

His face became shuttered, as it always did when she asked him a direct question. She felt a sharp jab of irritation and disillusionment. This is how it always was, she told herself sourly. How it always *would* be. He would always keep something of himself back. She'd already spent years of her life with a man who'd put himself first; so had Algernon, for that matter. If it had just been *her* mistake to repeat… She bit her lip and decided not to think about what she might do, if that was the case.

"It's just … this place. It doesn't like outsiders poking around in its business." He ran a hand through his dark blond curls, tousling them in agitation. "I want to make sure you're being careful, that's all."

"I'm just here for tea," she said shortly. "I don't *need* to be careful."

But if I do, I can look after myself. The rest of the sentence went unsaid, but he obviously heard it regardless, because he stepped back, indicating for her to go.

"As you were, then. Don't let me hold you up."

Then he turned as though to leave himself. But he didn't. She could feel his eyes on her all the way to the staircase.

Chapter Nine

The note had been left at the door of his lodgings, wedged into the splintering timbered frame at an angle, as though it had been jabbed into the crack in a fit of temper. He retrieved it, tucking it beneath the arm of his well-worn shop coat as he reached for the brass handle. The door swung open seamlessly, belying all expectations based on its outer, decrepit appearance. But then, so it should, thought Matthias Weaver, with a grim sort of satisfaction. It was his job to keep everything around here running smoothly, after all. He'd been doing it for as long as he could remember. Longer than almost anyone here could remember. There were few members left now who were old enough to recall The Aquitaine before he'd been a part of it. The place was like the wife he'd never had.

Indeed, he reflected, their relationship had lasted longer than many modern marriages, although, like any spouse, the club wasn't always the easiest to manage. She was a fussy mistress, but a splendid one, like a creaking galleon, full of holes but regal nonetheless. Their relationship was mutually beneficial: he took care of her, and she returned the favour. Or at least, she always had. Until Annabel Drayford had come along. Now, everything he'd known was changing. Including his beloved Aquitaine. And he wasn't sure how much longer he was going to be able to keep her.

He stumped through the darkened doorway, pausing to click on the lamp on the sideboard. A sepia-yellow gloaming bled across the room, just about illuminating its contents. But he knew what greeted him, and it was probably best not to see it too clearly. The peeling plaster, the damp creeping up the walls. The lamplight shone through the rotting window, sparkling off the condensation already building upon the old panes. He placed the candlestick he was carrying down on the scrubbed kitchen table, slapping the crisp white note after it with rather less reverence.

He fumbled for the box of matches he kept by the stove, fingers already growing numb from the seeping cold that seemed to imbue his house like a cloak on days like this. He tried to strike the light, but the box was damp, like everything else, and he had to try again and again, until desperation began to grow in him. In his weaker moments, he wondered how many more winters he could take in this place, how much more will he had in him. He tried not to think of his old lodgings above the stables; they'd been faded, yes, but comfortable, and warm, too, once he'd got the fire going nicely. More important than anything, though, they'd been dry. That was something you never appreciated until you'd had to live in unrelenting damp like this. At first, he'd tried to keep it at bay, patching up the plaster, resealing the windows, scrubbing the mould from the corners with a firm-bristled brush. But it was indomitable, returning within days each time, soaking through the layers of wallpaper, blooming across the ceiling like a rash.

It should never have been like this, he thought brokenly. He was supposed to have his home for life; that was the promise that had been made to him all those decades ago, when he'd first joined the club's staff as a green young man. A place for as long as he wanted it. A job and a home, all in one. It had been made to them all back then, a relic of a time when the club had treated its staff like family. He was the only one left now, but the promise still held, enshrined in the typewritten contract he'd signed.

Unfortunately, while it had been made with good intentions, it had been done so in a simpler, more trusting world – a fact that the club's new manager was only too ready to exploit.

He would never forget the day she'd marched into his house – the only time she'd ever crossed the threshold – and declared that his flat was required for turning into some sort of spa – *wellbeing rooms* was the term she'd used, he thought, although he'd been so stunned he'd scarcely been able to take in her words.

Her voice had dripped false sympathy, he remembered bitterly, but her eyes had given her away. They'd positively gleamed with triumph as she'd handed him her copy of his contract, then waited smugly while the anodyne solicitor she'd brought with her read out the legalese in a pompous, reedy voice. He'd listened numbly, staring at his juvenile signature at the bottom of the page, its ink faded with time. He hadn't understood a word of it, but he didn't need to. Essentially, it stipulated that while the club had to offer him a place to live, there was no specification that it had to always be the same place, or even one of his choosing. In fact, as it turned out, it didn't *have* to be anything at all. Not even, as it turned out, habitable. Something Annabel Drayford had taken full and immediate advantage of.

He'd promptly been moved to the gardener's cottage at the boundary of the estate, unlived in since old Ernie Bloomfeld had retired to Portugal in the late eighties. The gardeners since then had all been dailies, and the cottage, listed and therefore undemolishable, left to crumble out of sight. And now he, too, was out of sight, pushed to the farthest point away from the club, and pushed, too, to the limits of his endurance.

But that was as far as she could go, he reminded himself, striking at the match again, with renewed determination. She couldn't actually force him out. Only he had that power, and as long as he could keep clinging on, there was nothing she could do. On the darkest and coldest nights, the knowledge of that – and how much it must infuriate her – was the only thing that kept him going. Every day he stayed, he thwarted her a little more … and kept one more piece of his beloved Aquitaine alive with it.

Because he wasn't the only part of the old Aquitaine she wanted to see the back of. She had plans, he knew. She wanted to change this place, make it something it wasn't.

He'd had a feeling the first day he'd set eyes on her, striding through the snug, heels clacking on the flagstone floors. She'd looked utterly out of place, with her angular suits, her harsh make-up. A corporate robot, he'd thought dismissively, nothing behind the eyes but the bottom line. There was no way they'd hire *her* for the job; she was an anathema, the very opposite of what the club represented.

He still couldn't understand what had happened. How he could have been so wrong.

He struck the match again and eventually it caught, the flame gasping upwards. He lit the gas stove and put the kettle on, gathered a mug from the shelf. Began the well-trodden ritual of making a cup of tea. He slugged whisky into the mug, taking a gulp. As the warmth began to suffuse his bones, so did a renewed sense of purpose. He picked up the candlestick, gripping it with hands scarred from a lifetime of work; of fixing things, protecting them against the harsh passage of time. He fiddled with the drip tray, which had come loose from the stem. Easy enough to remedy and more than worth the minor effort. It was a beautiful piece, this, finely moulded, from a time when everything had been made with care and individual attention. Things like this … they deserved to last.

Things at The Aquitaine weren't supposed to be perfect. It just wasn't that sort of place. To say it had charm would be wrong; that was too twee, too neat. No, what the club had instead was that most English of traits – it had *character*. Stubborn, brilliant, inimitable *character*. It had a life of its own. Its idiosyncrasies were what made it, from its awkward pipework to its uneven floors. It wasn't the most up-to-date place to stay; it wasn't the most comfortable, either. That wasn't why people came. The things they came for couldn't be mapped on a corporate graph or plotted on a spreadsheet.

And Annabel Drayford simply couldn't understand that.

She'd said, in her opening speech to the staff, that she wanted to bring The Aquitaine into the twenty-first century. Instead, she was killing its very soul. Every inch further she got her sensibly buffed claws into the fabric of the place, the more the magic of it was fading. On the surface, it still looked much the same, but beneath it all, the decay was apparent. The warmth and eccentricity were bleeding away, the cracks being subtly buffed out, the staff too terrified of being anything less than perfect to show any kind of humanity, instead going about their business with blank, humourless faces.

Except him. He was the one thing here that couldn't be bought, couldn't be tossed aside. And he would hang on for as long as he had strength in his bones to do so. Until it killed him, if necessary.

His eyes travelled downwards, to where the white rectangle glowed insistently against the gloom. His eyes could just make out the vague shape of the club's logo, the familiar, imperious handwriting beneath it. More orders from on high, no doubt, delivered, as usual, with minimal ceremony, maximum contempt. His lips pressed together, bile rising in his throat.

With a sudden, swift movement, he brought the knife downwards, driving it through the ink and paper into the wood, where it shivered.

Chapter Ten

The next morning descended in the sort of perfection that only an October day could bring: the sky a blank, pearlescent blue, the sunlight stark and white upon the world below, casting jagged shadows and scintillating off the surface of the river. It was so dazzling that Felicia had to shield her eyes as she opened the front door of the cottage on Water Street. She bent down to retrieve the milk from the bowed stone step, unable to resist pausing as she straightened, just for a moment. The view that greeted her might be familiar, but it was impossible to imagine ever tiring of it.

The old milliner's cottage she'd grown up in was miniscule in dimensions, but it held one of the finest positions in town, mere metres from the water, with uninterrupted views across its tree-lined banks. On a quiet day, surrounded by the rustling of willows, one could almost forget one was right in the heart of town.

She retreated into the dark interior of the cottage, squeezing down the narrow hallway into the low-timbered kitchen.

It was a room, which, like the rest of the house, could be described in several conflicting ways, depending upon who was doing the describing – namely, whether you were an estate agent, American tourist or someone who actually had to live within its sloping walls.

To both of the former, the dark, craggy beams and deep-set, diamond-paned windows would be charming and olde-worldy; the collection of well-worn, mismatched furnishings her father had rescued from the auction's unsold pile eclectically rustic, the burly ginger tomcat curled up in the fruit bowl a cosy marker of country life. However, to the latter group, the reality was that it was cramped, underheated, stuffed with items that were unwanted for a reason, and the cat was actually savage – a fact that anyone foolish enough to get within a foot of him would swiftly ascertain. Also, Felicia happened to know that there was fruit in that bowl, beneath that furry orange rump. Fruit that was now looking decidedly less appealing than it had a few minutes ago.

"Good morning, darling," she said to Algernon, who was showering cereal into a cracked bowl with the natural early-morning perkiness he certainly hadn't inherited from her.

Then she saw that her son wasn't alone at the table.

"Don't you mean darlings?" Dexter grinned, lowering the broadsheet that had been propped up around him like a tent.

Felicia felt her eyes narrow, the good mood brought on by the promising morning already beginning to fade.

She really shouldn't be surprised to see him here, she told herself. If anything, she ought to be pleased that he was spending as much time as possible with their son. After the years he'd spent gallivanting around the world in pursuit of fame and fortune, he had a certain amount of making up to do in that department.

And she *was* pleased, she added firmly. Of *course* she was. It was just … did he have to sprawl about the place *quite* so much? She noticed he was well-installed, steam curling off the cup of coffee in front of him – a very *European* habit, her father always said, coffee first thing – crumbs from a half-eaten crumpet flurried across the tabletop, a spoon stuck into the blackcurrant jam at a rakish angle. Blackcurrant jam she'd only just picked up at the weekend, and which he'd obviously taken the liberty of opening; that little fact alone caused a fresh surge of irritation.

"Is the kitchen in your flat not working?" she asked, not really bothering to disguise any pointedness. Dexter didn't really do subtlety. You had to be direct, and even then, it usually went over his head.

"*Well…*" Dexter hedged, lounging back in his chair. The one with the wobbly leg, she noticed, thinking that now would be a highly satisfying time for the wood to finally give way.

She folded her arms, spearing him with a glare, but before she could say anything else, Algernon chirped, "He says he'd rather eat our food. Besides, he doesn't know how to turn on the oven."

Felicia smiled as Dexter groaned in mock exasperation.

"Honestly, son, sometimes I wonder if I've given you anything. You've certainly inherited none of my guile."

"Thank heavens," Felicia shot back. Perhaps a little too sharply; Dexter's eyes moved searchingly to hers, and she turned away quickly, pulling a crusty loaf out of the bread bin.

Then Dexter's voice said softly, "You once thought it one of my finest qualities."

Once being the operative word, Felicia thought, reaching into the fridge for the jar of marmalade. Lemon and lime, a flavour only she liked. It was about the one thing in the house safe from being purloined in her absence. Her fingers closed around the cold, frosted glass, pausing as her mind unravelled backwards, to that bittersweet place before life and time took its toll on her opinion of the man sitting behind her. Beneath the dreaming spires and across the manicured quadrangles of their university city, he'd seemed indescribably perfect. Of course, it had helped that Oxford itself was a bubble of unreality, fantastical and esoteric; it wasn't real life, the rules didn't apply. But they couldn't stay in that suspended reality forever, and what in that context had been dashing charm and cavalier attitude began to seem, in the cold light of adult life, rather less romantic.

The thing about Dexter, she concluded ruefully, was that he was always the same. In any place, any circumstance, at any point in time; he was like a cartoon character, ageless, impervious to the winds of change.

But she wasn't. And in the end, that had become like a wall, rising up between them. There'd been no way around it.

"I think 'finest' is a bit of a stretch," she said tartly, spreading marmalade across the singed surface of the bread.

"Most diverting, then."

"Maybe. For a while." The next sentence fizzed on her tongue; she fought to keep it there, failed. "But you can have too much of a good thing, can't you? I know I did."

No-one could possibly miss the barbed undertone this time. There was a beat of silence from the kitchen behind her. Felicia gripped the knife, closed her eyes. Then came the merciful sound of scraping as a chair moved away from the table, breaking the suddenly awkward atmosphere.

"I'd better go, Mum." As usual, Algernon showed no reaction to the febrile atmosphere between his parents, a fact which half broke Felicia's heart. "We've got assembly this morning."

"All right, darling." She turned at last, fixing a smile on her face; a smile which immediately wavered at the sight of him in his blazer and tie, schoolbag over his shoulder. It was ridiculous, of course, this sudden bittersweet wistfulness, the lump clogging her throat. She'd seen him in his uniform countless times since he'd started at the school six months ago, and yet suddenly, this morning, with the pale October sunlight igniting his bronze hair, he looked different, grown up in a way she couldn't have seen coming. Like it had happened overnight. How did children manage that?

She fought the impulse to throw her arms around him and cling on, instead patting his shoulder in a restrained, mother-of-teenager fashion. She was proud of herself for that, and for the airy tone she managed next.

"Have a good day. I'll see you later."

He nodded, shovelling a last spoonful of cereal into his mouth.

"Seven o'clock, right?"

"Yes." She hesitated, wondering whether to say more. "Look, you really don't *have* to come tonight. I know Lucia invited you, but I can say you're busy. It's Halloween, after all." Woe betide that his friends thought she was stopping him from hanging out with them so he could go to some fusty dinner with his parents.

"It's okay." Algernon shrugged, hitching his bag further

onto his shoulder. She'd picked that thing up once or twice and it weighed a ton; since then, she'd been keeping an eye on his posture. She didn't want him to end up like Richard III, with one shoulder higher than the other. "It's only hanging out at Septimus's house, and I'll be there for some of it. We're going over straight after school. Then Dad's going to pick me up before dinner."

"I see. You seem to have it all organised." She tried not to feel a little stab of jealousy that it was Dexter he'd turned to.

"I'll be there." Dexter waved his piece of toast in confirmation. "Now, go and raise hell, son. That's what your schooldays are for. Elysian fields, and all that."

Algernon's eyes met hers, and they shared a knowing look. Immediately, any lingering hint of resentment vanished. Dexter might love his son, but he would never understand him like she did. They just weren't made in the same mould. For one thing, Algernon was about the most unlikely hell-raiser to walk the planet.

"Sure, Dad," he said indulgently, as he headed for the door. Felicia watched him go, still with that rather maudlin feeling that had settled upon her this morning. She couldn't even blame the weather, she thought, frowning at the sunlight streaming through the warped glass of the windows.

"All right," she said pointedly to the newspaper, which had risen once more in a solid blockade of print around her ex-husband. "What's going on? Clearly you know something I don't."

The paper twitched but didn't lower. Instead, a vague voice emerged from behind it.

"I would say I know many things you don't, dear heart. Which one are you referring to this time?"

God, but he could be *such* a pain in the proverbial sometimes. Felicia gritted her teeth.

"About why exactly our twelve-year-old son is suddenly so keen to come along tonight."

She felt a twinge of anxiety even as she said it. Algernon had always been an unusual child, dreamy and full of contrasts, and in many ways, far too old for his time. Felicia had never wanted him any different, and from the start, she'd encouraged him to be who he was and not bow to pressure. She'd never regretted that course of action, but nonetheless, it hadn't always been easy to watch as a parent. He didn't naturally gel with his peers, as a rule, and she'd worried incessantly about his starting at the school in Stamford. But to her surprise – and intense relief – he'd fallen in almost seamlessly with a nice crowd.

Seeing her son having friends for the first time made her happy beyond measure, but, as she was finding, it also brought with it a gnawing sense of fear. She couldn't bear it if anything went awry, and she remembered all too well what the societal fabric of teenage life could be like. "Nothing's … happened, has it? With his friends?"

"Everything's fine." Dexter flipped the paper in half, creasing it neatly before dropping it onto the table. "Stop fretting. He just wants to avoid the blood and gore, that's all. You know how squeamish he is."

Felicia paused, toast halfway to her mouth.

"What blood and gore?" Good grief, what did they have *planned* for tonight?

Dexter gave her an amused look.

"No ritual sacrifices, don't worry. Just a few horror films,

I understand. Apparently, all teenagers have a predilection for scaring themselves witless."

"Not all." Felicia felt her heart sink. "Algie *hates* horror films." He'd had nightmares after watching *Home Alone* the Christmas before last.

Dexter nodded.

"Which is exactly why he has commissioned me to run a little interference." Dexter dolloped an obscene amount of blackcurrant jam onto the last piece of his crumpet. "I've agreed to 'take one for the team,' as I believe the expression goes." He adopted a forbidding expression, dropping his voice to an ominous tone. "In tonight's performance, I shall play the wicked father to his downtrodden adolescent. Denying him even the smallest crumb of freedom or pleasure, insisting cruelly upon a life of duty and servitude instead." He placed a hand upon his chest. "I think I shall rather relish the role."

Felicia was very glad she hadn't taken a bite of her toast in the end, because she would have choked on it if she had.

"*You*?" she scoffed. "A *stern* parent? You wouldn't know where to *start*."

"I have been practising," he said portentously. Only to then ruin the effect by wiggling his eyebrows. "Do you want to see?"

She smiled; she couldn't help it.

"No, I'm all right. Save it for tonight."

"Oh, go on." He leapt up, stretching his arms above his head as though limbering up. "I'm dying to show somebody. I have a speech and everything. I've even invented us a family motto, which I intend to bark in his face when the moment's right. I toyed with a few iterations, but in the end I decided to keep it punchy and go with 'duty, duty, *duty*!' – it'll be louder in the actual performance," he added, almost apologetically. "I don't want to scare the cat."

Godfrey, who'd been washing behind his bitten-off ears, gave a characteristically antagonistic hiss.

Felicia laughed, reaching over to collect the coffee pot from the table.

"It sounds like you've got it covered. I look forward to hearing all about it later."

There was a pause, then he said, almost hopefully: "Say, you could come along if you wanted. Make it a double act."

Felicia felt her breath draw in sharply. Suddenly, she was aware of the situation; how close they were standing, this all-too-familiar glow in her chest. This was what Dexter did best, almost without trying; he wore down defences, slipped around walls designed to keep him out, and before you knew it, there he was, back in your good books again. Except, it was only ever temporary.

No, she'd learned too many times that Dexter was better off at arm's length, both literally and figuratively. This time, she was determined she was going to keep him there.

Since the spring, she'd thought things had felt … different. Both of them back in Stamford, thrown together by murder, by something bigger than their own problems … she'd allowed herself to think of them as a team again, of sorts. But she'd been a fool, naïve. She'd soon learned that the main love in Dexter's life was still himself; that, and his desert-booted television alter ego. The fame and adulation *Treasure Seeker* had brought him was something she knew she could never hope to compete with.

She stepped to the side, subtly but firmly putting distance between them as she moved around him to the sink. She made a show of filling the cafetière with soapy water, trying to keep her voice totally flat as she said: "I don't think so. Anyway, it was you he asked." She paused, watching an errant soap bubble float upwards, the sunlight piercing it as it passed in front of the window. For a brief moment, it shimmered in a kaleidoscope of colours, then abruptly burst. She knew the feeling. "I hope you appreciate that, by the way." It had been a while since Algernon had relied on his father for much.

"Naturally." Dexter sounded slightly irritated, and she felt a mixture of satisfaction and relief, hoping that was a sign he was actually listening for once.

"Okay." And she was going to leave it there, she really was. But she knew Dexter too well. She wanted to make sure he was taking it seriously. "Just … don't let him down, all right? If you say you'll be there, *be* there. No gallivanting off on one of your whims at the last minute."

He sighed deeply.

"Oh, *I* see what this is. You're still annoyed with me about last night, aren't you?"

She grasped willingly at the excuse, in part because actually it wasn't entirely inaccurate.

"I'm not best pleased, no. There are things I'd rather be doing tonight. Instead, you've roped us all into this—" she waved a suds-coated scrubbing brush in the air, trying to come up with the word she wanted and ending up rather pathetically with "—thing."

"By *thing*, I take it you mean the four-course dinner at one of the most lavish and exclusive eateries in town?" Dexter sounded disbelieving. "Because you're making it sound like we're all having a spell on the rack."

"That may be more enjoyable," she muttered, knowing she was being petulant but unable to help herself.

Besides, she added silently to herself. It wasn't *just* dinner.

"If you come early, you'll be able to catch this ancient Halloween tradition they do," Lucia had said last night, eyes resting lingeringly on Dexter. "It's really *spooky*, apparently. Quite a spectacle. Mummers, they call them. It's a medieval tradition, almost forgotten these days; they tell me that here's one of the few places you can still find an authentic performance."

"Oh, don't be so dramatic." Dexter was folding his arms now; how she could tell that just by the tone of his voice, she couldn't explain. Just years of proximity, she supposed. "And I'd love to know how exactly I'm supposed to have 'roped us into it.' From what I recall, we were *invited*. More to the point, *you* were the one who accepted!"

"Well, I had to, didn't I?" she retorted, finally spinning around. He *was* folding his arms – not that she'd ever doubted it – and looking at her mutinously. She persisted, undeterred. "And if *you* hadn't flirted so outrageously with her, maybe Lucia wouldn't have got the idea in the first place."

"I was being *polite*," Dexter protested. "You told me she was an old friend of yours; being a boor didn't seem the done thing."

"I never said she was a friend, as such," Felicia muttered. "We were… Oh, I don't know. It was complicated."

"Why are you so against going tonight? Really?" He raised an eyebrow. "Not afraid of a little ghoulish fun, are we?"

"Of course not," she said lightly, but her voice hitched a little on the white lie.

Because how could she explain it to him when she wasn't

even sure herself? It wasn't really about Lucia; she sensed that was just a smokescreen, a rational reason for her mind to grab onto to disguise the fact that her unease was more nebulous in origin. Perhaps it was the season, or more precisely, the day. Felicia didn't exactly subscribe to the idea of the undead roaming the cobbles all night, but equally, it was hard not to pick up on some of the atmosphere, as the nights drew in, black and cold, and the trees shivered off the last of their leaves.

Or maybe it was the club itself. Despite the gilded grandeur and jaw-dropping resplendence, she couldn't help but feel there was something strange about the place. All those people, doing the same things, in the same order, even down to having the same seat at tea each day… There was nothing wrong with routine and tradition, but surely there was a point where it became unhealthy? And that manager, with her cold, penetrating stare…

Last night, she'd thought to herself that she'd be quite happy never to set foot back in the place again. Now, it appeared she would be doing exactly that.

Despite the warmth of the kitchen, and the glorious sunshine outside, the thought made her feel strangely cold.

Chapter Eleven

The bar at The Aquitaine was a thing of gilded myth, seen by few but talked about by many – and mostly in reverential, hushed tones, at that. Reports were of a dazzling sweep of Art Deco glass and chrome, floor-to-ceiling mirrors lining every inch of wall, reflecting back upon each other into a kaleidoscopic infinity, and rows upon rows of crystal-cut decanters, exquisitely backlit to glitter off the countless facets like a constellation of diamonds.

Normally, the subject of such breathless, extravagant rumours could only be expected to disappoint in reality. But not this one. The Aquitaine's bar more than lived up to any description; in fact, if anything, words tended to undersell it. As did photographs. It was one of those places that had to be *seen*; really seen, with one's own eyes.

Alas, it rarely was, reflected Leo Wild, as he drummed his fingers on the shimmering bar top and rearranged a pile of cocktail napkins that hadn't been touched since the last time he'd done it. Which had been all of – his eyes moved to the stainless-steel clock set high into the wall, encased within a sunburst of glass – five minutes ago, give or take. Each hour seemed to stretch for eternity in this place.

To be fair, this was guaranteed to be the quietest time of day. Teatime was when most of the guests were ensconced in the snug or library, drinking something a little less potent than cocktails and chasers. The denizens of The Aquitaine were nothing if not creatures of habit, and teatime was just that: for tea, nothing more.

They more than made up for it the rest of the time, though, he thought to himself dryly. No, the problem certainly wasn't lack of demand for his services. Bloody Marys at breakfast, an Irish coffee mid-morning, champagne cocktails before lunch … and that was just the first half of the day. In one sense, he'd never been so busy at any bar he'd worked at. The members here certainly made sure the club's liquor license paid for itself, he conceded. The issue wasn't so much what they were drinking as *where* they were drinking it.

He speared a pimento olive with a cocktail stick, chewing on it disconsolately as he looked out over the empty room. It ought to have been a place of buzzing activity, always with someone to be found, whether lingering on after a long lunch or business meeting, or simply propping up the bar, whiling the hours away until dinner. But the members seemed to have an aversion to this space, instead ordering drinks to their beloved snug, or to one of the other myriad cosy nooks tucked around the sprawling townhouse. Somewhere with squashy chairs and faded rugs and the air of noble decay the English seemed to have such a fondness for. It had taken him a while to work it out, but he'd realised eventually that the bar, in all its magnificent 1920s excess and glamour, was simply *too* grand for them.

This left him at something of a loose end. After all, mixing the drinks was only a small part of a barman's job; he could practically do *that* with his eyes closed. No, by far the larger share of his time ought to be taken up by talking to people. Or more specifically, listening. It was a cliché, of course, that people liked to talk to a barman, but it was also true, and people like these, with too much money and time on their hands, were no different. If anything, they were probably worse. In the absence of anything real to worry about, they became adroit at inventing problems instead.

But what did it matter to him whether the problems were real or not? Granted, it was hard to swallow the whining sometimes, the self-pity, but swallow it he did, and with a smile at that. He'd learned early on that a handsome face, combined with an engaging manner and a willing ear, could generally get him where he wanted to go. It wasn't hard to feign interest, and the more people could be encouraged to stay, the more outlandish the tip at the end. Whether said tip was fuelled more by gratitude or shame on their part, he didn't lose sleep over. They could afford it, after all. And thanks to their pathetic need to share, he was well on his way to being able to afford some of life's nicer things himself. It seemed like a fair trade.

But he couldn't listen if there was no-one to talk to. And the job that had once looked so promisingly rosy, so full of opportunities, had rapidly lost its sweetness.

Although, he reminded himself, if all went to plan, he may not have to put up with it for much longer.

He began to move amongst the mirrored tables, setting

them carefully, albeit more in hope than expectation. He doubted any of them would be in now; no-one would want to miss this evening's entertainment, after all.

Nonetheless, appearances had to be maintained. He reached beneath the bar, producing a club notecard, upon which he wrote something. Then he propped it up on the bar, in front of the smoked almonds. As he did so, he heard the sound of high-heeled shoes crossing marble. He felt his shoulders stiffen but arranged his face into its default laid-back expression. That was how people liked their barman, he'd found: affable and easy-going. So, to all outer observers, that's what he was.

"Good afternoon, Miss Drayford."

He said it formally enough, but with a lingering note on the '*Miss*', which made her look at him sharply. Then, immediately, like a bird of prey, her eyes swooped upon the bar top, spotting the anomaly in moments.

"What's this?" There was nothing merely curious about the question; her tone was emphatically accusatory. She picked up the card, examining it with disapproval. "A new cocktail?"

She uttered the word 'new' as though it was the most offensive thing imaginable. He felt a twinge of irritation but kept his reply breezy.

"A signature Halloween cocktail," he enlightened her. "Designed by me, for one night only."

She narrowed her eyes at him.

"You should have run this past me first." She sounded angry, but there was an edge of worry to her voice. Up close, he could hear it.

"Why? You know I can mix a drink." He took the card from her fingers, returning it to its spot on the bar. "After all, that's why I'm here, isn't it? Only the best and brightest for The Aquitaine."

She must have caught the sarcasm in his voice, because she flushed slightly, her mouth tightening. Her eyes flicked back to the card nervously.

Christ, she's wound up tight, he thought. *What does she think's going to happen? That I'm going to poison them all? Although I'd probably be doing the world a favour.*

"Look, it's nothing too controversial," he said, persuasively. "Marmalade and blood orange, with a blend of spices. Warming, aromatic … it's autumn in a glass. A crowd-pleaser."

Not, he added privately, that most of them probably would drink it. It didn't matter what it was. They were just too set in their ways. The unwritten job description of The Aquitaine's barman wasn't to innovate, it was to memorise; to know exactly what everyone drank when and to serve it to them without them even needing to ask for it.

"Hmm." She still didn't look convinced. "And the 'bloody twist'?" She pointed at the words.

"Ah, that. Just a little touch for Halloween." He grinned. When she didn't unbend in the slightest, he sighed. "Just a cranberry syrup drizzle, that's all." The effect was remarkably effective, mind; when laid over the crushed ice, it glistened just like real blood.

She scowled, clearly unimpressed.

"It sounds tacky, Leo. The Aquitaine doesn't do gimmicks."

"It's supposed to be *fun*." His patience was starting to wear thin, laid-back mien cracking slightly. Could she not let *anything* go? "I thought that's what this whole Mummers thing is meant to be about." He dropped his voice to a mere murmur, leaned in close, until his lips almost brushed her ear. "I know you can have fun, Annabel."

Her eyes widened. Then she stiffened, stepping away. She regarded him with something approaching fury. At once, he knew he'd made a mistake.

"For the *guests*," she hissed, "it is fun. For *you*, it is a privilege." She paused, then added, meaningfully, "One I'd *really* hate to have to revoke. But we both know there are plenty who'd be willing to take your place."

He stared back at her, knowing she fully meant the threat. Knowing she'd do it just to punish him. She was spiteful like that.

"You're very quiet all of a sudden." She cocked her head on one side, a jubilant glint in her eyes. "I take it you'd rather I didn't do that?"

The temptation to tell her where to stick it was overwhelming. But he held himself in check, reminding himself of what he had to lose. So he swallowed his pride, hung his head in a show of contrition.

"No, Miss Drayford," he said dully, not sure who he hated more in that moment; himself or her.

Her eyes scanned his face suspiciously, as though unsure of his sincerity. Then she pulled herself upright.

"Good. Then you'd better start taking things seriously. Do your bloody job. And for God's sake, get rid of *this*." She swiped at the card, knocking it from the bar onto the floor. It was a rare outward show of pique – at least in a public part of the club, within potential view of the members – and she had cause to regret it immediately as movement shimmered beyond the frosted glass of the doors.

The two of them reacted instantly, each of them rearranging

their face into a professional smile as they turned to greet the incomers. And just in time. The doors swung open, a dazzling vision of snow-white fur and blonde hair sweeping into the room. The entrance somehow managed to be dramatic yet elegant at the same time, and with an air of ceremony usually reserved for the red carpet. Upon seeing who it was, Leo felt his false smile turn into a real one.

"Ms. Johnson." He spoke first, as Annabel remained uncharacteristically silent next to him. "I trust you had a good walk?"

Nobody looking at her would possibly deduce that that's where she'd been, he thought, as she shrugged off her ermine coat – *vintage of course, darling* – and draped it in the direction of Annabel, who had no choice but to take it. She looked rather annoyed, which he found particularly raised his spirits.

"Oh, yes. It's *so* atmospheric out there." Cymbeline Johnson – no-one was sure if that was a stage name or her real one, but she was so well known by that moniker that anything else would have seemed wrong – perched elegantly on a bar stool, smoothing a strand of caramel hair away from her face. It was in a swirling updo today, somehow managing to look artless yet complicated at the same time. It was held up by diamanté clips, which would have looked overdressed on anyone else but somehow, on her, perfectly acceptable as daywear. She didn't really do dress codes, Leo noticed; she just wore what she wore, whatever the occasion. It was just one more thing he liked about her. She was a breath of fresh air in this place. "You can really feel the *thrum* of energy. It's electric."

"Well, Stamford is a bustling place," Annabel put in, in her formal, measured way. Next to Cymbeline, Leo thought, she looked dull, lifeless, like a pebble next to a diamond. "There's always plenty going on."

Cymbeline looked at her, an expression in her violet eyes that was half pity, half incredulous. The eyes that had made her famous, all those years ago, gazing out from the television screen on a Sunday evening; he'd seen the reruns, and they still looked much the same, give or take a few fine lines. Leo had seen a lot of bad cosmetic work done in his years behind a bar, so he knew that whoever was helping Cymbeline Johnson to keep the passage of time at bay, they were doing it well. If you squinted slightly and knocked thirty years off your mental calendar, you could almost be convinced that she was still the same eighteen-year-old girl who'd had her breakout role as a pirate's daughter in the soapy smash, *Over the Emerald Waves*.

"Not *real* people, darling." She drew out the long 'a' in the last word. "Well, not anymore, anyway. I mean the *spirits*. You *do* know that the veil between the worlds is at its thinnest tonight?" She paused, then added, "Well, I *think* that's what they were saying at my Om chanting circle, anyway."

Leo smiled to himself as he decanted some ice. Cymbeline still moved in quite arty London circles, and she was an absolute sucker for any kind of fad. She would latch onto it as though it were her dearest passion in life, only to promptly forget all about it the minute it was no longer in vogue. At the moment, it seemed to be all things dubiously spiritual.

"Well…" Annabel began doubtfully, but she was saved from having to comment further. Cymbeline wasn't in need of an answer; like most of her questions, it had been rhetorical. She carried on dreamily:

"But you know, I really *got* what they meant. I'm very receptive to these things, you see, and I could *feel* the channel of energy, wide open. It was thrilling to experience." She gazed enthusiastically at them both. "If you have a moment, you ought to go down to one of the churchyards, soak it in. You'll never feel more alive."

Annabel looked like there was nothing on earth she'd be less likely to do. Leo pictured her stomping around the churchyard in her sombre suit and sensible heels, barking enquiries at the gravestones. He coughed to cover a laugh, then, when both women turned to look at him, hurriedly followed it with a question.

"Aren't you taking tea this afternoon, Ms. Johnson?"

"Heavens, no." All hint of mysticism rapidly vanished – as if some imaginary director had shouted 'cut' in her head, Leo thought – replaced by a more worldly tone as she slapped down her cream leather gloves on the mirrored surface of the bar. "Something *much* stronger is required on a night like this. It's freezing fog out there." She saw the card on the floor, bent to retrieve it. "And the Universe responds! A Halloween cocktail, too. How *divinely* wicked." She waggled the card coyly in his direction. "Say, Leo darling, how about whipping me up one of these? And don't stint on the bloody twist."

She said it all casually enough – she was an actress, after all – but there was a twinkle in the way she looked at him that told him there was nothing artless about it. She must have heard the exchange between him and Annabel after all. The two women had never got along, and Cymbeline couldn't seem to resist baiting her at any opportunity.

"Coming right up," he said, allowing his lips to quirk up at the edges in a small smile of acknowledgement.

"So refreshing to have something different around here for a change," she said, a touch over-loudly, and obviously for

Annabel's benefit. He looked at the woman in question, staggering beneath a mound of white fur. A vein in her temple was beginning to twitch; a sure sign she was annoyed.

"Yes, well," Annabel said stiffly. "Many of our guests *appreciate* tradition." She paused, then added, meaningfully, "But if it's not to your taste, please don't feel obliged to come to the performance tonight. I wouldn't want you to be bored."

If Cymbeline noticed the passive-aggressive slant to Annabel's suggestion, she didn't show it.

"I wouldn't miss it for the world," she declared. "It sounds absolutely thrilling. And so novel; I can't imagine any of my Om chanting circle has been to anything like this."

Clearly the thought was one to relish.

"And with the spirits at large, who knows what might happen?" she continued, almost cheerfully. "No, it seems like this is the place to be tonight if you want drama."

"The only drama tonight will be from our performers," Annabel said, with a thin smile. "And we have strong locks on these old doors. Trust me, Ms. Johnson, no spirits will be disturbing our festivities tonight."

Cymbeline raised her eyebrows.

"Provided, of course, that the evil isn't already within."

She said it lightly, but the effect on the room was anything but. The barman paused, hands on the cocktail shaker. Annabel had gone white; her lips trembled slightly.

"I…" she stuttered faintly. "Why would you say…"

"Just a joke, darlings!" Cymbeline clarified quickly, with a tinkling laugh, and in an instant, Leo felt his senses returning to normal. Dimly, he became aware of a burning pain in his hands; the frigid cold of the metal cocktail shaker had been seeping into his skin, and he hadn't even felt it.

"Oh." Annabel gave a little laugh in return, but it wasn't very convincing. She still looked faintly ill. "Of course. Now, if you'll excuse me, I must…" She backed away, her usual self-possession deserting her as she almost bumped into a chair in her haste. "Preparations for tonight … still *so* much to do…"

"Well, she seems extra skittish tonight," Cymbeline said, although she avoided his eye, Leo noticed. "Ah, and here's Florian," she said, sounding, he thought, distinctly relieved by the interruption heralded by the arrival of her son – a distinction that was hers alone, thought Leo privately. Personally, he found the boy unnerving.

"Mother," Florian said, almost reproachfully, glowering at her from beneath thin black brows. He had a habit of that, tilting his chin down so he was forced to look up at people, even if they were smaller than him. They were the straightest eyebrows Leo had ever seen, each just a perfect horizontal slash in his forehead, without any hint of an arch. Against his pale skin, they stood out angrily. "You're not at tea."

"No, dear," Cymbeline said lazily, apparently unbothered by his censure. She lazed against the bar like an unrepentant cat. "I'm not."

"But…" Florian blinked furiously several times. "You *said* you'd be there." His voice was a petulant whine. "I was looking all around the club for you."

"Well, that was foolish of you, darling. I should have thought anyone would guess to look for me here first." When he just carried on staring at her, she sighed and patted the stool next to her. "Oh, *do* stop moping, sweetling. It's terrible for the complexion. You know me, I go where the wind blows." She took a healthy sip of her cocktail, nodding appreciatively. "And it's blown me in the direction of this utterly *divine* drink.

Won't you have one with me, darling? It's a Halloween special. Clever old Leo here made it just for tonight."

"Mother!" Florian looked scandalised. "I'm seventeen."

"Are you?" she said vaguely. "I thought you were eighteen by now. Well, all right, if you will be so stuffy, a mocktail, then? They have one that tastes just like a Jaffa Cake, apparently. Isn't that clever?"

He sighed in a deep, soulful way.

"You *know* I can't have sugar, Mother. It interferes with my creative process."

Cymbeline responded with a snort that strayed dangerously close to unladylike.

"Never interfered with any of *my* processes. Just as well, otherwise you wouldn't be here."

Florian looked blank. Leo wondered if he'd even understood the innuendo.

"Fine." Cymbeline pouted, when it became clear that no reaction was forthcoming. "At least have *something* with me. A beautiful lady should never drink alone."

"If you insist," Florian said sulkily, gingerly manoeuvring himself onto a bar stool, where he perched like a baby bird, gripping the edges. "I'll have a still water. Just lemon, no ice. The cold affects my teeth."

"Spoilsport," muttered his mother, although not without affection. "You know, darling, you don't have to suffer *quite* so much for your craft. It's perfectly possible to enjoy yourself and produce decent art. Look at me; *I've* done all right, haven't I?"

There was a beat of awkward silence. Clearly, neither of the men knew how to respond without pointing out the obvious, which was that Cymbeline Johnson had never had another significant role since *Over the Emerald Waves*. And that in itself hadn't been anything one could even tenuously describe as 'art'. Not with a straight face, anyway.

"So, er, will we be seeing you both tonight?" Leo ventured quickly, rescuing the moment. He dropped a slice of lemon into the water.

"Just me," Cymbeline chirped. "Florian's not keen on the idea of the Mummers. He's a sensitive soul; aren't you, sugarplum?"

Florian had been poking morosely at the lemon in his drink, but he looked up now.

"Actually, Mother, I've changed my mind," he said haltingly. "I might come after all. It will be very … interesting … to see it."

He sounded almost robotic at times. Leo looked up at him, and their eyes met. The returning gaze was dark, expressionless. He felt himself flinch involuntary, then hoped it hadn't been obvious.

"Well, *that's* a turn up for the books!" Cymbeline clinked her glass with Florian's. "My son, the daredevil! It must be the magic in the air tonight. Who knows, by later on he might even be letting you make him one of these." She indicated her cocktail by means of swooping it through the air. As she did so, syrup dripped over the side of the glass. "Oops. Butterfingers. *So* sorry, Leo darling."

"Oh, I won't be here later," he replied casually, as he fetched a cloth to wipe up the spill. "But don't worry, my stand-in will be available and willing to make up as many of these as you desire."

"I see." She gave him a knowing, red-lipped smile, clearly

understanding perfectly. "Well, *wherever* you may be … and I'm sure it'll be nowhere near here…" She winked.

"Absolutely not. Not even remotely." He tried not to grin.

"Well, I wish you a successful evening. And, dare I say it, a *profitable* one."

Apparently, she understood even more than he'd thought. But before he could respond, she'd raised her glass again.

"To All Hallows' Eve," she declared loudly to the empty room, apparently unperturbed by the lack of audience. "May the spirits be kind to us all."

Leo nodded, but his throat felt strangely tight. On the bar top, thick drops of dark red glittered beneath the lights. Quickly, he wiped them away.

Chapter Twelve

Annabel Drayford gripped the cold rim of the porcelain sink, staring at her drawn reflection in the mirror. She looked exhausted, haunted. Like it was all catching up with her. But then, perhaps it was.

The en-suite bathroom attached to the manager's office had been installed in the 1920s, and it hadn't been updated since. Nor had the plumbing, which creaked and groaned like a banshee trapped within the walls of the building. It probably had lead pipes, too, although she tried not to think about that. Because despite all of this, the room was still a very welcome perk – or perhaps, as the long-gone manager who had had it fitted realised, a necessity for a job that rarely allowed for sleep and held little regard for sociable hours. She'd learned early on to keep a duplicate of every product she used in the vanity unit above the sink, and it was impossible not to notice that the bottles here ran out much sooner than the ones in her own bathroom at home.

She unscrewed the gold lid on a jar of face cream, dabbing

it across the deepening crease in her forehead. It was a futile endeavour, and she knew it. The long hours and unrelenting pressure were showing on her face, and no amount of expensive promises from beauty companies could reverse it. But still, she told herself she had to try. This was a job that required perfection, unwavering and flawless. But it also required consistency. Consistency made people feel calm, reassured. They liked things to stay exactly the same; that was the secret of The Aquitaine, and it extended to the people who were part of it.

Of course, sometimes changes *did* have to be made. The truth was, The Aquitaine wasn't quite as impervious to the winds of change as it liked to make out; even it had to adapt from time to time. The only important thing was that the guests didn't see it happening. Keep them snugly believing that everything was as it always was – *that* was the secret.

Her head was throbbing, and in a moment of impulse, she pulled out her hair pins, letting the wavy curtain tumble around her shoulders. She so rarely saw it down anymore, it looked strange on her, like someone she vaguely recognised but couldn't place. Little Annie, with the mane of golden curls … she'd worn them down to her waist then.

She closed her eyes on the memory, breathing deeply as she kneaded her scalp in circular motions. She was beginning to feel the familiar panic, the sense that things were slipping out of her control. It was the one thing she couldn't stand, to lose control. Knowing it all, predicting it all before it happened, leaving nothing to chance … *that* was where safety lay.

She dropped her hands with a frustrated sigh. None of her relaxation techniques were working today. She was still unsettled, edgy, in a way she couldn't shake. She'd never liked

Halloween much, although not because she was afraid – growing up, she'd learned that the real things to fear in life were far more tangible than ghosts and ghouls.

And yet, it did almost feel like some puckish spirit was taunting her this evening, derailing her carefully laid plans. To start with, the pumpkins for tonight's soup had failed to materialise, forcing them to fall back on butternut squash as a replacement. That bungling caretaker was suddenly nowhere to be found, and just when she'd needed him to light the chandeliers in the dining room before dinner…

And now, to top it off, it seemed that Felicia Grant would be back tonight.

That was the straw that had tipped her already frayed nerves over the edge, Annabel decided bitterly. She may only have met the woman yesterday, but like anyone else in Stamford, she was well aware of her reputation. It was impossible not to be. The press might laud her as the crime-busting auctioneer, Annabel thought, with a curl of the lip, but all *she* saw was someone who had a predilection for trouble … and someone she was going to have to keep a very close eye on tonight. Whatever Felicia Grant was snooping around here for, she would find herself disappointed.

A deep sound reverberated through the building, shaking her from her introspection. The gong, announcing that it was time for the evening to begin. She scooped up her hair in one hand, twisting it with a ruthless flick of the wrist. She yanked it tighter and tighter, until her scalp screamed, bright tears springing to her eyes. The pain would be good tonight, she told herself; it would keep her focused. She secured the chignon, then, looking deep into the mirror, she rearranged her drawn, worried expression into one of serenity and competence. Smooth forehead, just a hint of a smile about the lips. It was no longer just a part. It was her alter ego.

As far as any of the guests would be aware, what lay ahead was an evening of folklore, mystery and entertainment, with just enough of an unsettling edge to thrill. And it *would* go off without a hitch. She would see to that if it killed her.

Chapter Thirteen

If there was one thing Cassandra Lane was good at, it was talking. From the moment she'd uttered her first word at nine months old – duck, apparently, although her father maintained it had sounded more like something decidedly less polite – she'd pretty much never stopped. Some might have called it a trait – and not always an appreciated one at that, as many an exasperated school report could attest – but Cassie saw it differently.

It was a *skill*. A skill to be able to talk to anyone, about anything, in any situation. To be able to bend people to your point of view, talk them down off a ledge, sell yourself, and all in a mere conjuring of words. She didn't care what anyone said; it was, in her opinion, her most valuable asset. She'd used it to get into her first job and out of her first speeding ticket – in the same week, come to think of it. She'd used it for years bringing up Robyn on her own, filling the space where another parent ought to have been with everything from sage advice to mindless chatter, ensuring there would never be silence, never emptiness, for her little girl. And it had proven utterly invaluable in her new career as the town's mayor. Cassie had always maintained that even if she was powerless to do a single other thing in a situation, she could at least always talk. Even if it was just to fill the silence, to keep fear at bay. She could talk and keep talking, for as long as it took. *Here lies Cassandra Lane,* her epitaph might read proudly, *who was never once lost for words.*

Or at least, the *old* Cassie had been, she reminded herself hastily. That was something she was working on; being more sensitive to others' moods. *Listening* more. Apparently, the downside of talking a lot was that you didn't really hear other people. Who knew? She and Alain were working together on her 'filter' – currently non-existent, apparently – along with myriad other 'red flags' she seemingly exhibited. Cassie just nodded along, pretending she knew what half of it meant. To be honest, it had never occurred to her that there'd been anything wrong with her before. That anything needed fixing – or *'healing'*, as Alain preferred to call it. But after what had happened in the summer … after Gavin…

And there it was, back again. Emblazoned across her mind's eyes, despite her best efforts to stop it. The moment that haunted her. He'd pointed the musket at her, and the hate in his eyes … it still made her shiver. She thought it probably always would.

"You all right, Aunt Cass? You look worried."

Cassie blinked, looking down into the young, serious eyes of her godson, who was walking at her side. In the setting sun, his bronze hair was ablaze, a halo of flames around his small face. He looked as though he belonged to another, more fantastical world, incongruous against the restrained, formal backdrop of the townhouse-lined street.

"Just thinking about this performance tonight," Cassie lied with a smile, suddenly feeling an overwhelmingly maternal need to reassure him. Trust Algernon to notice her shift in mood; he'd always seen too much, understood things too deeply for someone his age. It was unfair, really. Being a teenager was supposed to entitle you to be self-absorbed and oblivious. She put an arm around him, gave him a squeeze. "Apparently, these Mummer people are meant to be quite scary. We might have to protect your grandfather. He looks like a screamer to me."

Algernon grinned, and his whole face seemed to melt back into boyishness. Cassie felt her heart respond in kind.

"What's that you're saying, duck?" Peter Grant, who was walking up ahead with Felicia and Dexter, was peering back over his shoulder. "You after me for something?"

"No, no," Cassie said innocently, as Algernon clapped a hand over his mouth to stifle a laugh. "We're just talking about the Mummers, that's all." She paused, then added, casually, "We were wondering if you might remember when they did shows before? Maybe when you were younger..."

He scowled at her suspiciously.

"Aren't they medieval?"

By now, Algernon was struggling to contain his mirth. Cassie smothered a grin.

"Good point. My mistake."

Even Felicia, who'd been looking rather wan, was smiling complicitly. Peter cast a distrustful look around them all, eventually landing on Cassie, who just blinked at him sweetly.

Then she remembered that baiting Felicia's father was

something Alain would probably frown upon, a disappointed look in his dreamy blue eyes, and she sighed internally. This being-a-better-person thing was *hard* work.

"Did I miss a good joke?"

Lucia was standing on the steps, a vision in black lace. Her makeup was perfectly done, her dark hair a shining curtain, half swept away from her temples. She looked, Cassie couldn't help thinking, like a vampire's wife. Glamorous and ageless, almost untouched by life. From a distance, she could almost be the same young woman they'd parted ways from at eighteen.

Cassie was all too aware that the same couldn't be said for *her*. Her waistline had thickened, her stomach covered with stretch marks from bearing four children. Her skin showed the ravages of bringing up said four children. Only her hair, ironically always her most hated feature, had stayed exactly the same, a frizzy, cloud-like mass of blonde that haloed her round face. At once, she felt like an almighty frump in her floral dress – too summery for an October night, but so much better than one of her dreary, mayoral power suits, she'd thought – her hastily done at home manicure already chipped by having to prise apart two stuck-together building blocks for a howling toddler. At once, she wished she was back in Alain's office, with him sitting cross-legged on the floor telling her how to breathe through this feeling, how to stem the rising panic that she was all wrong, that she was failing at everything a modern woman was supposed to be.

"You okay?" Felicia's hand was on her shoulder, her voice low and sympathetic. Felicia, who she already knew looked fantastic under her marshmallow pink coat, in a shimmering silver column dress plucked from her London wardrobe, which skimmed her willowy body and matched her eyes.

Felicia, who'd been sensible enough to just have the one child, who'd kept her body and her sanity and always seemed to know exactly the right thing to say.

Suddenly, irrationally, Cassie felt a bolt of hatred towards her best friend, and she shrugged her away, muttering: "I'm fine. Just cold. Let's get inside."

Dexter had already bounded up the steps and was linking his arm through a tittering Lucia's, reassuring her in silken tones that she hadn't missed a thing.

"We're all in anticipation for this performance tonight. We haven't missed anything, I hope?"

"Oh, no. Although we'd better go straight in; they've just struck the first gong." She drew him away, leaving everyone else to trail in their wake. "I have to confess, I haven't the faintest idea what it's all about, but they all seem very energised about it." She tilted her head girlishly at him, gazing up into his face. "Lucky me, though, to have a famous historian to teach me. *Won't* you give me a lesson, Professor?"

Cassie distinctly saw Felicia roll her eyes and fought the urge to do the same. Of *course* Lucia would be all over Dexter; most women were, in Cassie's experience.

"Oh, well..." Dexter had a stab at not looking insufferably smug, and failed dismally, in Cassie's opinion. "I mean, this isn't strictly my *field*, but I confess, I did manage a little light reading up earlier... I'm sure I can give you the salient points."

"Grand; we could all do with some of those," Peter boomed, managing to insert himself between the pair so shamelessly that Cassie couldn't help but wonder if he'd done it on purpose. "Let's get a drink and you can tell us what this fandango is all in aid of."

"*Grandad,*" Algernon murmured, as Annabel Drayford

came striding towards them, a forbidding look on her face. "Maybe you shouldn't call it a fandango out loud. They might hear you."

"Welcome, all," the manager said, with a tight smile. Cassie thought she looked unbelievably stressed; there were dark circles under her eyes, and her face was pale. "Tonight's performance will take place in the snug; please, make your way through, get comfortable, order some drinks. We have traditionally brewed mead, if you really want to get into the historical spirit of the evening, or else our barman will mix up whatever your heart desires. We'll be starting shortly."

And then she was gone, disappearing through one of the myriad doorways that led off the resplendent foyer. Cassie turned to see that her party was already heading through another; she followed, finding herself in a heavily timbered, atmospheric room, all shadowed corners and glowing firelight. This, presumably, was the famous snug. It felt, Cassie thought with a little thrill, like a place where dark, *dramatic* things might happen. Exactly right for a night like this.

"I'm excited about this," she whispered to Felicia. "I hope it's going to be suitably spooky. Trick-or-treating's too cutesy these days; I spend half my time going round with the kids hoping for a really decent jump scare. But there never is one. It's all friendly zombies and vegetarian vampires and jolly ghosts." She gave a disapproving snort. "Where's the fun in that, I ask you?"

Felicia gave her friend a fond look. She was about to remind Cassie that they'd always had to agree to disagree when it came to the concept of scares for pleasure – Felicia having spent many a cinema trip in their teens hiding behind the popcorn – but just as she was opening her mouth, a voice hailed her from behind.

"*You!*"

Chapter Fourteen

Felicia turned, warily – as an auctioneer, being flagged down wasn't always a good thing. After all, selling antiques was an unpredictable business, and the bidding could go either way on the day. Added to that the hopes and cherished expectations of old heirlooms, and her valuations could either make her very popular or *very* unpopular. For every person pleased to see her, there was always another who still resented her for a disappointing result or for breaking the news to them that Aunt Polly's tea caddy wasn't Queen Anne, as she'd always vaunted, but a rather commonplace Victorian reproduction instead.

She needn't have worried in this case, however. The face that was puffing towards her across the snug was wreathed in smiles.

"I'm *so* glad I caught you," the woman wheezed. Felicia recognised her as the unfortunate sister who'd been pouring the tea yesterday. She was clutching a mound of knitting, the ball of wool unravelling in her wake, leaving a turquoise trail back towards the wingback chairs by the fire. "I always like to introduce myself to the new faces."

Her own face, already glowing magenta from the short pursuit, seemed to light up even more as she looked Felicia up and down. "My, but you're so *pretty*! And so *tall*, too. I've always wished I was taller, but alas, not to be." She gave a merry laugh, eyes twinkling with the kind of innate good humour that left Felicia feeling rather at a loss. She thrust out a hand, which Felicia took, marvelling at how warm and almost unbelievably soft it was. "Sybil Greenlake. My sister and I are local, so we don't stay, but we're here most days. Are you new members, you and your … friend?" Her eyes had strayed, not so subtly, to Felicia's bare, ring finger. Felicia smothered a smile.

"Felicia Grant. And no, just a visitor."

Sybil stilled.

"A visitor, you say?" She cocked her head. "Well, now, how *exciting*. We don't get many of *those*."

The look she gave Felicia was filled with such hungry curiosity that it began to feel distinctly uncomfortable.

"Although, that tea might just change my mind," Felicia said quickly, taking a calculated gamble that this was a topic that might just distract her new companion. "I've never seen anything like it."

She'd judged correctly. Sybil clapped plump pink hands together in a sheer, girlish expression of delight.

"Oh, the *tea*!" She all but swooned. "Isn't it just *divine*? Such a *treat* to have a proper English tea these days, with all those old-fashioned things like parkin and seed cake and Bath buns. Proper ones, with a lump of sugar right in the middle…"

As her breathless soliloquy continued, Felicia found her

attention diverted to the doorway, through which Aurelia was entering, accompanied by two adults who could only be her parents. The father was in a sharp suit, which even from this distance Felicia could tell was lavishly expensive, although not necessarily in the right sort of way. His hair was blond and he held himself like someone used to being obeyed. He came in first, a certain swagger in his step, letting the women trail after him. Aurelia's mother, by contrast, was a surprisingly small woman, hunched over her daughter, her face pinched in concern. Aurelia had a look on her face that could best be described as forbearing.

"Nowhere else really knows how to make those things anymore," Sybil concluded ruefully, and Felicia dragged her attention back, feeling a touch guilty to have zoned out. "It's turning into a lost art. I always say, you know, thank *heavens* for The Aquitaine! It keeps these traditional things going that would otherwise slip away. And they're *important* things, you know? Things we *mustn't* lose. Old English recipes. Now, I've nothing *against* these new foreign things like cappuccinos…"

"You've been able to get a cappuccino on these shores for a good forty years, Sybil," a deep, dry voice said, as her sister materialised at her side like a well-heeled bat, clad head-to-toe in black. "It's hardly the cutting edge."

"*Oh.*" Sybil twitted self-deprecatingly. "Have I just said something *very* foolish?" She looked to Felicia. "You must think me very out of touch, my dear. I never notice a thing that goes on, Lavinia here always tells me. Head in the clouds, she says."

"You haven't noticed your knitting's unravelling again." Lavinia dumped the tangled skein of wool on top of the pile in her sister's arms. "The waiter almost tripped over it. But I won't waste my breath telling you to be more careful."

"I wouldn't," Sybil agreed cheerfully. "Mind like a sieve. You're always saying so, aren't you, Lavinia, dear? She says that if someone put a marble in one of my ears, it would just roll straight out of the other one."

"One of these days, perhaps someone will try it," Lavinia replied, her angular face as flat and inflectionless as her voice. She turned to Felicia, with eyes so dark the pupils were barely visible. It made her even harder to read, if such a thing were possible. "I must apologise if my sister has been boring you. She has little sense of boundaries, I'm afraid."

"Not at all," Felicia replied immediately, feeling a touch defensive on Sybil's behalf. She looked between the two women, trying to see any sort of family resemblance and coming up completely empty.

"Wouldn't pick us for relations, would you?" Sybil said cheerfully, obviously reading her mind. "We're a family of two halves; one terribly clever and successful, the other rather dim and with rotten luck." She gave her merry laugh again. "Guess which side *I'm* from."

"I don't think that's much of a challenge for anyone, dear," Lavinia said tonelessly. "Now, let the unfortunate woman go. She's got better things to do than stand around listening to your inanities."

For a half second, Felicia thought she saw the flush on Sybil's ruddy cheeks deepen, and she wasn't the only one who'd noticed; from across the room, Aurelia was watching the exchange, her face twisted in sympathy.

But Sybil rallied quickly, the expression on her round, jolly face barely flickering.

"Of *course* she has. *So* sorry, my dear." She smiled, but it didn't quite reach her eyes this time. Eyes that were suddenly rather bright with moisture. "You must think me *such* a nuisance, prattling on like this. I didn't mean—" Suddenly, she was distracted by something over Felicia's shoulder; her mouth fell open as she gasped, "Oh, my. Look at her. Doesn't she look *breathtaking*?"

Felicia turned. There, standing in the doorway, stood none other than Cymbeline Johnson.

It was amazing, Felicia thought, how you could immediately recognise a face that you hadn't seen in over thirty years, and even then, only as a two-dimensional image on a screen. At once, she was catapulted back to her early teens, huddled on the bed in her pyjamas with Cassie watching *Over the Emerald Waves* on a Sunday night. They'd paint their toenails, devour ice cream straight from the tub, and swoon over the love story between the pirate's daughter and the Commodore's son. She felt a rush of nostalgia and looked across the room to see Cassie staring at the actress, practically bouncing up and down in her seat in excitement.

Although, she was far from the only one looking. It seemed as though the whole room had momentarily stopped what they were doing, a hush descending as all eyes fell upon the vision in their midst.

And a vision she was, Felicia admitted, as Cymbeline sashayed into the room, pretending for all the world not to have noticed the attention. She was wearing a bias-cut, pink-silk Schiaparelli dress, and its vibrant hue shone like a beacon amongst the muted colours of the room. Her caramel-coloured hair was down in tumbling, starlet curls around her slender shoulders, framing a face that had barely changed in a third of a century. The effect was magnificent, only slightly marred, Felicia thought, by the sullen-looking boy trailing in her wake. The serious boy from the snug yesterday, she realised. So *this* was his mother.

"Honestly, that *woman*," Lavinia looked thunderous. "Always has to make a scene wherever she goes. Why doesn't somebody tell her it's not a catwalk?"

"Oh, but it's her *job*, Lavinia," Sybil said breathlessly. "We're *so* lucky to have her here as a member," she added to Felicia in an undertone. "I couldn't believe it the first time I saw her. A celebrity in our midst! Who'd have thought it? I mean, there are plenty of important people here, but they're not half as glamorous and thrilling as a real *star*…"

"She's hardly that, Sybil," Lavinia snapped, eyes flashing. "I don't know why you're so obsessed with the woman. She's a third-rate actress, and a has-been." She shook her head regretfully. "The Aquitaine used to have better taste."

Cymbeline Johnson swished across the room. Lavinia turned away as she approached, clearly having no intention of greeting her, but Cymbeline had other ideas.

"Lavinia," she said, loudly, to the other woman's back, "what a *delight* to see you."

Lavinia's eyes narrowed, but she had no choice but to turn around.

"Good evening, Ms. Johnson," she said coolly. "Still here, then?"

"Oh, yes. I wouldn't miss tonight. Apparently, it's one of The Aquitaine's great traditions; as members, we should certainly see it – don't you think so, Florian?"

The teenage boy just glowered at the floor. Cymbeline

didn't seem perturbed by his lack of response. Instead, she flicked a hand towards Lavinia's sober, high-necked gown.

"You've dressed appropriately for the date, I see."

The tip of Lavinia's long nose went pink, but otherwise she didn't show any reaction to the slight.

"Well, at least one of us has," she said, and this time her tone was glacial. "Dressed appropriately, I mean."

Her words fell into an empty silence. It seemed everyone in the room was listening in. For a brief moment, Cymbeline Johnson looked utterly furious. Then she gave a brittle laugh.

"Always a pleasure to talk to you, Lavinia. Now," she opened her arms to the room, "which of you lovely gentlemen is going to offer to fetch me a cocktail?"

Several men leaped to attention. And just like that, the moment was broken. Conversation resumed, the hubbub flowing across the room.

"Ah, *Leo*!" Sybil all but snatched at a passing man, clearly desperate for a diversion from the awkward moment that had just passed. Lavinia had lapsed into frosty muteness, apparently still brooding on it. "The club's barman," she explained to Felicia. "And a *very* talented chap. He can make any drink in the world, can't you, Leo dear?"

"Oh, I don't know about that," he replied modestly, with just a hint of a smile. He was athletic-looking, tall with broad shoulders. The sort of boy you'd expect to find as the star of some university sports scholarship rather than working behind a bar. "But I do my best."

"Leo," Cymbeline Johnson called across the room. "What are you doing here?" Her lovely violet eyes sparkled meaningfully. "Haven't you got another engagement tonight?"

"Just checking in," he replied easily. "You know me; always

the perfectionist." He beckoned to a waiter, who was carrying a tray of amber-hued cocktails; surveying the drinks with a critical eye, he finally nodded, muttering instruction in an undertone before turning to the ladies around him. "Can I tempt any of you to a signature Halloween cocktail? My own creation."

"Goodness, no!" Lavinia spoke up irritably, swatting at the tray as though it were a persistent moth. "We won't be wanting any of that. Sherry, dry as you can get it. You know my usual."

"Ooh, I'd better not. It'll go straight to my head, and Lavinia tells me I'm addle-brained enough as it is," Sybil giggled. "I'll just have a small glass of my violet liqueur, please, Leo dear."

"I'll have one," Felicia took pity on the barman as disappointment flickered across his face. She picked one off the tray. "They look fabulous."

"Are you all right, dear?" Sybil asked Lavinia, as Leo was dispatched with their drinks order. "You seem a trifle distracted."

She wasn't as unobservant as she seemed, Felicia thought. Indeed, Lavinia had been subtly glancing around all evening, clearly looking for someone.

"Just wondering where Dr. Rauceby has got to, that's all," Lavinia said, with a vagueness that didn't suit her at all. "It's unlike him to be late."

"For Christ's *sake*, Maureen, leave the girl be!" An angry voice rose above the melee, causing Felicia, who'd just been about to take a sip of her cocktail, to freeze. "How's she ever going to do anything for herself if you're always fussing over her?"

There was a plaintive rejoinder, which Felicia couldn't quite hear. By now, though, others were starting to notice, heads turning, conversations trailing off. Now Felicia could see the source; Aurelia's father, standing over their table, his face a dull red.

"You're half the problem, you know that? Putting ideas in her head that she's ill, that she's helpless... She's never going to live her life again if you won't stop bloody *suffocating* her..."

Someone moved into Felicia's line of sight, and she missed the rest. Not that there was much more. The next moment, Aurelia's mother was scurrying from the room, head down. Felicia could tell from her body language that she was quietly crying. She looked back to Aurelia, who was sitting there, face immobile. Like she'd shut it out, gone somewhere else in her mind.

"I need a drink," her father was saying roughly. He eyed a passing tray of cocktails with disdain. "And none of this bloody muck. What's a man got to do to get a whisky around here?" He clicked his fingers imperiously, to which none of the waiters responded. "You want something? What about a mocktail? You need perking up a bit; you're sitting there like a wet weekend."

"No thanks, Daddy." Aurelia's voice was faraway. "It's got marmalade in it; you know I can't stand the stuff. I'll have a cherry cola instead."

"Suit yourself." With a disgusted sound, he gave up clicking. "This lot are useless. I'm going to find that barman."

Aurelia didn't respond. She just sat there, looking into the middle distance unseeingly. Felicia hesitated, wondering whether to leave her alone. But something in the girl's hunched shoulders made her decide otherwise. She moved across the room until she was standing over her.

"Hello again."

The young face blinked, looked upwards … then came alight.

"You came back." She said it almost in wonderment.

"Yes, my friend invited me to see the performance tonight." Felicia sat next to her.

"Well, I hope you're not easily scared. Mummy hates it. She only came because I did."

"Aurelia," Sybil had followed Felicia over, and was hovering. "Is your dear mother *quite* all right? Only I saw her leave, and…"

"Oh, er … yes, thank you, Sybil." Aurelia pinkened. "Just one of her dizzy spells, that's all. She decided to go back to the room for a lie down."

The words were perfectly plausible, but the delivery made it less so. An awkward pause settled on the group. Felicia searched for a way to break it.

"Oh." A glint of something had caught her eye; she brushed Aurelia's hair aside to reveal a pair of aquamarine studs. "These are *lovely*."

"Aren't they?" A shadow fell over them. Aurelia's father was back, whisky in hand. "I picked them for her myself. Antique," he added, with obvious pride.

Felicia hesitated. Just for a second. She didn't even need to look at the earrings closely to tell that they were nothing of the kind. If they were made as long as ten years ago, it'd be a surprise to her. Someone had clearly seen him coming and told him what he wanted to hear in exchange for what had no doubt been an eyewatering amount of money.

But she wasn't in her professional capacity now, she reminded herself. She wasn't doing a valuation on them, and there was no need to tell him any of that. So instead, she smiled and said truthfully, "They're beautiful stones. And they suit Aurelia's colouring perfectly."

"I know my girl," he squeezed Aurelia's shoulder. "Better than anyone, in fact. She doesn't like to think so though, do you?" Aurelia didn't answer, but it didn't stop him. He persisted. "*I* was the one who first saw how good she was on a horse. Her mother would never have let her get up there. But I saw the competitive spirit, the will to win." He turned to Felicia. "It's still there. That fire. Wouldn't think it, but it is. She could be up there again, if she just stopped moping about."

"Daddy, you know that's not true." Aurelia's face was shuttered, miserable. "I'll never get on a horse again; they've told us that from the start."

He made a dismissive sound.

"There's more to life than horses. And that's coming from me." He grasped her wrist. There was a determined flush high on his cheeks that Felicia recognised. She suspected that whisky wasn't his first tonight. "You know what; get up now. Let's walk across the room. No, leave the frame. You can lean on me."

Aurelia's face registered panic.

"Daddy, I can't."

"Course you can." He gave her wrist a sharp tug, looking irritated. "You'll never get better if you don't put some effort in. After all the money I've paid those bloody specialists, and you don't even bother to do the exercises. You're not trying hard enough. Well, no more. I want to see some results."

"No, *please*. I don't feel…"

The deep sound of the gong thundered through the room, silencing everyone immediately. Aurelia's father let go of her wrist, and it fell limply to her side. Felicia turned to see the sharply suited form of Annabel Drayford silhouetted in the doorway.

"It's time, everyone," she intoned. "The Mummers have arrived."

Chapter Fifteen

Molly Dunster pushed her cleaning trolley along the landing, its wheels soundless on the plush, ice-blue carpet. The whole upstairs of The Aquitaine was hushed, an atmosphere only made more apparent by the contrast of the revelry going on below. The sound of clinking glasses, of laughter … of *life* … was audible, yet at the same time muffled, distant. It ought, perhaps, to have made the quiet emptiness up here feel isolating, even a touch eerie. Especially since everything that made these corridors look sumptuous and characterful in the daytime – paintings cramming the walls, furniture and statues occupying every nook – took on a more sinister cast at night, creating deep, inky shadows. Some members had even complained that the eyes of the portraits seemed to follow them after dark, that it gave them the uneasy feeling of being watched.

Such stories were inevitably dismissed as fantasy by most, but Molly knew differently. She'd felt it herself, many times, in fact. It had frightened her, too, at first, made her dread these lonely shifts. But these days, she no longer minded. Whatever ghosts The Aquitaine might possess were almost like old friends to her now.

Besides, she preferred to work in peace. Her job was to be seen and not heard, and whilst many might have taken umbrage at that, it suited her perfectly. She didn't *want* to be seen. When she did occasionally come across a guest, it was all she could do not to shrink away. She kept her exchanges polite but brief, retreating as soon as she was able. She always worried that they would sense that she was different somehow, that she wasn't like the rest of the staff. She didn't intend to hang around long enough for them to start working out why.

She knocked discreetly on the door of the next bedroom on her roster. She waited a moment, ear cocked to the panelling, before letting herself in with her key. The Aquitaine still used proper keys – electronic key cards were practically a thing of science fiction here – which, whilst undoubtably charming, meant that she was forced to carry a huge brass set of them around with her with each room's duplicate on it.

She held her breath upon entering, a reflexive action caused by one too many incidents of finding the occupant inside after all, most often in some sort of compromising position. But a quick glance around was enough for her to release it, her lungs deflating in relief. Empty, as they all had been thus far. That was at least one good thing about this whole whacky Halloween tradition of theirs, she decided; it got everyone out of her way.

Not that she'd ever actually *seen* the Mummers performance herself, she conceded silently, as she began her turn down routine, which was so familiar now that she didn't need to concentrate; her hands just did it by rote, freeing her mind to wander. She'd heard plenty about it, though, from the other staff members – not that she mixed with them much, but still, things found their way into her ears. To be honest, historical or not, it all sounded utterly crazy to her. That people would be willingly robbed of huge sums of money and call it *entertainment*...

Although, if there was one thing she'd learned in her time working here, it was that the rich had some truly strange ideas of what constituted fun. They seemed to occupy not only a whole other world, but a whole other universe; one which she'd long given up on ever beginning to understand.

But then, it wasn't her business to, she reminded herself firmly, as she briskly plumped the pillows, clicking on the bedside lamps to bathe the room in a soft, inviting glow. She did a final scan of the room, satisfying herself that all was in order. Then she retreated into the corridor, pulling the door gently closed behind her. Apart from the turned-down bed, it would be as though she'd never even been in there. This was her life: creeping silently in and out, rarely seen, almost never acknowledged. Like a ghost, she thought, the aptness of the description not lost on her, tonight of all nights. A pillow mint-dispensing ghost.

She returned to her trolley, continuing her route along the landing. As she raised her hand to knock on the next door, however, something made her pause. Something wholly unexpected.

Voices. And what's more, they sounded ... she could be wrong, but it *almost* sounded like...

She strained to listen, eyes widening. Then, slowly, she let her hand fall to her side. She moved back to the trolley, chewing her lip indecisively. Bending down, she retrieved an envelope from where it had been tucked amongst the clean towels. Before she could change her mind, she darted to the door and slipped the envelope underneath.

Something shivered across the back of her neck.

She shot upright, heart in her mouth, head swinging one way, then the other. But there was nothing, and no-one. Just the portraits on the walls. Those old familiar eyes, on her as always. Except, for once, they didn't feel quite so friendly.

For once, she wished she wasn't *quite* so alone.

She heaved against the trolley, pushing it forwards. And with barely a squeak of the wheels, she disappeared deeper into the heart of the building.

Chapter Sixteen

"The tradition of Mumming is an ancient one," Annabel Drayford began. She was standing in front of the fireplace, looking out at them all intently. An expectant hush had fallen over the room; the air practically crackled with expectation. "It has taken many forms down the centuries; those of you who have heard of it may associate the practice with theatrical performances – singing, dancing, plays. But here at The Aquitaine, we honour its earliest incarnation."

She paused meaningfully. Then a low, thumping knock echoed on the closed door to the snug.

"Every New Year, groups of men and women would disguise themselves and traverse their towns and villages, knocking on their neighbours' doors," Annabel Drayford continued. She motioned to a porter, who moved towards the door, grasping the handle. "Convention decreed that if the Mummers came to your house, you had to admit them. You had no choice."

There was a gasp from someone, and Felicia turned her

head to see that the Mummers had begun to file into the room through the low doorway. She had been prepared for something out of the ordinary, but even she felt her heart thud in alarm at the sight of the nightmarish figures who were advancing slowly through their midst.

They were clad in a variety of rough, motley-looking costumes. Some wore coats adorned with multiple strips of fabric that fluttered as they moved. Others wore long tunics made of hessian. Each one, without exception, was embellished with natural finds; some wore long straw capes over the top, others had feathers or grasses woven into their dress. But the most disturbing feature of all was what they wore on their heads; every single member was masked in some way. Several wore animal heads woven of wicker; Felicia saw a stag, a fox, and a hare amongst them. Others wore masks of a single flat, wooden panel, with two holes cut for the eyes, and devil-like, curving horns protruding from the forehead. A couple of them wore hessian sacks over their heads, modified in the same way. They processed slowly, steadily, like a funeral march, their long capes dragging along the flagstone floor with a dry scraping sound.

The effect on the room was immediate. The atmosphere, previously so convivial, was suddenly leaden, apprehensive. It was as though a pall had fallen over the assembled company. Felicia cast a surreptitious glance at Algernon to see how he was taking it; he was watching avidly, but he looked tense, his face already slightly pale.

Annabel Drayford had begun to speak again, as the Mummers reached her side, flanking her in a menacing wall.

"Once inside, they would engage in dice games – several of which we still know the rules to, and which you will get to have a go at tonight. They may seem simple, but beware; the Mummers are notoriously tricky to beat." She gave a knowing smile. Behind her, the featureless faces stared outwards. Not one moved. "A long-lost tradition, still very much alive within these walls. And now I, too, shall be silent, except of course to say," she lifted her palms to the ceiling, "let the games begin! And may luck be on your side tonight."

As one, the Mummers moved, fanning out to position themselves at the various tables and nooks around the snug. One stood in front of Felicia's group; it – she couldn't tell whether it was a he or she, the costume was that all-encompassing – was the hare she'd spotted earlier. The huge wicker head was even larger up close, the moulded sockets of the creature's eyes blank and empty. The Mummer said nothing; for a moment, it simply stood there, looming over them all. Then it raised an arm and dropped three dice onto the table.

"Ah!" Felicia jumped to see Dexter shift forward in his seat, his face suddenly intent. "I know this one. Raffle, I believe."

"Very impressive, Mr Grant." Annabel Drayford had materialised amongst them. "Usually, we have to explain to newcomers, but I suppose I must remember that we have a famous historian here with us tonight."

"It's a well-known medieval dice game," Dexter explained to the rest of them. "Very simple, really, and the precursor to a lot of modern gambling – slot machines, scratchcards, that sort of thing. You just have to roll three of the same number." He picked up the dice. "Anyone for a go? Cassie? You're usually game for a bit of a flutter."

"Oh, er…" Cassie, who'd been bent over her phone, looked up guiltily. "Maybe in a sec. I just have to check something.

What about you, Lucia? I bet you've been in some glamorous casinos in your time."

Lucia gave a demure smile and reached for the dice.

"Well, I suppose ... how hard can it be?"

Dexter pulled out his wallet and placed a note on the table. The Mummer stared down at him, arms folded.

"I think you might have to do a bit better than that," Peter murmured, looking rather pleased by Dexter's discomfort. "He doesn't seem too impressed. We're in a fancy place now; wouldn't do to be a skinflint."

Dexter gave a nervous laugh, glancing sideways at Lucia. With visible reluctance, he put down another few notes.

"Cass," Felicia hissed, taking the opportunity while the game got into its stride. "Are you okay? What's going on?" Her friend was staring at her phone in visible anxiety, chewing her lip. "Is it one of the children?"

"What?" Cassie started, then flushed, her ruddy face turning scarlet. "Oh, no. They're fine. It's just ... it's nothing."

Felicia plucked the phone from her hand – not something she'd do with anyone else, but when you'd known someone for as long as she had Cassie, certain rules didn't apply – and immediately, her eyes widened in disbelief. "I don't *believe* this! You're messaging Alain right now!"

"I just wanted to ask his opinion on gambling," Cassie muttered defensively. But she wouldn't meet Felicia's eye. "See if he thinks ... you know, if it's all right for me to be doing it. From a moral perspective."

"You can decide that for yourself, Cass." Felicia put the phone firmly away in Cassie's bag. When her friend didn't look convinced, she added, "Besides, I don't think Alain would begrudge you letting your hair down a bit." Actually, she thought sourly, he probably would, but she wasn't about to tell Cassie that. "Surely that's got to be good for the soul? What's that you told me the other day?" She mentally sifted through the many bumper-sticker phrases she'd been bombarded with over the past few months. "You have to fill your own cup first, or you have nothing to give to other people."

"Oh, blast!" An unladylike expletive from Lucia made them both turn. She was pouting, a frown creasing her forehead. "I don't think this game is for me. I haven't won once."

"That's not surprising," Dexter said easily. "Considering the dice are most likely loaded."

"What?" Lucia looked incensed. "But that's … that's outrageous!" She looked sharply at Annabel Drayford, who was standing there with a rather supercilious smile. "Is it true? Did you know about this? I think she *knew*, Dexter. Look at her face."

"Yes, she knows," Dexter said quickly, with an apologetic glance at the manager, who just looked back serenely, apparently unconcerned by the slight. "But it's not what you think. It's part of the tradition." As they all looked askance at him, he extrapolated, "The people they were playing against back then would likely have known, too."

"I don't understand any of this." Lucia folded her arms and stuck her nose in the air petulantly. "It doesn't make any sense. What's the point in playing if they're just going to cheat?"

"It's an ancient custom, Lucia," Cassie said mildly, picking up the dice. Felicia was pleased to see that her words – recycled as they were – had obviously got through to her friend. She looked more light-hearted than she had in weeks. "And an English one, at that. Even now nothing we do makes sense; we're famous for it worldwide. You just have to get into the spirit of it." She rolled, then let out a whistle. "Damn. Put some more cash down, Dexter. He's cleaning us out here."

Dexter opened his mouth, then, catching Peter's eye, sighed and reached for his wallet again.

"Think of it like trick-or-treating," Dexter coaxed Lucia. "That's probably the easiest way to understand it. That's basically consensual extortion: you give me something nice, or else I'll do something unpleasant to you. And the penalty could be really quite nasty back in the day; it wasn't exactly much of a choice. Of course, people tend to shy away from the 'trick' element of it now, but the sentiment is still there in the name."

"That reminds me of what I wanted to ask you." Felicia turned to Annabel Drayford. Out of the corner of her eye, she could see the other games going on; Sybil was laughing merrily at a move she'd just made, Lavinia sitting stonily by her side, not looking to be enjoying any of it. Aurelia's father seemed to be demonstrating to her the correct way to roll the dice for a win. Cymbeline Johnson was attempting to flirt with her Mummer, if looks were to be believed. Florian was gazing across the room – initially, Felicia assumed into space, but the intense expression on his sensitive, poetic face made her follow his line of sight ... directly towards Aurelia's bent blonde head. She smiled inwardly, then realised that the manager was looking at her in expectation of the rest of her sentence. She hastened on. "You said earlier that this was originally a *New Year*'s tradition?"

"It was. But we've always felt it more appropriate to honour it at this time of year."

"Because this is where it ended up." Felicia nodded. "It led into what we now think of as trick-or-treating. I understand that. But how?"

"It's difficult to say, exactly." Dexter, never one to miss an opportunity to explain something, took on the mantle. "Many people think of Halloween as a gimmicky, modern celebration, but in fact it's as ancient as the hills, and the traditions associated with it are more complex than almost any other time of year. For thousands of years, the idea that the veil between the worlds is at its thinnest right now has existed, along with the concept of the undead walking amongst us. Dressing up in costume, or disguising oneself, was seen as a way to hide from roaming evil spirits."

He crossed one long, wisteria-hued leg over the other in a motion that Felicia knew indicated they were in for a lecture.

"The idea of scaring each other wasn't on the agenda back then, however. It was more of a reflective festival, a time to honour the dead. Yuletide, on the other hand, which Mumming initially belonged to..." He paused to take a sip of his cocktail. "We think of Christmas now as a time of comfort and goodwill, but in the medieval period, it wasn't quite so warm and fuzzy. There was an unsettling sense of anarchy to it, of hierarchies upended and rules going out of the window."

"Well, *this* is certainly unsettling," Lucia said, looking at the Mummer warily. It just replied with a low, husky drone, a repeated 'mmm' sound. It was the only thing it had uttered all evening. Lucia shrank back, looking agitated. "Why does it keep *doing* that? It's giving me the shivers." She clung to Dexter's arm. "Make it stop, won't you? Why doesn't it *say* something?"

"Because they can't," Dexter replied. "They can only make that sound. Hence why they're called Mummers."

"But *why*?"

"To preserve their anonymity, of course. Mumming was an opportunity for the lower social order to break free of their constraints for a while, get one over on their betters. Then it was back to a life of oppression and servitude for the rest of the year." He raised his eyebrows. "You can imagine how that might have gone to people's heads. They would have relished the chance to be as frightening and intimidating as possible, without fear of recrimination. Some of them probably even got a little carried away, took it too far. You certainly wouldn't want your feudal lord recognising you if that was the case."

"So, what changed?" Peter was sitting forward in his seat, looking intrigued – surprisingly so, thought Felicia. Despite running an antiques auction, her father wasn't really much of a history buff. Not usually, anyway.

"As is often the case with history, many different factors. Christmas became more of a jolly, religious celebration, for one. The idea remained, but it became a much more honest practice; the Mummers became performers, doing plays and dances in exchange for their money instead. The disguises were taken off during the course of the evening, as identities were guessed, so the anonymous figures who arrived on your doorstep left as people you knew." He motioned to the Mummer, who was standing there, motionless. "But as with most of our pagan traditions, it never really died out. They're pervasive things; they adapt, morph, shapeshift. They switch names, seasons, they blend into something else. This is what we think happened with Mumming. There was an existing Hallowtide practice at the time called souling, where children carrying hollowed-out turnips with a candle inside went from house to house saying prayers for the dead in exchange for food and ale. And in Scotland and Ireland, there was guising, where children visited houses in costume and were rewarded for seeing off evil spirits. We believe that all of these things went into a melting pot to create what we now think of as modern trick-or-treating."

He paused, indicating he'd finished. Felicia tilted her head on one side, looked at him with a hint of a smile.

"I thought you said you'd done a little *light* reading?"

He had the grace to look faintly abashed.

"Well, I suppose my idea of light reading *is* probably rather different to most people's."

Simultaneously, they all seemed to become aware of a kerfuffle across the room. Aurelia's father now appeared to be trying to argue with their Mummer, which of course wasn't getting him anywhere except more and more irate. Annabel Drayford stood to attention immediately.

"If you'll excuse me." She strode away to deal with the issue.

"You fancy a go, son?" Peter held the dice out to Algernon. Felicia looked down at him and immediately felt terrible; he looked as white as a sheet.

"Are you all right?" she murmured.

He nodded, but not very convincingly. She put a hand on his back as she rose to her feet, encouraging him to do the same.

"Come on. Let's get some air."

They went into the foyer, Felicia immediately enjoying the blast of cool breeze after the intensity of the snug. With so many people crammed in there, and the fire blazing, it had been getting uncomfortably warm. She looked around for somewhere for them to sit out of the way, eventually spotting a little window seat up on the landing, which she made a beeline for, all but dragging a lacklustre Algernon with her. Settling him on the seat, she unlatched the window and, after a good shove, managed to crack it open just enough to get a channel of cold, night air through.

"There." She pushed Algernon's bronze hair away from his forehead. "Let's just sit for a minute, shall we?"

He nodded, leaning back against the wall and closing his eyes. My, but he looked dreadful, she thought, with a lurch. His heart-shaped face was smaller than ever, his features pinched. Was he doing all right? *Really*? And she didn't just mean tonight. He told her he was happy with life here in Stamford; he certainly *seemed* happy. But so much had happened since they'd been back here; he'd been through so much. Things no-one should have to go through, let alone a young boy. How could she be *sure* he was truly all right? Once, she would have just asked him; but he was twelve-and-a-half now, moving towards adulthood, and the barriers between them were shifting. She could no longer assume she knew everything about his life, about what went on in his mind. And she couldn't keep trying to. He would only resent her interference.

Of course, telling herself that didn't stop her worrying. Not in the slightest. She would worry forever, she already knew that. She'd be worrying about him when he was forty-five, if she was still around by then. Actually, never mind if she wasn't; it wouldn't make any difference. She'd probably manage to worry about him from beyond the grave.

A floorboard creaked, and Felicia jumped. But it was only one of the elderly brothers she'd seen in the snug yesterday, playing their quiet game of chess. They'd been over in the corner together tonight, watching the activity but not participating. He didn't see her and Algernon sitting there; instead, all his attention seemed to be on making his way down the staircase. He gripped the bannister, obviously struggling. Felicia glanced at the door he'd emerged from; a discreet plaque indicated that it was a cloakroom. She couldn't help but wonder why he hadn't used the one downstairs, just off the snug. But then again, she reminded herself, perhaps he just liked the exercise; she knew several elderly people who swore that using the stairs regularly was the only thing that kept them mobile.

Swallowing a sigh, she turned her head and gazed through the sliver of an opening down into the night-cloaked garden. The weather had closed in remarkably fast, the clear twilight having rapidly been smothered in a dense, swirling fog whilst they'd been inside the club.

A figure came into view, moving purposefully across the lawn below. Felicia didn't need to look twice to tell who it was; his white hair shone even in the murky conditions. The objectionable Doctor Rauceby from yesterday, Felicia thought. So that's where he'd got to.

He disappeared from view. Felicia was about to look away again when something else caught her eye.

Something else moved.

It was nothing, really. A mere ripple across the grass. But she saw it. Felicia leaned closer, peering through the narrow slit. What she saw made her blink, her breath catching in her throat.

A long, billowing cape, the silhouette of two curling horns...

"Ms. Grant, isn't it?"

Felicia started, whirled around.

Lavinia Greenlake stood over them, the sinewy lines of her face rendered dramatic by the low lamplight of the landing.

"Miss … Greenlake," Felicia said distractedly. She turned to look back out of the window. But there was nothing there now. The garden was just an empty rectangle. Felicia took a steadying breath of the fresh air, wondering if she was letting this whole evening get to her head. God only knew what kind of dreams she'd have tonight. "My son just needed a bit of fresh air," she explained, even as she wondered why she felt the need to. But there was something about the woman's hawkish look that made her feel as though she'd been caught somewhere she wasn't supposed to be. "It's so hot in there."

"I'm fine now, Mum." Algernon was looking guilty, too; obviously, he was feeling the unspoken censure as well, because he stood. "Let's go back. I want to see if Dad's managed to roll a triple yet."

"Or run out of money," Felicia said dryly.

They went downstairs, followed closely by the disapproving presence of Lavinia Greenlake. Perhaps she hadn't liked them being upstairs, Felicia thought. Where the bedrooms were. But then, Sybil had said they didn't stay, so why should it bother her?

When they re-entered the snug, it was to find that things had ratcheted up in their absence. A particularly vigorous game was going on by the fire, and people were drifting away from their own games in order to watch.

"A triple three!" Sybil's face was flushed from the flames. She took another sip from the virulently purple drink in her plump hand. She looked flushed with triumph, her round face pink and shiny. "I'm winning, Lavinia! Look!"

"Don't be asinine, Sybil." Lavinia strode over, looking annoyed. "Of course you're not going to win."

"But I am!" Sybil's expression had changed from its usual jovial benignity. She frowned crossly. "You just don't think I can do anything. You don't *want* me to do anything, because that would threaten you, wouldn't it? The clever sister, the *successful* sister. You need me as your foil, to make you look better." She was more scarlet than pink now, Felicia noticed, with some alarm.

"You're making a spectacle of yourself," Lavinia said icily. "I suggest you call it a night."

Everyone was trying not to look as though they were staring, and failing dismally. Felicia took the opportunity to let her eyes scan over the room, specifically the costume-clad figures standing mutely by. She began to count in her head.

"*Oh.*" Sybil's face crumpled; the word was almost a wail of contrition. She looked around at everyone, dazed but evidently mortified. "Goodness. I don't know what's come over me. I'm feeling … so very strange. Everything's spinning."

"It's just the heat," Lavinia said shortly. "You've got too close to the fire. Come away."

But Sybil didn't move. She just stood there, as though she hadn't heard, swaying from side to side.

"Didn't you hear me?" Lavinia snapped. "What's *wrong* with you? Are you completely featherbr—"

But she never got to finish. Because at that moment, Sybil's legs crumpled beneath her. With a splintering crash and an explosion of glittering shards, she collapsed onto the table.

Three dice fell from her motionless hand, rolling across the flagstones.

Chapter Seventeen

D r Jonathan Rauceby picked his way across the gardens in the gathering twilight. The weather, so fine and crisp earlier in the day, had begun to close in as evening approached. Bruised clouds clustered the horizon, making the air dense and purple, filled with a cold mist that threatened to sink into the bones if one stayed out in it too long. He looked behind him, slightly longingly, at the glowing windows of the club, within which he knew fires would already be blazing, then back out into the wall of inky gloom ahead. With a grimace, he forged onwards, hoping that what had dragged him out on this filthy night would be worth it.

He wasn't an outdoors sort of man. He wasn't averse to pottering around a garden or two, but he liked them to be attractively ordered, neatly landscaped, and with plenty of places to sit and admire the effect of nature put firmly in its place. The Aquitaine's plot usually lived satisfyingly up to that description, with its profusion of clipped topiary, its mirror pond and meticulously managed kitchen garden. That was the most pleasing place of all; the vegetables marching in rows, the fruit trees pleached into submission against the brick wall.

He put his expensively shod foot in a rabbit hole, stumbled, muttered a low curse at the reminder that he'd left that world of manicured order behind at the last dahlia border. Now, he was traversing into the farthest depths of the grounds. It was clear why no-one ever came out this far, Rauceby thought irritably, shaking soil from his brogue. The place was almost stubbornly untamed in contrast to the rest of the garden. They really should sort it out; it wasn't exactly in keeping with the standards of the club.

He drew up short at the edge of an avenue of trees, annoyed with himself as he hesitated at the opening. He peered into the black void, telling himself that he was a man of reason. That there was no such thing as atmosphere, ominous or otherwise. The only reason people had an aversion to yews was because they associated them with graveyards, funerals, and ultimately, death. What they conveniently forgot was that those same yews had also been standing there on their wedding day, and they hadn't found them sinister then. It was just another depressing example of how the human mind was on the whole weak, credulous, easily given to base superstition. Really, most people were barely above Neanderthals in their thinking.

Even so, as his eyes roved over the gnarled, writhing forms of the trees, he wondered why the club didn't just cut them down. They were such unsightly things; of course, they were often protected, but that oughtn't be too much of an issue for a place like this. Red tape was for the masses, the unimportant. Given the calibre of the members here, concessions would no doubt be made.

He moved gingerly along the path, which seemed like a veritable obstacle course: overhanging branches overhead, twisted roots bursting through the ground underfoot. *This* was why nature shouldn't just be left to its own devices, he thought, feeling vindicated. With every step, it seemed to grow wilder, darker, more unpredictable.

After what seemed like an eternity – but was in fact probably only about a minute – the leaves overhead parted, and a dark mass loomed before him, the tip of its spire already beginning to melt away into the encroaching fog.

The door of the chapel was unostentatious, and, surprisingly, given what the building was used for, unlit. How any of the staff managed to get to and from this place, especially carrying a load, was beyond him.

Something rustled behind him. He froze, spun around, his heart automatically jumping into his throat. But everything was still. Not the slightest sign of movement.

He caught his breath, scolding himself for reacting so ridiculously. Overimaginative children feared monsters in the dark; logical adults knew better. It was probably nothing but a rabbit in the undergrowth, or a bird in the trees.

He turned back to the door, ignoring the niggling voice in his head that told him it hadn't sounded like the shifting of twigs or leaves. If he had to put his finger on it, he'd say it had sounded almost like … *straw*. A dry, rasping sound he recalled from summers spent working on a farm in his youth. The sound it had made as the bales dragged along the barn floor…

He shook the thought off as soon as it had come. After all, where would you find straw in the middle of Stamford? And in late October, too?

He turned the handle, and the door moved inwards. It was open, then, as he'd hoped. They were expecting him.

The fact that it had swung open so seamlessly, without the anticipated creaking sound one would expect from an ancient church door, would have seemed odd to anyone who didn't know what to anticipate inside. But he knew differently; nothing about this dilapidated little chapel was what it seemed.

He slipped within, his heart beginning to patter again, although this time it was out of excitement, not fear.

The interior of the chapel was in darkness, too. He hovered in the doorway, wondering if perhaps he'd got it wrong after all. But as his eyes adjusted to the gloom, any hint of disappointment was replaced with wonder.

Huge wooden racks loomed before him, stretching the full length of what had once been the aisle. What had once been *everything*, he corrected himself, looking around. There was nothing left of the contents of what had once been this most holy of spaces. These days, it was the container of far more worldly pleasures.

The sound of his footsteps followed him as he walked through the echoing space, between the huge racks filled with more bottles than could be counted in a lifetime.

Dr. Rauceby was as far away from a spiritual man as you could get. But as he ran his hand lovingly along the dust-covered bottles, he felt something close to religious fervour, the adoring worship others spoke about in terms of their faith. Except, he told himself, for one crucial difference. They were fantasists; what they revered didn't exist. This, on the other hand … this was real. *This* was heaven.

His mind swam as he pulled out bottle after bottle, gasping

at labels he'd heard about but never seen, names he'd thought were mere myth. It was, by any measure, the finest collection of wine he'd ever encountered; his head pounded just trying to calculate how much it might all be worth. Not that it was about the money, of course, he reminded himself hastily. People who thought of wine only in monetary terms weren't serious oenophiles; they were mere guzzling Philistines.

At once, he heard another sound. Not a rustling this time; more of a scratching. He jumped guiltily, wary of being caught snooping, dropping the bottle he was holding in the process. He lunged for it, catching it just in time, and slotted it carefully back into its rack with shaking hands.

"Hello?" he called. There *was* a light, he realised now. He'd been too absorbed to notice it before, but there it was, glowing from the far corner. He moved towards it now, striving for a blustery tone, hoping his transgression hadn't been noticed. "It's Dr. Rauceby. I received your invitation."

More scratching, but no further response than that. As Rauceby grew closer, he could see why. The light was in fact coming from high up, shining down from a square hatch above his head. Then his toes hit the edge of something, and he looked up the length of an impossibly tall wooden ladder. He was standing beneath the bell tower, he realised. The next moment, he realised something even worse.

He was going to have to go up.

The thought didn't fill him with relish. That ladder had to be … what, forty feet? But clearly they couldn't hear him from down here, so…

He looked back at the racks of wine, glittering so appealingly in the low light, and braced his shoulders. It was worth it. He'd waited a long time to be allowed in here.

He began to climb. As he approached the hatch, the light grew brighter. Presently, he saw that it was a lantern, blazing with a hot white glare. He put a hand up to screen his eyes, the ladder wobbling slightly as his weight shifted.

The scratching was intensifying, growing almost manic. At the top, Rauceby turned to look down; somehow, it seemed to be even higher than it had looked from the ground. As he did so, a shadow flitted across the open doorway, catching his attention.

He looked … and then immediately wished he hadn't.

A devil stared back at him. Clad in a cape of straw, its face a grotesque, terrifying mask. Horns protruded from the top of its head. Rauceby felt his throat go dry, logic giving way to blind terror. With a fear-fuelled strength, he launched himself upwards, into the mouth of the hatch.

With a blood-curdling screech, a dark shape plummeted towards him. Rauceby felt his entire body jerk in shock, his fingers scrabbling as the ladder slipped away from him.

The last thing he knew, he was falling into the night.

Chapter Eighteen

Detective Sergeant Pettifer was thoroughly enjoying his Halloween. He was collapsed on the sofa with the missus – granted, being forced to endure some incomprehensible period drama, where the women communicated in irritatingly coy glances and every other man who appeared was called William – but at least he was sitting down. And the house was blissfully quiet and empty. The years of Halloween parties – nightmare-inducing in themselves, with the carpets soaked from apple bobbing and all the food having to look like eyeballs or severed fingers, and herding hordes of screaming, sugar infested children away from the more prized knick-knacks – were long in the past now.

His own three, now teenagers, had slunk off to various gatherings, and if he'd happened to notice that their outfit choices weren't the traditional Halloween fare – in his daughter's case, there wasn't much outfit to speak of at all – he'd decided to turn a blind eye for tonight, and take his policeman's hat off, so to speak. They weren't here, moaning at him about money or raiding the fridge for carbohydrates; that was enough for him. So long as their antics didn't land them at Welland Police Station during the course of the evening, he'd be content.

The sound of the doorbell echoed from the hallway, breaking into his pleasant torpor. A pointed glance from the other sofa cushion quashed any hopes that he might be the one staying put, and with a gusty sigh, he heaved himself to his feet.

Bloody trick-or-treaters, he thought, as he shuffled down the hall in his slippers, collecting the bowl of sweets from its position of readiness next to the front door. And there his evening had been looking so promising. He should never have been so complacent; of course there was no hope of peace, not on this of all nights. His suggestion that they leave the inevitable pumpkin on the doorstep unlit this year in a bid to dissuade all but the most tenacious of visitors had seen him branded a grinch in his own household. All very easy for them to say, he thought ruefully, as he helped himself to a chocolate toffee – no-one liked those anyway, so he reasoned he was doing a public service – when *they* weren't the ones who'd be up and down like a jack-in-the-box all evening.

At least he'd managed to draw the line at wearing a costume this year, he thought dolefully, chewing vigorously on the already much-regretted toffee. He'd always made a particularly unconvincing vampire, with his build. He looked like he'd eaten the whole person, not just drained their blood. And the year the kids had persuaded him to be an Egyptian mummy, everyone had mistaken him for the Michelin Man.

Not that he even needed a costume to be terrifying, judging

by the number of small children he made cry just by opening the door. That was something else he got reprimanded for every year, too; apparently, he had a 'forbidding expression.' Whatever *that* meant. He'd been reliably informed by many who knew him that he was famous for only having one expression. In which case, could it even be called an expression at *all*, or was it simply his face? Because if it was the latter, then technically, it couldn't be his fault, could it?

Deciding that such philosophical meanderings were pointless, as he'd be told off by Mrs. Pettifer in any case, he tried to arrange his features into something more genial this time as he unlatched the door.

"*Christ*, Sarge." Constable Jess Winters stood on the doorstep. "What have you come as this year? A strychnine victim?"

Pettifer immediately let his face drop into a scowl. There, that was a lot more comfortable.

"A little old for trick-or-treat, aren't we, Constable?"

"I'm afraid I'm here on business. Although as you're offering…" She eyed the bowl, still in his outstretched hand, and selected a sweet, which she proceeded to unwrap. "Apparently a report's come into the station about a missing person."

That got Pettifer's attention. He stopped chewing the interminable toffee, looking at her intently.

"Missing? From where?"

"The Aquitaine Club." Jess raised her fair eyebrows meaningfully. "One of their guests has disappeared."

Pettifer gave a low whistle.

"The Aquitaine, hmm? Isn't that the snooty members' club across town?"

"I'm not sure that's how they'd choose to describe themselves, but yes, sir, it is."

"Well, that's a turn up for the books." Pettifer was already reaching for his overcoat. "Must be something for *them* to get in touch."

As far as he was aware, they'd never contacted the station about anything. Damned secretive place, by all accounts. It was one of the few places in town he'd never set foot inside. You'd think nothing untoward had ever happened there, which of course, couldn't possibly be true. They must hush it all up, keep it internal.

And yet *now* … a missing person. And they were reaching out for help. It was interesting. The most interesting thing, in fact, that had happened in a good few months. A good mystery was just what his jaded palette had been craving. Suddenly, he was feeling a lot more cheerful. He shrugged the coat over his massive shoulders, turning up the collar against the chill he could already feel was waiting for him out there.

"How long's this person … sorry, this *guest* … been missing for, then?"

"Well, um…" Jess shuffled her feet. "This is the part I'm not sure you're going to like."

Was it his imagination, or did his constable look rather sheepish? His hands stilled on the buttons of his coat.

"What won't I like?" he asked ominously.

"He was last seen…" She looked up at the blank, overcast sky, and he could have sworn she was counting to ten in her head. "At five o'clock," she said at last.

"Yesterday?"

She winced.

"I'm afraid not."

"*Today?*" Pettifer could hear his voice rising in angry disbelief. "He's been gone for two *hours*? That's not missing! That's out for a walk or having a drink somewhere. Are they off their rockers? Who the hell reported him missing? And who the *hell...*"

His mouth set in a grim line. There really wasn't any need to finish that question.

"The DCI's insistent that we follow it up," Jess said, apologetically. "Apparently, with The Aquitaine being such an important institution..."

She was paraphrasing that; he could practically hear those words coming from Heavenly's well-moisturised lips, in that supercilious tone of his. *Important institution.* Yes, of *course* he would be all over this. Their superior was an insatiable social climber, permanently disgruntled at having to exchange his cushy role in London for the decidedly less starry and more down-to-earth one of running a tiny rural station. The prospect of swanning around The Aquitaine, with its gilded clientele, would be like catnip for him. Pettifer only wondered that Heavenly wasn't taking on this particular case himself.

Apparently, Jess read his thoughts, because she added, "I think he was a bit put out not to be able to go himself, to be honest. But he's at some dinner, thrown by the Chief Commissioner."

Of course, Pettifer thought dryly. Couldn't possibly think of leaving a policeman's dinner to do some actual police work. *That* would be risible.

But he didn't say it out loud, much as he might have liked to. The DCI was still their superior, like it or not, and call Pettifer old-fashioned, but that counted for something in his book. Jess might pick up on his lack of admiration for the man, but he was careful never to say anything openly disrespectful. He had to set an example.

"All right," he sighed, trying not to think about the ambrosial spread likely on offer at the aforementioned dinner. Food that would go largely untouched by his DCI, a man rarely seen to eat anything beyond a plain oatcake or once, it was reported although not confirmed, a small satsuma. All these formal dinners were entirely wasted on him, Pettifer thought ruefully. Send *him*, now, and it would be a different story. There'd be no food wastage then. "Well, this sounds like a waste of time if ever there was one, but orders are orders." He patted his pockets, checking his gloves were present. "But listen, it doesn't need both of us. You get off home, lass…"

He paused. She'd moved into the light, and for the first time, he saw what she was wearing: a black leotard that sparkled as she moved. Two pointed ears were nestled in her blonde hair, and three black lines were drawn on each cheek in what looked like eyeliner. "Or wherever it was you were off to," he finished diplomatically, in a tone that suggested he *really* didn't want any details.

She shrugged.

"Just a Halloween party. My house mates were making me go. I won't be missed."

He shook his head firmly.

"You should let your hair down. You work hard enough." Generally, he didn't do fatherly advice; he was sure she must have her own father somewhere, although he'd never asked her about it. Work time was for work talk, in his opinion. But at times he felt someone ought to tell Jess to take a break. That the world wouldn't fall apart if she relaxed every now and again. It would make her a better officer in the long run.

"But the DCI…" she chewed her red-stained lip, "he asked me to come and fetch you. If he finds out I didn't attend the scene with you…"

"Don't worry about Heavenly. I can deal with him." Their superior had a habit of automatically calling Jess for everything, something which Pettifer had tried several times to put a stop to. The lass did enough donkey work as it was, being the youngest member of the team, and the only woman to boot. But whether it was actual misogyny, or simple thoughtlessness, Heavenly continued to do it anyway. "It's not like I'm up to anything pressing." He indicated over his shoulder, to where the television could be heard gushing: "Oh, *William*, I thought you'd *never* ask!"

Pettifer quirked a wry smile.

"See? You'll actually be doing me a favour. Now, you go and enjoy yourself. I'll see you in the morning."

He bellowed a goodbye to his wife and stepped out onto the pavement, turning towards the clustered spires on the horizon that pinpointed the centre of town.

"I *really* don't mind, sir." Jess, far from leaving, instead followed, falling into step with him. "Honestly. And I'm here now. I might as well help."

He stopped dead, turning to look at her suspiciously.

"Constable Winters, do *not* tell me that you'd rather come to work than go out to a party."

"Of course I would! As, I'm sure, would you." She gave him a playful prod in the arm. "You're not exactly a party animal yourself, sir."

"Not now I'm an old family man, no," he said with dignity. "But when I was young, like you, it was a different matter. I liked a knees-up back then."

"The fact you're calling it a knees-up tells me how long ago it was," Jess said dryly.

"Enough of that cheek, Constable." His eyes took on a faintly wistful look. "Ah, yes, I had some moves in those days."

"Really?" She eyed him sceptically. He frowned.

"Yes, Winters, *really*. How else d'you think I snagged Mrs. Pettifer?" He jerked a thumb back towards his house. "Finest lass in Barnsley, she was. Could have had her pick. And I was no oil painting, even before this," he tapped his broken nose, "but I tell you, when I took a girl onto the floor … my hips had a life of their…"

"Argh! Enough!" Jess's hands flew to her eyes, as though she could block out the mental picture. "All right, you win. I'll go back to the party when we've finished. Please, just…" she added entreatingly, "no more details. And *certainly* no demonstrations."

They lapsed into silence after that, the only sound their footsteps ringing on the paving as they wound through the streets towards the glowing lights of town. But when Jess risked a peek across at her superior, she saw something very odd. In fact, later she would tell herself it must have been a trick of the dark. Because the sergeant's granite-like face wasn't fixed, for once, in its usual dour expression. It displayed something else, something she'd never seen before.

If she didn't know better, she'd say it had looked *very* much like a smirk.

Chapter Nineteen

"Well, Constable," Pettifer put his hands on his hips and surveyed the splendour that surrounded them on all sides, "it would appear we're going up in the world. We're certainly not in Kansas anymore."

"Or Stamford High Street," Jess agreed faintly, looking slightly dazed. Her head was swivelling this way and that, as though she was struggling to take it in. "What kind of people can afford a place like this?"

"We're about to find out." Pettifer elbowed her lightly in the side, bringing her to attention as a sharp-suited woman bore down on them. "You're in charge here, I presume?" It was a guess he was prepared to make. She was young, but everything about her, from her body language to the look of strained authority on her face, screamed management. She might as well have had it written on her forehead. He held out a hand the approximate size and shape of an average paving slab. "DS. Pettifer and PC. Winters. Welland Police."

She didn't respond immediately. Instead, she noticeably

looked them up and down. Her expression remained outwardly bland and professional, but the sense of disdain that radiated from her was enough to make even Pettifer, usually immune to opinions on his appearance, find himself shifting uncomfortably under her scrutiny.

They probably didn't look at their most encouragingly professional tonight, he admitted, with himself in an old rugby shirt, Jess in her Halloween cat costume. They certainly stood out in the plush, cultivated surrounds of The Aquitaine's foyer; and not in a good way. Still, he reminded himself robustly, squaring his already extremely square shoulders, it didn't make them any less official in capacity. He had a feeling he might need to make that plain to this woman, who already didn't seem enchanted by their presence.

Eventually, she spoke, taking his hand and giving it a surprisingly firm shake.

"Annabel Drayford, manager. Apologies for the wait. We've had a little incident here tonight; I was just checking on progress."

"An incident?" Pettifer raised his bushy eyebrows.

"All under control." The manager's tone was smooth, but a small dent appeared in the middle of her forehead. Pettifer got the impression she was annoyed with herself for mentioning it, or annoyed with him for asking; which, he couldn't tell. "One of our guests had a turn, that's all. The paramedics are with her now." She folded her arms; Pettifer noticed she was tipping forwards onto the balls of her feet, as though she was itching to get moving again. "Now, please, how can I help you officers?"

For a moment, he thought she was being disingenuous. But he looked at her again and realised that the question had been posed in earnest. She really *didn't* seem to know. He and Jess shared a look, then he cleared his throat.

"We're here in response to the call, Miss Drayford." When she continued to look blank, he persisted. "The telephone call? About the missing guest of yours? I'd assumed you were the one who placed it."

"*Me?*" She looked astonished; it was such a departure from her previous mien that Pettifer couldn't decide if it had to be real or could only be fake. "No, it wasn't me. And I can't imagine…" She seemed to gather herself then, suggesting neutrally, "A mistake must have been made somewhere. Perhaps you could try one of the other hostelries in town…"

"So you *don't* have a missing guest?" Pettifer tried not to look too hopeful. If this all turned out to be some Halloween prank … well, he'd be a *very* happy man. In his mind's eye, his beloved sofa was already beckoning invitingly to him. But he mustn't get ahead of himself, he thought reluctantly; he believed in always doing a thorough job, however unpromising it appeared. So he persisted.

"A doctor…" He looked at Jess queryingly.

"Dr. Rauceby," she supplied immediately, as he'd known she would. Jess was excellent with names. In fact, she was excellent with factual information generally, the drier the better. He sometimes wondered if she had one of those photographic memories you read about. As for himself … well, he often got his own children's names muddled up, and last week he'd called for his wife and ended up accidentally summoning the cat. That hadn't gone down well on any side, not least because the blasted feline then expected an early dinner.

"That's the one." He clicked his fingers together

triumphantly. "We were told he's gone missing. Are you saying that's incorrect?"

"Utter nonsense, I'm afraid." She shook her head. "I'm sorry your time's been wasted. And on your evening off, too," she added, with another, none-too-complimentary glance at their attire. "Some crossed wires, perhaps. Or high jinks. It is that time of year." She began to usher them towards the door. It was subtly done, so much so that Pettifer didn't even realise she was doing it until they were halfway across the foyer. "You can rest assured, however, that this *won't* be taken lightly. I shall look into this miscommunication myself. And I'm sure Dr. Rauceby will be mortified to hear that you've been dragged out here on his behalf…"

"Wait." Jess stopped dead, almost causing the manager to walk into her. "You mean to say that he *isn't here*?"

Annabel Drayford's face twitched as she realised her slip-up. A brief spasm of irritation, quickly papered over. But not before both officers had observed it.

"Not … currently, no," she said, in a clipped voice.

"And you don't know *where* he is?" Jess pressed. Pettifer hid a smile. Annabel Drayford had yet to realise the full extent of her mistake. She'd got his constable's suspicions up, and Jess was like a dog with a bone when she thought she was onto something. There'd be no shaking her off now.

"We don't keep tabs on our members, Constable," Annabel Drayford replied tightly. "They come and go of their own free will." When neither Jess nor Pettifer made any sign of moving, she gave an exasperated sigh. "I *assure* you, there is absolutely *nothing* to be concerned about. Of course, if I thought there was…" She turned away; a clear dismissal this time. Pettifer felt a flicker of disbelief at the woman's arrogance. "I do, of course, thank you for coming out. It's good to know our local police are so active. But it's a false alarm in this case. Now, if you'll excuse me, this is a busy evening for us, and I must be getting on. You'll understand if I ask you to see yourselves out."

It wasn't a question. So perhaps it was fitting that she didn't wait for an answer, but simply walked away, her back ramrod straight, her stockinged legs eating up the floor in purposeful strides. Jess stared after her in open indignation.

"What a bloody *cheek*!" she spluttered. "She treated us like we were door-to-door hawkers, not police officers here on official business. Our warrant cards might as well have been library cards for all the impact they had on her."

Privately, Pettifer agreed. But he didn't see any point in adding fuel to the fire.

"Well, in any case, it seems that's that." He blew out his cheeks in a sigh. "Come on, lass; let's be shifting. With any luck, I'll have just missed the ending of Mrs. Pettifer's latest bodice ripper by the time I'm home."

"Wait…" Jess looked at him in disbelief. "You can't be serious, Sarge. We're not *actually* leaving?"

"Course we are." He risked a sideways glance at her and knew he was going to have to explain further. "Look, our hands are tied. *She* insists he's not missing, and considering the timeline we're working with…" He shrugged. "Two hours does not a missing person make, Constable. There's no case to answer here."

She still didn't look mollified. If anything, she looked more stubbornly incredulous. He couldn't help but wonder how much this newfound zeal for the case owed to irritation at the way they'd just been summarily dismissed.

"So we're just going to give *up*? Is that it?"

"No," he said levelly. "We're going to chalk it up to a job done diligently and accept that we can't do any more." When she continued to look mulish, he frowned. "Look, what do you want us to do? We wouldn't even know where to begin looking for him."

"Actually," a soft voice said behind him, "that's not entirely true."

Pettifer whirled around – as fast as his bulk would allow, anyway; he suspected it resembled more of a jerky rotation – and immediately felt his expression darken ominously.

Felicia Grant stood there, watching him apprehensively. As well she might, he thought grimly. She must have known he wouldn't be pleased by her presence. Why was it that *every* time there was something suspicious going on in this town, there she was? Just for once, he'd like to bump into her under normal circumstances, and yet, the only time their paths ever crossed was…

Well, usually over a dead body, come to think of it. The thought did *not* improve his mood.

"What are *you* doing here?" The question came out more roughly than he'd intended.

She obviously decided it was more prudent not to answer, because she continued as though he hadn't spoken.

"I saw him crossing the gardens about half an hour ago."

Jess's ears pricked up at that.

"You're *sure* it was him?"

Felicia nodded.

"Definitely. He's quite distinctive."

Jess looked at him then, her fair eyebrows raised meaningfully.

"Doesn't really seem the night for horticultural appreciation, does it, Sarge?"

Pettifer remained flintily silent.

"He looked like he was heading for somewhere specific," Felicia added. "But I'm afraid I couldn't tell you where. I'm brand new to this place."

Jess had already whipped out her phone and was pinching the screen, zooming in on a satellite image of the club. She made a triumphant sound under her breath.

"There's something at the far end of the garden. It looks like some sort of small church, or chapel. You can see the tower on here." She held it out to show Pettifer, eyes shining. "Surely, it's got to be worth checking out, at least? Seeing as we're already here."

Pettifer looked between the two women and felt his shoulders drop in resignation. He nodded.

"All right, Constable. Lead the way, then. It looks like we're going to church."

Chapter Twenty

The garden was a brumous, purple soup, shrouded in a fog so dense that it was only possible to see about three feet ahead. Pettifer and Jess made their way cautiously through it, crossing a lawn as flat and perfect as a bowling green, occasionally having to alter course as a flower border or stone fountain reared up suddenly out of the blank wall of nothingness.

"So, you're telling me this church belongs to the club?" Pettifer said, as he narrowly avoided toppling into an ornamental pond. The carp within looked at him with an expression he could have sworn was disdain before swimming back down to the depths. Even the bloody fish in this place were snooty, he thought, not entirely humorously. "Funny sort of thing to have in the garden, isn't it?" He paused, then added, because he knew they were both thinking it, "Even by Stamford's standards."

And Lord knew, the place had more than its share of oddities. Multiple millennia of history were bound to leave a mark, after all. The people of Stamford thought nothing of living next to a medieval hospital, or doing their shopping inside a converted church, or passing an ancient piece of castle wall on their way to work. To them, it was just part of life in their town.

And that was just the stuff that really *existed*, Pettifer thought sardonically. If he had a pound for every time someone spouted one of the town's famous – and innumerable, it seemed – myths and legends at him during the course of his work… He'd even heard tales of tunnels running beneath the streets, a secret network linking up to the cellar system. It was all utter rhubarb, of course; the product of an overly imaginative rural population with not a lot else to entertain them. People had always made up stories, only in most places, folk were too sensible to pay them any heed. Pettifer's own personal opinion on the matter was that history was probably a much duller place than most liked to imagine. Not to mention a far less hygienic one.

"Technically, sir, it's a chapel," Jess corrected him. "Not a church."

He scowled into the darkness.

"Don't be a swot, Winters."

"Sorry," she said, not particularly sounding it. He'd bet anything she'd been a prefect at school. He, meanwhile, had done well to scrape through till sixteen. "But it's actually rather interesting, you know. It's built on the site of an ancient shrine…"

Pettifer gave an inward groan. Why was everyone in this town such an insufferable history buff? Even his own bloody constable; he couldn't even get away from it at work now.

"How do you know all of this, anyway?" he asked

exasperatedly, cutting her off. They'd been here all of ten minutes; how had she *possibly* had time to find out…

She held up her phone, which she was also using as a torch, having taken pity on her poor troglodyte of a sergeant and given him the analogue model.

"There's quite a bit about it, most of it on architectural and historical websites. Too much to read in the time, naturally, so I got an AI chatbot to summarise it for me, and…"

"All right, yes," Pettifer said hastily, hoping the fog covered up the utter befuddlement that had set in somewhere around the word 'chatbot'. "Well, er, good work, I'm sure."

"Oh, it was nothing, sir."

She said it so airily that he had the sobering impression she wasn't being disingenuous. He was beginning to feel more and more like a dinosaur. He couldn't help but wonder, in his darker moments, how much longer the force would see the value of old-fashioned plods like him.

"And you say they keep wine in there now?" He forced himself away from introspection. No use worrying; that was what he was always telling his children. If it happens, it happens. Fretting won't change a thing. "Are they even allowed to do that?"

She shrugged.

"It's all deconsecrated. Has been for centuries."

Pettifer pushed aside the low-hanging branches of a tree. Their progress was getting more challenging; this far part of the garden was in deep contrast to the meticulously groomed landscape they'd left behind. Here, it was wilder, almost overgrown in places. The trees formed a dark tunnel all around them, oppressive and menacing. Their roots knotted across what had once been a path, but now was a treacherous trip hazard. Even in the daytime, you'd have to watch where you put your feet; at night, in weather like this…

"Haven't they got a perfectly good cellar to keep it in?" he grumbled, as he narrowly avoided twisting his ankle in a rabbit hole.

"Maybe the cellars are kept for more nefarious purposes," Jess suggested. "Guests who don't pay their bills. I wouldn't put it past that ice queen of a manager."

Suddenly, a wall sheered upwards out of the brume. Jess skidded to a halt, causing Pettifer, who was slower in his reactions, to almost stumble into her. As he righted himself, he realised they were standing in an arched doorway.

"Well, go on, then, lass," he said, as she turned to him expectantly. "You do the honours. This was your find."

She nodded, reaching for the handle. There'd been no hesitation in the movement, but Pettifer could feel the nervous energy radiating off her, see it in the tense set of her shoulders. Always trying to prove herself, his Jess. Always wanting to impress, to be right. She'd be disappointed if they didn't find the doctor here, he thought. She'd hide it well, but she'd take it personally. As if she'd failed, made a mistake.

Personally, he thought they were likely on a wild goose chase. Why would anyone in their right mind tramp all the way out here on a night like this? It didn't look as if there was much to see; the whole place had an abandoned feel to it, from the overgrown vegetation scrambling across its surface to the fallen, crumbling pieces of stone that littered the ground around it. But he didn't want to tell Jess his doubts; this was the next logical line of enquiry, and she was following it, just as she should. He was supposed to be teaching her to do the job well; it wasn't always about results.

So he stayed silent as he followed her into the interior of the chapel. The first thing that struck him was the cold; it was nothing like the chill in the air outside. It was a numbing, penetrating, lifeless frigidity. The kind of cold that had reigned for years, decades, longer even, which was now as embedded into the fabric of the building as the stones from which it was built.

There was nothing sadder than an empty church, didn't they say … or wait, was it an empty theatre? Either way, it felt like an odd place, this, devoid of its original function, of all the things that would have made it inviting, and which he recalled so well from the Sunday mornings of his childhood: sunlight streaming through stained glass, the drone of the organ, smartly-dressed folk filling the pews … not that there were any pews in here, he observed, looking this way and that. Not anymore. Instead, as Jess found the light switch, and the low sconces on the walls flickered to life, the view that greeted him was something far stranger.

The vaulted space was filled, floor to ceiling, with enormous wine racks. Light glinted off the glass of countless bottles. The effect was undeniably impressive, but also discombobulating, claustrophobic. It made him feel uneasy, the police officer in him not liking the amount of dark corners, blocked views. Anyone could be in here with you, and you'd be none the wiser.

As though responding to his thoughts, a scuffing sound came from the other end of the chapel. He and Jess looked at one another and understanding passed between them. As one, they began to advance, moving between the racks. Looking down at his feet, Pettifer realised they were following the path of the original aisle.

"Doctor Rauceby?" Pettifer raised his voice, letting its deep tones rebound around the vaulted space. "Are you in here?"

No response. Pettifer paused for breath. Breath, which, he realised, he could see, forming in ghostly clouds in front of his face. Bloody hell, it was cold in here.

Then the sound came again; this time, it was apparent that it was coming not from the central body of the building, but off to the side. In their way stood a huge line of wine racks. He motioned for Jess to go one way around, himself taking the other.

"Doctor Rauceby," he called again, more softly this time. He didn't want to frighten the old bugger. There hadn't been any mention of his potentially being confused, but then, that manager hadn't been very forthcoming about anything. Best to err on the side of caution. "It's the police. We're just here to make sure you're all right."

He moved between the walls of bottles as carefully as he could, his broad shoulders mere inches from the glass bottlenecks on either side. Occasionally, he brushed one, making a tinkling sound; that, combined with the sound of his heavy boots on the stone floor, was probably undermining all his efforts not to sound threatening, he acknowledged ruefully. He wasn't a man built for stealth. That was what he had Jess for. Of *her*, he could hear nothing; she was as light-footed as a cat burglar. He was glad she'd decided to work on the side of the law, and not its opposite; she'd be a formidable foe to catch.

He reached the end of the rack, and ahead of him was an area of clearly unused space. As a result, there were no lights down this end of the church, and Pettifer found himself peering into inky, impenetrable shadow.

Or perhaps not, he realised, as his eyes adjusted. There was a glow of light, coming from somewhere above. He shifted his weight forwards…

And that was when he heard the footstep behind him.

Since the beginning of his career, Pettifer had made a study of the sound of his colleagues' footsteps. He could tell who was approaching his desk across the station without looking up; some might have called it just another of his 'quirky ways', but in his opinion, knowing who – or more importantly who *wasn't* – behind you was invaluable when in a vulnerable situation. He was pretty sure it might even have saved his life more than once.

And so he knew immediately that the person who'd crept up on him wasn't Jess. But he didn't wait to speculate further. He spun around, at a speed that would have been impossible for him without the burst of adrenaline currently pulsing through his veins, shining the beam of his torch directly in his pursuer's eyes.

Unfortunately for him, the torch was on its last legs, and only produced the most insipid halogen-fuelled sheen imaginable.

Felicia Grant blinked, her hand moving to shield her eyes before she evidently decided it wasn't necessary and let it drop.

"Sorry, I didn't mean to scare you."

"You didn't," he snapped, his tone sharpened to an edge by the blood still singing in his ears. He looked her up and down. She was wearing a silver dress; a strappy thing, no sleeves. Hopelessly inadequate for the time of year. She was clearly freezing, her arms wrapped across herself; for some reason, this realisation just made him feel even more annoyed with her. "It's a good thing, though. What the *bloody* hell are you playing at, sneaking up on a police officer like that?"

"I didn't sneak!" she protested, actually having the audacity to look offended, which he could scarcely credit. "You just didn't hear me, that's all." Her gaze moved towards his size-fifteen feet, clad in their clomping great boots. He scowled, unable to deny that she had a point.

"I haven't got time for this," he said shortly. "You need to leave. Now."

"I know, and I will, I just…" She hesitated, pushing her bronze waves away from her forehead. "Look, there's something I think you should know, and I didn't want to say it back there in the club. It might be awkward, you see, if it turns out to be nothing, but…"

"Sir!" Jess's voice, raised in alarm, cut through the musty air.

He turned to Felicia with a warning look.

"Stay here," he ordered roughly. "I *mean* it."

Then he broke into a run, plunging into the shadows towards the square of light, which was where he could hear Jess calling from.

"*Sir!*" she said again, although this time it was more of a yelp. He staggered to a halt as he realised he'd nearly fallen over her. She was crouched on the ground, and she wasn't alone.

A body was sprawled across the flagstones, lit dramatically from above, as though it were a corpse on a stage. But that wasn't even the strangest thing about the scene.

On its back sat a small, black creature. It looked at Pettifer with beady, malevolent eyes, and then, as he watched, it stretched out its sinewy wings, letting out an ear-splitting, heart-stopping shriek. Pettifer would swear forever afterwards that it had been a shriek of gloating. Of triumph, even. Of course, he would never truly know.

But what he did know was in that moment, he felt his blood run ice-cold.

Chapter Twenty-One

Felicia stood in the stark surroundings of the stripped church and watched Pettifer and Jess perform the seamless routine that had to be followed after the discovery of a body. Pettifer was calling it in, his face set in grim lines as he communicated in his trademark monosyllables. Jess was making notes, scanning the area around the lifeless form for any telling pieces of evidence. They were a good team, Felicia reflected, seeming to know what was required of one another without even having to say it aloud. There was something reassuring about watching their quiet choreography, so calm and understated that it managed to take the edge off the whole thing, make it just that bit less unbearable. She was intensely glad they were here; she couldn't imagine being on her own in this place right now.

She'd done what Pettifer had asked of her – for *once*, as he would no doubt say – and stayed in exactly the same spot. She hadn't moved an inch. She wasn't sure she could, in all honesty; her feet seemed bolted to the floor, her eyes glued on the pathetically crumpled form lying at an unnatural angle on the flagstones ahead of her. She'd come across her fair share of sudden death during her time back in Stamford, but it never got any easier, nor any less desperately perplexing, the mind unable to comprehend how someone you'd just seen alive one minute could be gone the next. Gone for good, the light extinguished.

She shivered – whether at the thought, or the more prosaic fact that she was freezing cold, she couldn't say. She sincerely wished she'd stopped to fetch her coat before rushing out here in what had to be the world's most insubstantial dress, but she'd been so bent on catching up with Pettifer, she hadn't given it a thought.

She tried to distract herself from her discomfort by surveying her surroundings, but there wasn't a lot to see, and what there was didn't exactly uplift the spirits. Of the fabric of the building itself, there were very few adornments remaining, the church having clearly been heavily targeted during the iconoclastic years following the Dissolution of the Monasteries – surprisingly so, she couldn't help but think, for such a small, unimportant-seeming chapel. The desecration in here had been as brutal as it was complete; every single niche was empty of the statue that would have once filled it, every single gargoyle that would once have glared down from the corbels had at least part of its face hacked away. The vandals had even taken the trouble to chip away at the carvings on the pillars, rendering them unidentifiable.

Just as she was beginning to think she might have been forgotten about entirely, Pettifer turned away from the body and made his way towards her. He didn't look any more pleased about her presence than he had earlier, but she couldn't entirely blame him for that, Felicia conceded, a little awkwardly. The truth was, she probably shouldn't have been here. But it was too late to worry about that now.

Pettifer appeared to be of the same mind, because he didn't launch into a reprimand as she might have expected.

"Well, there's no question what did for him," he said matter-of-factly. "Falling from that height … the only consolation is that he obviously hit his head when he landed; he would have gone instantly. Doubt he knew much about it."

"Presumably he wasn't aware of the bat colony when he climbed up there?" Felicia looked at the hunched black figures watching her malevolently from the top of the ladder, and tried not to shudder. As a rule, she didn't mind bats in the slightest, but there was something about these that made her distinctly uneasy. Or perhaps it was just the knowledge that they'd contributed to a man's death.

"I think we have to assume that," Pettifer agreed, also eyeing them warily. "No-one in their right mind would go up if they did."

As if to prove his point, Jess, who'd been gingerly attempting to climb the ladder, retreated with a yelp as she was instantly dive-bombed by several shrieking, wailing winged creatures.

"There's no way I'm getting up there, Sarge," she panted, ducking out of the way as they continued to swoop at her. "They're really riled."

"All right, lass. Don't try it again," Pettifer ordered. "We don't want you going the same way as the good doctor here."

Felicia wasn't aware of it, but she must have made some slight reaction to that, because suddenly, Pettifer was giving her a decidedly speculative look.

"Oh aye, it's like that, is it?" As Felicia opened her mouth to protest, he got in first. "And before you point out that he's dead, that's a nonsense excuse. He can't hear you now; you might as well say it as it is."

Felicia looked at the body again and felt a fresh wave of pity. Immediate or not, it must have been a terrifying way to die. Nonetheless, Pettifer had a point. She wouldn't help the dead man by avoiding the truth.

"I only met him yesterday," she said cautiously. "But … well, he seems to have been rather a difficult man." She hesitated. "Actually, we had a bit of a run-in with him."

Pettifer's expression hadn't changed. But she could sense his interest.

"About what?"

Her eyes flickered to the dead man, then away again. She focused on a doorway to her right, set at the bottom of a few shallow steps; the zigzag carving above it suggested that the origins of this church were Norman, much older than she would have thought. That carving had been left alone, clearly not having been considered suitably blasphemous by the iconoclasts. To the left of the door, adjacent to the handle, she noticed what she at first thought was a rare survivor: a single gargoyle in the shape of a woman's head. But a second glance told her otherwise; it was a reconstruction, well done but clearly only carved in recent years. The realisation was a sad one; she'd liked the idea that one part of the church's personality had escaped to tell its tale for generations to come.

"If you must know," she sighed. "We were sitting at his favourite table."

It sounded even more absurd out loud. Pettifer's eyebrows raised infinitesimally, which in itself spoke volumes. She could tell he was wondering disbelievingly what kind of madhouse it was he'd stumbled into.

"What *are* you doing here, Felicia?" When he spoke again, his voice had changed in tone. It was quiet, intense. He folded his arms. "And this time, I want an actual answer."

"I met an old schoolfriend of mine and Cassie's here yesterday. She's staying for a few nights while she sorts out some business in town." She didn't feel the need to elaborate on what kind of business; it wasn't exactly relevant to his investigation and she had confidentiality to keep. "And she invited us all back here tonight; they have this ancient Halloween tradition they re-enact, then we were going to go to dinner…" Her stomach flipped at the mere thought of food. There was nothing like finding a dead body to kill your appetite.

"And the doctor; he wasn't at this … re-enactment, I take it?"

"No." Felicia frowned as a thought struck her. "Actually, it was commented upon. I got the impression he was expected to be there. He must have changed his mind at the last minute."

"Or someone changed it for him."

He said it quietly, but with such assurance that her chin jerked up in shock, and their gaze clashed.

"You don't mean…"

In response, he indicated over his shoulder, towards the small, square hatch in the ceiling.

"That light up there … it's a camping lantern, turned up to its highest setting. Those things are designed for pitch darkness; you can't even look directly at it. I tried, and I'm still seeing spots."

"Not exactly the natural thing to have in a nest full of bats,"

Felicia admitted. Then she clapped a hand over her mouth in horror. "*Oh.*"

"When Winters and I came in here, the place was in darkness. That light would have been visible all through the church."

"You think someone *lured* him up there?"

"Someone had placed the lantern way back from the entrance to the hatch, in the corner where the bats were roosting. We can only assume the intention was to deliberately disturb them, make them angry; at this time of year, they've probably only just gone into hibernation. It also rules out the idea that the doctor took it up there himself; scuff marks from his shoes on the rungs indicate that he fell off near the top of the ladder, so likely he never made it all the way up." He took a breath. "So, to answer your question, I can't believe I'm saying this – maybe this bloody bonkers town has finally turned my brain – but yes, I actually do." He dropped his voice, muttering to himself, "Bats in the bloody belfry, I ask you. Anywhere else, *any* other town, they'd laugh me out of the force."

Felicia scarcely heard him; a creeping numbness was stealing over her, a mixture of delayed shock and cold. Her teeth were beginning to chatter.

"I still can't…" she said faintly. "I *just* saw him. He was *fine*. And now…"

He'd been so vital, so brimming with energy; peevish, irritable energy, granted, but still…

Pettifer obviously sensed the shift in her emotions, because he abruptly changed tack.

"For God's sake, lass, I can't look at you shivering away like that any longer," he said curtly. But he was already shrugging off his enormous coat, which undermined the sting in his words. He draped it awkwardly around her shoulders; Felicia politely tried to ignore the way the pockets crunched and jangled as he did so. "You'll catch your death."

Too late, he seemed to realise what he'd said, but clearly didn't know how to rectify it. There was a pause.

"Actually," Felicia said, in a small voice. "That's not technically a belfry; it doesn't have a bell in it. It's just a church tower."

Pettifer rolled his eyes, but the ghost of a relieved smile played around his lips.

"I know you're doing all right when you correct me."

"Sarge." Jess was standing in front of them, her soft face determined. She looked every inch the detached professional. But Felicia noticed that the little silver-moon stud in her ear – which she twisted absent-mindedly when she was stressed or anxious – was turned on its side. "I've finished with the area around the body. I'm just going to do a sweep of the rest of the chapel now. Then we should probably inform the club what's happened on their premises."

Pettifer nodded, but he didn't seem in any hurry to move. Instead, he looked back at Felicia.

"There was something you wanted to tell me. Before."

"I saw someone out there in the gardens with him." She reconsidered. "Well, not *with* him, exactly, more…"

"Following him?"

Felicia gave a rueful shrug.

"I can't say for certain. I only got a brief glimpse." At once, she felt rather foolish for having rushed out here after him, like some true-crime obsessive making everything seem suspicious. They could have just been out for a perfectly innocent, unconnected stroll. And yet, something in her said they hadn't been. Something in the way they'd moved, stealthily, low to the ground…

But without explaining that to Pettifer, she could only sound vague in the extreme. Pettifer obviously thought so, too; she sensed an edge of exasperation to his voice as he asked his next question.

"Any idea who it was?"

"Yes, actually." Thank God, something she could be concrete about. "It was one of the Mummers."

He looked at her blankly.

"Say again?"

She sighed, drawing the coat closer round her shoulders. Not that she needed to; it probably could have wrapped around her whole body three times over.

"Okay, bear with me. I'll try and give you the condensed version."

But he was already shaking his closely-cropped head.

"You know me better than that by now. I don't just want the headlines; tell me everything."

And so she did. Almost. When she got to the part about Sybil collapsing, he held up a mammoth hand to stop her. It was the first time he'd interrupted.

"This would be the 'incident' Miss Drayford referred to, I take it?"

"Yes. They think she must have overheated." Felicia hesitated, her mind picturing Sybil swaying in front of her. The spaced-out look, the huge, dark pupils. The niggling sense in her mind that it was familiar, that she'd seen something like it before. But it was just more conjecture on her part; she had no real grounds for it. And it was Dr. Rauceby who'd died, not

Sybil. So she said nothing more. And Pettifer seemed to take it at face value.

"Probably. With the fire, and the alcohol flowing as it sounds like it was. You were drinking cocktails, you said? They can be deceptively strong."

"Not Sybil, though." Felicia felt a strange need to defend the jolly, kindly woman she'd met. "She just had a small glass of violet liqueur."

Pettifer drew up short.

"That sounds revolting."

"Apparently, it's her favourite. They keep it in just for her."

He frowned, so obviously wondering what was wrong with a pint of bitter that it almost brought a smile to Felicia's face.

"Okay, we're done here." Jess had reappeared between them, snapping off her gloves. "Time to seal the scene for forensics."

"Nothing of note, I take it?" Pettifer didn't sound hopeful.

"Unfortunately, no. They haven't left any trace. There's only the one entrance and exit; the door behind you there looks like it maybe goes down to the crypt. And the lock's soldered shut. No-one could have come or gone that way. The only way our killer could have left is through the same door we came in. Judging by how recently he died, we may well just have missed them." She looked regretful. "We may have to accept that they're long gone by now."

But Pettifer didn't seem disappointed by the news. Instead, he looked thoughtful.

"Or else we simply passed them." He pulled himself up. "We need to get back to the club; I have a feeling that's where our answers might be. And with any luck, our killer, too."

Chapter Twenty-Two

The harlequin-patterned windows of The Aquitaine shone invitingly from the outside, the flickering glow of firelight scintillating across the rippled glass. Through the thin panes and ill-fitting frames, the sound of merriment spilled forth, revealing the celebrations still ongoing within.

Felicia sat on the edge of a stone fountain in the courtyard, willing herself to go inside. That's what she'd assured Pettifer and Jess she'd do, after they'd accompanied her back to the club. And she'd meant it. Except now, faced with the reality of having to walk in there, she found herself immobilised, unwilling to break the spell.

After all, no-one inside had any idea yet of what had happened. To them, the evening was still a festive one, Sybil's collapse only having thrown it into temporary jeopardy. As soon as it had become apparent that nothing terrible had happened to her, the rest of the company had quickly settled back into the swing of things. As soon as Felicia went in there, though, she would be bringing the horror with her. Even if she said nothing, it couldn't be long before people noticed the police officers amongst them. Pettifer and Jess had disappeared to follow up their next lead, but by the looks on their faces, and after what had been said back in the chapel, she knew that they were set on this having been no accident. Soon, they would be rounding the guests up, wanting to question everyone, and they would all be plunged back into the unreal, claustrophobic atmosphere of a murder enquiry.

Worse still, what if Pettifer's suspicions were right, and the person they were looking for was in there with the others? Someone she'd talked to, spent the evening with? It was a chilling thought, and in the cold night air, Felicia found herself beginning to shiver violently, wishing she hadn't given Pettifer his coat back.

"There you are. I was about to send out a search party."

Felicia looked up, and there was Dexter, standing over her. He looked so wonderfully normal, so familiar, so annoyingly handsome in his ridiculous lilac trousers – which she'd really hoped he wouldn't be able to carry off – that she had a sudden, overwhelming urge to fling herself into his arms. It was so powerful that her body rocked forwards on the edge of the fountain, as though pulled towards him by a magnet.

Luckily, she managed to stop herself, because the compulsion only lasted a moment or two. Almost immediately, she cringed at the thought of what she'd almost done. She couldn't run to Dexter anymore; he wasn't her husband. Even though that had been her choice, it was something she seemed to keep on forgetting.

As soon as he saw her face, his expression changed. Gone was his usual urbane nonchalance, replaced with something she didn't often see in him: concern.

"Something's happened, hasn't it? I know that look."

Of course he did. He knew everything about her. It was just a shame she clearly couldn't say the same of him anymore.

But there was no point in keeping any of what had happened from him. He'd know soon enough. They all would. So she told him as concisely as she could, the words scratching the sides of her throat as though they didn't want to be spoken aloud.

He listened patiently, although rather ruining the effect by sipping his cocktail – which he'd brought out with him; he couldn't exactly have been *that* worried about her, Felicia thought sourly – at intervals. For once, however, he managed not to interject, so she had to wait until she'd finished to hear his verdict on the matter. Once she had, however, she was immediately reminded why you should be careful what you wished for.

"Killed by a bat on Halloween?" He tapped his chin thoughtfully. "Well, you do know something about your murderer, at least. They've got a sense of humour."

"Dexter!" Felicia was horrified by his flippancy.

"*What*?" He held up his hands, looking a bit defensive. "I didn't say it wasn't a vile sense of humour, did I? But you can't deny it."

Begrudgingly, Felicia conceded that he *might* just have a point. Doing it like that … it had been risky. So many things could have gone wrong. Why not just bonk the doctor on the head, or drown him in an ornamental pond? This place was full of hazards, if they'd wanted to make it look like an accident. Although Felicia wasn't even sure the killer had been bothered about that; after all, they must have known the lantern would cause suspicion.

Or then again, maybe not; she'd come to realise that not all investigators were as observant as Pettifer. Could their murderer have been banking on a different police officer choosing to believe the simpler story of an accident? Honestly, she couldn't even make a guess. Either way, though, Dexter was right; there was no denying that the murder had an element of whimsy, even playfulness to it... She could feel goosebumps rising up on the back of her neck.

Belatedly, she realised that it wasn't only the macabre thought that was causing the physical reaction; she became aware of the sensation of being watched, her mind catching up on what her body had known several seconds before. Jerking her head around, she saw someone in the shadows of the garden. For a moment, her heart lurched in fear at the grotesque mask, but then her eyes adjusted, and she realised it wasn't what it seemed. It was just a man, but the lantern he was holding threw stark white light up onto his craggy face, rendering it almost like one of the gargoyles that would once have adorned the chapel.

Seeing he'd been spotted, he turned, melting away into the swirling mist. But not before Felicia had time to realise the significance of the lantern in his hand. It was a camping lantern, just like the one Pettifer had described as being placed in the chapel's tower. She leapt to her feet, suddenly unaware of the cold, the damp ground underfoot.

"Fliss?" Dexter looked up in alarm. "What are you doing?"

But she was already setting off in pursuit.

"I need to find out where he's going. You go back inside; make sure Algie's all right. I won't be long."

"Algie's fine; he's with your dad, and... Oh, bugger it." He was following her; she could hear his long strides eating up the grass behind her. She wanted to check back and see if he'd brought his cocktail, but she had to be mindful of where to put her feet in the mist-soaked turf. Her silver heels were sinking in with every step, but she ploughed on, determined. She could see the light from the lantern up ahead, swinging back and forth. Even in this visibility, it wasn't hard to follow; the hot, white beam slicing through the fog, guiding the way.

"I don't need an escort, Dexter," she fired irritably over her shoulder. "I'll be fine."

"You always say that, and you never are," he pointed out, not unreasonably, damn him. "And besides, I'm not running the risk of Sergeant Pettifer finding out I let you tramp off on your own again. I don't fancy my odds against him in a fight."

She was glad she was up ahead so he couldn't see the smile that crossed her face at that image. But he must have known he'd won her over, because he jogged the next few steps until he was by her side. She didn't look at him, but nor did she tell him to leave again.

They continued to follow the light in silence as it bobbed and weaved through the night. It was heading towards the cluster of yew trees, and for an unpleasant moment, Felicia feared she was going to have to go into that dark, sinister tunnel once more, but to her relief, the light veered to the right, skirting around them instead.

The ground out here was bumpy, uneven, becoming more like parkland than lawn. Felicia was almost tempted to take her shoes off and continue the chase barefoot, when suddenly, she spied a ramshackle building ahead; it looked abandoned, the tin roof peeling and caving in, the windows practically falling out of their frames.

"The light's disappeared." Dexter was looking around him

uncertainly. "Whoever you saw, Fliss, I don't think they're here. We must have lost them along the way."

A ball of disappointment lodged itself in Felicia's throat as she scanned the fogbound garden, the eerie shack in front of them shrouded in darkness. Then her eyes travelled upwards, and she saw something that made her freeze.

From the top of the collapsed chimney, smoke was curling softly.

"You're wanting me, then?"

Felicia started at the gruff voice, grabbing Dexter's arm as she whirled around. The old man was standing by the door to the shack, watching her suspiciously. The lantern was still in his hand, but the light had been put out. Without that, he almost seemed to blend into the stone wall behind him, in his faded brown, shop coat, his squashed tweed hat the colour of dry bracken.

Felicia nodded, and in response, he gave the splintered door a shove.

"You'd best come in then, hadn't you?"

———

Meanwhile, Pettifer and Jess stood in front of a much more refined kind of door, also contemplating a way inside. The landing outside the doctor's room was quiet, but Pettifer could hear the sound of revelry still going on downstairs. Soon enough, they'd have to burst that bubble, but for the time being, he wanted to keep the advantage. If no-one else knew the body had been found yet, that may well include the killer.

"Sir," Jess whispered. She was chewing her lip, clearly unhappy with the breach in protocol. "Are you *sure* about this?

Don't you think we ought to just ask Miss Drayford for the key?"

Pettifer paused, his shoulder to the door, and gave her a level look.

"You're right, Winters. That *is* what we ought to do. But that doesn't mean we're going to. I don't trust that manager of theirs; she's already made it clear she doesn't welcome our presence here." He braced his shoulder once more. "I'm not about to give her a chance to potentially interfere with our evidence."

"All right, I see your point." Jess darted over and grabbed the handle, trying to make him stop and think. It was unlike the sarge to be gung-ho, she thought. Annabel Drayford must have got to him a lot more than he'd let on earlier. "But just … please. Let's not cause any damage if we can help it. Imagine what Heavenly will say." As his expression wavered, she added, persuasively, "Imagine the *lecture*."

Pettifer's face took on a look of dread. There was nothing their superior relished more than giving condescending lectures on how *his* force should be run. The last one had gone on for three hours. With no tea breaks.

"All right, lass." Pettifer moved away from the door reluctantly. "Let's do this by the book. What d'you suggest?"

Honestly, she had no idea. She'd just wanted to prevent him breaking down the door. But now he seemed to be expecting a solution, so she racked her brains hastily.

"Um, maybe we could find a cleaner, see if they've got a master key?" She bent down to peer at the lock, and as she did so, the handle twisted beneath her palm. To both officers' astonishment, the door swung open, with almost mocking ease.

"Or, we could just check it isn't already open," Jess added, weakly.

But Pettifer was already inside, his expression keen as he scanned the luxuriously appointed room. She recognised the intense energy radiating off him; he was a mild man, the sarge, despite his intimidating appearance, but once he'd got the bit in his teeth over a case, there was no-one better. She felt lucky every day to work with him.

"Right, Winters, something tells me we don't have long before news of our presence here is noted. I have a feeling this is the kind of place that has ears. So we need to be quick. Let's find out what the hell sent him out to that chapel tonight, when he was supposed to be downstairs in a nice warm parlour with a drink in his hand." He was already searching as he spoke, rifling through the books on the bedside table. He moved to the bed, ruffling the duvet. As he did so, something fell out. A cream envelope, slit open along the top seam; he caught it, his voice turning distracted as his eyes scanned it with interest. "Or anything that might tell us more about our victim. You know what to look for."

Jess, meanwhile, had picked up something from the writing desk.

"Like these, you mean?"

His head turned at the tone of her voice, his attention diverted to the box in her hand. He gave a rare smile.

"And we're off to the races." He gave the box a once-over. "Medication?"

"Yes, but not anything I recognise." She pulled out her phone. "I'll do a quick search. See what comes up." After a moment, she looked up with a frown. "Sarge, this is something strange. It's migraine medication. But get this; it's a *trial* drug.

Still not approved for use." She skimmed some more text, her fair eyebrows descending even further. "And it may never be. It seems to be controversial in the medical sphere, lots of experts unconvinced about the side effects."

"He was a private GP, wasn't he? It's not unreasonable to suppose he had the contacts to get hold of the stuff, but still…" Pettifer was looking at the box, clearly troubled. "It was a hell of a risk, him even having this in his possession. If he'd been caught… Any chance it was for his own use?"

"None. That's the other thing; they've been testing it for women's use specifically."

"So, he was procuring it for someone else." Pettifer blew out his cheeks. "The question is, who?"

"I can answer that for you." The floor-length blue curtains moved aside. From the recess in front of the window, two bespectacled eyes looked calmly back at them. "I think you'll find, Sergeant, that those are mine."

Chapter Twenty-Three

"So do you fancy telling me, Miss Greenlake," Pettifer looked at the old lady seated primly across the table from him, "what *exactly* you were doing in Doctor Rauceby's room?"

Lavinia stared back at him through limpid blue eyes. The colour, that was. The expression in them was anything but. It flashed with the fire of annoyance, the kind only produced by protracted time on Earth.

"Don't be tedious, Sergeant. I despise false ignorance in a person. We both know you're perfectly aware of the answer to that."

"I'd still like you to tell me."

"Fine," she huffed. She inclined a gracefully coiffed head towards the box of pills sitting on the coffee table between them. "I needed those; I'd run out, and I simply can't do without them. I knew where they were, and as they *are* mine..." She shrugged. It was a neat movement; a small hitch of the shoulders, that was all. The rest of her body remained unaffected. Her posture remained upright, her hands still clasped in her lap. This was a woman who was perfectly bred, perfectly proprietous … she had that 'once presented at court' aura to her; rarely seen nowadays of course, but Pettifer had dealt with enough wealthy country sorts to recognise the signs.

And yet, and *yet* … Pettifer mused to himself. She had a temper. He'd just seen it, clear as day. A temper so strong that all the polish and carefully learned politesse couldn't paper over successfully. That was something to make note of.

"You thought it gave you the right to break in?" he suggested mildly.

She gave him a haughty look down her long nose.

"I did no such thing, I assure you. The door was already open. I suppose you *could* attempt to charge me with trespass, if you really have nothing better to do. But it would be rather embarrassing for you. I advise against it."

Pettifer felt his teeth grit, but he kept his expression bland. In his mind, he added another descriptor to this woman: *peremptory*. Clearly, she was one of those types who had a very high opinion of their own intellect, to the point of convincing themselves that no-one else could possibly know better than they did. The temptation to disabuse her of that notion was strong, but experience told him to hold back for the time being. So instead, he tried another tack.

"Perhaps you can tell me what the pills were doing in Doctor Rauceby's room in the first place? If, as you say, they belong to you?"

Her eyelids fluttered in palpable impatience.

"You're doing it again, Sergeant. Pretending to be stupider than you are. It might work on other people, but not me. Surely you can guess, based on the context."

"He procured them for you?"

"Yes, he did."

He sat back, drumming his fingers on the cracked-leather covering of the armchair he was occupying. His eyes moved to the pills.

"You *are* aware that those are a trial drug? That they haven't been approved as safe to use yet?"

"Well, of *course* I am," she all but tutted. "Why would I go through all of this ridiculous rigmarole otherwise?" She folded her arms, jutted her chin mutinously. "The stuff my own doctor's fobbing me off with is weak as water; a child would barely feel the effects. I might as well be taking a placebo." She raised a thin grey eyebrow. "There's no need to look so disapproving, Sergeant. I'm perfectly entitled to put what I like in my own body."

"Not legally, you're not," he corrected her sternly. "Not in this case, anyway. I take it this wasn't the first time Doctor Rauceby had done this for you?"

She gave him a cool look.

"*That* very much depends."

"On what?"

"On how much trouble I'm likely to get in."

He sighed, leaning back in the squashy armchair. He'd chosen it for its proximity to the fire, not that it was doing much good at the moment. In the interests of privacy, he'd brought them into a little lounge named The Morning Room – and indeed, he could see that it would be a cheerful space in the daytime. Its buttercup-yellow walls would no doubt be radiant with the sunlight streaming in, but under artificial light, they were rendered an unfortunate, dirty beige colour. The room was cold, too; clearly, no-one was expected to use it after noon, and although the staff had hurriedly lit the fire for them, it was yet to have much effect on the night-time chill that was creeping through the single-paned windows.

He made a rapid calculation; Lavinia Greenlake wasn't yet aware that the doctor was dead. As far as she knew, he was only interested in the man for being involved in the supply of illegal medication. He intended to keep it that way until he was ready, but he would have to tread carefully. One slip-up, and she'd be onto him.

"Look," he said at last, in a reasonable voice. "What you've done isn't legal. We both know that. But I'm sure you also appreciate that my main focus here is on catching the supplier, *not* the purchaser. If you can tell me something that might help me do that…" He leaned forward. "I highly doubt you're the only person he's been supplying; my guess is there'll be quite a list of names. Now, if one of those *happened* to slip my attention —" he opened his palms with a helpless shrug "—well, I don't think anyone could blame an overworked investigator for the oversight. Do you?"

She assessed him hawkishly for a moment, then gave a regal nod.

"All right, then. To answer your question, yes. Doctor Rauceby has been obtaining those on my behalf for a while now. I believe he has to bring them over from America." She waved away his next question before he'd even opened his mouth. "And no, before you ask, I don't know any more details about how he does it. I've never seen fit to enquire."

Pettifer was inclined to believe her, so he didn't persist.

"How exactly did your arrangement with the doctor come about?"

"I was complaining one day in the snug about how I had

one of my dreadful, debilitating migraines coming on, and the doctor … well, he must have been listening in, because he came to see me later on. Told me that he could help me with my problem."

"For a fee, I presume?"

"Naturally." This was said drily. "A rather steep one, I might add. But I wasn't in a position to barter. At the time, my migraines would last two, even three whole days. But now, with just one of these pills…" she snapped her fingers, "an hour, and it's gone. Worth every penny, especially at my age. One doesn't have time to waste lying in a darkened room for days on end."

"So you … what? Met him here? For the exchange?"

"My sister are I are here most days anyway. And the doctor stays regularly. It's not hard to arrange an overlap once or twice a year. It's a very convenient and discreet system, really. No fuss, and no *talk*." She sighed, and it would have sounded almost wistful if it weren't edged with frustration. "Can't you just give him a rap on the knuckles, Sergeant? I don't know what I'll do if you arrest him. I've become quite dependent on the service he's providing."

A soft knock sounded on the door, and Jess's head appeared, blonde hair hanging down in a shimmering curtain. She'd taken off the cat's ears, he noticed, but the whiskers had obviously been impervious to scrubbing; the faint shadow of them still showed on her cheeks.

"Sarge? A minute?"

"Excuse me a moment." Pettifer placed his hands on his knees and heaved himself out of the chair, trying not to wince at the familiar creaks and cracking sounds the movement prompted. His aborted career as a rugby player had left him with the body of a pensioner before he was twenty-two. Not to mention a face like a turnip that even the most worthy of wonky veg boxes would toss aside. Even so, he didn't regret it – often. On nights like this, when the air was cold and damp, and the chill got into his joints, he did wonder why he hadn't just got a nice job at the local biscuit factory like his father had, and his grandfather before that. It might not have had the thrill of professional sport, but at least half his bones wouldn't be held together with pins. Not to mention he would have been entitled to a lifetime's supply of shortbread.

"You found more of it?" he murmured, dropping his voice to keep their conversation private. Well, as private as it could be in a place like this, with people coming and going constantly. He couldn't imagine a worse place to carry out an investigation.

Jess nodded.

"*Lots* more. I asked them to override the safe code, and there it all was. All different types of medication, and all illegal in this country for one reason or another. I think we can safely call this an established sideline."

Although they'd have a devil of a time getting anyone else to admit it, Pettifer thought dourly. Most weren't as plucky as Lavinia Greenlake.

He turned to the woman in question, who was making absolutely no pretence of not listening in to their conversation.

"You were due to meet him tonight, I take it? That's why your medication was already out of the safe."

She sniffed.

"He was *supposed* to hand it over to me during the Mummer's performance. It was a good opportunity; dark, everyone distracted … but he never made an appearance."

"So, you went to look for him?"

"I most certainly did. I can't abide shoddy service. But when I got to his room, he wasn't there. I knocked several times. In the end, I gave up. Decided to try again later. Then, when I heard that the police were in the building, looking for him…" She arranged her dark skirts primly. "My hand was rather forced."

"And you didn't see him again this evening? You're certain?"

"No, I didn't, and neither will you, I'd wager. If he's caught wind that you're after him, he'll be long gone. And you'll do well to catch him. Like most of the members here, he has friends in high places."

"Oh, don't worry, Miss Greenlake." Jess said ominously. "He won't be getting away from us now."

"Well, I don't mind saying that I jolly well hope he does," she retorted fiercely. "And I find it hard to believe that this is really worth your time. Aren't there any proper crimes you could be out there investigating?"

Pettifer sought to be conciliatory.

"Miss Greenlake, I understand you think he was helping you, but—"

"Now, you two listen to *me*." The reply was a clap of thunder, making both of the police officers start in surprise. She folded her bony arms, looking between them both forcefully. "Whatever conclusions you might have leapt to about Doctor Rauceby, you're quite wrong. Yes, he can be a difficult man, really rather insufferable in many ways. Abrasive, and terribly pernickety," this was said without a hint of self-awareness, Pettifer noticed, "but he isn't simply some refined version of a street dealer, pedalling dangerous drugs for profit. He's a maverick, a *visionary*. He truly believes that many of the regulations we have here are too limiting, too precautionary. One might even say too *safe*. And he's far from the only one of that opinion; that's why people seek his help. Those who have done so, did so willingly, and with full knowledge of the risks." Her eyes bored into them. "So you'd do well to rethink those insinuations of yours."

Outside in the hallway, a gong sounded, its deep note reverberating through the wooden panel of the door. Instantly, Lavinia rose to her feet.

"Now, if that's all – and I can't imagine what else you could *possibly* have to ask me – I have somewhere to be."

It was so fantastically imperious that for a moment, Pettifer was almost stunned enough to let her sweep past him.

Almost.

"Actually, there is one last thing," he said suddenly, as much to be contrary than anything. "Did you see anyone else? Anyone who can corroborate your story?"

She looked pleasingly incensed at the suggestion.

"Is my *word* not enough?"

He smiled blandly.

"For my sort, unfortunately not."

She narrowed her eyes at him.

"As it happens, yes, I did. I was with Felicia Grant. I understand from the newspapers that you two are firm acquaintances; in which case, perhaps her word will satisfy you, even if mine doesn't."

Felicia hadn't mentioned *that*, Pettifer thought, slightly annoyed to see a self-satisfied smile touch on Lavinia Greenlake's lips. But then, with everything that had gone on, perhaps it just hadn't seemed important. Perhaps it *wasn't* important. At the moment, he couldn't be sure.

"Thank you, Miss Greenlake. We won't keep you any longer." A thought occurred to him, and he added, more gently, "I understand you'll be wanting to get back to your sister."

She stared at him as though he'd grown two heads.

"Why would I do that? I'm going into *dinner*. That was the gong."

He tried, and failed, to hide his surprise.

"I'd have thought you'd be staying in your room tonight."

"I don't see why. After all, *I'm* not the invalid. Besides, my sister is in good hands. One of the staff members is a first-aider; they're sitting with her. In which case, I might as well enjoy my meal in a civilised manner."

"What a harpy," Jess blurted out, once Lavinia had swept grandiosely away out of earshot. "I'm almost inclined to wonder if her sister feigned being indisposed on purpose to avoid her company tonight. *I* would."

"I certainly wouldn't want to rely on her to pull me out of a burning building," Pettifer agreed mildly. "She doesn't seem to have many loyalties, that one."

"Except to Doctor Rauceby. She was quite the defender of him, wasn't she?"

"You're thinking it's unlikely she would do him in? On the face of it, I'm inclined to agree. But that doesn't mean one of his other patients might have felt differently. These drugs are counted as risky for a reason; there must have been some complications, some bad reactions. We need to find out who else he sold to."

"I'll get onto his practice. It's after hours, but I might be able to track down his secretary. It's unlikely he'd have shared his illegal activities with her, but you never know. She might be able to get us into his computer, if nothing else."

"Grand. Then I want you to look into that phone call. The one that tipped us off that the doctor was missing. See if you can pin it down to a precise extension."

Jess's eyes widened.

"You think it came from within the club?"

"I'd stake my badge on it," he replied grimly. The question was, had the caller been a friend or foe of the doctor? Clearly, they'd wanted the police to find him … but alive, or dead?

Pettifer looked down at his holey rugby shirt with a grimace.

"Christ, we need some proper clothes. We can't conduct a murder investigation looking like this. I'll call the station, see what they can send over. After that, you'll find me in Annabel Drayford's office, pulling on our next thread. I think you'll want to be there for this one." As Jess looked at him quizzically, he explained, "We're going to ask her why she pretended not to know where we could find Doctor Rauceby tonight."

Jess started.

"You think she lied to us? She knew he was in the chapel all along?"

In response, Pettifer produced the card he'd picked up in the doctor's room, turning it round for Jess to see.

"Given that she was the one who told him to go there," he said quietly, "Then yes, Winters. I most certainly do."

Chapter Twenty-Four

Felicia followed the stooped figure into the cottage, ducking to avoid banging her head on the door frame. Whatever she'd been about to say next died on her lips as she straightened, taking in the interior for the first time.

She'd been expecting a storage shed of some kind; instead, she saw a home. But not the kind that filled one with a warm, cosy feeling. Once, the cottage that surrounded her had no doubt been quite comfortable, but those days were long past; now, it was in a state of terrible disrepair. The wallpaper was peeling and covered in sinister-looking dark patches, the damp seeping through the walls and thickening the air. The floor tiles were cracked, jagged sections missing. The room was freezing, windows rattling in their rotted panes in the worsening weather, and Felicia tried not to shiver too obviously. Over her shoulder, she heard Dexter draw in a breath, and for once, she didn't shoot him a warning look. It was shocking, hard to take in that someone might live in such conditions.

The man leaned heavily against the coat rack, shaking off his boots.

"I suppose we'd better have tea, if you're staying," he growled. Now in lumpen socks, he stumped over to the far corner, which was occupied by a kitchenette in a virulent green Formica. "You'll have to excuse my lack of airs and graces; it's been a long while since I've had visitors."

He picked up a stovetop kettle. Felicia noticed that while it was clearly well-used, it was nonetheless buffed to a shine. In fact, she observed, looking surreptitiously around her, the same could be said for everything in here. The fabric of the building might be falling to pieces, but the objects within it were a different story. Everything was old and worn, but lovingly cared for. Neat, even. The effect was one of quiet pride. Dignity, even in these conditions. Felicia felt a wave of sympathy for the crabbed little figure, even as he snapped and fussed at them.

"Well, don't just stand about like that. Find somewhere to sit." He turned on the tap, which made a deafening, screeching sound not dissimilar to foxes mating. Unperturbed, he simply raised his voice over the din. "Don't mind all that," he added, still shouting even as the tap abruptly ceased its wailing. He indicated the kitchen table, which Dexter was eyeing uncertainly. "I like to bring my work home, is all."

The table was the only part of the cottage that wasn't neatly organised. Instead, its surface was covered with a jumble of detritus, the red tablecloth underneath only just visible in patches. Some of the items were identifiable: there was a three-branched candlestick – probably early Regency, Felicia thought, her valuer's brain jumping in before she could stop herself – a half-disassembled lamp, a gilt frame with part of the moulding detached. But most of it seemed to be component parts, bits of metal and wood that could be distinguished only by a brain far more practical and hands-on than her own.

Dexter, whose brain was decidedly *less* practical and hands-on than her own, gingerly moved a roundel of wood from a chair, inspecting the seat with a wary eye.

"Just sit *down*," Felicia hissed across at him, hoping their host's hearing was as poor as appearances might suggest.

Dexter gave her a wounded look.

"But these are new trousers."

"I don't care. Stop being so precious." She grabbed his arm and dragged him down onto the chair just in time. The old man turned back to face them, a bottle of Scotch in his hand.

"Fancy a nip in your brew? It's turning wild out there."

"Absolutely." Dexter perked up immediately. Then, catching Felicia's raised eyebrow, he muttered, "Well, we don't want to appear rude, do we?"

Felicia stared at him in disbelief, then wondered why she was bothering. She took a breath, focusing on their host's hunched back.

"You're the caretaker here, I suppose?"

He continued clattering cups and teaspoons unabated.

"I am at that."

"And have you … been here long? Working, I mean?"

"Longer than anyone. Longer than most can even recall."

Felicia left a pause, waiting for him to say more. But he didn't. She looked at Dexter, who shrugged. Fat lot of use he was. Felicia thought for a moment, pondering another approach. What would Pettifer do in this situation?

The answer came immediately. He would get straight down to brass tacks, that's what he'd do. The upfront approach. See if he could surprise an answer out of them. She'd seen him do it more than once.

"You were watching us, weren't you? Back there, in the garden?"

She waited for a response, however slight. But there was nothing. Felicia was beginning to feel as perplexed as she was frustrated. She sensed he wanted to talk; he'd *wanted* them to come here, she was sure of it. And yet, now they were, he'd clammed up. Something was holding him back; but what?

"I suppose you've heard what happened this evening? There's been an incident," she said, watching him carefully as she spoke. "Actually, a very serious one. A guest has died."

Finally, a reaction; he flinched, shoulders tensing. But he didn't turn around. When he spoke, his voice was as gruff and monotonous as ever, although there was a definite artificiality to it this time.

"Aye, well, that's a shame, I'm sure. It's happened once or twice. Some of our members are very old."

"It wasn't natural causes," Felicia said shortly. "Someone lured him to his death. The police are looking for a killer."

Silence. Then he opened a cupboard, pulling out three glass tumblers. He turned, banging them down on the table and uncorking the scotch.

"Bugger the tea." He sloshed tawny-coloured liquid into the glasses with a scowl. Picking his up, he tossed it back. "What do you want with me? Are you with the police?" At her surprised expression, he gave a crooked grimace. "Aye, I know they're here. I can spot police a mile off, however they're dressed. And I saw *you* with them. Coming back from the chapel."

"Yes, I was there." Felicia felt she had to choose her words carefully here. "But I'm not with the police. I just happened to be there, when…"

He looked at her shrewdly with his small black eyes. She thought she detected a flicker of dread in their unfathomable depths. Afraid, she realised, in a rush. That was it. He was *afraid*.

"That's where it happened, then?"

He was trying to sound disinterested, but as he topped up his glass, Felicia noticed his hand shook a little. A hand that had been perfectly steady before; would have to be steady as a rule, to repair these objects that surrounded them with such finesse and delicacy.

"I knew this would happen one day," he muttered to himself. "That place is cursed. For what they did … they'll never be forgiven. The dead can wait. Wait for as long as it takes."

Dexter gave him a look that was chary in the extreme, edging away along the bench. But Felicia leaned in. She had the feeling that this was it; that they were getting somewhere at last. She just needed to tread lightly.

"Who'll never be forgiven?" she asked, keeping her voice soft, encouraging.

"I won't walk there if I can help it," he said. He wasn't looking at her, but rather through her, his eyes glazed over. "Not through those trees. That's where they were, you see. The monks. That was their graveyard. But they wanted them gone. When they rebuilt the house, some three hundred years ago. Didn't like the idea of graves in the garden, I fancy, so—"

"So they took the tombs out?" Felicia guessed. It wasn't uncommon; there'd been no such thing as planning laws back then, and it was largely a case of the rich doing what they liked on their own land. Any number of precious historical sites had been disturbed or demolished across the centuries thanks to aristocratic whim or the vagaries of fashion.

"Aye. But they're still there, underneath … sometimes I think they're still watching." He shuddered, and the motion seemed to bring him back to the present. Back to this miserable, pathetic room, to the two people sitting across the detritus-covered table from him. When his eyes met Felicia's, they were utterly lucid. "I'm not a superstitious sort, as such, but I'm a country-raised lad, and I was taught how to respect certain things. *Unknown things*, as my old mother would have put it. Too deep and complex for the mortal soul to understand, she'd say. Things you shouldn't tamper with. But they did, and now…" He looked at her, almost beseechingly. All trace of his earlier cantankerousness was stripped away, and suddenly, all she saw was a frail, frightened old man. "But I just did as I was told. I never had any choice." His voice trembled. "It was what she wanted. Please, you have to believe me. You have to make the *police* believe me. Can you do that?"

Dexter raised his eyebrows at her, as if asking her the same question. Felicia sat back in her rickety chair, exhaling a long breath. Then she said gently, "You know, I don't even know your name. If I'm going to help you, I think I ought to, don't you?"

"It's Weaver. Matthias Weaver."

"Well then, Mr. Weaver. I think it's time you told me all about it."

The shadow moved silently through the empty rooms of the club, its long cloak fluttering behind it. It flitted across the snug, weaving between tables littered with drained glasses and dishes of appetisers, making its way, as the room's previous occupants had some time before, towards the Great Hall. It paused in the doorway, allowing itself a brief moment to drink in the sight of a full dinner service in this most magnificent of rooms.

From beneath the eye holes of the wooden mask, its gaze roved over the lavishly laid tables, the blue-and-gold-clad waiters bearing silver trays of steaming dishes. Laughter swirled, glasses tinkled, cutlery clinked against fine china, all within a glittering constellation of candlelight.

The eyes moved to the chandelier, dazzling with flames, suspended above the company, the rope that held it straining beneath its colossal weight. It was the brightest star of all. And everyone beneath, so oblivious to what was going on outside their own gilded bubble. Well, that would change soon enough.

Instinctively, the shadow turned its head, looking out through the window into the fogbound street, to the world beyond these walls. It felt its lips curve in a satisfied smile.

Soon, they would see that this place couldn't protect them from everything.

Tonight, for one night only, it would not be business as usual here at The Aquitaine. Far from it.

Tonight, it was the turn of chaos.

Chapter Twenty-Five

"I don't believe this." Annabel Drayford leaned forward, hands braced on the walnut desktop. Her face was pale, whether with shock or anger, Jess couldn't tell. "You went into the chapel? Without coming to fetch me first? This is unacceptable."

That was what she was thinking about right now? Really? When they'd just told her that one of her club's members, a man she'd known, was dead? Jess felt her thoughts fighting to show on her face, as they always did, much as she might strive for the stony impassivity Pettifer did so well. She knew she wasn't supposed to judge; she was trained to stay distant, to view the suspects as just that: through the objective lens of investigation. But it was hard, with a woman like this. She was so icy, so *inhuman*. It gave Jess chills just being in the same room as her.

"I would have thought your main concern would be for the deceased," Pettifer said. He spoke levelly, but there was a vertical crevice between his unruly brows that Jess recognised by now as well-disguised disapproval. Immediately, she felt better; clearly, she wasn't the only one struggling to contain her censure. Annabel Drayford, similarly, must have picked up on it, because she looked, for the first time since Jess had encountered her, faintly shamefaced.

"I'm sorry. Of course. It's just…" She took an uneven breath, smoothing her jacket – which really didn't require it. Jess suspected it was a habit, a means of steadying herself. "My mind went straight to the practicalities. Automatic, I'm afraid, but I must think of the club, the other members…" She shook her head. "It's so *baffling*. The chapel is always kept strictly off limits; some of the wine in there is priceless. I just can't understand what he would have been doing there."

"Can't you?" The words slipped out of Jess's mouth before she could stop them, hard and sarcastic. Pettifer shot her a reprimanding look, and she immediately quailed. The Sarge wasn't often sharp with her; despite his dour mien, he was one of the most patient and understanding superiors she'd ever come across. But in this case, she knew she'd gone too far; it was one thing to have private opinions about a suspect, something else entirely to show them openly. She needed to rein it in. Jess made a show of writing something in her book, crouching over as an excuse for letting her pale blonde hair fall across her blazing cheeks. Hoping Annabel Drayford had been too preoccupied in her own thoughts to notice the slip.

No such luck.

"And what do you mean by *that*, precisely?" The manager snapped, eyes narrowing.

Pettifer swallowed a sigh; brilliant, now Annabel Drayford was on the defensive. *Not* what they needed. He didn't look at Jess, but then, he didn't need to; he could see her out of the corner of his eye, her shoulders hunched over again in mortification. He already half regretted glaring at her like that, although really, she ought to know better by now. But the damage was done; the only thing to do was forge on. Throw the softly-softly approach he'd planned out of the window and go all in, as they said in poker. He reached into his pocket, slapping the notecard – now removed from its envelope and in an evidence bag – down on the desk between them. From here, the scrolling handwriting was illegible, but still distinctive, standing out in stark black ink.

"She means," he said, almost conversationally, "that you knew full well what he was doing there."

Annabel Drayford stared down at the note silently, eyes scanning back and forth across the single line of text. She didn't make any effort to pick it up. Pettifer waited patiently, observing her.

He'd seen people react in any number of ways when confronted with the evidence of their guilt. There was by no means a universal response. Some broke down in tears, some panicked, some withdrew into themselves, resigned. Some became angry. Some even appeared relieved. Relieved it was all over, that they didn't have to pretend anymore.

But none had ever reacted quite like this woman did. She simply pushed the card back towards him once she'd finished, steepling her fingers on the desk and surveying him impassively. He saw no fear in her eyes, nor anything else for that matter. She appeared completely unmoved – if anything, he thought, she looked more composed than ever.

"Surely this is some sort of jest, Sergeant?" Her tone was incredulous. "You can't really believe I sent this?"

"You deny that it's signed by you?"

"Signed with my name, certainly. But not by me." She stood, beginning to rifle through the papers on her desk. "I'll find you a sample of my handwriting. Just give me a moment."

Pettifer took the opportunity to survey her office. It was plush room, although decidedly masculine in style. He suspected that was how she had inherited it from previous incumbents. There was probably some arcane rule that stipulated she wasn't allowed to change anything, he thought. Such a presence out on the club floor, she looked strangely small and slight in these surroundings, dwarfed by the hulking pieces of furniture, including the enormous, ormolu bureau plat, which she stood at now.

Looming behind her, flanking the entire back wall of the office, were a number of inbuilt pigeonholes, each with a shiny, brass plaque beneath. Pettifer squinted, trying to read what they said and acknowledging, not for the first time, that he really needed to get his eyes tested. He ought to have taken advantage of the fallow period when people weren't getting themselves killed, he thought, with a stab of dark humour. In the end, he gave up, rising to his feet to take a closer look. Annabel Drayford didn't even stop what she was doing, which didn't surprise him. That was the good thing about being a police officer; you were entitled to be nosy. In fact, people almost expected it.

"These are places in Stamford," he observed, when he was an embarrassingly close enough distance for the letters to come into focus. His eyes roved over the familiar names: St. Mary, St. Leonard, Red Lion, Bath Row, Blackfriars…

"Also, the names of our rooms," she informed him. "It's long been the custom here. Many members request to stay in the same each time, to correspond with their favourite place in town. Not that there's any real link, of course. We put a few pictures up of the place in question, but..."

"Aye, well, people are sentimental like that," Pettifer said mildly. He looked at the contents of the pigeonholes with some curiosity; they were filled with paperwork, as one might expect. Folders, letters, the usual sort of thing. In itself, not at all strange, and yet... He pulled out a slim file; it was clearly old, its once red cover faded and curling at the corners. Opening it to a random page, he read:

Mr. Swan — goose-down pillows (four), Assam with splash of milk a.m., Scottish whisky only...

It went on. Perplexed, Pettifer shut the file. On the cover, in faded ink, was the year: 1973.

"I expect you think that's a little curious." He looked up to find that Annabel Drayford had finally stopped what she was doing and was observing him coolly.

"I'll say." He frowned down at the file, then back at the pigeonhole it had come from. At once, he saw what had bothered him; almost everything else in there appeared equally dated. It looked more like an archive than a current filing system. "What exactly *is* this?"

"It's how we do what we do. Meticulous records have always been kept for each guest. Likes, dislikes, matters of routine ... it's the secret to how we deliver such a personal service."

"And all filed by room?"

"Yes, it is rather an antiquated system. From a quainter time. I myself, would reorganise it more efficiently, but..." She stopped herself, with visible effort. "As I said, though, most guests still favour one room in particular. So the system *just* about functions."

Her tone made it clear how unsatisfactory she found it. Pettifer wondered how much it must irritate her, having her hands tied in so many ways by the spider's web of rules and regulations this place seemed to have. Because *they* might call it tradition, but that was just a pretty word for it, in Pettifer's opinion. From what he'd observed, for all the olde-worlde charm it played on, the true nature of the club was suffocatingly rigid, everyone terrified to put a foot out of line. Bowing to ancient laws that no-one even knew the origin of, let alone the purpose, was just one small example of that control.

"Well, if you don't mind me saying, I think it's time you had a clear out," he remarked, putting the folder back where he'd found it. "Most of these must be long past use to anyone now."

"Maybe. But you never know." At his quizzical look, Annabel Drayford explained, "We hold on to everything. Just in case a guest comes back."

Jess, obviously having felt she'd done her penance, piped up disbelievingly:

"After fifty years?"

"You'd be surprised. Stamford is that sort of place. People who've been here once, long ago … they always remember. They always wish to come back some day. And many of them do. Even if it's just for one last time."

Pettifer couldn't argue with that. Many had passed through Stamford in their time; it was, after all, perfectly placed off the old Great North Road, hence its rise to prominence as a famous coaching stop in Georgian times. And it was a place that struck people; it emblazoned itself on the mind. They were curious to come back, to see if it was still the same … whilst knowing, of course, that it would be. That was why they wanted to come, really. In a world where so many places had changed so fast, where else could you count on to be the same after half a century?

And to come here, to the club they'd once visited, and to find *that* exactly the same, too. Not only that, but to have waiting for them, perhaps, the paper they'd once read in their room, a cup of their favourite tea placed at their elbow, made to their preference, without them having to ask. After all that time … as though none had passed at all. Yes, he could see that would seem like magic.

But of course, he didn't say all of that. It would have been an unprecedentedly long speech for Pettifer. Generally, he restricted his verbalisations to a single sentence or couplet; a brief paragraph if the occasion warranted it. So he expressed the sentiment in his own, succinct manner.

"I see," he said.

They lapsed back into silence for a moment while Annabel Drayford continued her search. Then Pettifer remarked languidly: "Not a very popular room, I take it?" He pointed up at a pigeonhole marked 'Barn Hill' that was conspicuously empty. It seemed surprising; after all, the picturesque, cobbled lane, with its grand mansions and moneyed atmosphere, was one of the most photographed locations in town. He'd have thought it a prime choice.

"Oh, we keep that for sentimental reasons. It's an old room, since amalgamated into another to make a suite." She straightened, handing him a sheet of paper. "This should do. It's the welcome letter included in the information folder in every bedroom in the club; you can use it to verify that *that*," she looked pointedly at the notecard, "is not in my hand."

Pettifer looked between the two dubiously.

"They look fairly similar to me."

Annabel Drayford folded her arms.

"I didn't say it wasn't a *good* copy. But a copy it is. Careful study will show some differences."

"And the card itself? It's club-branded stationery."

"Available in all guest rooms, plus behind the reception desk."

"You don't seem very concerned," Pettifer pressed, not comprehending her attitude. My, but she was a cold fish. "If what you're suggesting is true, then someone's deliberately tried to involve you in this."

"I'm not given to overreacting, that's all." She gave him a look that was supercilious in the extreme. "It's clearly just a prank of some kind. A joke that went horribly wrong. Those bats are a real menace; they're aggressively territorial when disturbed. We'd have done something about them, but it turns out they're some sort of endangered variety." Her brows drew inwards. "Like so much else in this place, they are untouchable."

"I'm not given to overreacting either, Miss Drayford." Pettifer returned her look levelly. "This was no prank. And if I were you, I'd be on your guard."

Silence. Then she spoke, very carefully, as though picking up each word and turning it over to inspect it before allowing it to leave her lips.

"I'm going to have to ask you to explain yourself further. I was told that he fell off the ladder to the tower. Surely that could only be an accident?"

"Not if you stop to ask yourself what he was doing up that ladder," Pettifer replied shortly. "Someone opened the trap door to the tower, then left a lit lantern inside to lure him up there. Someone who clearly knew what would happen when he reached the top."

Her mouth opened, then closed again. He took advantage of her temporary incapacity to forge onwards with his questions.

"Who knew about the bats?"

She swallowed, but responded calmly and with admirable clarity for someone who'd supposedly just had a shock. Either she had nerves of steel, thought Pettifer, or the news hadn't been such a surprise after all. Time would tell which.

"Well … all of the staff. It's one of those workplace legends; *never go up to the tower*, that sort of thing. They sometimes tease the new starters that they'll be sent up there as an initiation, but they never actually do it. They know how dangerous it would be."

"And the members?"

"No. I mean, I don't see why they would know. Like I said, they're discouraged from going near the place."

So they had to work on the assumption that Dr. Rauceby hadn't known what was awaiting him up there, concluded Pettifer. He'd never stood a chance, the poor bugger.

"He was on that ladder," he said quietly, studying the face of the woman across from him intently. "Because he was led to believe that the person he was meeting was up there. That person – in his mind, at least – was you, Miss Drayford. I need you to tell me why." The note had been decidedly lacking in revealing information; just an invitation to the chapel, and a time: 7:15 p.m. "*Why* would he accept a summons like that, on what was apparently a whim, to go out into a night like this, when he was supposed to be elsewhere?"

"I wish I could tell you, Sergeant." She shrugged regretfully. "I really do."

It had been perfectly delivered. But she'd paused before she said it. And Pettifer never missed a thing like that.

"That's a shame," Pettifer said softly. Meaningfully. "It really is. And here was I so hoping you'd be able to help us. Now it seems I'll have to do this the hard way." He stood, Jess taking her cue to do the same. "This whole club is locked down until I say otherwise. No-one leaves; you understand? I want a list of everyone who's here tonight. Oh, and nobody goes near that chapel. It's now officially a crime scene."

"But…" She paled. Finally, he'd got to her, Pettifer thought, with some satisfaction. She looked distinctly rattled at that last statement. "You *can't* … we need access at all times…"

"I think your guests can survive off the contents of your bar for the time being," Pettifer said acerbically. That room had contained more alcohol than a distillery; including, he'd noticed, an entire wall of wine racks. Why they needed an entire chapel-full, too, was anyone's guess.

"I don't… None of this even makes any *sense*," Annabel Drayton was muttering, almost more to herself than the two police officers in the room. "I mean, even if someone *did* send him a note in my writing … that wouldn't be so difficult to arrange. But how did he get *in* there? I'm the only one who—" She broke off, obviously realising what she'd said as the rest of the sentence hung ominously in the air.

I'm the only one who has a key.

As though roused by an invisible force, Annabel Drayford began opening drawers in her desk, riffling through them with a briskness that soon began to flavour of desperation.

Eventually, her hands stilled, and she looked up at Pettifer with a bleak resignation in her eyes.

"It's not here."

Pettifer gave a brusque nod. Then he turned to go, pausing for a moment with his fingers on the door handle.

"Oh, I almost forgot," he said, in a light, conversational tone. "One last thing. Were you aware that the doctor was dealing controversial off-market medications right here at the club? Under your nose, one might say."

She stared at him, her blue eyes unblinking.

"Of course not. That's... How shocking. I had no idea. No idea at all."

But her armour had slipped; she no longer sounded even remotely convincing. Pettifer gave a hard smile and pulled open the door.

"I suggest you keep yourself easy to find, Miss Drayford. We'll be talking with you again."

Chapter Twenty-Six

When Felicia found Pettifer, he was pacing up and down, phone suctioned to one of his cauliflower ears. He was listening rather than talking, and whatever the information being relayed was, it evidently wasn't to his liking. His heavy brow was corrugated, his mouth set in a terse line. When he spotted Felicia, however, he held up a finger, silently asking her to stay as he ended the call with a few brusquely muttered words.

"Algernon get off all right?" he asked, walking towards her.

"Yes. Thank you for letting my father take him home. I'm aware that they're technically witnesses."

He waved that away with a spade-like hand.

"We can get their statements later. That lad of yours has been through enough of this sort of thing this year." Pettifer knew that all too well; he'd once saved Algernon from almost becoming a murder victim himself. "Besides, he might have dubious taste in sweets, not to mention a much better vocabulary than yours truly, but I highly doubt he's our killer in this case."

Felicia smiled. Despite his gruffness, Pettifer could be quite softhearted when he wanted to be. Although he'd be horrified if he thought she'd noticed.

"Developments?" She nodded towards the phone, still gripped in his hand.

He clicked his tongue in annoyance.

"No, something else." He hesitated, evidently wondering whether to say more, then: "You remember Henry Bunting's old house? Up on Barn Hill?"

"I'm hardly likely to forget it," Felicia said dryly. She and Dexter had been the ones who'd found the elderly recluse's body; she could still see the blood-soaked bedsheets if she closed her eyes. "What's happened?"

"Someone's broken into it, that's what."

"Oh." Felicia frowned, assimilating this information. In a way, it wasn't surprising, perhaps, although it was on the depressing side. After all, the house had been sitting there empty for the best part of six months now as probate dragged on, Bunting having died without any close family to automatically inherit. "I thought the solicitors had put in extra security?"

"They had. But that's no obstacle to someone who really wants to get in. Especially if it's a professional job."

He had a point there, Felicia conceded.

"Did they take anything?"

"They don't know yet." He huffed out a sigh. "And Christ knows how they ever will; if I recall rightly, the place was chock to the rafters with junk."

"It was full of *antiques*," Felicia corrected him pointedly.

Pettifer had no time for anything that didn't come flat-packed, she knew, but sometimes she wondered if he was as obtuse about it all as he made out, or if he was just being deliberately aggravating. Bunting's house had been a treasure trove; a chaotic, overstuffed one, granted, but still. She could only dream about the wonders hiding in there. "And what about the inventories? The ones you lent to Dexter? They seemed pretty comprehensive; you should be able to work out from those if anything's missing."

"I suppose so," he said gloomily. "But we just haven't got the time or manpower for that kind of fine-toothcomb work. We'll have to pass it over to the solicitors." He shoved the phone irritably into his pocket. "What the hell do they expect me to do about it now, anyway? I'm in the middle of a bloody *murder* investigation, for crying out loud."

Felicia tilted her head on one side, observing him hesitantly.

"You seem a bit … *stressed*."

He regarded her through suspicious eyes.

"You say that like you're about to make me even more so." When she didn't answer, he groaned. "Bloody hell, Felicia. Spit it out, then. What have you gone and done now?"

"Found your killer." As his head shot up, she added hastily, "In a sense, at least. I know who put the lantern up in the church tower."

Pettifer stepped closer. There was a keen light in his eyes she recognised well.

"Who?" he asked, his voice low and urgent.

"The caretaker. Matthias Weaver, he's called. He lives in a cottage on the edge of the grounds." She winced. "Although 'cottage' is probably too grand a word for it. It's more like a hovel. You should see the state of it, the conditions they're allowing him to live in…" She looked around them, at the opulence, the splendour. The contrast was sickening.

But Pettifer wasn't listening. He was already in full deductive mode, turning over this new development, working out its ramifications.

"I suppose he'd have known about the bats – probably better than anyone, in fact. He'd have known how to handle them, too, how to get up there without disturbing them so he could set the trap. The question – apart from the obvious *why* – is *how* he got in? Annabel Drayford claims the key's gone missing."

"Then she's lying to you." Felicia folded her arms and looked at him levelly. "Weaver's got it. She gave it to him."

Pettifer had been about to resume his pacing, but he stopped abruptly mid-pivot, resulting in an ungainly wobble on one leg.

"She did *what*?"

"He claims she instructed him to do it. All of it."

"But…" Pettifer scratched his stubbly head in apparent disbelief. "He didn't think it was … *odd*? That it might even be dangerous, at that? Didn't he think to question it?"

"Apparently, she told him the exterminators were coming out the following day. But even if she hadn't…" Felicia paused, trying to put her impressions into words. She'd got the sense that there was no love lost between the manager and caretaker; that perhaps wasn't to be wondered at. After all, Annabel Drayford was an exacting perfectionist; her goal seemed to be taking the club in a slicker, more modern-luxury direction – a picture that Matthias Weaver, with his moth-eaten appearance and crabby ways, certainly didn't fit. But all the same, Felicia couldn't help but feel it was more than just that.

Pettifer had obviously picked up on something of her thoughts because he suggested quietly: "You think he's frightened of her?"

She shook her head.

"It's not quite that. More like … beholden, somehow." Suddenly, she felt uncommonly tired by the whole thing; she sat down on a baroque trousseau chest, trying not to look at it too closely in case she realised how valuable it was. Too valuable, she suspected, to be sat on. "You know, he thinks this is all part of some curse on the place. There are a load of monks buried under the yew walk, apparently. Their gravestones were removed when the house was converted in the eighteenth century."

Pettifer gave her a look out of the corner of his eye as he sat heavily next to her. The chest groaned in response. Felicia tried not to openly wince.

"If you're about to suggest to me that vengeful phantom monks set angry bats on our victim…"

"Of course not." Felicia rolled her eyes. "I think a very real person did." She hesitated as the thought struck her. "And I suppose now we know exactly which one." It was odd, somehow, to think that might be it. As though it were all too simple somehow, unsatisfyingly unfinished. But not all murder cases were going to be complex, Felicia told herself. It was Pettifer himself who often reminded her sternly of that fact.

It was only then that she became aware that the man in question was still sitting next to her. She frowned, perplexed at the lack of dynamism. She'd seen him at this point in a case before, when he'd got his killer cornered; usually, he'd be leaping up – or at least creaking to his feet – with a look of determination on his squat face. Instead, he looked pensive, his gaze far away.

"You'll be arresting her now, then, I suppose?" Felicia ventured, attempting to jog him into action. "Or at least taking her in for formal questioning?"

"Winters would jump at the chance," he agreed easily. "But me … well, you know what I'm about. Like to have all my ducks in a row." He folded his arms. "Tell me, these instructions she gave him … did she deliver them in person?"

"No. Apparently, she rarely has direct contact with him. She—"

"She didn't, by any chance," he continued, uncharacteristically interrupting her, "send them in a note?"

Felicia stared at him.

"How on *earth* do you know that?"

He gave a thin smile.

"Just a hunch."

He produced an evidence bag and handed it to her. Inside was a notecard, beautifully embossed in gold and pale blue. Felicia skimmed the handwriting underneath, her hand moving to her lips as she read.

"Well, that's pretty conclusive, isn't it?" If anything, it only strengthened the case against her, as far as Felicia could see.

"It would be … if she wrote it." He gave a rueful shake of the head. "Thing is, she swears up and down that she didn't, that someone's copied her hand. The problem is, if they have, they've done it well. And I'm not qualified to judge either way."

"Can't you get a handwriting expert to look at it?"

"I can, but not at this time of night. And even then, they're not exactly ten a penny. Even if I put the pressure on, it could take days to get it looked at. And we don't *have* days." His frown darkened. "If she did this, I need to know now. And if she didn't…" He trailed off, looking grim. "Well, I need to know even more."

Felicia decided she didn't want to know what he meant by that. Instead, she looked down at the note thoughtfully. The handwriting was distinctive, businesslike – as one might expect from a woman like Annabel Drayford – yet with some rather quaint little idiosyncrasies. An idea began to form.

"I don't suppose you've got a confirmed sample of her handwriting on you?" she asked slowly.

He eyed her sardonically.

"Are you going to announce that you're a handwriting expert now, on top of everything else?"

"Not in the slightest. But I do have some expertise when it comes to antique silver marks." At his raised eyebrow, she sighed and picked up a little silver dog ornament from the ledge behind her. "You're a very untrusting person, aren't you? I can see I'm going to have to show you." She flipped the figure to show him the base, pointed at the four symbols punched into the metal. "Seen these before?"

"I'm not a total cave dweller, Felicia, even if you think otherwise. I'm aware of what a hallmark is. It's something…" He trailed off with a grimace. "Oh, I haven't the blazes what it means. But all silver has it; I know that much. If it doesn't have a hallmark, it's probably plated metal trying to look like silver." As she looked impressed, he added, "I found that out when I had to clear out my late father's house."

Felicia nodded, knowing all too well. That was when most people got their crash course in hallmarking; until then, they'd blithely assumed that anything shiny and silver-coloured around the house was probably the real thing. With the real thing's value attached. It didn't help that it wasn't uncommon for makers of silver plate to stamp their pieces with fake hallmarks in an attempt to make them look authentic.

"It's basically a code," she explained. "British sterling silver tells you all about itself, but you do need to speak its language." She tapped the first symbol, a dark square, within which a set of initials floated. "This tells us *who* made it." She moved to the next. "The lion here; that says that it was made in England, and the symbol next to it … that's the assay, or city mark. It shows us where the piece was approved and hallmarked. In this case it's a crown, so Sheffield."

Pettifer inclined his head approvingly at the ornament.

"A fellow Yorkshireman, then."

She gave him a quick, fond look.

"You're quite delightfully quirky, really, aren't you? You pretend you're not, but—"

"And that?" He ignored her, pointing to the last mark: a single letter in a swirling script.

"*That* is the date mark. Each year is denoted by a letter."

"What do they do when the run out of letters?"

"They go around again. And again. We've been hallmarking silver exactly like this for about five hundred years. So there are quite a few of each letter out there, as you can imagine. And yet, each one has to be utterly unique, otherwise it would be meaningless."

"And the only way to do that," he said slowly, finally understanding where she was going with this, "is to change the font."

"Exactly. However, there are obviously only so many

differences you can create, and to be honest, a lot of them end up looking pretty similar to each other. Often, the difference between one year and another comes down to the minutest of details. A serif here, a flourish there..." She carefully put the dog back where she'd found it. "So you see, while I'm no handwriting expert, I'm the closest you'll get here tonight." She held out the card to him, meeting his gaze.

He knew what she was doing; offering her help, but not pushing it on him. It was typical of her, but nonetheless, he saw the glimmer of caution in her eyes. She wasn't sure how he'd respond, and no wonder. Last time there'd been a murder, he'd made it quite clear he didn't want her involvement.

And he'd well and truly learned his lesson there, Pettifer thought dully. Not only had she solved the damned thing first, she'd managed to put herself in danger anyway – the very thing he'd been trying to protect her from by keeping her out of the loop.

He puffed out his cheeks, then exhaled heavily.

"If Heavenly knew, he'd have my scalp. But as he's not here..." He produced the writing sample Annabel Drayford had given him, handing it over. "What the hell. Have at it."

He waited while she studied the two side by side, her bronze hair falling across her face in a curtain, shading her expression from view. Then, knowing he shouldn't distract her but unable to resist, he asked, "So, when was it, then?"

"Hmm?" She didn't raise her eyes from the page. "When was what?"

"The year on that dog." He folded his arms. "Which one was it?"

"Haven't the foggiest," she replied distractedly. "I'd have to consult my book of hallmarks."

"Oh." For some reason, that felt like rather a cheat. "I see."

"Are you disappointed?" She looked at him, then, amused. "I think if I could retain over half a millennia's worth of hallmarks in my head, I'd be the subject of experimentation by now."

"I suppose," he conceded, begrudgingly.

"I bet you were that child who always insisted on finding out the sleight of hand behind every magic trick, then felt let down by the answer." She handed the pages back to him. "Here you go."

He looked at her in surprise.

"You've finished? Already?"

"I've seen what I needed to see."

"And?"

"In my not-so-expert opinion? *Not* the same person. Like you said, it's a good attempt. It's certainly not something that was dashed off on a whim; someone's been practising. But nonetheless, the tells are there." She craned to look at the sample. "See these loops on her 'l's? They're very elongated; they almost come to a point at the top. *Almost*, but not quite. The pen carries on smoothly; it's one fluid motion. Whereas here, in the note…" She pointed. "Look. There's a small notch in the ink. The pen clearly paused at the top of the loop before carrying on into the downwards slant."

"Someone was trying to copy the shape," he agreed. He could see it now she'd pointed it out; it was as clear as day. But he would never have noticed it on his own.

"And then there's this."

"She writes her 'r's backwards. Yes, I'd noticed that."

"On the surface, a bit of a gift for any would-be imitator. It's so distinctive that at a glance, anyone would immediately assume this was written by Annabel Drayford. But it's also completely unnatural for anyone who hasn't always done it. You can see that here in the note; there's a hesitancy about the way the 'r's are formed. They look forced." She shrugged. "But that's just my impression."

"Well, it's enough to convince me," he said, tucking the papers away in his jacket pocket. "Thank you." At her sceptical look, he insisted, "I mean it. I'd been staring at those words for ages. I knew something was there; I just couldn't see it. You could."

"Something tells me you didn't really need much convincing," she said softly, regarding him with those perceptive grey eyes.

"Aye, well, perhaps I didn't," he admitted gruffly.

"A feeling for her innocence, perhaps?" she suggested sweetly.

He glared at her.

"More like logic and experience."

"In what way?"

"Well, think of it like this: if Miss Drayton was going to murder someone in her own club, she'd be a damn sight more intelligent about it than to leave a load of clues pointing in her direction, wouldn't you say? At the very *least* she would have removed the note from the doctor's room before we had the chance to find it. That's what anyone with half a brain would do."

"True. Although you often tell me that people do remarkably stupid things when they commit a crime."

"They do. But not people like her." She was cunning, that

one. A survivor. He'd met the type before. "If anything, I reckon she's *more* intelligent than she lets on, not less. If she did this, she'd cover her tracks, lead us a merry dance. We might catch her in the end, but she'd make us work a hell of a lot harder than this."

Felicia had gone quiet, taking in his words.

"For what it's worth," she said at last, "I think you're right. But if you *are* … well, you do realise what you're suggesting?"

"That I've got not only a murder on my hands, but someone being framed for it as well?" His lips quirked in a humourless smile. "So much for thinking I'd be home in time for the ten o'clock news, hey? It looks like it's going to be a very long night."

As though in confirmation, the air at that moment was shattered by a huge crash, so powerful that it seemed to shake the floor upon which they stood. For a long, agonising second, Pettifer and Felicia just stared at one another, stunned into immobility. Breath held, waiting for what came next.

Then the screaming started.

Chapter Twenty-Seven

The Great Hall was a scene of utter devastation. Pettifer stood in the middle of it, hardly able to take it in. What had once been a table lavishly laid for dinner like the others that still surrounded it, was now a mass of jagged wood, broken crockery and glass, all buried beneath the carcass of an enormous chandelier. Half-burned candle stumps littered the floor around it, but some remained in their sockets, still smoking. The whole thing was sodden, dripping water and foam, filling the air with an acrid tang that stuck in the back of Pettifer's throat; he was fighting the urge to cough as Jess appeared behind him, her face sombre.

"I've put the other diners in the snug. They didn't protest much; to be honest, they all seem pretty stunned."

"I don't doubt it," Pettifer replied leadenly. He'd been on the other side of the building, and the sound of the impact had been enough to make him freeze in shock. To actually be in the *room* with it…

His gaze moved towards the other chandelier, still in place

up in the rafters, still secured by its rope to the far wall. The things probably weighed a ton, and it must all have happened so fast. No-one underneath could possibly have got out of the way in time.

"It seems rather naïve to ask if it might have been an accident, given recent events," Jess ventured, almost apologetically. "But…"

Pettifer sighed.

"No, you're right, lass. We have to consider all possibilities. Despite what our fictional television counterparts might be fond of saying, there *is* such a thing as coincidence. But in this case…" He beckoned her towards the wall, where the frayed edge of the rope hung limply. "Take a look at that."

Jess crouched down.

"It looks like it's been cut."

"It has. Twice, in fact." Pettifer pointed to the saw marks. "In the first instance, it's been cut almost all the way through – to weaken it, so when the time came … it would only have taken one more small cut to make it snap." The rope was almost as thick as the average arm; sawing away at the entire thing would have been impossible to do unnoticed in a room full of people. But this way … it would have been but the work of a moment. "Who was sitting here?" he asked abruptly, motioning to the table nearest to them.

"A Mr. Spencer Torrent and his daughter Aurelia. Wife, Maureen, has been in their room all evening lying down with an attack of dizziness. You might have heard of him if you're horsey; he's a famous racehorse breeder."

Pettifer's eyes bored into her.

"Do I seem like a horsey person, Winters?"

"Well, no," Jess admitted, colouring sheepishly. "But I

didn't think it was polite to just *assume*…" She gathered herself. "But anyway, it isn't quite that simple. From what I understand, the pudding trolley was parked here throughout dinner. People were coming up to it all the time."

"Of course they were." Pettifer's reply was weary but unsurprised. He should have known this killer wasn't going to make it that easy for them. "Why isn't it still here?"

"They had to move it to get to the fire extinguishers, I think."

Pettifer looked at the smoking, dripping hulk in the centre of the room, and his mood deteriorated further. He understood why they'd had to douse it; with that number of candles, the whole thing could have gone up in a fireball. But it meant that any forensic evidence was going to be severely compromised.

His eyes moved to the base of the wreckage. From underneath, a hand protruded, the fingers curled limply in on themselves. Fighting a rising tide of bile, Pettifer turned away from the sight.

"Why would anyone want to kill these people, Winters?" The question was torn from him roughly. First Doctor Rauceby, and now Lavinia Greenlake. His mind was still spinning from the suddenness of it. It seemed so random, so savage, and yet … there had to be a connection. A *reason*. Why these two, out of everyone here? "I mean, from what I can tell, neither of them was exactly a popular sort…"

"The kind to make enemies?" Jess suggested.

"Perhaps." There was something very *definite* about these crimes, Pettifer brooded. There was a *point* to them; the planning involved, the outlandish methods … they could have just conked the victims on the head, but no. They were willing to take a risk. They wanted to *play*. That troubled him more than anything else. "Doctor Rauceby, certainly. He was dishing out rogue medicine. That makes him potentially the target of some serious hostility. People who've put their hope in him, only to be disappointed, potentially even angry … it's a highly charged situation. Deep emotions involved. I don't suppose we've got any further on his other clients, by the way?"

Jess shrugged helplessly.

"I've been trying to get through to the secretary at his clinic, but…"

"Understood. It's after hours. We can't expect much." He shook his head and looked at his watch. Half past nine. That was two murders in as many hours, and what was already feeling like the longest evening of his life.

"Any updates on when we can expect some back-up?" he asked, more in hope than expectation. The Welland Police was a toytown institution, really, crammed into a single-roomed station and counting a total of five officers on its books. One of which was Heavenly, whom even the most generous person would struggle to describe as an active investigator. It had been set up to tackle the kind of crime one might expect from a bucolic backwater like Stamford: the odd theft from the market, a tourist dropping litter, teenagers playing loud music on a park bench late into the evening. There was no such thing as back-up, or a forensics team; for anything more serious, they had to call in for help from further afield. Help that didn't always arrive as fast as one might like.

His suspicions were confirmed by the face Jess pulled in answer to his question.

"We're on the list, but everyone's tied up at other incidents."

"Aye, well it is Halloween." Of all the nights to choose to

commit murder, Pettifer thought ruefully, this had to be one of the most inconvenient from a policing point of view. With all the high jinks and misguided pranks going on out there, resources were rarely more stretched. "All right, so it's just you and I for the time being. We can't afford to hang around until they get here, though; we have to forge ahead now, even if we're missing a lot of the answers. We need to work with what's in front of us." He looked at the lifeless hand, and immediately regretted it as his stomach turned. "The question is, who would want to kill an old woman like Lavinia Greenlake?"

"Apart from her sister, you mean?" Jess suggested, only half in jest.

But Pettifer wasn't listening. His mind was already turning over, attempting to answer his own question.

"She's the only person we know of who definitely used the doctor's services. The only person who definitely knew about what he was doing. That *must* be our link."

"So, either she was more involved than she let on, or—"

"Or she knew something."

"Perhaps something she wasn't even *aware* she knew."

"Bloody hell." Pettifer was feeling a decidedly sinking feeling in the face of so many unknowns. "Never mind the news. We won't be home for *breakfast* at this rate."

Jess looked uneasily at the doorway that led back to the snug.

"We're going to have to tell them what's been going on, aren't we? We can't exactly keep it from them any longer."

"Yes, we are." Pettifer rubbed his face exhaustedly. He didn't relish the thought of telling a room full of people that a murderer had been at large while they'd been obliviously enjoying their evening. He'd thought that keeping the doctor's death under wraps would give the investigation an advantage, help them flush out the killer. Now, he was wondering if he hadn't made a colossal error of judgement. "We'll need to get statements from every single one of them. Find out what they saw, no matter how minor the detail." He gritted his teeth in frustration. "Our killer was right *here*, Winters. Where we're standing. They had to walk up to this point, in front of an entire dining room of witnesses … someone *has* to have seen something." He knew he was trying to convince himself of the fact as much as his constable. "Let's get in there and find out what."

He strode towards the snug, face set determinedly, gaze fixed forwards, Jess scuttling in his wake. He barely noticed the figure he brushed past just inside the doorway.

Felicia watched Pettifer go thoughtfully, her eyes following his broad back as it cut a path through the crowded room.

The snug, usually such a cosy, convivial space, now hosted a distinctly sepulchral atmosphere. The laughter and chatter were gone, replaced by cloying silence as everyone sat numbly, shock written all over their faces. No-one was really looking at one another; they were lost in their own thoughts, their own horrific recollections. Or at least, *nearly* all of them were, Felicia reminded herself, with an inward shudder; if the conversation she'd just overheard was correct, then one of these people was putting it on. One of them had walked calmly up to the rope, and with the flick of a knife, they'd signed Lavinia Greenlake's death warrant. But which one?

Her eyes moved around the room, taking in the people she'd met tonight. The people whom ultimately, she knew so little about.

Pettifer was making a beeline for the Torrents; perhaps unsurprisingly, as they'd been sitting the nearest to the rope mechanism. Aurelia sat with rounded shoulders, staring down at the floor. She had changed her walker for a stick, Felicia noticed – presumably to appease her father, who was standing rigidly behind the sofa she sat on like a patriarch in a portrait, his face expressionless. To their left, Annabel Drayford stood near the door, as though on guard. Her face was pale, but otherwise she looked as composed as ever. The dashing young barman from earlier was moving around the room, serving small glasses of brandy for the shock, and although most people were clutching a glass, Felicia noticed that only a few had roused themselves enough to actually partake of the tonic. Matthias Weaver had been fetched from the garden and was lingering by the window, as though not wanting to get too close to anyone else. His small black eyes roved back and forth furtively. Florian was sitting on a low chair, his head hanging between his knees, as though he felt faint. Cymbeline sat next to him, one leg elegantly crossed over the other. Felicia thought she looked uncharacteristically nervous. Next was Lucia, sitting by the fireplace, and beside *her*…

"Cass?" Felicia was at her friend's side immediately, and her heart lurched at the tear-streaked face that greeted her. She knelt down beside Cassie's chair, putting her arms around her.

"Oh God, Fliss." Cassie had her face buried in Felicia's shoulder, her voice a muffled moan. "It was *horrible*. I've never heard a sound like it."

Felicia couldn't respond to that with anything meaningful, so she didn't try. Instead, she just squeezed tighter.

"I'm sorry I wasn't there." She'd sent Cassie into dinner with Lucia on her own, citing Algernon's mystery illness as an excuse. She'd hated lying to her friend, but she'd promised Pettifer that she'd keep the doctor's murder a secret, and she hadn't seen any other way around it. Even so, it didn't stop her from feeling dreadful now.

"You couldn't have done anything," Cassie sniffed. "No-one could. It all happened so fast. One minute she was just sitting there, having her dinner, and then…" She trembled. "God, look at me shaking. I wasn't even sitting nearby. It's just … what a bloody *tragedy*." She blew her nose on a cocktail napkin, blinking at Felicia with red-rimmed eyes. "Where's Dexter? I assumed you two would be together."

"No, I sent him on ahead. He was supposed to be joining you." Felicia frowned, but then quickly dismissed the thought. The man was a law unto himself; she didn't have time to worry about him right now. Besides, those lilac trousers should be enough to scare off any would-be murderers who happened to cross his path. Chances are, he was perfectly safe.

"Listen, Cass." Felicia dropped her voice, then hesitated, wondering if she was about to do the right thing. But her gaze went to Pettifer; she took in the bleak look on his face, the pessimistic downwards slope of his shoulders, and she shook off her misgivings. If the official channels weren't working, she had her own methods of getting the information they needed. And the most potent of all was sitting right here next to her. "I need you to find something out for me. Something to do with the people here. Can you do that?"

Cassie's face creased in confusion.

"I don't understand. That's the sort of thing you ask me when you're on one of your cases, but this was just a terrible accident. Those chandeliers were a disaster waiting to happen, surely? Why would you…" She trailed off; slowly, her head swivelled round to Pettifer, then back to Felicia again. A look of horrified understanding flooded her features. "Oh, no," she said, her voice rising frantically. Felicia bit her lip nervously as Lucia looked around. "Absolutely not, Fliss. Do *not* tell me this is another one of your horrible murders! I couldn't take it; I really couldn't."

"There's no-one better than you at getting people to talk," Felicia pressed coaxingly, deciding to overlook the '*your* murders' comment for the time being, although it did sting somewhat. Cassie made it sound as though she caused them somehow. "And right now, it's gossip I need."

"Well, you'll have to look elsewhere," Cassie retorted, with a sniff. "I don't do that anymore, Fliss. You know that. Gossip is beneath me. Alain says that great minds discuss ideas and small minds discuss people."

Did Alain make these quotes up, Felicia wondered, or did he have a book somewhere?

"Cass, *please*," she implored, although with a firm edge to her voice. "Two people have died. This is no time to stand on ceremony."

Cassie's eyes bulged.

"*Two*?" she squawked, and Felicia winced.

"Pettifer will explain everything in a moment," she said, in an undertone. "Right now, though, I need you to trust me. It's for the greater good, Cass. I promise." As Cassie opened her mouth, she hurriedly added, "Look, tomorrow, you can go back to being a bastion of discretion, and Alain need know nothing about it. But for tonight…" she looked her oldest friend in the eye, and said softly, "I need the old Cassie back."

For a moment, Cassie wavered. Then she sighed.

"All right. Tell me what you want to know."

Pettifer, much as he hated to admit it, was beginning to feel despondent. With every witness he interviewed, it became more and more apparent that their killer had pulled off the seemingly impossible. No-one had seen the murder happen. No-one had ever seen anything that might be counted as suspicious. They'd practically all been up to the pudding trolley to browse during the meal; worse still, it seemed that their adversary had thought through the timing. They'd waited until the final course had been laid out, a cornucopia of fresh fruit and nuts to accompany the cheeseboard that had replaced the puddings on the trolley. That meant that by every single plate, there had been a fruit knife – small, but more than sharp enough to cut the last remaining cords of the rope, and even more depressingly, foldable, and therefore eminently concealable in a sleeve or pocket. The perfect weapon, right there at the scene. The killer hadn't even had to bring their own blade. If it wasn't his job to catch them, he might have been begrudgingly impressed by such efficacy, Pettifer thought bleakly. As it was, the knowledge was enough to make him consider filing for early retirement from the force.

"Sir." He heard Jess's breathless voice behind him. As soon as he turned, he could tell that something had happened; she looked excited, her eyes shining. She was rocking back and forth on the balls of her feet, as though it was taking all of her effort to stay in one spot.

"Please." He tried not to sound as desperately hopeful as he felt. "*Tell* me you've got something."

"I think so. But it's strange, Sarge. I don't know what to make of it."

What about this case *wasn't* strange, Pettifer thought ruefully.

"Which one?" His eyes moved questioningly across the assembled company in the snug.

"None of them. That's the thing." She drew him away towards the door, dropping her voice so they wouldn't be overheard. "I was approached out there in the foyer by one of the other members. A Mr. Richard Warner. He saw something that worried him, and he thought we should know."

"He wasn't at dinner?"

"No, he's been out all evening at a cricket-club AGM elsewhere in town, but he was feeling tired so he came back earlier than planned. And that's when he saw them: someone hovering around the dining-room door, watching the people inside. He said they looked furtive."

"Who? Did he recognise them?"

"Well, that's just it. Yes and no. It sounds like they were wearing some kind of demon costume, the way he described them. Bloody terrifying. Although, he says he knew exactly what it was." She tucked a loose strand of baby-blonde hair behind her ear. "Apparently there was a performance here earlier? The ... what were they called? Mummies?"

Pettifer felt a cold sensation in his chest, like he'd been hit by an icy fist.

"Mummers, Winters," he said distantly. "They're called Mummers."

His mind was racing, his throat constricting as he replayed the conversation he'd had with Felicia. She'd mentioned something about that, hadn't she? About one of them being out in the garden with Dr. Rauceby, just before his murder? With everything else happening, he'd half dismissed it, marked it as something to follow up later. Except, there hadn't been a later; this killer moved faster than anyone could have imagined. There hadn't been a moment to breathe, let alone pick up loose threads.

Now he was wondering if he might have missed a major lead.

Of course, he assuaged himself quickly, even if they were involved, there was no way they could actually have *cut* the rope. Not themselves. Unobservant as this lot might be, even they were sure to notice someone dressed up as a bloody great monster waltzing up to the pudding trolley.

Or could they? The question popped into his mind, uncomfortable but impossible to brush aside. How easy would it be to wait, watching proceedings, then, when the time came, to slip off the disguise and enter the room as themselves? To move towards the looped end of the rope, blade concealed within a palm, or swept off a table as they passed... There were people coming and going all the time; who would have thought anything of it?

That in turn opened up a new, even more unpalatable idea: that their murderer might not even be here in this room, as he'd supposed. They might not have been at dinner at all. They could have been anyone, anywhere in the club... His mind went to the list that he'd been given, the names of everyone on the premises tonight. So many names ... and yet only now he realised that some were conspicuously absent.

"You hold the fort here, lass," he said shortly, already making his way across the room to a familiar figure. "There's someone I need to talk to."

Chapter Twenty-Eight

"You know, Miss Drayford, when *most* people are asked by the police to do something as part of a murder investigation," Pettifer clasped his hands together on the desk and glowered across the polished mahogany surface at her, "they do it. *You*, however, seem to think the rules don't apply to you."

She returned his look unrepentantly. In fact, she had the temerity to appear affronted.

"I think that's a *little* unjust, Sergeant. Haven't I complied with every one of your requests thus far?"

Just about, Pettifer thought grudgingly. But in his opinion, she'd done the bare minimum, and no more. Whether that was in aid of the ridiculous veil of secrecy this place insisted on wrapping itself in, or something more, remained to be seen. But he wasn't about to let her get away with it for a moment longer.

"I asked you for a list of *everyone* who's been at the club this evening," he persisted. "No exceptions."

"Isn't that what I provided?"

He pulled out the sheets of paper she'd given him – a list of members, and a staff rota – and slapped them down on the desk with force. Suddenly, he was feeling thoroughly vexed by her smug, supercilious attitude – which, incidentally, seemed to have recovered fully after briefly slipping in their earlier interview.

"*No.*" The word was like a boom of thunder. "It is not. There was a troupe of performers here earlier this evening; they're not on this list. I'll be needing their booking information so we can track them down." He paused, then added ominously, "*Now.*"

But she didn't seem remotely cowed. In fact, she seemed to regard it as almost amusing, her lips curved in a faint smile.

"There's no need for that, Sergeant. They're all still here."

That brought Pettifer up short.

"I don't follow," he said slowly.

"The Mummers are an in-house band. They're formed of members of The Aquitaine's own staff."

Pettifer sat back in his chair, assimilating that information.

"Isn't that rather a conflict of interest?" he said at last. "I mean, they take money from the guests, don't they?"

And that wasn't the only liberty they took, he added silently. The performance, from what he gathered, seemed to be as much about power as financial gain. Were the pampered, self-important members of this club, who paid through the nose to call themselves that, aware that the very people who usually waited on them hand and foot were behind those costumes, mocking them?

Annabel Drayford didn't move. She didn't even blink. And

yet, somehow, she managed to make the room temperature feel like it had dropped by several degrees.

"You make it all sound so very underhand, Sergeant."

"Isn't it?"

"Of course not," she snapped. Then, obviously sensing that this wasn't enough to convince him, she seemed to unbend slightly. "Look, between you and me, the members are fully aware of the situation; they're not technically supposed to be, but it's an official *un-secret*, if you will. They play along, pretend they have no idea; it's part of the game."

"So, they know who they are?"

"Not specifically, although they can probably work out some of the players, depending on who mysteriously 'disappears' from their shift just before the performance." She pointed to the rota. "See how here there are two names coupled together? And here? That's because we've had to get in double the staff, so there's someone to cover each person who's performing. The ones with a small 'm' next to their name; those are the people who were down to be a Mummer this year."

Pettifer's head snapped up.

"It changes, then? I'd assumed it'd be the same people each year."

"Oh, no. There's an annual selection process." She drummed her fingers on the desk. "It's actually quite an honour to be asked; you have to prove yourself first."

"*Prove* yourself?" This was getting more bizarre by the minute, Pettifer thought. "How, exactly?"

She'd obviously gathered the direction his thoughts were taking, because she raised an eyebrow.

"Just by working well, Sergeant. No sinister rites or virgin sacrifices, I assure you."

"I see. And when the performance is over? What then?"

She shrugged.

"Well … then it's over. They return the costumes, go back to their shift … like nothing happened. Until next year, of course." She gave him an evaluating look. "But surely, none of this can be relevant to your investigation."

"On the contrary, Miss Drayford." It was time to reveal part of his hand. "One of them is a suspect for the murders."

"*What*?" There was no disguising her genuine astonishment. "But … that's impossible. I told you…"

"I know, but you were wrong. Clearly someone's decided not to give up their role." As she opened her mouth to protest, he held up a hand. "They've been observed by multiple people. There's absolutely no doubt about it."

She shook her head obstinately.

"No, I'm sorry, but there must have been some mistake. I'll show you." She picked up the phone on her desk, punching a series of keys. "Hello? Yes, it's me. I need you to check on the Mummer costumes, confirm they're all there." She waited for a moment, then her face drained of colour. "I see. Which one? All right, well … thank you."

She put down the phone with a hand that, Pettifer noticed, wasn't entirely steady.

"Well, Sergeant," she said stiffly. "It seems that you were right; there *is* one costume missing."

"Whose was it?"

She hesitated. It was brief, subtle, but he saw it nonetheless.

"I'm afraid I can't say. The costumes weren't allocated."

She was lying. He knew it immediately, innately. He felt a flash of anger.

"Miss Drayford, do I need to remind you that this is now a *double* murder investigation? And we don't know what else this killer has planned. Until they're caught, I cannot guarantee the safety of your guests."

"You keep calling them *guests*, Sergeant," she said icily. "I thought it was impolite to correct you before, but here at the club, we take details seriously. They are *members*. And they are my first priority. I'm sorry, but like I told you, I can't help."

Pettifer held her gaze, then kept holding it, until it was beyond comfortable. But she just looked coolly back at him. Patently, she wasn't about to back down. His eyes moved around the office that surrounded them; like a museum, beeswax-scented, heavy on the dark wood and gilt-framed hunting prints. There was nothing in here that told him anything about this woman; about who she was outside of her role here. It was as though she was part of the fabric of the place itself. And clearly, she would defend it to the hilt.

"Well, I'm very disappointed to hear that," he said softly, rising to his feet. "I sincerely hope we don't all live to regret it."

As he was heading out of the door, her voice summoned him back.

"Oh, wait. I've just remembered; there *is* someone else here tonight." She clicked her fingers. "A photographer; I hired him to do some new promotional shots of the club. He's freelance, so he won't be anywhere on the rotas."

Pettifer felt his face go rigid.

"His name?" he asked, through gritted teeth. Something told him he already knew the answer he was about to get. And it wasn't one that filled him with benevolence.

"Riding. Jack Riding." She cocked her head to one side at the expression on his face. "You know him, I take it?"

"Oh, *yes*," Pettifer said darkly. "I know him all right."

"I want you to look at something for me." Pettifer handed Felicia the two pieces of paper. "These are the names of everyone who's been here at the club tonight."

"Right." Felicia took them, scanning her eyes over the reams of neat handwriting – *that* she recognised; it was Annabel Drayford's, the same as the sample she'd been shown earlier. Now she knew its quirks, it was unmistakable. But what it said was another matter; she knew several of the members by now, but of the vast majority of staff … the only one she could potentially place was a Leo Wild. Hadn't Sybil called him Leo earlier tonight? "Wait, why is this one crossed off?" She pointed to a name halfway down: Arthur Talbot, she thought it said, beneath the heavy slash of ink.

"Oh, he doesn't work here anymore. Annabel Drayford says she had to let him go yesterday evening. That's why he was still on the rota."

"Let him go?"

"Yes, apparently he made a mistake at tea, and it was the last straw." Pettifer sounded impatient to move on. "I think he had a complaint made against him."

Felicia felt a distinct sense of unease blooming in her chest. Her mind flashed back to Lucia and Annabel, heads together the previous evening. She recalled the unhappy look on the manager's face… It would make sense, certainly.

But no, Felicia told herself, slightly desperately, surely

Lucia wouldn't actually have … she'd promised to let it go. *Promised*.

And yet … Felicia felt a twinge of misgiving as memories began to surface. The truth is, it was *exactly* the sort of thing she'd do … because she'd done it before, many years ago. There'd been a teacher at school who'd mysteriously disappeared midway through a term. A teacher who, the gossip mill claimed, had recently failed a fourteen-year-old Lucia in chemistry. Another girl who'd moved schools after a flurry of salacious rumours had made her life miserable; rumours that had only started after the girl had suddenly blossomed into her looks, becoming a head-turner overnight. Lucia had no longer been the prettiest girl in the year … until, of course, she was again, her competition conveniently shunted out of the way.

But even so, to believe that her old schoolmate would do something so vindictive now, so pointlessly spiteful … it was too uncomfortable to countenance.

"Why are you showing me this?" She shoved the papers back at Pettifer irritably, knowing she was taking her own emotional turmoil out on him, but unable to contain it.

"I want you to tell me if anyone's missing."

"How should I know? I don't know the names of everyone. I've only been here a couple of times. I can't help you."

"*Can't* you?"

Something about the softness of his tone made her go still.

"You could have told me your boyfriend's here," he continued, sounding almost conversational. But she knew him well, and he wasn't as detached as he made out; there was an undercurrent shimmering in his tone.

"My *what*?" Then her face cleared. "*Oh*. You mean…"

He didn't even wait for her to finish.

"Don't play coy with me, Felicia; I'm really not in the mood." He folded his arms, a posture that only made him look more monolithic than ever. "You knew that Jack Riding was on these premises tonight and you didn't see fit to tell me?"

His voice remained at the same level, but a distinct bite had crept into it. Felicia winced internally; all right, so he was *definitely* angry.

"I didn't! I had no idea." She immediately went to protest, then realised it wasn't quite the truth. "I mean, all right; yes, I knew he *was* here. But that was yesterday." Her mind was racing as fast as her pulse. Jack was here right *now*? "I haven't seen him tonight; he didn't say…"

"Oh, so you had a good long chat with him, then?" Now Pettifer had abandoned all pretence of indifference and was practically bellowing. "Bloody *brilliant*, Felicia. So now *you're* lying to me on top of everyone else. This is all I need."

That was so patently unreasonable, and so unlike him, that any potential annoyance Felicia might have felt at the accusation was immediately quashed, replaced instead with concern as she looked into his exhausted, grey face, the unkempt stubble forming on his jaw. He looked completely wrung out.

"Look, we're going round in circles here," she said gently. "Why don't you tell me what this is all about?"

He sighed, scrubbing a hand across his face. His huge shoulders dropped in resignation.

"That Mummer you saw in the garden earlier … they've been seen again." His voice was so low it was scarcely audible. "Just before Lavinia Greenlake was murdered."

Felicia drew in a sharp breath. With everything that had

happened since, the brief sighting that had so unsettled her earlier had shrunk into insignificance. The trail had seemed to be pointing in another direction entirely, and she'd managed to convince herself that what she'd seen was perfectly innocent, just one of the performers taking a quick break in the fresh air. But if they were still around … well, that put another spin on it entirely. The show had been over hours ago; there was no reason for anyone to still be wandering around in costume. No good one, anyway.

"So now you see why it's vital that I know everyone who's unaccounted for," Pettifer concluded.

His words jerked her back to the present. She stared at him, not wanting to believe what he was suggesting.

"Of course I do, but … you can't possibly think it's *Jack*? Why on earth would he do such a thing? He has no connection to this place beyond a brief commission."

"Aye, well, that's another thing." Pettifer was looking grimly pleased with himself; Felicia felt a responding wariness. She had a feeling she wouldn't like what she was about to hear next. "It was *supposed* to be a brief commission. But it seems he's dragging it out. According to Miss Drayford, our lad wasn't even down to be here tonight; he was meant to have finished up yesterday. But suddenly he throws some sort of artistic hissy fit and announces that none of his work is up to scratch and that he needs to start all over again." Pettifer raised an eyebrow. "Now, why'd he do a thing like *that*, I wonder?"

Felicia tried not to let her expression change, but underneath, she couldn't deny a flicker of disquiet. That didn't sound anything like Jack; if anything, he had almost the *opposite* of an artistic temperament. He was so measured and unreadable it drove her mad at times.

"What, no bright ideas?" Pettifer pressed sardonically. "Well, that's all right, because I've got one of my own. Clearly, he's deliberately arranged to be back here tonight. He's up to something and no mistake."

"That is a *wild* leap, and you know it." Felicia put her hands on her hips. Jack was the one subject she and Pettifer were always guaranteed to fall out about, the fly in the ointment of their odd but otherwise mutually respectful acquaintance. "There are plenty of perfectly natural explanations for why he might have canned those shots." She hoped her own lack of conviction wasn't showing in her voice; just in case, she compensated by glaring at him. "Why do you *always* insist on thinking the worst of him?"

He returned her look unwaveringly.

"Because I know him, Felicia. Far better, might I add, than you do."

"You know *of* him," she retorted. All of Jack's transgressions, such as they were, had been long over before Pettifer had been transferred to Stamford. Pettifer's entire view of Jack was based on what he'd been told by his fellow officers and predecessors. That was what irked her the most, in truth: that he hadn't even taken the time to forge his own opinions. He'd just adopted the official verdict, still bandied about by resentful former officers and local busybodies irritated that their town's black sheep had, as they'd seen it, never been properly punished for his misdemeanours. Even more irritated that he was still around, a permanent reminder of the fact, taunting them with his very presence. What they didn't realise, of course, and probably didn't wish to, was that Jack *had* suffered. He'd done plenty wrong, but he'd also been wrongfully accused, and it had tainted his life and, Felicia couldn't help but feel, his trust of the world. From other people, Felicia could maybe understand such a wilfully blinkered view, but from Pettifer – a man she usually counted on to take people as he found them – it perplexed and infuriated her in equal measure. "That's not the same thing. *I* know because he told me."

"Oh, and you believe him, do you? A proven miscreant and liar, over the word of respectable townsfolk and professional law enforcement?"

Felicia's lips had immediately formed around a defiant affirmative, but now, she found that no sound was coming out. She hesitated, hating herself for it but unable to deny the crash of confusion and doubt his question had thrown up. *Did* she believe Jack? Honestly, when it truly came down to it?

The answer came immediately, but it wasn't any more comforting.

She believed what he'd told her about his past. Absolutely, unswervingly. But did she trust him *now*, in the present? Could she honestly say that he would always be straight with her? That she could always count on him to be on the right side? The fact that she couldn't was the very reason why she'd put distance between them these past few months. Why she couldn't allow herself to get pulled in any closer. The truth was, Jack's life had been hard, and it had made him the same by consequence. He was distrustful of everyone, secretive, and believed solely in looking out for himself, which, while perhaps understandable in its way, made some of his decisions seem decidedly greyscale when it came to morals.

"Well?" Pettifer demanded, holding her gaze. Refusing to let her look away. "What's your answer? I'd like to hear it."

She knew what he was really asking. In his mind, it was his

word or Jack's; there was no way for her to answer without betraying someone, so she just looked back at him, frozen.

"Am I interrupting?"

Jess was beside them, head swivelling between them warily. Felicia felt a rush of gratitude for the blonde-haired constable; rarely had she been so relieved to see anyone. She opened her mouth to reply, but Pettifer got in first.

"No. Felicia was just leaving."

He said it expressionlessly, but he was still looking at her, and what she saw in his eyes told her otherwise. She swallowed, knowing that even though she hadn't answered his question, he'd taken a response anyway from her silence.

"Actually, Sarge, I think she should stay." Jess was twisting the silver moon in her earlobe; she looked keyed up, her eyes bright. "The station has managed to trace the call we received earlier tonight. The tip-off that the doctor was missing. You were right; it came from right here in the club. One of the guest bedrooms."

Pettifer wasted no time with words. His response was a monosyllable, stark and urgent.

"*Who?*"

Jess's eyes flicked to Felicia, then nervously, almost apologetically away again.

"Lucia DuFontaine."

Chapter Twenty-Nine

"This is simply *outrageous*." Lucia was practically quivering with indignation as she stood by the bed, arms folded. "You can't just barge in here and go riffling through my room, like I'm some sort of common criminal! Do you have any idea who my husband is?"

Pettifer obviously didn't feel that warranted a response, because he simply pointed to the phone, which Jess was busy trying to fit into an evidence bag. It wasn't proving easy; it was a cumbersome, rotary dial model, probably from about the 1930s, if Felicia had to guess from this distance.

"Have you used that telephone this evening?" Pettifer's question was brusque; evidently, he wasn't going to waste time warming up his witness.

"No." Lucia looked put out, but she replied readily enough. "I used it this morning to ring for my breakfast, but not since then."

"Are you sure?" Pettifer's eyes bored into her. "I'm going to give you a chance to think carefully. You might wish to reconsider your answer."

"Yes, I'm *sure*," Lucia shot back. Her eyes narrowed. "Listen, what *is* all this about? I have a right to know, if you're going to interrogate me like this."

The faintest of smiles touched Pettifer's lips.

"Oh, this isn't an interrogation, Mrs. DuFontaine. Believe me, you'd know if it were. No, we're just having a friendly chat, is all." He sat on the bed; deep within the mattress, a muffled *boing* indicated the death of a spring. "But you're right, it's only fair you know why I'm asking. It's quite simple: somebody placed a call from *that* telephone at 7:35 p.m. this evening. A call connected to Doctor Rauceby's death."

He stopped short of saying that the caller could well have been the murderer themselves, Felicia noted. She saw immediately what he was doing; despite the seeming directness of his approach, in reality, he was circling Lucia carefully, drawing her in. If she tripped on her story, it would be of her own accord; he wouldn't force it. But it didn't mean he hadn't engineered it. Felicia had seen him at work multiple times now, and regardless of her feelings towards him at the present moment, she couldn't deny that it was impressive.

Lucia's impeccably groomed eyebrows rose in surprise.

"Well, whoever it was, it wasn't me. I was downstairs in the snug at that time. With everyone else, I might add." She glanced across the room and seemed to notice Felicia for the first time. "Wait, Felicia was there. *She* saw me." She indicated Pettifer with a dismissive swipe of the hand, as though he were a mere serf. "Tell him, Felicia. Tell him I was there all the way through the performance."

Felicia hesitated. When she spoke, she did so slowly, choosing her words with care.

"As far as I know, she was."

It didn't go down well. Lucia stared at her in open consternation.

"What on earth does *that* mean?" Her voice took on a peevish buzz. "What's the matter with you? Why won't you just tell him I was there all the time?"

"Because I don't know that for sure," Felicia replied calmly, even as her pulse quickened under the other woman's hostile gaze. "*I* wasn't there all the time, remember? I took Algernon outside for a while around then."

"This is beyond ridiculous." Lucia's face was taut with suppressed rage. "You said you'd gone up to the landing. I would have had to *pass* you to get to my room."

Felicia shook her head.

"Not necessarily. This is a Georgian house; there's always more than one staircase. You could have come up the servants' stairs."

"For God's sake, Felicia!" Lucia's composure finally snapped. Her hands were clenched at her sides, knuckles white. "Whose side are you on here? I'd expected some kind of loyalty from you, after all the time we've known one another." Her lipsticked mouth curled in a sneer. "But then, you always *were* on the outside looking in, weren't you? You and Cassie. You never really understood how to be part of the gang." Her eyes glinted. "Is that what this is all about? Some sort of petty revenge for not being popular enough back then?"

In that moment, Felicia knew that Lucia was more than capable of having that waiter fired on a whim. She hadn't wanted to see it, but her old schoolmate was still just that; she hadn't really changed at all. A lot of things about the girl she'd remembered – that coldness beneath the smile, the calculating way she got what she wanted – they were still there. They hadn't gone away with maturity, as she'd hoped; instead they'd simply grown a more sophisticated face.

A face, which, at the moment, was twisted with malice. Felicia swallowed, but stood her ground.

"What you *mean* is that I wouldn't lie for you back then just because everyone else did. And I won't now." She sighed, then turned to Pettifer, who'd been watching the exchange with an unreadable expression. All that said, she couldn't preach truthfulness and then hold back, loath as she was to help Lucia in any way. "But you could ask Dexter; he was sitting next to her all evening. She wouldn't have been able to leave without him noticing."

"Thank you," he replied curtly. "We'll do that. Now, I'm going to have to ask you to excuse us for a moment, if you don't mind."

Felicia nodded and moved to leave, only realising belatedly that it wasn't her he'd been addressing. He was looking at Lucia, who immediately bristled.

"You're asking *me* to leave? My own room?"

"Just while we finish up here, yes." Pettifer didn't make any effort to sound apologetic. "I need to confer with my colleague."

"Which one?" Lucia said bitterly, her eyes lingering on Felicia. Then she swept out, nose in the air.

Pettifer exhaled gustily into the ensuing silence.

"Well, if that's what private school is like … I'm not so sorry I went to the local comp now. It seems like a rose garden by comparison."

"You have no idea," Felicia stated flatly. "That's just the tip of the iceberg, believe me."

"Sarge," Jess broke in, looking agitated. She'd given up trying to put the telephone in an evidence bag, Felicia noticed. "You know, if Dexter *does* confirm her whereabouts at the time of the call…"

"I know, Winters, I know." Pettifer rubbed the back of his neck wearily. "It throws the whole thing wide open again. We'll need to find out who else could have had the opportunity to slip away. Who wasn't there for the whole performance. That's our only hope of finding out who did this."

Even as he said it, he knew it was an impossible task; by all accounts, the room had been dark, everyone riveted by the show … it would have been the easiest thing in the world for someone to duck out for a moment. And it *would* only have been a moment; that was the most damning thing of all. By using Matthias Weaver to set up the murder for them, their killer hadn't even needed to go to the chapel. Their sole job would have been coming upstairs to place the phone call, something that would only have required them to leave the snug for a few minutes at most. A negligible absence, and one that, even if vaguely observed by anyone else in the room at the time, was unlikely to be recalled afterwards.

It also cast the net prodigiously wide; as with Lavinia's murder, it could easily have been done by almost anyone sitting in that room. That meant they still had a large number of suspects, with very little way of whittling them down, of focusing on any one thread. Although presumably their killer had been well aware of that; they seemed to have thought of everything else, after all.

Pettifer had the chilling sensation, and not for the first time, that this was all a game of sorts. That this killer was enjoying running rings around them, blowing smoke in their eyes. He didn't often doubt his capabilities as an investigator, but now, with the prospect of having to go back to the start in this case all over again, he couldn't deny a small, doubtful whisper in the back of his mind that asked if he hadn't met his match this time. If he just wasn't good enough to crack this one.

"Is it, though?" Felicia was talking to herself, softly, but Pettifer heard. He rose from his ruminations, blinking.

"What's that?"

"Sorry, I was just … thinking aloud." Felicia faltered, wondering whether to expand further. Normally, she would feel comfortable giving her input, but with the atmosphere between her and Pettifer at the moment … it didn't feel appropriate, somehow. The doubting thought continued to gnaw at her, however, the pressure to voice it growing. She bit her lip, then heard herself blurting out, "The thing is, I can't help wondering … even if they did manage to sidle away unnoticed, how would they have got into the room? Lucia isn't some trusting, small-rural-town kind of person; she's lived all over the world. And she has some *very* expensive things here with her." Belatedly, she realised she might have said too much; before they could begin to wonder how she knew that, she hurried on. "She'd never have left the door unlocked. I remember from school how careful she used to be about securing her locker. She said her father had drilled it into her to never leave her valuables vulnerable."

Pettifer didn't look pleased by her logic. He frowned darkly.

"That's as may be. But if it wasn't her who placed the call, then it's irrefutable. *Someone* managed to break in here. We may not know how they did it, but…"

Felicia looked around. Then her eyes fell upon the perfectly made bed. The straightened coverlet, the little mint on each lushly plumped pillow.

"Unless," she said slowly, "they didn't need to break in at all. Because they already had a key."

Chapter Thirty

"Thank you for coming." Pettifer indicated the seat opposite him. "Please, sit. This shouldn't take up much of your time."

Molly Dunster obeyed, although with visible reticence. She perched warily on the very edge of the seat cushion, as though poised to make a bolt for it at a moment's notice. Her fingers played nervously on her lap, and she clamped them hastily between her knees. Pettifer, regarding her, couldn't help recalling Felicia's words from back in Lucia's bedroom.

"You know, there was *someone* who would have been up here while everyone else was downstairs at the performance," she'd said, her grey eyes alight in that way he'd come to recognise during the course of their investigations together. It usually meant the game was about to change, that what she was about to say next would turn everything they'd previously thought on its head. "Someone no-one would miss. Potentially that no-one would even notice."

Pettifer looked at the club's cleaner now, taking in the way her posture shrank in upon itself, how her long fringe cast her eyes – and with them, most of her discernible expression – into permanent shadow. Someone who could easily be overlooked, indeed. And yet, he had the feeling that the effect wasn't accidental, but rather deliberately cultivated. That intrigued him.

"We're speaking to every staff member here tonight." He sat down, resting his forearms on his knees. Making the interview less formal, trying to put her at ease. He knew this type well; outwardly diffident as she might seem, she would only talk if she chose to. "I understand you were on the turn-down service this evening?"

"I was, yes." Her voice was barely audible above the crackling fire.

"And you visited the doctor's room as part of your route?"

"I visited all the rooms. There aren't very many of them; one person can easily do the whole round."

"And at what time did you enter his room?"

She blinked rapidly.

"Exactly? I mean, I can't be…"

"Just roughly," he assured her, sensing she was about to go into a flap. "As accurate as you can be. It might be of help to the investigation."

"Um, okay." She squeezed her eyes shut, as though picturing it. "Well, let me … wait." Her eyes flew open. "The gong. I heard it as I was going along the landing."

"The first gong? Or the second?"

"The second, definitely. So … just before seven o'clock." Her cheeks were pink with relief, her voice a breathy rush, as though she'd just passed a test of some kind. "Yes, that's when I was there."

"Thank you." He nodded across to Jess, unnecessarily as it turned out; she was already scribbling furiously. Her determination to record absolutely everything was impressive, and he didn't doubt it was an approach that would probably crack many a case over her career, but sometimes he had to remind her to look up a bit more. What you saw and observed in this job was often just as important as the cold, hard facts. And what he was observing right now was a woman who was practically vibrating with nerves. So much so that it was obviously taking a lot of effort for her to keep her body still.

Molly Dunster, it occurred to him in that moment, was utterly terrified. The realisation hit him square in the chest, making sense of what had been just scattered jigsaw pieces. But the question was, of what? Something? Or some*one*?

"And he was present, the doctor?" He kept his voice neutral, determined to stick to a factual line for the time being. Soon enough, an opportunity would present itself. He just had to be patient. "You saw him?"

Her leg, which had been jiggling up and down, stopped. She stared blankly at him for several long moments.

"Yes." Her voice was scratchy. "Yes, I did."

"Were any words exchanged between you?"

"A few. He wasn't a chatty guest on the whole. He tended to ignore you, to be honest. But he did mention that he'd be going down for drinks in a few minutes; that he'd lost track of time, and he'd be out of my way in a minute."

"And was he?"

She swallowed, nodded.

"I finished up and let myself out."

"He implied that he was going to attend the performance, then?"

"Y-yes."

She stuttered on the word. Even if Pettifer didn't already know she had to be lying, he would have spotted it there and then.

"Interesting." He raised an eyebrow, folded his arms. "And you believed him, did you?"

"Of course." She was trying to sound shocked by the question, but it didn't quite ring true. "Why on earth wouldn't I?"

Enough playing, Pettifer decided then. It was time to get down to brass tacks. He reached into the inside pocket of his jacket and pulled out the notecard, which he laid on the table between them.

"Because of this."

She stared down at the card, and her face drained of colour. Her hand flew shakily to her lips.

"Your prints are all over it," Pettifer said coldly. "Both on the envelope *and* the note inside, so don't deny you read it. We already know you did."

The official back-up might still be conspicuous by its absence, Pettifer thought, with a touch of pride, but that didn't mean they were entirely without resources. Jess had managed to pull some prints with the aid of some ash collected from the fireplace and a spare makeup brush from behind the front desk. The results, once sent back to their colleagues at the Welland Police Station, had been good enough to find a match.

"Oh, God," she whispered. Her hands moved upwards, covering her whole face. But Pettifer was no longer feeling sympathetic; he pressed on mercilessly.

"You gave this to him, didn't you?"

"Yes," she moaned. "But I had no idea what was in it then, I *swear*. How was I to know it was anything sinister? I just saw it on my cleaning trolley…"

Pettifer cut her off brusquely.

"Was that usual? For communications to be left for you to deliver?"

"Well, no. But it's a hectic night, half the staff caught up in the performance, the other half making up the slack. I just assumed someone was cutting a corner. It was in one of the club's envelopes; it's got the watermark on the back if you look… I had no reason to think…" She took a breath. "It was no trouble for me, at any rate; I just slid it under the door and told myself I'd done a good turn for someone."

Pettifer felt his face freeze.

"You've made a slip there, Ms Dunster," he said, in a quiet, silken voice, trying to conceal his growing fury. "A small one, granted, but you're dealing with me now, and I'm fond of my details. You never even saw the doctor, did you?"

For a moment, she feigned innocence, but then her face crumpled.

"I'm sorry."

"Wait, what?" Jess's head shot up so fast she made an ink blot in her notebook. "That was all made up?" She looked disbelieving. "That whole conversation…"

"Never happened, I think you'll find," Pettifer said flatly. "We're dealing with quite a fabulist here, Winters. Rather wasted in her current profession, I'd say. We ought to point her in the direction of *The Stamford Bugle*; they're in need of new writers at the moment, I've heard."

Molly Dunster coloured magenta.

"I just thought if I said I'd seen him alive, you wouldn't

think I'd…" She sighed. "Look, it's hard to explain, but I had my reasons. If you only knew…"

"Not at all," Pettifer said easily. "In fact, I understand perfectly."

She drew back, looking wary.

"You … do?"

"Mmm." Pettifer looked down at his huge hands, still clasped together on his knees. "You know, something struck me about you, Ms Dunster, the minute I saw your details. If you don't mind me observing, you're a little different to the other staff here, aren't you?"

She blinked, looking startled by the sudden change of tack.

"I … uh, well, I mean, I'm a little *older*, I suppose…"

"Thirty-eight, to be precise," Jess supplied, flipping through her notes. "With grown-up children."

"Twin boys." Her eyes were darting between them now, nervously. "They're eighteen next month."

"Hardly in your dotage, then," Pettifer allowed. "But the others working here … they are *very* young, aren't they? I don't think anyone's a day over twenty-one. Why exactly is that?"

"I'm not sure…" She looked confused. "I mean, that's normal, isn't it? For club work?"

"I wouldn't have said so. Myself, I'd expect a range of experience, especially in a place like this. Some familiar old hands. Reassuring, capable. Part of the furniture, as it were." He sifted through the paperwork in front of him. "But you know, the staff here … they're an interesting bunch. I can't quite put my finger on why. In many ways they differ … they're all from different backgrounds, so it's not that. But they are all young. They're all ambitious. And they're *all* without blemish. Except, that is, one."

He looked at her.

"Ah." She sat back in her seat, looking defeated. Somehow, though, she simultaneously seemed to relax, lose a little of her skittishness as the weight of pretence slipped from her. "Of course. I should have realised; you've matched my prints. That means you've seen my record. You know about my past."

"Quite a colourful past, as it turns out. Almost … *psychedelic*, one might say."

Her gaze hardened.

"I was young, and I was stupid. It's no defence, really, but it's the truth. I fell for the wrong man, fell for a lot of the wrong things, but once I'd had my boys … well, I knew I had to change. I wanted to be better. Except, it's not that easy, it seems." A definite bitterness flavoured that last sentence. "It follows you everywhere, taints everything you touch. You can never shake it off."

"Does Miss Drayford know about your history?"

"Of course! You think I'd lie to her?" She seemed to realise the irony in that, because she continued swiftly, "It's not even like I could; my record's easy enough to find, with the right contacts. And she knows everything, that one. Leaves no stone unturned."

Did he believe her? Pettifer found he couldn't say. On the one hand, she had a point: Annabel Drayford seemed to make it her business to know everything about everyone who passed through the hallowed walls of her club. But equally, he found it hard to credit that she would hire someone with a criminal record, with her lofty standards. Unless, of course, there was something else; something he wasn't seeing yet.

Molly Dunster obviously read his face, because she flushed defensively.

"Look, I can't say why she chose to go with me. That's her business. But I do wonder sometimes if…" She hesitated. "Well, if she understands. If her life hasn't been as easy as you'd think. You get to recognise one another, when you come from the kind of place I do. Fellow survivors." She gave a faint smile, which almost immediately vanished again. "She's not as bad as everyone makes out, you know. She's always been good to me. This job might not seem much, but compared to some of the things I've had to do… I never thought I'd get to work in a place like this. I pinch myself most days."

"I wonder how *good* she'll be towards you when she finds out you've just become our chief suspect," Pettifer said levelly. "Let's find out, shall we?"

A look of sheer panic crossed Molly Dunster's face. If Pettifer wasn't still so furious about her deception, he'd be feeling sorry for her right now. As it was, his resolve didn't waver.

"Please, no! I *can't* lose this job." She took a shaky breath. "Look, I might not have seen the doctor, but he really *was* there. In his room, alive and well. I heard him." She faltered. "Him and … someone else. That's why I didn't go in. It didn't sound like something I ought to intrude upon. So I just delivered the note and decided to come back later for the turn down, once they'd finished."

"Are you referring to something of a…" Pettifer did his awkward cough, "romantic nature?"

"Not that. An argument." She picked at her nails nervously. "I try to avoid any kind of confrontation these days."

"Who was it?"

"I don't know." When he looked disbelieving, she quailed. "Honestly! I don't. Their voices were too low. I couldn't even

275

tell you if they were a man or a woman. But I can tell you they weren't friendly."

"So you can't be sure that one of them even was the doctor himself? It could have been two completely different people in his room."

"No, it was him. He has … *had* … a distinctive voice. Sort of a deep baritone to it. It carried, even when he was speaking quietly."

"And you weren't worried for him at all? You weren't concerned for his wellbeing?"

"No, I … it's hard to explain, but it wasn't that kind of argument. They didn't sound threatening, more like they were pleading with him."

"And yet, obviously you changed your mind later." Pettifer held her gaze unwaveringly. "When you reported him missing."

She stared at him, slack-jawed. If Pettifer had been of a more showy disposition, he might have taken some pleasure in these moments of showmanship, the rabbit emerging from the proverbial hat as he dragged a deception into the light. Things folk thought they'd hidden so well. As it was, he'd much rather they'd just told him in the first place.

"How did you—"

"Never mind how I know. Just tell me what happened."

"There's really not much more to tell. When I next popped downstairs to refill my trolley, I overheard that he hadn't turned up for the performance. That seemed strange; he never missed it. And I don't know, I suppose that argument was in the back of my mind…"

"The argument that hadn't worried you in the slightest?" Pettifer said dryly.

She gave a conceding grimace.

"All right, so maybe it *had* bothered me more than I'd thought. The person he was with … they'd sounded almost desperate. In my experience, desperation is more dangerous than anger … more dangerous than anything." She seemed to shiver at a memory. "I don't know why I went back up there, exactly. Perhaps I was hoping he'd be there, and I could put it out of my mind. But he wasn't. And then I found the note. It was lying on the bed, already opened, and I read it. I knew then that something was very wrong."

Pettifer got that prickle across the back of his neck. The sense that something important was about to be said next. He tried not to lean forwards too eagerly in his chair.

"As far as I can see, there's nothing in here to cause alarm." He flicked the envelope with the back of his hand. "It seems like a perfectly innocent invitation."

"Yes, but an impossible one." At his quizzical look, she expanded, "For one thing, Miss Drayton would *never* have double booked herself during the performance. Between you and me, I think she felt she needed to keep an eye on it. It can get rather … lively."

"Have you ever taken part?" Jess piped up.

"Oh, God, no. I stay away from it. The whole thing makes my skin crawl." Molly Dunster shook her head, making her fringe dance back and forth in front of her eyes. "But look, you have to understand, that chapel … it's *strictly* out of bounds. None of the staff are allowed to go in there without express permission. And the members are discouraged from even going near it. Miss Drayford has always been most adamant about that. The thing is, Doctor Rauceby fancied himself a bit of a wine buff; he was always trying to wheedle a look in there, but she shut him down every time."

That explained why he would have been so willing to drop everything at the last minute, then, Pettifer mused. Clearly, the note was meant to imply that the manager had changed her mind.

"Do you know why?"

She shrugged her shoulders. Broad, athletic shoulders, he noticed. At odds with the slightness of the rest of her frame. She was stronger than she looked, no doubt honed from years of hard manual labour.

"Insurance? I've heard some of the bottles in there are priceless. Or health and safety, maybe. The place is half falling down."

"So … you were suitably concerned," Pettifer concluded, folding his arms. "Enough so that you decided to alert the police."

"Yes, I…" She looked down, casting her face in deep shadow. "I'm not sure what I thought … that I could prevent something, perhaps."

"Not *so* concerned, however, that you didn't think to save your own skin first."

Her head snapped up.

"That's not fair."

"Isn't it? You very carefully made the call from another room. You made sure you covered your tracks. And you've failed to come forward since, despite the fact that the missing person you were supposedly so worried about turned up dead." Pettifer began to gather up the evidence, shaking his head disgustedly. "You've withheld information. And in doing so you might have helped a murderer go free."

"It wasn't like that." She looked hurt, her voice shimmering with tears. "I just … couldn't afford to get mixed up in this. Not with my record. I just want to be left alone, to get on with my life quietly. Is that really too much to ask?"

Pettifer paused, feeling conflicted. In truth, he could understand why she'd done it. And yet…

"You don't always get to choose what you're mixed up in, Miss Dunster." He stood, nodding to Jess to indicate that she should follow. "None of us do."

If they did, he reflected, his job would certainly be an awful lot quieter.

Chapter Thirty-One

F elicia was unsurprised to find Dexter sitting within the mirrored cavern of the bar, comfortably furnished with a dish of olives and a half-finished martini. He was deep in decidedly un-earnest conversation with Leo, who was in the process of already shaking up another cocktail.

"I sincerely hope that's for me," Felicia said, with an arched brow, sliding onto the neighbouring bar stool. "Although, it should probably be champagne. I've just heard that Sybil is out of the woods. She's going to make a full recovery; they say she could even be up and about tomorrow, if she feels up to it."

Leo gave a relieved exhale.

"Thank God for that. We needed some good news around here tonight."

"Well, I say it's marvellous," Dexter declared, draining his cocktail. "In fact, we should probably have a toast in her honour. To her health."

"Mmm," Felicia said, glancing at him out of the corner of her eye. The question of where he'd been for half the evening – why he hadn't been at dinner with Cassie and Lucia – was on the tip of her tongue, but she resisted asking it. It wasn't her business, she reminded herself coldly. "That's very charitable of you, I'm sure." Then, slowly, a smile stole across her face as a thought occurred to her. "Although, you know, if you *really* want to honour Sybil, it should be with a glass of her favourite liqueur."

Dexter narrowed his eyes at her, and she beamed back innocently.

"That stuff that looks like toilet cleaner?" he muttered, under his breath, "Christ, you can't be—"

But Leo was already reaching for the decanter.

"That's a nice idea. But I hope you're prepared; she's the only person I know who can stomach the stuff. It tastes like potpourri." He smiled fondly as he poured it into a glass and pushed it towards Dexter. "To be honest, we only keep it in for her. I've never known a single other person drink it."

He placed the decanter on the bar, causing the drink inside to swirl and eddy. As it did so, Felicia noticed a fine sprinkling of dust drifting through it and wondered exactly how long the unpopular liqueur had been languishing on the shelf for. If Sybil was really the only person who drank it, it could have been…

Dexter picked up the glass gingerly. The liquid within glowed a radioactive purple under the lights. He grimaced, then visibly braced himself.

"It sounds like down in one's the only way." He raised the glass high. "To you, Sybil. May your taste in drinks improve along with your health." He tilted his head back.

Something was nagging at the edges of Felicia's mind, an

uneasy sense that she'd overlooked something important. What was it, exactly, that Leo had said?

Sybil was the *only* one who ever drank it. *My* violet liqueur, she'd called it earlier tonight, when she'd asked Leo to bring her some. The decanter all but belonged to her. In fact, always in Lavinia's shadow as she'd been, it was potentially the only thing in this place that was hers and hers only. Presumably, that was common knowledge around the club.

Which meant their killer must have known it, too. And if they had…

"Wait!" Felicia's hand shot out and closed over Dexter's, stopping him in his tracks. "Don't drink that!"

He frowned, lowering the glass.

"I'm sure it can't be that bad, Fliss. I've imbibed worse things on my travels for the show. That sheep's brain, for starters…"

"No, it's not…" She prised the glass off him, peering into its ultraviolet depths. "Look; what's that?"

She fetched a long-handled spoon from the bar and fished it out: a slender spine in a deep shade of green.

"It's probably just a lavender leaf or something." Dexter was eyeing her strangely. "Are you feeling quite all right? It's been a long evening. Perhaps I should ask Pettifer about taking you home."

"It's a *violet* liqueur, not lavender," she shot back. "And in any case, that's no lavender leaf. It's far too dark. And look," she turned the napkin this way and that so the leaf caught the light, "see that shine on it? No, this is from an evergreen of some kind." She looked up, a sudden feeling of dread in the pit of her stomach as the realisation finally fell into place. "More than that, I think I know *exactly* where it came from."

"Yew trees?"

Pettifer looked at the gnarled trunk closest to him. It twisted and turned, one branch sagging to the floor, having clearly collapsed under its own weight. And yet, the tree continued to grow, nonetheless. Even with his limited knowledge, he could tell that these were truly ancient specimens.

Felicia nodded. Her face was lit from beneath in the halogen glow of the torch; it cast her skin in a bloodless tint.

Pettifer looked up at the sky. The fog was still dense but beginning to lift, marginally; he could just about see the outline of the moon now, a hazy, shimmering wash beneath a veil of cloud. Then his gaze moved back down to the black tunnel of trees that yawned in front of them. He'd been rather hoping he wouldn't have to come back here; there was something about the place that he found unsettling. And yet, whichever way he turned in this case, all roads seemed to lead him back to this bloody chapel, and the crabbed, hunched silhouettes of these trees, which guarded it from the world.

"You think someone poisoned Sybil Greenlake's liqueur with yew?" he repeated, just to be sure he was understanding correctly. "But that's…" He scrubbed a hand over his head and sighed. "You know, I was about to say crazy, but considering the context of the rest of this case, it's actually not at all." He looked at her resignedly. "What made you think she was poisoned? Everyone else seems convinced it was just a turn."

"Well, I always wondered…" she faltered, then, before she could continue, an eager Jess piped up.

"It makes sense, though, doesn't it? I mean, yews are

famously toxic. It only takes a few leaves to fatally poison someone. And all of these just … sitting here, right within reach. It would be *so* easy for someone to…"

"Would it, though?" Pettifer disliked interrupting her, but he could tell she was beginning to get carried away. She was a good officer but had a romantic side to her; one that tended to overlook the facts when a good story was presented to her. Someone had to be the hardheaded sceptic, and apparently, that task fell to him. "I mean, do *you* think you could drink a mouthful of these…" he plucked a spine from the nearest tree and held it between thumb and forefinger, "without noticing? I know I couldn't."

"Well…" Jess thought for a moment, then deflated. "No. I suppose not."

"Sorry, lass, but I'm just not buying it." Pettifer shrugged his massive shoulders at Felicia. He patted the trunk next to him. "For once, these trees aren't to blame. You know, they get a bad reputation, perhaps unfairly; I can remember my mother religiously sweeping the path each day where one grew over it, terrified that the dogs would eat the berries. Although, funnily enough, I found out years later that they're not even poisonous! Turns out they're the only part of the whole tree that isn't."

"The *flesh* of the berries isn't poisonous," Felicia said quietly. "But what's inside them very much is. Your mother knew what she was doing." She folded her arms across her body and suppressed a shiver. "When I looked in the decanter, there was sediment floating in it; I assumed it was just dust, but now…"

He stared at her.

"You're suggesting that someone *crushed* the berry stones?"

"It's only a theory, but it would be the easiest way to get it past her lips undetected. And the stone is the most toxic part of the whole plant; only a tiny amount would be deadly."

Pettifer blew out his cheeks.

"Except it wasn't, in this case. They miscalculated." And thank God they had, he thought; otherwise it would be another death on their hands.

Felicia was obviously thinking the same thing, because a pained expression settled across her features.

"I felt there was something strange about it all when it happened," she said, her voice barely above a whisper. "The way she looked just before she collapsed; her pupils were dilated... I'd seen it before."

As had he. Pettifer nodded curtly, knowing that neither of them much relished being reminded of that day. The theatre at the Arts Centre, and Caroline Boughton crumpling onto the stage ... Her eyes had taken on that same dilated look, pupils flaring. Except, that time, the consequences had been fatal.

"I wish I'd said something earlier." Felicia's voice shook on the words. "But I second-guessed myself. And now..."

Pettifer, who could immediately see what she was doing, moved swiftly to reassure her.

"It's all right, lass. She's going to be fine. No harm done."

As a policeman, you learned how to cut off the what-ifs and might-have-beens before they took root in your mind. Guilt was a constant companion, but you couldn't let it consume you. He was trained for that, for dealing with it, but he had to remind himself that Felicia wasn't.

"You wouldn't have wanted to cause panic if you weren't sure," Jess added supportively, her eyes soft with understanding.

"It does raise a whole other question though." Pettifer was loathe to point this out, but it had to be done. "Why on earth would *anyone* want to kill Sybil Greenlake? From what I understand, she's a blameless sort of person, liked by everyone."

He posed it casually, but in truth, her attempted murder threw a huge spanner into the works of whatever theories he'd had swirling around. Dr. Rauceby and Lavinia had been difficult, antagonistic people; it had been a tenuous link between them, perhaps, but at least it had been easy to see how they might have made a mortal enemy of someone. Whereas Sybil … she was different.

"She was always suctioned to her sister's side," Jess ventured. "Perhaps whatever got Lavinia killed she also knew about, and the killer needed to ensure her silence."

But Pettifer shook his head.

"If they wanted to kill them both, why not just do it together? They were *both* supposed to be sitting under that chandelier, remember? No. Something about this just isn't adding up."

Felicia seemed to be wavering uncertainly, about to say something. But as she opened her mouth, a ringing sound came from her pocket. She rummaged for the phone, squinting at the bright rectangle of screen.

"It's Cassie. I'll put her on speaker."

"You owe me a very large bar of chocolate," Cassie's voice boomed into the surrounding darkness.

"You've done it?" Felicia asked, scarcely able to believe it. Even with her friend's talents, that was prodigiously fast.

"Of course I've bloody done it. It wasn't even that hard. All the banging on about secrecy and discretion in this place is a load of old cobblers; I've never met such a bunch of leaky sieves. They couldn't wait to snitch on each other."

"What exactly is she talking about?" Pettifer was giving Felicia a suspicious look, but she waved him away, straining to hear Cassie's voice above the quickening breeze.

"You wanted someone who had an issue with both Lavinia *and* Annabel?" Cassie was saying. "Well, I've got them for you. Someone who, by the sounds of things, had a very good reason for wanting them both out of the way."

Chapter Thirty-Two

This time, Pettifer didn't waste time with the delicate approach. He had a feeling the person sitting opposite him was a lot tougher than they liked to make out.

"Were you aware that Lavinia Greenlake was vying to have you kicked out of this place?"

Cymbeline Johnson winced, arranging the floating layers of her scarf around her shoulders.

"Rather a *vulgar* way of putting it, Sergeant, but I suppose there's little call for poetic prose in your line of work." She sighed. "Well, I suppose it was always going to get around. Apparently, even murder isn't enough to stop the gossip mill in this place. Although you'd think people would have better things to think about tonight."

He'd take that as a yes, Pettifer decided.

"That must have been very aggravating for you," he observed.

She waved the idea away as though it were a cobweb floating in the air.

"Oh, not at all. I mean, yes, she was being a *teensy* bit meddlesome. Trying to suggest to Miss Drayford that I'm not a suitable type to have here at The Aquitaine." She muttered something that sounded decidedly like, "Not stuffy enough," but hastily followed it with a beatific smile. "But you see, when one is a *free* spirit like myself, one can't expect to be everyone's cup of tea – or gin sling, as might be more appropriate in my case." Her eyes twinkled mischievously. "Honestly, I've long since learned not to care what people think of me. I've had to, as a prominent actress. You couldn't *imagine* the things the fans get into their heads; once, my character, Cordelia Montrix Le Bleu, pushed her sister down the stairs in a fit of pique… Well, the letters I got afterwards! *Death* threats." Her voice quivered dramatically, and she put a beautiful, long-fingered hand to her chest. "They really thought *I* was *her*. They blamed *me*." The hand moved to her forehead, violet eyes fluttering closed. "After years of that, it's just become water off a duck's back. Easy come, easy go these days for me."

"Except it wasn't just talk." Pettifer, who was beginning to find her theatrics rather irritating, said bluntly. "She was actually *doing* something about it. Something that would have been very problematic for you if she'd succeeded."

The lovely face hardened, the dreamy vagueness gone in an instant. Cymbeline Johnson, Pettifer thought in that moment, was perhaps a better actress than people gave her credit for.

"You're not going to give up, are you? You're just going to keep probing away, asking your nasty little questions, insinuating things, until you get what you want. So yes, all *right*." She drew herself up. "The old bag had only gone and pulled rank on me. You wouldn't think that was possible, in this day and age, but here … well, it's all about hierarchy, even amongst the guests. Florian and I are relative newcomers, whereas she's been a member for yonks. So when push came to shove, her or us…" She shrugged, but it didn't look very nonchalant. "That was that. We were out. Given our marching orders."

"Miss Drayford told you that?"

"Well, no. She hadn't spoken to me yet. But she was going to; Lavinia made that *quite* clear." Her eyes glittered bitterly. "You should have seen her earlier this evening; she was insufferably smug about the whole thing."

"So, this would have been your last stay at The Aquitaine, then?"

"If she'd lived, you mean?" At the surprised expression on Pettifer's face, she rolled her eyes. "Well, come on, that *is* what you were implying, isn't it? That I bumped off the old carbuncle to keep my membership here?" When Pettifer didn't reply immediately, she gave a sudden hoot of laughter, making Jess, who'd been silently taking notes, jump in her seat. "I'm right, aren't I? Oh, that's simply *too* much!" She wiped tears from her eyes, spluttering, "I tell you, Sergeant, you should go on the stage; you're wasted in the dreary old police."

"I doubt the costumes would fit me," he replied flintily. Jess was looking extremely diverted by the idea. This, Pettifer decided darkly, was quite securely his *least* favourite interview so far. "And please, do tell me what's so entertaining about the suggestion. It's what in my trade we'd call a solid motive."

She continued to laugh, unmoved by the warning in his voice.

"But … it's fantastical! No-one would commit murder for such a ridiculous reason. No, Sergeant, you *must* be having me on."

"You'd be surprised what people would kill for," he said mildly. But that wasn't uncommon, he added silently. In fact, most would. What you learned in his job, above all, is that nobody was as many steps away from becoming a murderer as they might like to think. "And in this case, I don't think it is such a ridiculous reason. Certainly not to you. In fact, I think that to *you*, the prospect of losing your membership here ... it was deadly serious."

The laughter stopped. She looked at him with a kind of fear in her eyes.

"I ... don't know what you're talking about."

Pettifer abruptly retracted his earlier statement about her being a better actress than advertised. His children could do a better deflection than that.

He sat back in his chair, gestured expansively around the room.

"What do you think, Constable?" Jess, surprised at being addressed, promptly sat to attention as Pettifer continued languidly. "Is this the sort of place an avant-garde, free-spirited lady would naturally choose to stay, in your opinion?"

Jess looked around her, then said slowly:

"No, sir, I don't, now you mention it."

"Old-fashioned, hierarchical, regimented, all these obscure little rules and regulations to follow..." He pointed to Cymbeline now, including her in the conversation. "Ms. Johnson here used an excellent word earlier to describe it. What was it, now?"

"Stuffy," Jess supplied obligingly, ever quick to catch a cue. "It was stuffy, sir." She tapped her notes. "I have it written right here."

Cymbeline flushed a fetching peony pink.

"That was *not* part of the official interview," she said stiffly. "I want that struck from the record."

Pettifer pretended not to hear her. Instead, he carried on thoughtfully, "And yet, despite that, you desperately wanted to get into this place. We've been having a browse through the file they keep on you here … it makes for very interesting reading. It seems you were actually *rejected* for membership several times. You were very persistent, it seems."

Jess raised a fair eyebrow.

"Not exactly easy come, easy go, then?"

"It would appear not, Constable. In fact," he leaned in, as though holding a private conversation with Jess, although keeping his voice loud, "rumour has it she only got in eventually because a certain high-profile gentleman put in a word for her."

Jess's eyes widened in mock surprise.

"That was lucky for her, sir."

"Well, it probably helped that she was having an affair with him at the time, according to the society papers."

"That's *enough*, thank you," Cymbeline snapped. "You can stop the double-act now. You've made your point." She sniffed, looking misty eyed. "He was actually a surprisingly athletic lover, given his age. I find myself rather missing him, funnily enough."

Pettifer was looking slightly queasy, so Jess stepped in.

"And yet you were the one who ended the affair, if rumour is to be believed … conveniently enough, just after you finally secured membership here. I wonder how he took that."

"We parted on excellent terms, I'll have you know," Cymbeline retorted. "Unfortunately, he died earlier this month. And of course, Lavinia saw her opportunity to swoop in;

didn't waste any time. She's been wanting me out for ages, but as long as he was around to support me... He was higher up in the pecking order than she was, so to speak." She hugged her arms around her willowy form, looking around her in distaste. "You're right, this place – this sort of thing – it makes my skin crawl, to be honest. I feel like I need a week in Bali to decompress after I've been here."

"Then why come?" Pettifer pressed. "I still don't understand."

"Because I am a *mother*, Sergeant. And I would do anything for my son." She sighed. "Florian takes after his father, I'm afraid; he's very insular. He doesn't *do* well in the world. But he has his art, and in that, he finds his solace. But what many don't grasp is that he's not just any artist; what he does is decidedly niche. He's a fresco painter, prodigiously talented when it comes to historical designs. He can recreate medieval church paintings, imitate marble or wood on walls ... his *trompe l'oeil* is simply stunning. It has to be seen to be believed. But he can't just dash something off on a canvas and sell it; he needs *commissions*. And the only people who have any call for his sort of work are those in stately homes. Ancient families. I might have a few connections left in showbusiness, but they're no good in this case. What's required is old money, old *class*. And despite how I might seem ... well, I grew up above a fish shop; this accent was learned from enunciation tapes. Cymbeline isn't even my real name." She looked nervous. "Although, please don't tell anyone about that."

Pettifer, who didn't think anyone had ever laboured under that misapprehension, simply nodded stonily, encouraging her to continue.

"A place like this ... well, it can bridge the gap. If you're in here, you're seen as 'all right' – so to speak. Suddenly, no-one's asking any more tricky questions about where exactly one might have come from, or who one's parents are. Look at that Spencer Torrent; frightfully vulgar chap. Very *nouveau*, if you catch my meaning. Even I think so, I'm a live and let live sort. Most people here would look down their noses at him if they met him anywhere else, but because he's *here*…"

"He's *all right*?"

"Magically so." She clicked her fingers.

A thought occurred to Pettifer.

"I don't suppose Lavinia liked his presence, much, either?"

"Oh gosh, no, she *hated* him," Cymbeline replied, with relish. "It's the only reason I can bear him, truthfully; knowing how much his being here irked *her*."

"Do you think she would ever have—"

"Given him the boot like me?" Cymbeline suggested archly. "I'm sure she would have *loved* to. But even *she* never dared try it with him. He's got friends in some *very* high places. Rumour has it he's managed racehorses for several European royals." The edges of her lips turned downwards sourly. "I don't expect *he* ever had to scrape and beg to get into this place. Sometimes life can be *so* demeaning." Her face softened. "But I'd do it again for my darling boy. And at least it's been worth it. Of course, one has to take one's time, build relationships a little … one doesn't wish to be seen as an *opportunist*… But doors are opening, certainly."

"Doors that presumably would politely but firmly close again should it become common knowledge that you'd been thrown out of here?"

She looked startled by the suggestion.

"Well, I mean … it would have been *delicate* to navigate, I'll admit." She tossed her scarf over her shoulder, tilting her chin. "But I'm an actress, Sergeant. My *life* is a stage. If anyone could bluff their way through it, it'd be me." When Pettifer didn't look convinced, she added, more firmly, "I *would* have found a way. Without the need to resort to anything drastic, I might add."

"Except, luckily for you, Ms. Johnson," Pettifer said, in a quiet voice, his gaze meeting hers, "now you'll never have to, will you?"

Chapter Thirty-Three

Felicia was on the verge of giving up.

She'd been all over the club, into every room she could access. She'd been upstairs, downstairs, out into the gardens. She'd even ventured as close to the chapel as she dared, although she'd drawn the line at going inside. In any event, she told herself, Jack wasn't exactly going to be hanging around in there, was he? Not with the doctor's body still sprawled across the cold stone floor, awaiting what seemed to be the county's least-responsive forensics team. Now, in her desperation, she was beginning to wonder if she shouldn't have checked after all. Because he certainly didn't appear to be anywhere else. Like the ghosts that were so often reputed to roam old buildings such as this one, he appeared to move around silently, be seen by no-one, leave no trace. The obvious answer, of course, was that he wasn't here at all, but she knew Jack Riding too well for that. He'd clearly planned to be here tonight, so here he would be.

"Where the *hell* are you, Jack?" she muttered to herself,

nudging a red ball across the green baize surface of the billiard table with her finger.

"I would be flattered you're looking for me," a voice came from the doorway, "but judging by that expletive before my name, something gives me the impression I shouldn't be."

She looked up, annoyed when her breath caught treacherously. It made her next words rather sharper than perhaps they needed to be.

"Where have you been? You *do* know there have been two murders and a poisoning here tonight?"

He picked up a cue, not seeming ruffled by her question.

"I gathered as much when I got here."

She felt a bolt of confusion.

"You … haven't been here all evening, then?"

"No." Leaning across the billiard table, he lined up a shot. The overhead lights lit his blond hair, turning it a rich gold, which Felicia tried not to find hopelessly distracting. "My last job overran, unfortunately. I only arrived about half an hour ago. Unfortunately, by then the place was crawling with police."

"I hardly think Pettifer and Constable Winters can constitute 'crawling'," Felicia said dryly. But inside, she felt a faint stir of hope; if Jack hadn't been here for most of the evening … that meant that Pettifer couldn't suspect him of anything, surely? Despite herself, despite how conflicted her feelings were for him these days, she still felt the need to defend him.

"Even so, I didn't fancy being spotted by them," Jack replied, neatly potting the ball. "You know what tends to happen every time I'm in the vicinity of a crime. I've spent quite enough of my life already in that police station."

She knew the bland carelessness in his voice was put on, but still it put her back up to hear it, especially in the context of the terrible crimes that had been taking place that night.

"And yet, you're still here," she said, acidly. "Why don't you leave? Slip away from trouble again; you're *so* good at that."

He didn't rise to the barb, which just made her even more irritated. Sometimes, she wondered if anything affected him at all.

"I came here tonight with a job to do," he replied simply. "I intend to see it through."

Now they were getting somewhere, she thought. The truth, which she would rather not admit, was that she hadn't really come looking for him tonight to protect him from the police investigation. She'd come because she wanted answers of her own.

"Work?" she said archly. "I hear you've been quite the prima donna over this commission."

He missed the next shot, biting off a muffled curse.

"Ah. You've heard about that, then?"

He did at least sound faintly rattled now. Felicia felt a flush of satisfaction; she doubled down.

"I have, and I don't buy it for a second. Neither does Pettifer, incidentally; he suspects you of having an ulterior motive for wanting to come back here tonight."

She'd fired her cannonball; now, she waited for it to hit its mark. But to her surprise, Jack replied calmly.

"Finally, the man's right about something. I'm astonished."

Felicia was taken aback.

"*What* did you say?"

"I said he's right. I do have an ulterior motive." He put down the cue, folding his arms. "But then, so have you."

And just like that, Felicia felt the balance of the conversation shift. First, she'd been on the attack; now, it appeared, she was going to have to defend herself.

"I don't…" she began, but he shook his head.

"Seriously, Felicia, don't bother. You're a terrible liar, anyway." He glared at her. "You want to know why I'm here? Because *I* heard *you* were going to be back here tonight. I *knew* something was going on with you yesterday. I *warned* you to leave it. And now … well, I was right, wasn't I?" He gestured towards the club beyond the door. "Here you are, surrounded by dead bodies again."

He looked at her as though it were somehow her fault.

"So you're … what? Keeping an eye on me? Is that it?" The thought was as humiliating as it was enraging. "And don't you *dare* pivot this onto me." She met his gaze uncompromisingly. "What are you really here for, Jack? The truth this time."

"I told you…"

"I don't mean tonight. I mean this whole commission of yours. It's clearly a cover for something; everybody knows The Aquitaine *doesn't* advertise. They don't need marketing shots. What are you involved in, Jack?"

He'd gone very still. The muscles in his face barely moved as he spoke.

"It's not true that they don't advertise. They just do it very discreetly. They send out feelers to people who … interest them, I suppose is the best way to put it. People who they want here. And this new manager seems to have some pretty big ideas; she wants to attract a fresh class of members. Shake things up. That's why she hired me; she wanted some more

299

modern-looking shots for the promotional material." He'd said all of this expressionlessly, though his eyes flashed as he added, "But it's good to know that your opinion of me is about in line with everyone else's now. I thought you … that we…" Suddenly, he gave way to motion, rumpling his hair agitatedly. "Christ, I feel like such a fool now. You know, when I saw you yesterday, I was so … I haven't seen you in so long…"

"You come into the office every month," she pointed out shortly. "You've seen me plenty."

"I've seen the back of your head or the heel of your shoe as you disappear around a corner. It's not quite the same thing." He took a sharp intake of breath. "I'm used to people avoiding me, Felicia. I know what it looks like. But I didn't expect it from you." The look in his eyes was devastating; Felicia felt her throat tighten. "I thought you knew me better than that."

"I don't know you!" she all but exploded, pushed to the limit. "How can I? You won't let *anyone* know you. I can't allow myself to have feelings for…" She broke off, horrified at what she'd so nearly confessed to. Something she hadn't even acknowledged in her own mind. Not since that midsummer day in his garden, when she'd been forced to realise that any potential between them could never blossom.

He'd had evidence in a quadruple murder case that he'd chosen not to come forward with; as if that hadn't been bad enough, he'd then tried to stop her from reporting it to Pettifer. His defence at the time had been that it wouldn't have made any difference to the outcome, and truthfully, he'd probably been right about that. But it hadn't been the point; Felicia felt that as strongly now as she had then. The admission had been the last straw in her already shaky trust in his sense of morality, confirming her long-standing sense of uncertainty about exactly where his loyalties lay.

"After everything that's happened since I moved home to Stamford," she said, in a low, controlled voice, "After all the terrible things I've seen, the danger I've been in … I need to know I'm with people I can rely on. There's no room in my life for somebody who's always just watching their *own damned back*."

She'd thrown his own words at him, and he obviously recognised it, because his golden gaze darkened.

Just then, a shriek tore the air, wild and desperate. Felicia's eyes clashed with Jack's, and automatically, they both began to run in the direction it had come from.

They didn't have to go far. As they rounded the bannister at the bottom of the main staircase, a heart-stopping sight greeted them. Aurelia was lying on the pale blue carpet, her fair hair fanned out around her bloodless face. A dark red stain was leaching into the pile around her head. Over her stood a trembling figure.

"*Lucia,*" Felicia gasped. "What on earth…"

Jack was already crouched down beside Aurelia's still form, his fingers pressing to the inside of her wrist.

"She's alive," he said. "Just unconscious."

"Lucia." Felicia grasped the other woman by the shoulders. "What happened?"

Lucia just moaned.

Suddenly, Felicia became aware of heavy footsteps approaching at speed. Only one person she knew could make that much cacophony whilst running; her gaze met Jack's, and understanding passed between them. She was giving him permission to leave, before the police turned up and saw him leaning over a body.

But he didn't act as she expected. He didn't move. Instead, he turned his attention back to Aurelia, placing one hand on either side of her head to keep it stable.

Pettifer appeared on the scene, followed closely by a worried-looking Jess.

"What the bloody hell's going on—" He broke off as he took in the tableau before him, his expression hardening as he saw Jack.

"Everybody move, please," Annabel Drayford's authoritative tone sliced through the air, as she strode into their midst. "My staff are qualified first-aiders; they need space to tend to Aurelia."

Jack stood aside as the wheels of efficiency got to work. Pettifer, clearly satisfied that the girl was no longer in immediate danger, turned a glowering face upon Felicia.

"We heard Lucia scream," Felicia felt she ought to explain.

"*We?*" Pettifer's eyes moved disapprovingly between her and Jack. "You two were … *together*, then?"

Felicia immediately felt as though she were fourteen years old again and had been caught with a boy behind the bike sheds. Reminding herself that she was, in fact, forty, and that Pettifer wasn't the school headmaster, she squared her shoulders.

"Yes, we were." She met his gaze challengingly. "But we arrived too late to see what happened. And I can't get any sense out of Lucia."

"I saw him," Lucia gasped. "He did it. I *saw* him."

"Who, Mrs DuFontaine?"

"One of those dreadful Mummers." Stricken, she pointed a

shaking finger towards the staircase. "He ran up there when he saw me. Oh, I've never been so terrified in my *life*…"

She swooned towards Pettifer's broad chest, only to find thin air. He'd already spun around and was charging up the stairs in Jess's wake.

Felicia turned to Jack, who was running a hand through his tousled curls.

"You stayed," she whispered dazedly. Her head was reeling, trying to understand. She'd given him the perfect chance to slip away, and yet … he hadn't taken it.

He shook his head, his gaze flicking concernedly towards Aurelia, who was being carefully tended to. She still hadn't come around.

And suddenly, the enormity of what he'd done hit Felicia square in the chest.

He *hadn't* run. Even though he knew what it would look like to the police, him crouching over Aurelia's prone body like that. Even though he really couldn't afford another strike on his record; he'd escaped prison once, he might not be so lucky again. They both knew that. And yet, when it had truly mattered, he hadn't cared about himself, or his own fate.

She looked up, to find he was watching her uncertainly, clearly trying to work out what she was thinking. From here, she could see the bronze flecks in his irises, the faint shadow of stubble around his jawline.

And then, before she could stop to think better of it, she leaned in and kissed him.

It wasn't the first time their lips had met. Although the last time had been accidental; this was completely different. It was reckless, she thought wildly, but that didn't mean it was any less intentional. Or any less right.

Because she was astonished at how right it *did* feel, as her body melted against his. He'd tensed briefly at first, stunned at the unexpectedness at it, but then immediately his arms had gone around her, pulling her closer, deepening the kiss...

"*Felicia!*"

Felicia started at the shrill squeak, pulling away to see Lucia staring at her, bug-eyed and slack-jawed. The expression was so delightfully unbecoming, and so far from her schoolmate's usual elegant mien, that Felicia rather wished she could bottle it.

"Yes, Lucia?" she said serenely, still wrapped in Jack's arms. "Can I help you with something?"

"What are you *doing*?" Lucia's eyes were darting between Felicia and Jack.

"I'd have thought that was somewhat self-explanatory," Felicia replied levelly. "But if you like, we can show you again." She leaned towards Jack once more.

"This place is a madhouse!" Lucia shrieked, throwing up her hands. "It's sent everyone doolally. Why on *earth* didn't I just go to The George?" She spun on her vertiginous heel. "I'm off to the bar. Getting sloshed's the only way I'm making it through this with my own sanity intact."

As she made to stalk away, there was a clink. She looked down; the pointed toe of her shoe had caught on something in the carpet.

"Why, it's a *watch*." She bent to retrieve it. "What's this doing here?"

"It could be Aurelia's?" Felicia disentangled herself from Jack to get a closer look. But immediately, she could see that she'd been wrong. The watch was clearly a man's, with a chrome case and battered leather strap.

"I can't imagine it would belong to *anyone* here." Lucia handed it over to her. "It's rather a shabby thing."

Felicia looked at the watch in her palm. And felt a strange tingling sensation in her chest as things began to come into focus, to form a clear picture, where before there had only been a blurred image.

"Looks can be deceptive, Lucia. It's worth more than you'd think."

Because this wasn't just any watch, Felicia thought, as her finger traced the tiny arrow symbol on its face. The same symbol she'd seen once before, glinting at her across the tea table.

She turned to Jack apologetically, but he got there before her, holding up his hands with one of his half-smiles.

"I know that look; you have to go. I can't possibly hope to compete with murder." He said it flatly, but his eyes were amused. "I know my place."

She stretched up on tiptoes and pressed a quick, feather-light kiss on his cheek.

"All right, but this isn't finished," she promised. "More like … paused."

Then she turned and ran for the staircase.

Chapter Thirty-Four

Jess took the stairs three at a time, leaving Pettifer far below her as she burst onto the landing just in time to catch a glimpse of trailing straw flapping round the corner. Once, the sight would have completely bemused her; now, it brought a smile of grim satisfaction to her lips.

"Got you," she muttered, urging her legs to go even faster. Coming upstairs had been a mistake in itself; now, if her memory of this place was sound, her foe was about to make an even bigger one. One that would end this for good.

She skidded round the corner, the breath whistling from her lips in a triumphant hiss as she saw that she'd been right. It was a dead end, usually populated by a solitary, life-sized urn … and now also a bizarrely costumed figure, head swivelling in visible panic as it dawned on them that they were trapped.

"All right." Jess pressed her hand against the wall, gulping for air. "Come on. It's over. There's nowhere left to go."

The figure froze. Just for a moment.

Then they reached for the window, hefting their shoulder into the frame to slide up the heavy sash. With a creak of ropes, the pane shifted, a slap of cold air whistling into the corridor. They turned to look back over their shoulder at Jess, uncertainty etched into their body language.

Jess put her hands on her hips, giving them her sternest look.

"Now you're just being ridiculous. There's no way—"

But she never got any further. With a sudden burst of decisiveness, the figure whirled back to the window and leapt through the opening into the night.

Jess bit off a curse, rushing over just in time to hear a cacophony of clattering tiles as her quarry slid down the roof.

"Christ alive," she muttered, not sure whether to be impressed or annoyed at such recklessness. "They're going to get themselves killed at this rate."

Her booted foot was already up on the sill, arms braced to heave herself through in pursuit … when suddenly, she was yanked roughly backwards by a powerful force.

"What the *hell* do you think you're doing?"

Jess looked up into her superior officer's furious visage, and tried not to quail.

"But, sir…" she protested, albeit weakly, as Pettifer looked ready to spontaneously combust, "he's getting away!"

"Then let him." Pettifer's response was brusque. "He's not worth risking my best officer's neck over."

The figure had tumbled down the slope of the roof and was scrabbling wildly at the guttering. With a yelp, they disappeared from sight over the edge. The sound of breaking branches came next, followed by an ominous, sickening thud. Then silence.

Both officers immediately leaned out of the window, straining their eyes in the darkness.

"I can't see him," Jess said, her voice rising anxiously. "You don't think—"

Then, without warning, a shadow staggered into view, beating a hasty retreat across the courtyard. It was moving awkwardly, dragging its leg behind it. Injured, but not as she'd feared. Not worse. Jess knew she should have felt relieved, but instead, the dominant feeling flooding her body was something else. Something that made tears sting at her eyes, to her horror.

"That was our chance." She could hear the bitterness in her own voice. She wiped at her eyes, hating her emotion, how easily it rose to the surface. "He won't be back; now we have no way of finding out who he is."

"Or maybe we do."

Jess and Pettifer spun to see Felicia hovering behind them. In her hand, she was holding a watch.

"We'll have to be quick, though," she continued. "Is your car nearby?"

"Just outside."

"Good. Then we might just get there in time."

"Hang on a minute," Pettifer thundered, as Felicia tripped away down the stairs. "Get *where*?"

"Absolutely no idea," she trilled back over her shoulder. "*Yet*. That's why we need to make a quick stop-off at Annabel Drayford's office first. Come on, both of you. There's no time to lose. Questions on the way!"

"She does know those are supposed to be *my* lines?" Pettifer grumbled as an aside to Jess. But nonetheless, he obeyed, and swiftly at that. He'd known Felicia Grant too long to hesitate when she had that light in her eyes.

———————

The Mummer stumbled through the silent streets of Stamford, their leg blazing in agony with every laboured step. The hem of their straw cape dragged along the ground, making a rasping, scraping sound on the cobblestones.

Not far to go now. They urged themselves onwards, keeping as close as they could to the shadows, staying away from the illumination of the streetlamps. They could only pray that no-one would be looking out of their windows at this hour; although given that it was still technically Halloween night, perhaps they would think little of it if they did. Just another costumed reveller weaving unsteadily home from the night's festivities. Why would they think otherwise? Who among even the most imaginative of onlookers would envisage anything even *close* to the truth?

The whole thing felt unreal, even now. It had got so out of hand, so quickly…

And now the only thing to do was run. Run and hide.

They reached the unobtrusive opening that led onto the lane, their breath coming in ragged gasps now, their vision beginning to blur at the edges from a pain so searing it no longer seemed to be confined to their leg, but instead was somehow everywhere, suffusing every cell. With trembling fingers, they unlatched the wrought-iron gate and staggered down the garden path.

Safe, they were safe. Or at least, almost.

They slipped into the darkened house, looking left and right. Then, reluctantly, their gaze moved to the stairs.

Gritting their teeth, they began the ascent. It took all of their strength not to cry out in pain as their leg gave way beneath them and they collapsed to one side with a thud. They froze, heart pounding, listening for any sound, and sign that they'd been heard. But there was nothing. They continued, crawling now. The much-hated costume dragged at them, almost as though it was trying to pull them backwards. With renewed strength, they forced themselves on. Just a few more steps now…

At last, they reached the safety of their bedroom, and they flung themselves inside. A small movement caught their eye, and they started, but it was only a cat's face, peeking warily out at them around the doorjamb. Belatedly, they remembered their unrecognisable appearance and they ripped off the cape savagely, sending straw fluttering through the air. They yanked off the wooden mask, too, gratefully gulping in a lungful of fresh air. The cat immediately relaxed, padding lightly towards them to wind itself lovingly around their legs. They reached down to stroke it, relishing the small feeling of normality. Maybe it really *would* all be all right. Maybe someday, this would all just be a dim memory, so vague and unbelievable that they could convince themselves they'd dreamed it all.

There was just one thing left to do first. They looked at the crumpled remains of their costume, knowing they had to get rid of it. Tonight. Erase all trace. Once that was done … they would be free.

"You'll have to burn it," a voice came quietly from the shadows. "It's the only sure way."

The Mummer gasped. They spun around. The darkness moulded itself into the shape of two figures, seated on the bed. Watching them.

The wooden mask slipped from their fingers, clattering to the floor. It spun for a moment, then settled against the wardrobe, empty eye sockets staring blankly out of the window at Stamford's fogbound skyline.

Annabel Drayford shut the door of her office behind her and leaned back against the polished wooden panel, closing her eyes with a deep exhale. She glanced at the carriage clock on the desk; a quarter to eleven. God, but it had been a *long* night. And it wasn't even half over yet.

The police had just been in here, asking her for an address. They hadn't given any details, but judging by the urgency in their tone, and the way they'd hared off afterwards, she could only assume they'd caught the killer at last. She knew that what she ought to be feeling now was an overwhelming sense of relief that this whole nightmare was over. And yet, for her, the work was only just beginning. There would have to be a cover-up, of course. They couldn't risk any of this getting out. More lies, more deception. She felt jaded just at the thought of it.

She massaged the back of her neck, turning it this way and that. Her eyes alighted on the pigeonholes, reminding her of the missive still awaiting her attention. For the first time since she'd taken this position, she felt a surge of resentment at what she was expected to do. After tonight, she'd had her fill of secrets.

She stalked over to the sideboard, unstopping the crystal decanter that was kept there for guests. She poured the tawny liquid into a glass and tossed it back, unable to suppress a shudder as it hit the back of her throat.

Sherry. She bloody *hated* sherry. Why was it even in her office?

The answer came immediately. Because it had been here before her, like everything else in here. Because it wasn't really *her* office at all, but a time capsule, a shrine to a past that ought to have been long consigned to the history books.

Her eyes roamed around the small room, taking in the leatherbound volumes, the antique globe, the heavy curtains. If she left now, there wouldn't be a single indicator that she'd even been here. She'd leave no mark, like so many others before her.

And suddenly she realised how naïve she'd been. All her efforts, all her dreams of putting her stamp on The Aquitaine, of bringing the club into a new phase … none of it had made any difference, had it? This place had still won in the end. It was always going to win. She'd only ever been a puppet, dangling in the air, arms and legs whirling but going nowhere.

She should leave, she decided. Walk away. But would they even let her? She knew better than anyone that once you'd become part of this place, you were never really free again.

She poured herself another sherry, banging the decanter down on the sideboard. To her horror, tears of bitterness and disillusionment were stinging the backs of her eyes. She hadn't cried in over a decade. She took a gulping breath, trying to steady herself, turning away from the sight of the hateful pigeonholes. Then she saw something that abruptly swept everything else out of her mind.

There was an object sitting in the middle of her desk. A pumpkin.

With a frown of perplexity, she moved closer. There was a note, propped against it. She unfolded it and a match rolled into her hand. Her eyes moved over the words, and for the first time all day, a genuine smile tilted the corners of her lips.

She looked at the pumpkin. It leered back at her, its carved mouth and eyeholes empty. Suddenly, a sense of defiance bubbled up inside her. She struck the match, raising the glass in her other hand in a spontaneous toast.

"Happy *bloody* Halloween," she declared, to the empty room. "May the spirits all bugger off back to where they came from."

She lowered the flame into the middle of the pumpkin, touching it to the candle wick.

She didn't even get the chance to realise something was wrong. There was a deafening bang, a blinding flash ... and in the space of a moment, Annabel Drayford's world was on fire.

Chapter Thirty-Five

"**S**it down, lad." Pettifer indicated the desk chair with a cordial sweep of the hand. "That leg must be killing you."

The boy looked at the chair, visibly swallowing as he observed that it had already been moved into a position to face the bed. Friendly as the policeman might sound, this was very much an interview set-up. But then a spasm of pain crossed his face, and he did as suggested, collapsing into the seat with a groan of relief.

"How did you know?" he asked flatly, levering his injured leg gingerly into position.

Pettifer shook his head, jabbing a thumb at Felicia, who was sitting quietly next to him.

"Not me, lad. Her. She recognised you. Don't ask me how."

Felicia held up the watch by its leather strap.

The boy lifted his wrist, eyes widening as he saw it bare.

"An Omega pilot's watch," Felicia said. They were very collectable. And easily identifiable by the Broad Arrow symbol on the dial. "You were wearing it yesterday, when you served my friend and I at tea."

She hadn't known his name then. But she did now; she'd seen it, crossed through on the rotas Pettifer had shown her. Cancelled out by the ruthless hand of Annabel Drayford.

Arthur Talbot. Rather a noble name, Felicia thought now, for the shivering, pathetic figure before them. He was barely more than a boy.

He looked fondly at the watch.

"I never take it off. It's very precious to me. It's been in my family since the war; my father passed it down to me on my eighteenth birthday." He dropped his head into his hands with a groan. "Oh God, my *parents*. If they knew what I've done … they're so proud of me. I can't bear the thought of letting them down."

"What *have* you done, exactly, Arthur?" Pettifer's gaze bore into him. The boy blanched.

"I didn't mean … look, none of it was supposed to *happen*. I didn't plan any of it."

"We know," Felicia said, ignoring Pettifer's glance of surprise. She indicated the heap on the floor. "That was never your costume, was it?" Her voice was soft, understanding. The lad's eyes shifted to her, his shoulders dropping in relief.

"So you *do* see. Thank God for that." He appeared almost pathetically grateful. "No, I wasn't selected to be a Mummer. Not that I was surprised. Miss Drayford never liked me much; she was always picking on me, finding something unsatisfactory in my work." He fiddled with a piece of straw that had landed on the chair, looking unhappy. "I tried, I *really* did. And it wasn't that I was stupid, or clumsy; I just get nervous sometimes, that's all."

"And she wasn't understanding of that?"

"She wasn't understanding of *anything*!" He spoke with sudden force, his eyes flashing, the straw ripping between his fingers. "You know that when my grandfather died last month, she wouldn't even let me swap my shift that evening? Even though I offered to organise it with one of the others myself so they wouldn't be short. It was like she…" He clenched his fists. "Like because *she* doesn't seem to have any feelings, or anyone who cares about her, no-one else is allowed to, either. I know I shouldn't say that, but…"

"She certainly didn't treat you very humanely earlier tonight," Pettifer agreed.

Wherever Felicia was going with this, he was prepared to follow along. "Sacking you on the spot like that, for a minor mistake. You must have felt it very unfair."

Felicia shifted in her seat, looking uncomfortable. Pettifer eyed her quizzically, but swiftly returned his attention to the lad in front of him.

"That's an understatement," came the bitter response.

"I presume your fellow staff members thought so, too? That's why they agreed to let you be part of the performance in secret?"

"I think they felt sorry for me, yes," he said, a little stiffly. "But you know, it was good of them. They were putting their own necks on the line if Miss Drayford had found out. And the extra cash … well, I couldn't afford to be too proud about it."

"Except you didn't stay for the money, did you?" Pettifer leaned in, his expression intensifying. "You slipped away from the show halfway through. *Why*?"

For a moment, he was afraid he'd been too blunt, but the

answer came readily, almost in a rush, as though the lad was relieved to have it out in the open.

"I didn't plan to do that. But I was feeling … emboldened. That's the best word. It's hard to explain, but there's something about being in that performance … about being a Mummer…" His eyes glazed. "I can see why people got a kick out of it, back then. You get this sense of power … taking money off the people you're usually bowing and scraping to, playing a joke on them, knowing you're scaring them…"

He seemed to come to with a shiver. "It sort of goes to your head, I suppose. That and the mead – I don't drink often, you see – it gave me a rush of confidence. False confidence, really. It was stupid, but I got the idea that I could confront Miss Drayford. Tell her exactly what I thought of her. After all, I had nothing to lose anymore, did I? So when she slipped out, I followed her." He hung his head. "I'm not proud of it. Fortunately, nothing came of it. When I found her, she was with him, and…" He screwed up his face at the memory.

Pettifer felt the hairs on his neck rise up. He looked at Felicia, and she was sitting forwards on the bed, her relaxed posture now alert.

"She's involved with someone?" He spoke urgently. "Someone here?"

Arthur blanched.

"I didn't mean to … look, it's none of my business … I mean, I can't say I *understand* it…"

"Who?" Pettifer boomed, standing up to loom over the lad, who shrank away.

"I can't … he's always been so nice to me. Heck, *he* was the one who suggested that I do the—"

Arthur clapped a hand over his mouth, looking horrified.

"The Mummer's performance," Felicia finished quietly. "It was Leo's costume, wasn't it?" A throwaway remark from earlier in the evening came back to her: Cymbeline had been surprised to see the barman amongst them. Because, presumably, she'd known he ought to be mysteriously absent. "You took his place."

At last, the boy let his hand drop from his mouth.

"Yes." The reply was resigned, more of a sigh than an actual word. He swallowed nervously. "Look, *please* forget I said anything. I'm sure he had nothing to do with … he's a good guy. I don't want to get him in any trouble." He looked thoroughly wretched. "God, this is *impossible*. I'm saying all sorts of things I never meant to. Talking to the police is a lot harder than they make out."

"Technically, only one of us is the police," Pettifer pointed out, slightly uncharitably, in Felicia's opinion.

Arthur's shoulders sagged.

"You know, I'm actually glad this is all over. It's been weighing on me so much."

Felicia felt her breath hitch at the admission in his voice.

Pettifer's gaze turned hawkish, but his voice was gentle, coaxing even, as he asked the most damning question of all.

"*Why* did you do it, Arthur?"

There was a pause. Then: "Honestly?" A resigned shrug. "I don't know. I wasn't thinking straight, I guess."

Felicia stared at him, stunned that he could be so offhand. Pettifer, however, had a more visceral response.

"*That's* your defence?" He growled. "Two people are dead, and all you've got to say is you weren't *thinking* straight?"

Felicia sensed that he was holding on tightly to his self-control. Rarely had she observed him so furious. A humour that wasn't improved by Arthur frowning at him as though he was being entirely unreasonable.

"Well of course, that's tragic, but I'm not really sure what it's got to do with *me*."

"I thought…" Pettifer drew back, confusion muddling his features. For once, he seemed utterly wrong-footed, and Felicia didn't blame him. "Wait. Let me get this right. You're … *not* confessing to the murders?"

Arthur's face drained of blood.

"Christ, no! You can't possibly think—" He looked between them in wounded disbelief. "But I would never kill anyone!"

"If you want to convince me of that, you'd better have *damned* good reason to account for your behaviour tonight," Pettifer snapped. "Because right now, all I can see is someone who was lurking around in disguise, who was spotted in the vicinity of each crime just before it happened. Someone who had the means, the opportunity … and, given your obvious grudge against the club, I'd say that's motive, too."

"Now, hang *on*!" Arthur held up his hands. "If I was nearby when the murders happened, then I certainly wasn't the only one. The club's not exactly a big place."

"You deny that you followed Doctor Rauceby out into the gardens, then?"

"Of course I do! I mean, all right, so I was out there. But not for him. I was looking for Miss Drayford, remember?"

"So you didn't go near the chapel at *all*?"

Arthur hesitated. But one look at Pettifer's face obviously cautioned him against attempting to lie.

"I suppose I … *might* have stumbled in that direction," he said cagily. "Just briefly. After I came across the two of them … together. I just wanted to get away, before they saw me. The yew trees seemed like the best cover." His face turned speculative. "Come to think of it, *they* weren't far from the chapel themselves. Either of them could have had the opportunity."

Hmm. So much for loyalty to Leo Wild, thought Pettifer dryly. The boy was a slipperier customer than he might appear. Nonetheless, it was interesting information. He filed it away for perusal later.

"It's *your* movements I'm interested in," he said sternly. He didn't like sneaks, on a personal level, even if they could prove useful to an investigation. "Did you see or hear anything while you were at the chapel? Anything that might be relevant?"

"Well, the door was open as I passed. But I didn't go in." He faltered. "I peeked in, out of sheer curiosity – I've never known it to be unlocked before – but then there was this … *sound*. A sort of hideous screeching." He shuddered at the memory. "It was like something from the bowels of hell. I've never heard anything like it; I hope I never do again."

"You didn't see what it was?"

"No, it was too dark in there. And I wasn't about to stick around and find out."

Pettifer's eyebrows shot up into his almost non-existent hairline. He looked at Felicia, and knew instantly that she was thinking the same.

"You do realise that was probably the moment the doctor fell?"

Two bright spots of colour appeared on the boy's cheeks.

"Well, I do *now*, obviously," he said, defensively. "But at the time… Besides, what could I have done?"

In reality, nothing. He couldn't have saved the man; death would have been instantaneous on impact. But the lad couldn't have known that at the time. And Pettifer wasn't entirely sure he deserved to know now.

"You're pretty fond of the helpless, innocent act, aren't you, Arthur?" Pettifer spoke quietly. "I expect it works on a lot of people, doesn't it? But not me. I'm not so easy to fool." He folded his arms over his colossal chest. "And d'you know what I think? I think you knew *exactly* what you were about when you donned that costume and went walkabout."

Felicia looked startled.

"You mean … he *wanted* to frighten people? But why? What was the point?"

"Because I *could*!" Arthur snarled, with such sudden, unexpected venom that Felicia flinched backwards. "And because they damn well *deserved* it. The people in that place have everything, and yet what do they do with it? Do they have a single shred of respect for the people who serve them, who didn't get the advantages they did?" His eyes glittered with bitter tears. "The way they used to look through me … like I was nothing. Not a real person, with thoughts and feelings. I hated how insignificant they made me feel. I *hated* it." His fingers curled into his palms. "I just thought about every guest who'd ever crossed me, made me feel insignificant. Every complacent, condescending, unreasonable…" A cruel smile twisted his lips, changing his boyish face into something ugly. "Well, I showed them, didn't I? They might have money, and power, but in a moment of terror, they just look as small and cringing as the rest of us. Fear is a great equaliser."

Felicia looked at him with something approaching sadness. Truthfully, she didn't know whether to despise him or pity him.

"And Aurelia? What did she do to you to deserve *that*?"

The light dimmed in his eyes.

"That, I really am sorry about. It was an accident; she fell and hit her head. I swear, I never meant for her to get hurt. I wasn't even trying to frighten her; she was just in the wrong place at the wrong time." He raked a hand through his already mussed hair. "The irony of it is that she's one of the few people in this place who *didn't* deserve it. She's always been so kind to me; I think she knows what it's like to feel out of place. Those parents of hers just don't understand her at all. Oh, she wants for nothing, in one way. Her father lavishes money on her; horses, clothes, jewellery ... you should see the ring he bought her recently; a hideous old gobstopper of a thing, couldn't suit her less, but presumably it cost a bomb, which is all he cares about – but it's all just for show. There's no real love there. She's just a trophy to him. She could have turned out so awful, so entitled, but she isn't; she's just the opposite." He hugged himself protectively. "She deserves so much better than all of this. I really hope she's going to be all right."

Pettifer looked at him in distaste.

"Believe me, if she isn't, I'll make sure you never forget it."

Arthur swallowed.

"Look, I know what you must think of me. I might be a coward, but I'm not a monster. I never wanted to do anyone any real harm. I know I took things too far, but..." He looked at Pettifer with wide, anxious eyes. "What's going to happen to me now?"

Pettifer's lips compressed.

"Well, first off, you've got to get that leg seen to. I've already called an ambulance; they should be here any minute."

"But..." Arthur blinked rapidly. "What about ... you're not going to arrest me?"

"Not right now, no." Pettifer hefted himself to his feet. "I think it's safe to say you're not getting far. If I want you, I'll know where to find you." He paused in the doorway, then added, "Oh, and by the way, your parents are downstairs. I'm afraid we had to wake them up; only way we could get in. I haven't told them much; I thought I'd leave the explaining up to you. You've earned it, I think."

And leaving that hanging over him, they departed.

"You know," Felicia ventured, as they drove away. Behind them, an ambulance was pulling up in front of the cottage, blue lights flashing. "When Heavenly finds out you didn't bring him in… He would have arrested him for less than he just told us."

"Heavenly would have arrested him for simply running away," Pettifer said shortly.

"We can't deny he had motive. He really seems to hate Annabel Drayford; it's not too much of a leap to think that he might want to frame her for murder. And not just her," Felicia mused. "The club's reputation would also be dragged through the mud. After all, The Aquitaine is doomed to be forever associated with these murders now. It would be the ultimate revenge."

"It's a tempting theory. He's certainly got a persecution complex, and we know he's the vindictive type. Nasty little sneaks like that can be more dangerous than people realise; I can certainly see him framing someone for murder just because they'd crossed him." He frowned, shaking his head. "But committing murder … that's something else. It takes a different kind of personality. I just don't think he'd have the stomach for it."

Privately, Felicia agreed. But she was beginning to feel a

creeping desperation; after all, it had seemed so certain that once they'd tracked down the sinister, rogue Mummer, they'd have found their murderer, too. If they hadn't, if this really did all turn out to be a blind alley … well, where did that leave the investigation? Worryingly close to square one, it seemed to her. Certainly, she didn't have any other bright ideas at the moment, and she suspected neither did Pettifer.

"Unless that explains why he arranged the murders like he did," she suggested, rather over-eagerly. "We just assumed it was done for practical purposes, to allow the killer to create an alibi. But what if it was actually about sheer, human fallibility? So Arthur didn't have to look any of his victims in the eye."

"A squeamish murderer?" Pettifer raised an eyebrow. "That's a new one."

They'd turned onto the lane now, The Aquitaine rose up in front of them, its façade as stately and placid as ever, betraying no sign at all to the outsider of the horrors that had been unfolding within its walls.

Except, Felicia realised, for one thing. Smoke was billowing out of a side window, spiralling into the cold, damp air. Black smoke.

Pettifer had seen it, too.

"That's Annabel Drayford's office," he said faintly.

And the look on his face made Felicia's blood chill in her veins.

Chapter Thirty-Six

The foyer was crammed with terrified onlookers, and Pettifer and Felicia had to fight their way through to reach the door to Annabel Drayford's office. When they got there, they discovered Jess standing guard, trying to field a barrage of questions.

"No, Ms. Johnson, there's no information yet. I'll inform you all when we know more … *Please*, Mr. Torrent. This is a crime scene. I need to ask you to move back." Her face registered relief as she saw Pettifer approaching. "Sarge. Thank God you're here. Can you help me explain…"

"Everyone bloody *shift* it!" Pettifer roared.

The effect was immediate, the space around the door clearing in a matter of seconds as everyone scuttled away, looking distinctly cowed. Even Spencer Torrent didn't dare raise a protest.

Pettifer turned back to Jess, his voice dropping right down the scale to a low, confidential murmur.

"What the hell happened here, Winters?"

"An explosion, sir. You could hear it throughout the building, but the damage appears to have been contained to this one room."

"Was anyone…" Pettifer hesitated. "Miss Drayford…"

Jess shook her head slowly. Felicia felt her stomach drop into her shoes. They'd been gone for *half an hour*, that was all. And in that brief, almost negligible amount of time … another soul extinguished, just like that; this time, of a woman who had positively crackled with life force, who'd seemed utterly indomitable. By a killer who was beginning to seem as relentless as they were unstoppable.

Pettifer's jaw tightened; she saw him swallow, but that was all the emotion he was obviously going to show, because the next time he spoke, it was in a brisk, businesslike tone.

"You were able to identify her?"

"Just." Jess looked unusually pale, Felicia noticed. She hoped she wasn't about to faint. She recalled that the young constable still wasn't that used to working on murder cases; she'd been thrown in at the deep end here in Stamford, that was for sure.

"Any idea about the source of the blast yet?"

"Well, the one bit of good news is that the forensics team finally turned up while you were out. They're in there now."

"About bloody time," Pettifer muttered. "We've been waiting for them for hours. What did they do? Ride sheep over here?"

"Well, they *are* always telling us how we need to make budget cuts in rural policing," Jess said feebly. Then, realising it probably wasn't the time for humour, bleak or otherwise, she forged on, "They've not told me much yet, but all the signs point to it having been…" She gulped, knowing that this next part wouldn't go down at all well. "A pumpkin."

Pettifer's gaze drilled into her. Not a single muscle in his face moved. Jess began to gabble, as she always did when she was nervous.

"Or, a jack-o'-lantern, to be more precise. It seems someone had rigged the candle; hollowed out the centre and inserted a small test tube filled with neat petrol."

Pettifer glanced at Felicia, who was still standing to one side. Although technically, she wasn't part of this conversation, he knew she'd been listening. And by the look on her face, she understood exactly what Jess was suggesting. As did he.

"So, when she put a match to it…"

He didn't need to finish the sentence. The smoke leaching out from underneath the door was enough to tell them all what had happened when a naked flame hit the petrol-soaked candle wick.

"Well, it certainly wasn't in there when I last spoke to her," Pettifer said, with an exhale. "It must have been left since."

"How could the killer guarantee that she would light it, though?" Felicia was looking perplexed. "I mean, she didn't exactly seem like the whimsical type."

"That, we do have an idea of." Jess, appearing to rally slightly, handed Pettifer a charred scrap of paper in an evidence bag. "There was a note with it. There's not a lot left, but from what can be made out, it seems to be some sort of apology."

"Of *course* there's a note," Pettifer muttered savagely, as he squinted at the barely legible words. He was getting sorely fed up with this killer and their coy little quirks. "If I never see another bloody note in my life... Wait." His finger stubbed against the paper. "Is that a kiss?"

"It looks like it, doesn't it?" Jess said mildly. "It's clearly from someone she had an intimate relationship with. Unfortunately, they haven't signed it." She shrugged. "But I suppose, if she had a lover, they wouldn't need to identify themselves, would they?"

Pettifer felt a glimmer of something within his chest. A quickening feeling, the kind he got when he began to see a way towards the truth. A feeling that he'd been beginning to despair of ever having in this case. He looked at Felicia, and a flash of understanding passed between them.

"No, they wouldn't," he agreed softly. "But *we* can."

"You've known who the mysterious Mummer was all along, haven't you, Mr Wild?"

The barman looked back at Pettifer evenly. He betrayed no hint of surprise, or guilt. A cool customer, Pettifer thought. That had been his first opinion of the young man, and it seemed he'd been right on the money.

"You don't deny it, then?" he pressed.

Leo Wild shrugged laconically.

"Why would I? You clearly know. I take it you've caught up with him, then?"

"Only after he almost broke his leg jumping out of a window whilst trying to escape."

That, at least, got a reaction. The barman closed his eyes briefly, swearing under his breath.

"I *knew* this would end badly." He opened his eyes, looking at them earnestly. "I told him no good would come of it. I begged him to stop, to go home…" He sighed, running a finger along the line of his brow. "Look, if you've spoken to him properly, I hope you've realised that he's harmless, really. He didn't mean anything by it."

"He petrified several innocent people," Felicia pointed out. "And he could have killed Aurelia with his antics."

Leo winced.

"I know. But trust me, he'll be tearing himself to pieces over that. She's always been a good friend to him; to all of us, really. She gets so bored moping around here, she often helps us with our jobs just for something to do. I even caught her yesterday evening helping Arthur out here in the bar while he was covering for me." He shook his head fondly. "Sometimes I actually forget she isn't one of us. In a way, I think she'd be happier if she were." Then his expression turned entreating. "But you've got to understand; to Arthur, being here … it meant *everything* to him. He was pinning his whole future on it. Losing it all like that … it really broke him."

"It's just a job, Mr. Wild," Pettifer said curtly.

Leo Wild looked at him for a long moment, and something simmered in the depths of his eyes. His lips parted and, for a moment, he seemed about to say something. Then he shook his head, sitting back in his chair.

"I should never have suggested the Mummers thing to him. It was idiotic of me; I should have seen he'd tipped over the edge."

"Then why *did* you suggest it?"

"If you must know, I felt for the guy. Look, he screwed up a bit earlier; he should have been more on the ball. You don't get to make excuses in this job. It's a one shot and you're out kind of place." He folded his arms, leaned back against the bar. "But even so, what happened to him, the way it was done … it wasn't right. I thought … a last little payday, on the club … it was the least he deserved." He looked between them, then reiterated stubbornly, "I just thought he should have the money, that's all. I thought it would help him."

"That must have divided your loyalties," Pettifer observed, in a silken voice. As the barman looked sharply at him, he added, "Given your relationship with Miss Drayford, I mean."

"Ah." Leo's lips twisted in a rueful smile. "So, you know about, do you? Listen, it was nothing, really. Just a fling."

He didn't exactly sound cut up about her death, Pettifer thought, with a hint of disapproval. Obviously, it showed in his expression, because the barman looked faintly shamefaced.

"Look, I know that sounded a bit callous. I didn't mean it to. And obviously, I am sorry about…" he swallowed, "about what happened to her. Nobody deserves that. But I can't pretend that she and I were anything more than a diversion to one another. I was bored, she was lonely; apart from that, we weren't the slightest bit compatible. If we hadn't been thrown together here, it would never have happened." An ironic smile crossed his lips. "To be honest, I don't think she actually liked me very much."

"Mr. Wild," Pettifer spoke slowly, making sure the barman was following his every word, "I'm going to ask you something, and I need you to tell me the truth. Did you leave something in her office this evening?"

"Something? Like what?"

"A note. And a…" Pettifer coughed awkwardly, "pumpkin."

"Why the hell would I leave her a *pumpkin*?" Leo looked so

genuinely mystified that Pettifer was in no doubt that he was telling the truth. "And a note? Not really my style. Like I said, it wasn't a romance; we weren't sending one another loving missives or anything. In fact, we didn't really communicate at all except about the logistics. Where, when, what we were into…"

"*Ahem*." Pettifer suspected he had gone the colour of pickled beetroot. "Yes, I get the message, Mr. Wild. You don't need to explain further."

"What did it say, anyway?" Leo was looking interested. "This note that was supposedly from me?"

"It wasn't entirely legible, but it seemed to be an apology of some sort. We'd assumed for a lovers' tiff. Had you done anything you needed to apologise for recently?"

"Oh, plenty, I'm sure. But I make it a rule to never say sorry."

"You wait till you get married," Pettifer muttered under his breath. But aloud, he said, "And it isn't possible she might have been seeing someone else? Someone who could have written this note?"

Leo Wild didn't look fazed by the suggestion that he might have had competition. He simply shrugged.

"Not that I'm aware of. To be honest, I'm not sure how she'd find the time. But who knew with Annabel? She was a force of nature."

She was that, Pettifer silently agreed. But it hadn't been enough, had it? Not to stop this killer. A killer who, he had a sinking feeling, wasn't sitting in front of him after all. Another dead end, then, in a case that seemed to be chock full of them. He was beginning to wonder who was even left to *suspect* in this God-forsaken place. Unless…

"And you don't think Arthur could have done it? He knew about your relationship with Annabel, after all. *And* we know he was in the vicinity of her office around the time the bomb must have been planted." He'd just been throwing theories around, really, but as Pettifer spoke the words, he realised the significance of them. When Lucia had come across Arthur, he'd been standing at the bottom of the staircase … which was *right* next to Annabel's office. Had he been too hasty in letting the lad go? Pettifer leaned forward intently. "You said he was harmless, Leo; tell me, do you really believe that?"

"Yes!" Leo had gone pale but remained firm. "And Arthur wouldn't do that to me. Not after all I've done for him."

Pettifer wondered if he'd be so quick to defend the other lad if he knew how he'd thrown him under the bus earlier. But before he could enlighten him, there was soft intake of breath from beside him. He looked askance at Felicia, who was already sliding gracefully from the bar stool.

"Thank you, Leo. You've been very helpful. I'm sure if Sergeant Pettifer has any more questions for you, he'll be in touch."

Pettifer gritted his teeth and descended – with rather less dignity – from his own seat to follow her. He waited until they'd left the mirrored cavern of the bar well behind them before he rounded on her with a thunderous face.

"What the *devil* do you think you're playing at, Felicia?" He jabbed a finger to his chest. "*I* decide when interviews are over, not you. Sometimes I think you forget who's actually the police officer here."

"Sorry," she said. But she didn't look it. Her eyes were shining silver, and she had a nervous energy about her. One that Pettifer recognised well. He looked at her sharply.

"What are you thinking?"

"I'm *thinking*…" she glanced at the clock, saying slowly, "that it's almost time for a midnight snack."

Pettifer drew back, bemused.

"Well, I suppose, technically…"

"Do me a favour, will you? Go to the kitchen and ask them for this." She named something that made Pettifer's eyebrows raise. He looked warily at her, wondering, not for the first time, if he really ought to be following her so trustingly. But in the end, he nodded.

He was out of answers, and, by the look on her face, it appeared she had them. He could only pray that they would turn out to be the right ones.

Chapter Thirty-Seven

"There you are. I've found you at last."

Felicia moved through the snug. The room felt strange like this, devoid of the buzz and energy of the dozens of people who usually populated it at all hours of the day. Now, for once, it was silent, the fire burning low in the grate, throwing amber light across the only occupied seat. "I heard you wouldn't go to hospital."

Aurelia, who was lying across a faded pink silk chaise longue, lifted her bandaged head and gave a weak smile.

"No. I've spent enough time in hospitals as it is. They said I just have to watch out for delayed concussion, but apart from that…"

"Shouldn't you at least be resting in your room?" Felicia perched on the opposite sofa, putting down the tray of tea and toast she was holding. The embers crackled softly in the fire to her left, the diffused heat caressing her cheek. "Surely you'd be more comfortable in bed."

"Believe me, I wouldn't. Between my mother in hysterics

that I wouldn't go in the ambulance and my father shouting and ranting at her…" She shook her head ruefully, then immediately winced in pain. Felicia leapt up.

"Here, lean forward and I'll put some more cushions behind you. You ought to be propped up."

She fussed around for several moments, pushing a bolster into the girl's back, plumping and rearranging, until apparently she was satisfied.

"It's slightly eerie in here at night, isn't it?" she commented, as she returned to her own seat. "I suppose everyone else has gone to bed, now the police have finally given them permission. I doubt they'll sleep well, though; I certainly shouldn't, with a killer still at large. Although, I'm rather hoping this place has seen its last murder tonight." As she spoke, the grandfather clock began to chime, echoing through the hushed room. Felicia gave a relieved smile. "Midnight at last. It's not Halloween anymore. I must say, I'm very glad to see the back of that particular festival this year."

She picked up a triangle of toast and began to spread it thickly with preserve. Aurelia raised her fair eyebrows.

"Isn't it a bit early for breakfast?"

Felicia gave a little laugh.

"Oh, this? I suppose it does seem rather odd, but I never did get dinner in the end, and … well, it seems foolish, perhaps, but I thought it would be comforting. It's the snack my sister used to make us when we woke up in the middle of the night, you see."

"You have a sister?" Aurelia shifted, looking at her with sudden interest in her wide blue eyes. "What's she like? Are you close?"

"Not anymore." Felicia pulled a face. "Actually, what am I

saying? Not ever. We're like chalk and cheese. But she did make *very* good toast," she acknowledged, with a smile.

"Still, at least you had someone to grow up with," Aurelia looked wistful. "I would have loved a sibling. Someone I could talk to, who'd understand what it's like living with my parents. At the very least, someone else would have divided Daddy's attention, given him another project to work on."

"It must have been hard," Felicia said sympathetically, "having so much pressure on your shoulders."

Aurelia nodded jerkily.

"When Daddy has an obsession, it's all or nothing. And my career has been an obsession for him. Competing, winning, trying to live up to what he wants … it's been my whole life. I couldn't even go to a proper school in case it distracted me. The closest thing I've ever had to friends is the staff at the places we've stayed."

"The staff here are certainly very fond of you," Felicia observed. "They seem to treat you like one of them. Part of the wallpaper, as it were."

"They're the only people around here who really see me. None of the members pay me the slightest attention. It was bad enough when I was just little Aurelia, trailing around in my father's shadow; now I'm *poor* Aurelia, whose life is over before it even began. They don't even offer me sympathy anymore; they just look through me. I'm an uncomfortable reminder of reality, you see." Her lips twisted as she glanced at her walker. "Of the fact that money and power can't protect you from everything."

"You've turned it to your advantage, though, haven't you?" Felicia said softly. "After all, it's helped you to kill three people."

There was a pulse of silence. Aurelia stared at her, face rigid with shock. Her mouth opened, but no sound came out.

Felicia struck a hand to her forehead, as though she'd just remembered something. When she spoke next, her voice was bright, even chatty.

"But wait, where *are* my manners? Would you like some of this?" She offered the plate, then drew it back. "No, of course. How forgetful of me. You hate marmalade, don't you? I heard you saying so earlier tonight, when you turned down a mocktail. And yet, that's odd, because I seem to remember you inhaling slices of marmalade swiss-roll at tea yesterday like it was going out of fashion." She tapped her chin in faux perplexity, then shrugged. "Ah, well. If you won't eat, how about a nice cup of tea instead?"

Aurelia just nodded mutely, looking cornered.

"You know, it seemed to me that whoever was doing these murders was leaving a lot to chance," Felicia said conversationally, pouring the tea. "Amidst so much meticulous planning, that just didn't seem to make sense. Until I realised: there was no guesswork about it. Our killer already *knew* what everyone was going to do. Because our killer knew The Aquitaine." She picked up the milk jug, continuing, "It's a unique sort of bubble, this place, isn't it? The members here … they're creatures of habit. And the club encourages this; it's very consciously a place where nothing ever changes, where every member's preference is already known, every quirk of routine down pat. They become, in essence, entirely predictable." Felicia's face hardened as she looked across at the girl she'd never suspected, not for a moment, of being capable of anything close to this. "And that made them easy prey."

It all seemed so clear now, in hindsight, Felicia reflected.

A bored teenage girl who spent her time mooching about the club, largely unnoticed; no doubt she'd become quite the adroit eavesdropper, and that, combined with her friendship with the staff, meant there was no-one better placed to know everyone's secrets. Information she had turned into a method of murder.

Aurelia had known about the animosity between Annabel Drayford and Matthias Weaver, known that she often left him notes rather than having to deal with him directly, and that he, in turn, would question none of her instructions. She had also known how desperately the doctor had wanted to get into the chapel, that he would go there whenever summoned.

She'd *known* that Sybil was the only person who ever drank the violet liqueur; that's why she'd felt safe to put the poison in the decanter. She'd known that Sybil would drink it tonight, that she wouldn't opt for mead, or the signature cocktail instead. She'd known that Lavinia wouldn't stay with her sister if Sybil was taken ill, that she would instead persist doggedly with her routine, going into dinner to sit at her usual table ... and therefore be in exactly the right spot when the chandelier fell.

Aurelia had been sitting at the table closest to the rope that had supported the chandelier, Felicia remembered now. She'd literally been the person with the most opportunity to cut it; Felicia almost felt slightly embarrassed now at how simply obvious that had been. So obvious, in fact, that she'd completely overlooked it at the time.

But then, she'd overlooked Aurelia in general, hadn't she? They all had. Sweet, angelic Aurelia, so placid and accepting of her lot in life ... how wrong they'd been.

Felicia pushed the teacup across the table towards the girl.

"Drink up. You don't want it going cold."

Aurelia picked up the cup with unsteady fingers. It was almost to her lips before she looked into its depths ... and gasped. The cup clattered down on its side, the poison ring rolling out into the saucer. Aurelia stared at it, momentarily stunned into silence. When she finally spoke, her voice was faint.

"You—"

"Stole it from you?" Felicia finished for her. "When I was plumping your cushions, yes. I suspected you'd probably be keeping it on your person somewhere, and there it was, in your pocket." She tilted her head apologetically. "A bit underhand, perhaps, but then, you *did* steal it yourself, so..." She took a sip from her own cup – which actually *did* have tea in it – and sighed. "Ah, that's perfect. They really know how to do tea here, don't they? Quite an overwhelming array they served us yesterday, in fact. All those plates and cake stands cluttering the table; no wonder we didn't notice Lucia's poison ring had rolled underneath one of them." Her expression hardened. "But *you* did, didn't you, Aurelia? And you knew what the ring was; you'd overheard what we were talking about as you approached. I presume you saw the opportunity and ran with it; quite impressively, I must admit."

"Yes, it turns out I'm quite good at thinking on my feet." Aurelia seemed to have recovered some of her composure; she actually looked quite proud of herself. "My original plan had gone to the wall; I didn't realise that Leo and Miss Drayford had chosen the area around the chapel as their place to meet, and they were there when I first went to try and collect the yew berries." She frowned. "So I missed my chance to put them in the decanter while Leo had sneaked away from the bar – it's almost never unattended otherwise. Anyway, when I heard you explaining about the poison ring, how it worked … well, I suddenly saw a way it could be done, even whilst someone else was around, and they'd never notice a thing."

"That's why you were helping Arthur last night, then?"

"I suggested we top up a few of the decanters in preparation for tonight. He never suspected anything. Bless Arthur; he's lovely, but a little dim. Exactly who I needed at that moment."

"Not so dim that he didn't notice the ring, though," Felicia took a certain amount of pleasure in pointing out. As soon as he'd described it, she'd had the sense that something didn't quite add up. Aurelia had told Arthur that her father had bought it for her … and yet, Felicia had seen the kind of delicate, ethereal jewellery he gave her with her own eyes. Spencer Torrent might not understand his daughter in many ways, but he clearly knew what suited her. He would never have bought her such a knuckleduster of a ring. All it had taken was a quick trip up to Lucia's room to check in her jewellery pouch, and the absence of the poison ring had been enough to confirm her suspicions.

Aurelia grimaced.

"No. That was unfortunate. As was what I had to do next. But I couldn't risk him telling anyone about it; that would have ruined everything … especially if it got back to your friend Lucia. I *had* to get rid of him. Luckily, Miss Drayford didn't need much persuading."

Felicia drew back in astonishment.

"Wait … *you* had him fired?"

She'd never seen that coming, she thought dazedly. So Lucia was innocent of that particular transgression, after all. And she'd been so *sure*…

"I put a few rumours around and let the grapevine do the rest," Aurelia said simply. "Everyone's so paranoid around here … it was almost *too* easy, to be honest."

"And yet, you didn't actually get rid of him, did you?" At Aurelia's confused expression, she gave a dry smile. "Oh, have I finally found something you *didn't* know? He's been here all night … although I'm not surprised you didn't recognise him."

Aurelia's eyes bugged.

"*He's* the Mummer?" She touched the back of her head, muttering, "He could have killed me earlier. What was he playing at?"

The irony appeared to be utterly lost on her. Felicia looked at the young woman in front of her, and tried to work out whether she felt abhorrence or pity.

"The only thing I don't understand is *why*, Aurelia?" Felicia leaned in, her voice gentle, cajoling. Inviting the girl to open up. "Why would you *do* this?"

"I'd like to know that too, lass."

Pettifer's huge, boxy frame blocked the doorway. He stepped into the room, eyes fixed on her face.

Aurelia, however, didn't seem fazed by his presence. If anything, it emboldened her. She threw back her head, eyes flashing defiantly.

"You couldn't possibly understand. Either of you." Her beautiful, otherworldly face soured. "You can't begin to know what it's like, to be forced to live a life that isn't your own. To be pushed, day in and day out, towards something you never even wanted."

Felicia and Pettifer remained silent, knowing exactly what she was talking about. Or, more precisely, who.

"I thought the day I fell off that horse would be the start of my life," Aurelia continued. "Finally, I wouldn't be of interest to him anymore; he'd leave me alone, and I could start making my own choices. But he wouldn't give up; he kept hiring more doctors, more tests. He found articles about people with similar injuries who'd made a full recovery, shoving them in my face, telling me I could have it all again..." She gave a bitter laugh. "Have it all? Go back to prison, more like. That's what that life had been to me."

"That's why you're not getting better," Felicia whispered, finally seeing.

"Psychosomatic is the term they're using. Apparently, it means my mind doesn't want my body to heal." She smiled thinly. "You can imagine how *that* went down when they told my father. It just made him even more persistent; he thinks it's something that can be broken, *toughed out*, as he puts it."

Felicia felt a sudden urge to put her arm around the girl, despite everything she'd done. What must it be like, to feel so utterly trapped, so under someone else's thumb, powerless to control your own destiny? She couldn't imagine. She didn't *want* to. No wonder Aurelia's mind had rebelled; shutting down her body probably felt like the only way to safety.

"You won't be fifteen forever, lass," Pettifer said gently. "I know it seems a long way off, but it does get better, if you just hang in there."

Aurelia looked weary.

"Not for me. He'll never let me go. I'm his legacy, you see. His shot at glory. No, I have nothing good ahead of me. For a while, that depressed me; I couldn't see the point in going on. Then, one day, I looked around at this place." Her lip curled in a sneer. "I've always hated it here, hated the kind of people my parents forced me to mix with. They call them lofty circles; to me, they're just entitled bullies. They trample over anyone who isn't as rich and powerful as they are, and no-one does anything about it. *No*-one stops them." Her gaze grew misty. "And suddenly, it occurred to me: *I* could. I was in the unique position of having nothing to lose; why not be the one to make other peoples' lives better?"

"By killing a doctor?" Pettifer looked disbelieving.

"He was no angel of mercy, let me tell you!" Aurelia's eyes snapped fire. "Doctor Rauceby was a *vile* man. He intimidated and mocked everyone he met; and he ruined God knows how many lives with his crusade against the medical establishment. It was nothing to do with helping anyone, either; he was simply obsessed with getting back at the people who had struck him off. He wanted to prove that he was right, and he'd use any amount of pressure and scare tactics to get people to go along with his experiments. You know even he tried to convince my father to take me abroad for an operation, *against* my will?" She looked between her two listeners. "How many more people were going to get hurt because of him? And not just them; their families, loved ones … they were all suffering, too. He had to be stopped."

"And Miss Drayford? Who was she hurting?"

"Annabel tormented everyone who worked for her," Aurelia snapped. "My friends. Worked them into the ground then tossed them aside the first time they made a mistake. The amount of panic attacks they have in the staff room…" She made a disgusted sound. "And I don't suppose you have the first *idea* what she was doing to Matthias Weaver, the caretaker here."

"Actually, I think I do," Felicia interjected quietly. "She was trying to force him out, I presume?"

"By making him live in squalor!" Aurelia spat. "She *knew* he had nowhere else to go; The Aquitaine is his home. He's given his life to it. He'd have held on until he died from something he caught living in those conditions; and it would have been *her* fault. She would have killed him … if I hadn't got to her first, that is." She folded her arms mutinously. "And Lavinia … well, I don't need to tell you about *her*, do I? You saw for yourself how she treated poor Sybil. Like a slave, taking advantage of her poverty, her lack of choices in life."

"So you saved them all," Pettifer said flatly. "How heroic of you."

"I *freed* them!"

"The people who were benefitting from the doctor's drugs might not think so," Pettifer returned. "And no matter what you say, there were plenty of them. People who saw him as a lifeline, and who'll now have to face the return of their suffering. Neither will the cleaner here, Molly Dunster, whom Annabel gave a job when no-one else would."

"Nor will Sybil," Felicia added. "She's been inconsolable since she heard of Lavinia's death, apparently. No matter how their relationship might have seemed from the outside, she really loved her sister. They were companions as much as siblings, all each other had in the world. Now she'll be completely alone."

"No. I don't believe you." The wide blue eyes were swivelling between them, panicked. "You're lying. Both of you."

"We're not, Aurelia." Felicia shook her head sadly. "The older you get, the more you see that things in life are never black-and-white. Nobody is all good, but they aren't all bad either; you don't just get to decide who the world is better off without."

Too late, Felicia saw the ring being slipped onto Aurelia's finger. In a second, the girl had flipped open the catch, throwing her head back to empty the black powder down her throat.

"*No!*"

Pettifer lurched forward…

Then skidded to a confused halt as the room exploded with an entirely unexpected sound.

"God!" Aurelia, eyes streaming, managed to rasp before she sneezed again. "What the—"

Felicia looked back at her serenely over the rim of her teacup.

"Well, you didn't think I'd actually leave the poison in there before I gave the ring back to you, did you?"

Pettifer rolled his eyes heavenward.

"So *that's* why you wanted some black pepper. I thought it was an odd choice to go with marmalade."

Chapter Thirty-Eight

"So, it was like a mercy mission of sorts, then?"

Felicia turned her attention reluctantly away from the window. All Saints' Day had dawned in a dazzle of sunlight and lupin blue skies, so determinedly bright and clear it was as though the weather itself wished to banish any lingering hint of last night's fog. Through the diamond-shaped panes, Water Street was a promising sight, the sun blazing through the scarlet and orange leaves, turning them into translucent sweet papers that rustled in a light, playful breeze, the river a scintillating millpond upon which the various water birds glided bucolically between the reeds. Looking at it, it was tantalisingly possible to convince oneself that nothing could possibly be wrong with the world; to forget, just for a moment, about the darkness and horror that had swallowed them all the previous evening.

And yet, the effect could only ever be temporary. As Felicia turned back to the kitchenful of people, all looking at her expectantly, she knew she couldn't hide from the truth forever. They deserved answers.

"In Aurelia's mind, yes," she sighed, toying with the mug of tea at her elbow. "She saw herself as a liberator, a saviour. She wasn't able to free herself from her bullying father, so she took it on herself to defend other people from bullies instead. She honestly thought she was doing a good thing; as far as I know, she still does."

"And no-one can make her see sense?" Peter asked, having to raise his voice to be heard above the sizzling of bacon and sausages.

Felicia shook her head.

"I doubt anyone will. And honestly, it's probably not surprising; Aurelia isn't a monster. Funnily enough, I'd say she's actually a kind and caring person. After killing three people, she needs to believe that she was in the right; it's the only way her mind will be able to cope with what she's done."

"And yet, she didn't have any qualms about poisoning Sybil, did she?" Dexter picked up the cafetière with a raised eyebrow. "Despite the fact that *she* was one of the victims she was supposedly trying to protect. What was she, simply collateral damage?"

Felicia paused. Truthfully, that was a question she'd been turning over in her mind all night, as she'd lay sleepless, listening to Algernon's soft breathing in the next bed.

"I don't think she meant to hurt Sybil," she said slowly. "Not seriously, anyway. If anything, I'm beginning to think it might have been the opposite. She wanted to save her life." As everyone looked puzzled, she explained, "Aurelia had meticulously planned out every aspect of the murders. There was nothing spur-of-the-moment about them; she'd clearly spent a lot of time thinking over every eventuality, doing her research, maximising the chance that her schemes would work in exactly the way she wanted. And yet, despite all of that, she only managed to mildly incapacitate Sybil with the dose of poison she gave her?" Felicia tapped her teaspoon thoughtfully against the rim of her cup. "That just doesn't seem to ring true. And with yew, of all things. It's a powerful toxin; you literally only need about three berry stones for it to be fatal. If anything, it was almost harder *not* to kill her. No, I think she just wanted Sybil indisposed, not dead."

Peter, who was cracking eggs into the frying pan, frowned perplexedly.

"But *why*?"

"To get her out of the way." A deep, rumbling voice came from the doorway, making them all start. Even Pettifer's heavy footsteps had been inaudible beneath the cacophony of a full English breakfast in the making. "So she wouldn't be at the dinner table when the chandelier fell."

He looked exhausted, Felicia thought, his face grey, eyes underscored by deep bags.

"Have you been at the station all night?" she asked.

He nodded wearily.

"I wanted to talk to Aurelia while I still could."

"And it's a good thing we did," Jess, who'd been invisible behind Pettifer's bulk blocking the doorway, added, her blonde head popping up over her superior's shoulder. "The station's already swarming with a retinue of big-name bulldog lawyers – all hired by her father, of course."

"And who are already doing their best to undermine our case against her," Pettifer added, tonelessly. "Not that she's helping them any. She seems determined to plead guilty."

Well, she *had* told the girl she'd had a flair for improvisation, Felicia acknowledged. And it seemed she'd left her most devastating flourish till last; getting caught had, in a way, given her a power over Spencer Torrent she'd never had before. With her confession, she had the opportunity to take him down with her, to tear down everything he'd built. His reputation would never survive this. There would be no more social advances, no more path to glory for him now. It was, in effect, the ultimate revenge; so much so that Felicia couldn't help but wonder if it mightn't have been part of Aurelia's plan all along.

"Pull up a chair, lad," Peter said to Pettifer, sounding uncharacteristically solicitous. "Sounds like you've done all you can for the time being. Join us for a fry-up; there's plenty to go round."

Pettifer seemed to perk up slightly as he craned to see what was in the frying pan.

"Black pudding?" he asked hopefully.

Peter glowered at him sternly.

"Of course. And none of that nonsense Americans call hash browns, either; only good old English fried bread in this house."

Pettifer relaxed back in his chair, mollified.

"She told you everything, then?" Felicia fetched two spare mugs for the police officers and filled them from the cracked teapot.

Jess nodded eagerly.

"There was so much we'd got wrong. For starters, we were completely fixated with the idea that someone wanted Annabel framed for the murders; that *that* was the killer's end goal. But actually, Aurelia had always planned to kill her. She just needed to use her authority to lure everything and everyone into position first. The framing itself was incidental; the purpose behind it was purely practical."

Pettifer sighed.

"I can't believe now that I never considered any of it from that angle; I just assumed the killer was playing some sort of game, that they were showing off how clever they were by using other people as pawns, moving them around a chessboard while keeping themselves at a safe distance. I never stopped to think that maybe they did it because they *had* to. Because they couldn't do everything themselves." He stared glumly into his tea. "That was a serious lapse on my part."

Felicia had been chastising herself about that, too. Like so many other things about this case, it seemed almost mockingly simple now. She'd unwittingly put her finger on it earlier, when she'd suggested human fallibility as the motivation; but the weakness she'd been talking about had been the mental rather than the physical kind. Of course, Aurelia had needed to be creative; she lacked the strength or speed to carry out most forms of face-to-face killing. In that context, the proliferation of notes, the manipulation of peoples' expectations, made sense, too. After all, Aurelia couldn't possibly have got all the way through the yew walk to the chapel to kill the doctor. Nor could she have climbed the ladder to put the lantern up there.

Of course, when she *had* been able to do things herself, she'd been ruthless in her execution. The poison in the decanter, the cutting of the chandelier rope, placing the pumpkin in Annabel Drayford's office… Felicia had no doubt that had been her personal handiwork. They'd been so distracted by Arthur's presence on the stairs that it hadn't occurred to anyone to wonder what the unconscious girl had been doing there. After all, Aurelia's room was on the ground floor; she had little reason to go near the staircase ... unless, of course, she'd been coming out of the office door just next to it.

"I never suspected her either," Felicia admitted. "She just seemed so..."

"Young?" Pettifer finished grimly.

A pall fell across the room at the reminder of who, exactly, was locked in the police station, potentially facing a lifetime in prison: a fifteen-year-old girl, barely out of childhood. In the course of her relatively recent association with murders, Felicia had already learned that finding the killer rarely led to the kind of unadulterated satisfaction and relief that fiction often portrayed. In reality, the conclusion was often sad, and conflicting; she'd thought that it couldn't get more so than in the last case they'd solved, but apparently it could. Aurelia, with so much life and promise ahead of her... The true tragedy here was that it wasn't only three lives that had been obliterated; in a sense, it was four.

"What's going to happen to her?"

Algernon was looking at Pettifer with wide, fawn-like eyes. Felicia tried not to think about the fact that he was only three years younger than the girl they'd just unmasked as a triple murderer.

"Well, she'll be charged as a minor." As ever, Pettifer answered him just like anyone else; he never tried to talk down to the boy. "And with the state of her health, along with other extenuating circumstances, I'm hoping the judge will be lenient."

"Well, I suppose that's that, then," Dexter said, refilling his coffee cup. "The only thing I don't understand is ... who was having that argument with the doctor in his room? The one the cleaner overheard?"

Felicia's gaze slid across to meet Pettifer's, and she bit her lip. She'd been rather hoping no-one would raise that particular question, in amongst all the other revelations. As it stood, only she and Pettifer knew the answer, and they'd made a promise to keep it that way.

It had become apparent to both of them, immediately after Aurelia had confessed, that it couldn't have been her; for one thing, she wouldn't have been able to get up to the first floor. And then Felicia had recalled someone else who had been on the landing around that time. Someone she'd seen with her own eyes. Not Lavinia; after all, if she'd been in the doctor's room earlier, she would have already been able to collect her medication, and wouldn't have needed to return as she had done. No, there'd been someone else; someone she'd all but forgotten…

The two elderly brothers had blended into the background of this investigation, keeping to themselves as they had. And yet, hadn't she thought it strange at the time, watching one of them struggle down the stairs when he could have used the cloakroom on the ground floor?

The conversation that had confirmed her theory had been quietly done, Pettifer excusing himself so as not to be alarming. Felicia had reassured the frightened old man – because that's what he was – that he would be in no trouble with the police for withholding what had happened. It would have been a hard heart who would have said otherwise, after hearing his story.

He, too, had been one of the doctor's clients, but unlike Lavinia, the drugs he'd been procuring had given him no hope of freedom. He was dying, his time trickling away like sand. Nothing could change that; he was simply trying to manage his symptoms, appear as normal as possible in front of the brother he'd not yet found a way to tell the truth to. And yet, last night, Dr. Rauceby had done something unexpected: he'd cut off his supply. Apparently, the drugs in question provided a false mercy; as time went on, and they built up in the system, the side effects they produced were worse than the disease. No amount of pleading had swayed the doctor; *that* was the argument overheard by Molly Gordon.

Felicia couldn't help but feel that it perhaps counted as one point in Rauceby's favour, even if it was now too late to be of any use. Clearly, he *had* cared about his patients, even if he'd had a strange way of showing it at times.

"We'll never know, I suppose," Pettifer said neutrally now, still looking at Felicia. "We don't always get all the answers in a real-life investigation, I'm afraid. Obviously, it had nothing to do with the murders, so…" He tailed off with a monolithic shrug.

At that point, they were saved from any further questions by Peter, who announced that grub was up, and everyone was promptly swept up in the business of passing plates, negotiating for the ketchup, and burning themselves trying to pick up their fried bread too soon. But Felicia found she couldn't join them; she looked down at her plate, her stomach turning to lead.

"Eat up, duck." Her father's voice, uncharacteristically gentle, met her ear. "You need your strength."

She dug her fork into the mushrooms, making a show of appetite. Belatedly, she became aware of a conversation taking place across the table.

"Can we tell them, Sarge?" Jess was looking at Pettifer, eyes pleading for approval.

He nodded curtly as he speared a piece of bacon.

"So long as it doesn't leave this room." He looked pointedly at Dexter, who frowned in affront.

Jess, meanwhile, was already leaning forward conspiratorially.

"You'll never guess who should walk into the station first thing this morning. Leo Wild, the barman. Claiming to have information for us about The Aquitaine."

Felicia looked up, feeling her interest stirring.

"What kind of information?"

"Absolute dynamite." Jess looked unprofessionally thrilled. "According to him, it's a vehicle for extortion and fraud at the highest level."

There was a stunned pause ... broken by Dexter, who let out a rather self-satisfied whistle.

"I knew there was something odd about that place. *Knew* it."

"Did you?" Felicia couldn't resist saying dryly. "You certainly didn't say anything when you were quaffing their cocktails or admiring their art."

"The club is, in essence, just a front, a way of luring people in," Jess continued, ignoring their miniature spat. "The glitter of prestige, of old-school exclusivity ... people are desperate to get in, be part of it. What they don't realise is that once they're in, they're under the place's power. Forever."

"All that fuss they make about knowing everything about everybody," Pettifer growled. "I dismissed it as just showmanship. But now... I think it has a much darker purpose. It's an excuse to spy on people ... in turn, to uncover their foibles, their weaknesses … and, in particular, their secrets."

"Secrets that can then be used to extract whatever they want," Jess added, biting into her fried bread with relish.

"And what *do* they want?"

"Everything," Pettifer said simply. "You name it, they deal in it. Every single person there is important in some way; they have connections, valuable information. That's why the club scouts them in the first place."

"Surely, not *everyone*, though…" Dexter gave a voice to the incredulity on everyone's faces. "I mean, what about Lavinia and Sybil Greenlake? Surely, they were just ordinary, if wealthy, old ladies?"

"Oh, they were," Jess said airily. "But they weren't always one another's only sibling … there was a brother once. *He* was high up in the secret service. Killed on the job. There were always worries that not all of his confidential files had been properly destroyed afterwards." She raised a fair eyebrow meaningfully.

Felicia sat back, dazed, trying to take it in. It just seemed so unlikely; all of those stuffy, bored people, going about their rigid little routines, fussing about minor things…

"By now, the club essentially 'owns' someone in just about every field, every sphere of society," Pettifer was saying, looking grave. "Someone they can get to do anything. We're talking at best, the extraction of classified information; at worst, actual interference, in stock markets, big business, medicine, even politics – presumably all at the behest of the highest bidder, although we're not quite sure of the setup yet. If it's true, the reach we're talking here, tentacles reaching into everything we think is safe…"

He trailed off, not needing to continue. The chilling implications of it had already imprinted on the minds of everyone in the small, low-beamed room.

"Apparently, the organised crime lot in London have had their eye on the place for a while," Jess explained. "But it's been impossible to pin anything specific on them. They have too many powerful people beholden to them for that."

"Even the staff were part of the racket," Pettifer added, bitterly. "Although to be fair, they didn't know that until too late. According to Leo Wild, they're carefully chosen, too – bright young kids, lots of potential but in need of a start in life. They give them an offer they can't refuse: they work at the club in the short term, putting up with the demands, the long hours, the crushing pressure to perform … in exchange for a step up later for those who perform well."

"They promise that with their connections, they can fast-track them into any field they like," Jess explained. "It's a golden ticket for their future, impossible to resist in today's job market. Of course, what they don't realise is they're being used. It's in the club's interests to funnel them into these positions. It expands their web; just more people beholden to them, forced to do their dirty work." Jess's mouth flattened. "Once you're in with The Aquitaine family, they never let you go."

"And Leo found out all of this from Annabel?"

Pettifer, who was mopping up baked beans with a piece of fried bread, nodded.

"She was the only one who knew the full extent of it. It must have been a lonely burden to bear, and in some more … ahem, *intimate* moments, she appears to have said more than she should to Leo. But ultimately, she was just a middleman, an enforcer." He frowned. "I noticed an empty pigeonhole in her office, marked Barn Hill. She told me it was an old room that no longer existed; but that wasn't true. Barn Hill was never a room in the club; that pigeonhole was used as a means of communicating instructions from her employers."

"So, who *are* her employers?" Dexter looked interested. "Who owns the club?"

"That, Mr. Grant, is the multi-million – if not billion – pound question. And it's turning out to be a difficult one to answer. At the moment, we're getting diverted from one shell company to another; whoever they are, they really don't want to be identified." He shook his head, looking quietly impressed. "Leo Wild planned to use the information he'd gleaned for his own ends, but after what he's seen recently, he's had a change of heart. He wants to do the right thing for once, he says, not just look out for his own interests anymore. And I have to say, it's brave of the lad. If what he's saying is true, he could find himself having crossed some *very* powerful people. He'll have to go into some sort of witness-protection scheme, I imagine." He shrugged. "But then, it's been passed on to someone much bigger than us now. I suppose we might never know where it all ends up."

It wasn't a reassuring note to leave it on, and sure enough, conversation hastily returned to brighter, more comfortingly ordinary matters. Felicia took the opportunity to slip away, heading out of the stable door at the back of the kitchen into the cottage's postage-stamp garden.

Cassie was sitting on a stone bench, ostensibly watching Algernon's guinea pigs – they'd managed to whittle the fourteen down to a mere four by dint of a successful rehoming campaign – grazing on the lawn. But as Felicia sat down, she saw that her friend's eyes were glazed, unseeing.

"You okay, Cass? Your breakfast's going cold."

She was trying not to sound worried by this, but in truth, it was unheard of for Cassie to refuse food. Not to mention that her usually gregarious friend had scarcely said a word since she'd arrived.

"Sorry." Cassie rubbed her face. "I must have lost track of time. I just … can't stop thinking about that poor girl. Parents can really screw a child over, can't they?"

Felicia looked back through the window, where she could see Algernon enthusiastically explaining something to Jess. There seemed to be a lot of arm movements involved; Godfrey the cat was looking decidedly wary. She certainly wasn't a perfect parent, and she worried constantly about what she wasn't getting right, but she'd always tried to allow him to be his own person. Now, she was thinking that that counted for a whole lot more than she'd realised.

"Lucia's gone home, by the way," Cassie said suddenly. "She got on a plane first thing. Back to her husband, with her jewels. I think she's changed her mind about trying to sell them secretly over here."

Felicia couldn't pretend she wasn't relieved to hear that.

"Minus one poison ring, I presume," she said archly. "That'll be in evidence for some time."

"Well, you might get to auction it one day. I understand she's told the police to do what they like with it once they're finished. She's waived all ownership of it; apparently, she thinks it's cursed."

Felicia pulled her knees up on the bench, hugging them to her chest.

"I don't believe in that sort of thing," she said quietly. "I think people are the problem, not objects." She sighed. "I made some terrible judgements about her, Cass. I thought she … well, I suppose I was still prejudiced by how she was at school. But I was wrong; I don't suppose she'll ever forgive me."

Cassie shrugged.

"Well, she was never really our sort, was she? It was always you and me." She put her arm around Felicia and smiled. "Weirdos together."

"I miss you, Cass." The words were blurted out, escaping from Felicia's lips before she could stop them. She flushed. "I know I shouldn't say that – it's probably some sort of unsupportive friend red flag…"

"Probably more of an amber," Cassie allowed, with a tilt of her head. But her eyes were soft.

Felicia, however, scarcely registered it. She was on a roll, her words tumbling over one another as they scrambled to get off her chest.

"And look, if you're happy, then I'm happy for you. I *am*. And I'll get used to it, I promise. It's just…"

Cassie put a hand over hers, bringing her to a faltering stop.

"Fliss, it's okay. I think I'm done with the therapy now." As Felicia's eyes widened, she explained, "It's served its purpose; I don't want to get stuck going over and over the past. It's time to move on. As me, though. Not some new, better, shinier version of myself." She squeezed Felicia's hand. "What you asked me to do … it reminded me how much good I can do, what a difference I can make, by doing things *my* way. I might not be everyone's cup of tea – I'm certainly not anyone's ideal – but I have my place, and my gifts, and I'm *needed* … just as I am."

Felicia felt tears sting at her eyes, and she clasped her oldest friend tightly.

"Thank *God* for that," she gasped. "Does this mean I finally tell you that Alain's about as French as a pork pie?"

"Oh, I already knew that." Cassie grinned. "He's from Nuneaton. Occasionally he forgets himself and a bit of West Midlands accent creeps back in."

Felicia threw back her head and laughed. Cassie joined in, and soon enough, it was like they were fourteen again – an effect compounded by Peter sticking his head out of the window and demanding to know what was so *bloody* funny, and to get back in here before he gave Cassie's sausages to Godfrey.

"He means it, you know," Felicia managed. "I wouldn't test him."

Cassie's eyes had fallen on a pumpkin, which was leering from a stone beside the pond.

"I don't think I'll ever look at one of those in quite the same way again," she said, with a sudden shiver.

Felicia stood and retrieved it, taking it to the green garden waste bin, where it made a satisfying *thunk* as it hit the bottom. Then she turned back to her friend, and smiled.

"Come on. Let's go and save your breakfast."

And arm in arm, they went back inside.

Chapter Thirty-Nine

As breakfast was being comprehensively dispatched within the walls of the lopsided, ancient cottage perched on the riverbank, across town, the front door of a very different kind of house was stealthily inching open.

After a moment or two, a head poked out into the crisp November morning, glancing nervously this way and that, scanning the neat, primly ordered cul-de-sac for signs of life. After confirming that no-one was around to witness what came next, bar a blackbird enjoying a leisurely soak in next door's birdbath, the door swung open more fully, the figure emerging into the daylight with a furtive tread.

Margaret Creaton tugged the lapels of her dressing gown more tightly across her hammering chest, as though covering every inch of skin would protect her from the morning air. But she knew it was no good; the sense of exposure she felt was something no amount of clothing could conceal.

With her heart in her mouth, she forced her eyes to move down to the doormat, where a cardboard box sat. The sight, although she'd expected it, was enough to make panic claw at her airways.

They'd been *here*. On her doorstep. The thought was too awful, too intrusive to contemplate.

She'd passed a terrible night, her sleep broken again and again by the same dream. The same face. That of a heinous monster, glimpsed through a window…

She'd woken, finally, to bright sunlight glaring through the cheap beige curtains into their bedroom. But any relief she'd felt at being free of that awful, cloying nightmare was cut short as her phone pinged.

Have you got my present yet?

Margaret had stared at the screen, frozen in horror. As she watched, another message came through.

Special delivery.

That had galvanised Margaret into action. She'd flung back the eiderdown, garbling her intention of fetching the paper. It was a flimsy excuse; after all, she'd never once risen before Colin in forty years of marriage. 'Morning jobs', as she called them, were a husband's duty. As were 'last-thing-at-night-jobs,' and anything involving refuse disposal. For once, though, she found herself inordinately grateful that Colin never questioned anything, no matter how strange or out of place. As far as she knew, he never thought about anything at all, except his blasted model-train collection, and when he would finally be allowed to open the good biscuits. Little did he know, he'd be waiting a long time on that second one.

That burst of energy had been brief, however. Now, Margaret found herself frozen once more, staring down at the nondescript cardboard box, until eventually, the sound of a garage door opening further down the street jolted her back into animation. She picked up the box with both hands, surprised to find how light it was. Nonetheless, she held it at arms' length as she conveyed it back into the house. She didn't bother to fetch the newspaper from where it was wedged into the letterbox; there was little point in shoring up her alibi. Colin had probably forgotten it already.

In the kitchen, she clicked on the kettle to cover any sound – although, judging by the cacophonous snoring from upstairs, that wouldn't be an issue – and with trembling fingers, pushed back the cardboard flaps at the top of the box. Flinchingly, her body already recoiling in anticipation of what she might find, she peered inside…

And blinked in surprise. Unable to help herself, she reached into the box and pulled out the unexpected object, holding it in her hand. As she did so, her phone pinged again from the depths of her dressing gown pocket.

Like it?

For a moment, Margaret fought with herself, caught in a tussle of indecision. But for once, prudence lost out. She punched the call button, feeling a rush of recklessness. Wondering if she'd finally cracked under the strain. After all, this was the number that made her heart race with terror, her stomach roil with dread. The voice she most hated hearing, and now she was seeking it out. It was the definition of insanity.

And yet … she had to know.

"What is it?" She turned it over in her palm; it was beautiful, no doubt about that. But also sinister. Frightening. "Why are you giving this to me?"

"Call it a little extra incentive," the familiar voice said languidly.

"I don't understand."

"Don't you?" The clicking of a tongue sounded down the line. "Come now, Margaret, don't deny you've been a little … distant lately. Avoiding my calls. It's a good thing I don't take offence easily, otherwise I might have found it rather hurtful."

Margaret pursed her lips, not willing to dignify that with an answer.

"I wouldn't want to think of you getting cold feet over our understanding," the voice continued silkily. "That would *never* do. We have such a good thing going, you and I."

Margaret looked down at the object in her hand and felt a shiver go through her.

"What *is* this?" she demanded again, more harshly this time.

"You don't need to trouble yourself about that. Just know that if you do decide to … let me down, shall we say … the police will be informed as to exactly where they can find it. Along with everything else you're hiding in that house of yours. Although I think you'll find they'll be especially interested in that particular piece."

Margaret shoved it back into the box as though it were contaminated, stuffing it down amongst the paper padding until it was no longer visible.

"I know I can trust you to look after it for me," the voice crooned. "Think of it as something else for your room of treasures."

"I won't do this," Margaret said, her voice shaking even as she tried to sound defiant. "I … I'll destroy it."

"Oh no you won't, Margaret." The voice sounded almost amused. "You're too much of a coward for that." A sigh.

"Come now, cheer up. It's not for long. I have big plans for that special little object."

Plans, which, presumably, *she* would be required to carry out, Margaret thought, suppressing a shudder.

"I'll tell you when it's time," the voice said. And Margaret didn't doubt they meant it.

As the line went dead, the kettle began to whistle, filling the kitchen with a high, keening sound. But Margaret barely heard it. She was staring at the box. She didn't know much about what was inside, but its presence in her home could mean only one thing.

She was in more danger than ever.

Epilogue

The telephone was ringing, a shrill, echoing tone that reverberated around the single-roomed cottage.

Matthias Weaver paused in the process of pulling on his gum boots, glancing across at the antiquated device sitting in a dish on the sideboard. It didn't ring often; in fact, it only rang for one reason these days.

For a moment, he hesitated, tempted to simply ignore it, to head off to his morning's work as he'd planned. But then he sighed, putting his boots aside.

He stumped unevenly across the room, picking up the battered old mobile. The screen glowed dimly, dulled to a misty matte finish by a plethora of scrapes and scratches. It showed no name, but the number scrolling across it would nonetheless be familiar to any of the town's regular book borrowers.

Jabbing at the call button, Matthias raised the phone to his ear with a gruff – and decidedly unwelcoming – "Yes? What is it?"

He waited, listening to the agitated voice on the other end of the line with growing impatience.

"Look, there's nothing to concern yourself about," he said shortly, after a few moments. "If there was, I'd have told you. Everything's under control." Another pause, then, "Yes, they did go into the chapel, but they didn't … look, you've *got* to calm down. It's safe, you hear me? The police are finished here now; they took the bodies this morning. No-one will be going near it again for a good while."

The line crackled with static as the caller expressed their doubts.

"No, *don't* come here. You'll only cause trouble if you do. I don't need you raising any more questions." A beat, then, irritably, "I don't care who you are, Aloysius; you've got your job to do, and I've got mine. And I say *leave it be*. I'm watching over it, just as I always have." And he would continue to do so, he added silently, for as long as he had breath in his body. Now Annabel Drayford had gone, so had the threat to his position. The thought gave him a quiet satisfaction.

He put down the phone, looking thoughtfully towards the grimy windows, through which the promising gleam of sunlight shone weakly. As he pulled on his boots, he felt a twinge of misgiving over what he'd omitted from the call. *Should* he, perhaps, have confessed about the man who'd been around here last night? He'd been surprised to see him again, for certain; he thought he'd told them everything they wanted to know, him and that woman he'd been with. But, it turned out, the man had had some questions of his own.

Questions that had skimmed uncomfortably close to a subject no-one had asked Matthias about in decades. A subject he'd hoped never to have to discuss again.

As soon as the word 'tunnels' had reached his ears, Matthias had felt his blood run cold. He'd kept his composure admirably, mind, although it had been the performance of his life to derisively laugh the suggestion off as mere lunacy, even as his heart had hammered painfully within his sunken chest.

Besides, the man hadn't struck him as any serious threat, Matthias reassured himself now. He'd been one of those posh city types, all ludicrously coloured trousers and put-on drawl. Chances are, he'd stumbled across something about Stamford's tunnels in one of the club's many old books while waiting to be released by the police. No doubt, his curiosity had been spawned more by boredom and an excuse to walk the grounds than anything more. He'd probably already forgotten all about it.

No, Matthias told himself, as he tugged on the door handle to the outside world. He'd done the right thing. He'd handled it, like he'd been tasked to do. There'd been no need to alert Aloysius; the man was already so jumpy, goodness only knew what he would have done. Someone had to keep a level head; it was the only way the truth could stay safe.

The door juddered open, revealing a day of unparalleled autumn beauty, which made every worry seem immediately small and irrelevant. The fog had lifted at last, replaced by a cloudless sky beneath which the garden shimmered in a jewel box of rich tones, streaked dahlias competing with waxen chrysanthemums in the mature borders.

The storm had passed, and the club had survived it, as it always did every challenge. Now, it was a picture of serenity once more. As he looked at it, Matthias Weaver picked up his spade and allowed himself what was, for him, the ultimate display of emotion: a small nod of approval. Then he set off across the gardens towards his beloved Aquitaine.

Towards home.

With thanks to Richard Warner.

'A fun read that kept me reading through to the end ... with a group of interesting characters, any one of which might have been a multiple murderer.' ☆☆☆☆☆

Who knew a harmless town fair could be so polarising – or so deadly?

When auctioneer Felicia Grant is talked into helping with the Stamford annual Georgian Fair, she expected the worst she'd have to endure was the corset. But when the headline speaker turns up dead in the hook-a-duck pool, and more murders follow in quick succession, she finds herself investigating a serial killer again – and this time the stakes are even higher...

Available now in paperback, ebook and audio!

ONE MORE CHAPTER

YOUR NUMBER ONE STOP

FOR PAGETURNING BOOKS

The author and One More Chapter would like to thank everyone
who contributed to the publication of this story...

Analytics
Imogen Wolstencroft

Audio
Fionnuala Barrett
Ciara Briggs

Contracts
Laura Amos
Inigo Vyvyan

Design
Lucy Bennett
Fiona Greenway
Liane Payne
Dean Russell

Digital Sales
Laura Daley
Lydia Grainge
Hannah Lismore

eCommerce
Laura Carpenter
Madeline ODonovan
Charlotte Stevens
Christina Storey
Jo Surman
Rachel Ward

Editorial
Rosie Best
Kara Daniel
Charlotte Ledger
Laura McCallen
Jennie Rothwell
Sofia Salazar Studer
Caroline Scott-Bowden
Emily Thomas
Helen Williams

Harper360
Emily Gerbner
Ariana Juarez
Jean Marie Kelly
emma sullivan
Sophia Wilhelm

International Sales
Peter Borcsok
Ruth Burrow
Bethan Moore
Colleen Simpson

Inventory
Sarah Callaghan
Kirsty Norman

Marketing & Publicity
Chloe Cummings
Grace Edwards
Katie Sadler

Operations
Melissa Okusanya
Hannah Stamp

Production
Denis Manson
Simon Moore
Francesca Tuzzeo

Rights
Ashton Mucha
Alisah Saghir
Zoe Shine
Aisling Smyth
Lucy Vanderbilt

Trade Marketing
Ben Hurd
Eleanor Slater

**The HarperCollins
Distribution Team**

**The HarperCollins
Finance & Royalties
Team**

**The HarperCollins
Legal Team**

**The HarperCollins
Technology Team**

UK Sales
Isabel Coburn
Jay Cochrane
Sabina Lewis
Holly Martin
Harriet Williams
Leah Woods

**And every other
essential link in the
chain from delivery
drivers to booksellers
to librarians and
beyond!**

YOUR NUMBER ONE STOP

ONE MORE CHAPTER

FOR PAGETURNING BOOKS

One More Chapter is an
award-winning global
division of HarperCollins.

Subscribe to our newsletter to get our
latest eBook deals and stay up to date
with all our new releases!

signup.harpercollins.co.uk/
join/signup-omc

Meet the team at
www.onemorechapter.com

Follow us!

@onemorechapterhc

Do you write unputdownable fiction?
We love to hear from new voices.
Find out how to submit your novel at
www.onemorechapter.com/submissions